Spiral

Spiral

Joseph Geary

PANTHEON BOOKS, NEW YORK

All rights reserved under International and Pan-
American Copyright Conventions. Published in the
United States by Pantheon Books, a division of Random
House, Inc., New York, and simultaneously in Canada
by Random House of Canada Limited, Toronto.

Pantheon Books and colophon are registered
trademarks of Random House, Inc.

Library of Congress Cataloging-in-Publication Data
Geary, Joseph.
Spiral / Joseph Geary.
p.   cm.
ISBN 0-375-42223-4
1. Biography as a literary form—Fiction. 2. Tangier
(Morocco)—Fiction. 3. New York (N.Y.)—Fiction.
4. Biographers—Fiction. 5. Painting—Fiction.
6. Painters—Fiction. 7. Gay men—Fiction. I. Title.
PR6107.E28 S65 2003
823'.92—dc21   2002035679

www.pantheonbooks.com
Book design by Anthea Lingeman
Printed in the United States of America
First Edition
2 4 6 8 9 7 5 3 1

For Sylvie

Every artist wants to throw himself into the gutter.

—Francis Bacon

The Writer

I

It was Barb who found Grossman, Barb who called Nick in the middle of the night, so stirred up by the turn events had taken that she forgot about the time difference between London and New York.

The middle of an English summer. The 3 A.M. dark of a West London basement. Everything changing because of a phone call. Later on, Nick saw it as the moment in which his life came apart.

"Does she even *realize?*" said Linda when Nick was back under the covers.

"She was drunk. You know how she gets."

Linda turned away from him with a disgusted grunt—yeah, she knew. Barbara Segal was one of two "rich old birds" she would have liked to rip out of his Rolodex, women he had gotten to know intimately in the six years he had been writing the biography of Francis Spira. Not that Barb was that rich, certainly not by New York standards. Her Upper West Side apartment was worth $800,000 tops, but forty years in the art world (she had started out writing for *Artforum* back in the sixties) and her closeness to the New York School's celebrity psychos, freaks and visionaries had left her holding a half-dozen blotched and spattered rectangles that were now worth serious money. And then there were the Spiras: six of them in all, all portraits of her from the late sixties, two of them gifts from the artist himself.

"So what the hell did she want?" said Linda.

Nick stared up at the darkness, getting little aftershocks of cognition, Barbara's news blooming in his head.

"She said she saw Jacob Grossman," he whispered. "In the street."

After Georges Pompidou had awarded Spira the Légion d'Honneur in 1971, the artist had gone out and found an Algerian trucker in Pigalle, taken him back to his room at the Crillon. He had shown up at the opening of the Grand Palais retrospective with a split lip that was only partly concealed by cosmetics. This was Spira's love life: roiling, libidinous, percussive, abandoned. But for all the wildness, he'd had only two significant others: Tony Reardon, the East End criminal who died the month Frank got his French medal, and Jacob Nathaniel Grossman.

Nick got out of the bed and stood there for a moment looking down at his feet. He was willowy but square-shouldered, and had the knotty hands and feet of his English mother.

"She said she saw him in the street."

Linda's head was an area of deeper darkness in the surrounding gloom. With the punky short haircut he'd given her, she looked like a boy.

"So she's hallucinating," she said. "It's not surprising with all the booze she puts away."

Nick pushed a hand back through his own butchered hair. For the past few months they had been hacking at each other as part of an ongoing economy drive, and her latest effort was particularly brutal.

"She saw him in the street, just a chance thing, and she followed him."

"But how could she even be sure who it was? I mean, after all this time it must be—"

"She said . . ."

Barb's voice came to him, flattened with the booze, slightly mushy on the consonants. *I followed him, Nick. This old bum. It's crazy, I know. But I couldn't just walk away. We must have walked around for hours.*

"She just knew," said Nick, trembling now, knowing that this was tremendous news, disastrous news. "She knew who it was."

He said it then, said that maybe he should go over to Manhattan.

Linda bumped the bedside lamp, grabbing for the light switch.

The room jumped into low-rent detail: a Dralon-covered armchair spotted with cigarette burns, a lethal disconnected storage heater. Papers and books stacked like dirty dishes around the walls. Linda reached for her cigarettes, then remembered that she didn't smoke anymore.

"Nick, we don't have the money."

Nick closed his eyes. This wasn't simply the truth. It was Linda invoking one of the darkest of their household gods. They were both hopeless with money, feared it, tried to live their lives as though it didn't exist. They'd go on in this way for long periods, and then a bill would come through the door, and they'd get into a panic, come up with some scheme that meant eating lentils for a month or, if they were really being strict, cutting back on the wine.

Beyond that, she was reminding him of Her Sacrifice. Five years ago she had agreed to his going freelance—he copyedited reports at a financial magazine in the City—had accepted the fact that he could not write this book and continue full-time. He'd tried it with his first book, and it hadn't worked out. Five years ago she'd agreed that for two years she would support him, would do this for him because it would make him happy. But deadline after deadline had passed, two years had become five, and for a long time now, they had been really struggling: renting videos rather than going out, eating cheap, making the minimum payments on the credit cards.

And the only reason Linda was still putting up with the situation was because of the Light at the End of the Tunnel, which had come into view when he'd delivered the manuscript to the Curlew Press four weeks ago. The £7,000 payable on delivery (the remaining third was due on publication) had also had its soothing effect. The idea that there might now be a further delay, more expense for her to shoulder, that they might be stuck in the tunnel for some time to come, was more than she could bear.

"Grossman's dead," she said, almost pleading. "And the *Life,* it's *finished,* Nick. You have a nine-hundred-page proof sitting on the table in the living room. You're supposed to be correcting, you're supposed to be handing it back at the beginning of next week."

He couldn't go back to sleep.

At 5 A.M. he was in the kitchen, brooding, scribbling notes, when Linda walked into the doorway.

"It's not as if there were actual evidence of his death," he said. "A burial certificate or an autopsy report. It's not like with Reardon. I mean, maybe Grossman's been wandering around all these years. And . . ."

He looked up, saw that Linda was holding a photograph in her hand. Two photographs.

"I mean, imagine it, Linda. Nobody knows anything, why he—what made him walk out of the clinic or—or where he's been all this time. Plus there's Tangier, the—the whole syphilis question."

"Nick, you covered all that. I mean, Tangier, that whole sordid episode. Oscar Nagel was down there, Laverne Taubmann, and you have *reams* of stuff from them. And then there's—there's Paul Mann, William Burroughs, Allen Ginsberg. There's Cecil bloody Beaton."

"But this is Grossman," said Nick, standing up.

He went to the refrigerator and took out the milk, and when he turned, Linda was standing directly in front of him, holding out one of the photographs. It was a copy of a Cecil Beaton, and it showed Spira and Grossman sitting in the shade of a date palm in Tangier in the fall of 1960. It was during this time that Spira had famously asked Grossman what he was going to do now that he had lost his looks, and from the expression on Grossman's face the question might just have been asked. Harsh sunlight struck a bar of shadow down from his nose, dividing the no longer beautiful mouth while Spira stared out from some dark place inside his head.

Franky. Destroyer and creator. The Anti-Midas.

"So?"

Linda had a tendency to stare when she was angry. A little sliver of white showed above the veiled blue of the iris.

"So what?" said Nick.

"Where was it taken?"

He tried to push it away, but she kept it in front of him.

"Tangier," he said finally. "October twelfth, 1960."

"Tangier—what, like at the beach?"

"Come on, Lind."

"No, really. I'd like to know."

"On the esplanade above the port. They had lunch at the Minzah and went out there with the Box Brownie."

She nodded, almost smiling. "Very good. How about this?"

Another print came up, a flimsy Kodacolor print. A holiday snapshot that trembled faintly in her bitten fingernails. They were standing in front of an old stone wall, each with a bicycle, their faces red with exertion. Linda had the kind of face that was transformed by a smile, an honest square face with pouchy eyes like the actress Diane Wiest. The eyes were a family thing, but the first time Nick had seen them, he'd thought they were a product of dissolute European ways.

He himself was frowning in the harsh sunlight. The slight thickening in the bridge of his nose made him look more easygoing than he really was. It could have been France. It could have been Italy, but then again . . .

He looked up, realized that this was the point.

"It's from the Life," said Linda, with a thin smile. "Ours."

Two days after Barb's call, Nick was back in Manhattan, looking out the window of her twentieth-floor apartment between the slats of a very dusty venetian blind, feeling like one of those cartoon characters that run right off the edge of a cliff but are fine as long as they don't look down—"down" in this case being the balance on the Visa card, "down" being the look on Linda's face when he'd told her he was going to have to come to New York one more time—her "Of course you do" somehow far worse than any reproach.

He hadn't been able to get a flight until Sunday evening, hadn't been able to communicate that fact to Barb until his arrival at the hotel on Sunday night (Barb was always forgetting to turn on her answering machine and carried a cellphone with a dead battery as though it were a lucky charm), by which time her meeting with Jacob Nathaniel Grossman had come and gone. Now it was Monday and she didn't want to talk about it.

Something had happened. Something unpleasant enough to make her want to talk about anything other than the matter at hand.

"So Linda, she's *angry* with you?" she said.

Nick turned and took in the room.

"For coming out here?" Barb insisted.

He shook his head. "She thinks I should be finished by now."

He crossed the room and sat in one of the low armchairs.

"Barb. I don't want to be a pain in the ass, but you were the one who called me."

Barb turned her head in a long, shuddering exhale and was for a moment lost in contemplation of a bloody rectangle on the other side of the room. Nick didn't have to look round to know what it was. It had been painted in July 1968: 34" x 22", oil on unprimed linen— Barb aged thirty.

At first glance it looked like a mistake, something that had been attempted in a violent flurry and then abandoned. It was only when you gave it a moment, gave your eye a moment to assemble the gouged and smeary marks that you really saw. Interconnecting blade-like planes looked like they were about to fly apart. The split and sutured face was impossible but somehow real, realer than real. This was Spira's trick. He tore things apart, turned them inside out, gave them back to the viewer quiveringly alive.

Three weeks ago a similar painting—same period, same subject, but nothing like the same quality—had sold for just over £2 million at Christie's in London.

"Poor Jacob," said Barb softly.

She shot Nick a look, mixing genuine distress with just a tiny bit of something else, something self-consciously alluring. It was very Barb. In this light and with the Cleopatra makeup she favored, she could have passed for fifty-something, but in the street looked older than her sixty years.

She was, by most people's standards, more than comfortable. She was witty, intelligent, had already lived through several lifetimes' worth of excitement, but it wasn't enough. She still wanted to exercise the pull she always had. Nick had realized early on that part of how they got along depended on how he dealt with her need to flirt. What was harder to take was her hostility towards Linda, which was some-how tied up with all the rest, as though Linda (whom she'd met only once) was in some oblique way a sexual rival.

Barb brought the cigarette to her mouth with a clack of amber ban-gles, her lips pinching hard on the filter.

"Barb, if you made a mistake, I'll understand. After all these years it would be perfectly understandable. You said yourself the light was fading."

"There was no mistake."

Her face darkened and she stood up. He had provoked her into saying something and she was annoyed. She wavered for a moment, the cigarette held in front of her mouth, then walked over to the liquor cabinet. Nick watched her break the seal on a bottle of vodka and pour herself a good two inches. She stayed at the cabinet, took a couple of sips. Then she was crying.

Nick rose.

"Barb?"

"It's okay." She snatched a Kleenex. "It's just seeing him after all these years, seeing what the years did to him. I'm telling you, it was . . ." She came back to her place on the couch, shaking her head. "It brought home to me how much we've all—aged."

Nick nodded, waited for more. Nothing came.

"But Barb, Friday night—I mean, Saturday morning you were all for it. 'Come on over,' you said."

"That's right," she said ruefully. "I just had to open my big mouth. And now everybody wants to know about poor . . ." Her chin puckered, and Nick thought she was going to cry again.

"Everybody?"

She flipped a hand at him. "Don't worry. I'm not talking to anyone."

"But why? What changed, Barb?"

"I *saw* him is what changed. More to the point, he saw *me*."

Saying it, reliving it, she shuddered, swallowed another mouthful of vodka.

Again Nick waited, but she'd said all she was going to say. It was driving him crazy.

"What—he was hostile, unfriendly?"

She groaned, let her head roll back on the couch, eyes closed.

"Nick, Nick, *Nick*. You're like—you're like a dripping fucking faucet. You know that? All these years. I mean, you know I think it's great, you wanting to chase everything down, wanting to get the story straight, but every now and then—can't you just *let up?*"

Nick looked down at his notebook. He had written GROSSMAN in block capitals, then drawn a box around it. Black lines radiated outwards.

"Did you ask him why he walked out of the clinic?" he said.

Barb brought the cigarette to her mouth and sucked down smoke.

"Did he look sick?" he said. "Come on, Barb, what difference does it make whether you tell me or not?"

She massaged her temples, blew a long blue stream at the ceiling.

She wasn't going to say anything unless he pushed her.

Then Nick had an idea.

"Was he missing anything?" he said.

She looked at him then.

"A nose?" said Nick. "Anything like that?"

"What the hell are you talking about?"

"Well, did he look like someone in the terminal stages of syphilis?"

She made a face as though she'd been fed a pickle.

"Jacob doesn't have syphilis," she said.

"No? That's interesting. I mean, you'd expect him to, right? If Spira had it, that is."

"Who says Spira had it?"

Nick smiled. They both knew the answer to that, the "who" in question being the nearest thing they had to a common enemy. His name was Martin Marion, and he was the "recognized authority" on Spira. He'd first come over to the States in 'sixty-five to help with the big Spira retrospective at the Guggenheim and had stayed on for thirty years of canapés and gin fizz. On the one occasion Nick had interviewed him, the great man had treated him with contempt, laughing at his questions, which he'd called "footling and futile." He'd insisted on talking off the record and made all kinds of crazy assertions, none of which could be used. Later on, word got back to Nick that Marion referred to him as "that plodding hack." The demolition of *Tortured Eros*, Marion's "firsthand" account of Spira's life, published within months of the artist's death, was in Nick's view long overdue.

It was in *Tortured Eros* that Marion had first developed his syphilis theory, and in which he had referred to Barb as a "Tenth Street groupie," something for which she had never forgiven him. Reviewing the book later, she'd attacked his idea that the bizarreness of Spira's late work could be explained by the effects of syphilis, arguing that there was no solid evidence for Spira's infection (although there were hints and rumors, the kind of thing that drove Nick crazy) and pointing out the suspicious similarities between Marion's scenario and the Faustus myth as per Thomas Mann's famous novel. The idea that Spira's artistic mastery and worldly success were due to the disease rewiring his brain, letting him see things that mortals didn't normally see, plugged him into the grandest tradition of Western artistic endeavor, put him right up there with Mann, Goethe, Marlowe. It also bound him, very attractively if you liked that kind of thing (and there were plenty of Spiraphiles who did), to the devil himself.

Marion had come back at her a month later with an essay which included an almost verbatim account of a conversation he'd supposedly had with Spira in his last weeks, in which the artist had supposedly admitted to the illness, saying that he hadn't been "right in the head" for thirty years or more. He'd also confirmed that it was Tony Reardon who'd given it to him while the two were living the life of Caligula in Tangier. The essay finished with a parting shot written in the grandest Marion manner: "The fact that Frank never spoke publicly of the illness, either to confirm or deny, is hardly surprising. Nor is it a surprise that certain 'supposed' friends should feel bitter that he never took them into his confidence. However, that they should choose to make scholarly play of the matter is beyond surprising; it comes, in fact, as something of a shock."

Why Spira's confession had been left out of *Tortured Eros* was, of course, a mystery, unless you took the view, as Barb certainly did, that it hadn't been included because Marion hadn't at that time felt obliged to make it all up.

Nick watched Barb's expression harden.

She raked at her frazzled hair.

"Jacob doesn't *have* syphilis," she said. "If he had syphilis, he'd be dead by now. Or crazy."

"Maybe he got some medical help early on."

Nick sat back in the armchair, watching Barb examine her fingernails, thinking it all through, a barely perceptible curl to her mouth as she savored the idea of putting a stake into Marion's fat heart. Because if Grossman didn't have syphilis, had never had syphilis, it was unlikely that Frank had been infected either.

"And with syphilis there are shades of gray," he said, giving her a final push. "With neurosyphilis, for example—"

"He was terrified," said Barb.

"Jacob was? Of what?"

"Of me. I don't think they told him he was going to have a visitor, and when I walked into his room . . ."

She closed her eyes.

"What?"

She was shaking her head, bewildered, lost.

"We were friends," she said. "We used to be close. When he went into the clinic, I was one of the few people who . . ." She closed her eyes again, a hard line creasing her heavily marked brows. "And then—yesterday—when he saw me. He was shouting, screaming. He thought—I don't know, he thought I was there to *kill* him."

She shuddered and took a drink. For a moment neither of them spoke. A fire truck went up West End Avenue wailing doom and destruction.

"Maybe . . ." Nick hesitated, then decided to say it anyway. "Maybe he *is* sick, Barb. That kind of psychosis—I read all around this, as you can probably . . ."

Barb shook her head. "No. He was lucid, sharp. After all this time he knew *exactly* who I was. And he was *terrified*. Afterwards, I spoke to the woman who runs the place. She was upset. She said she'd never seen anything like it. Said Jack—that's what they call him there—was one of her most placid customers. I could tell by the way she looked at me she thought I was some kind of hired assassin."

"Maybe with me, it'd be different."

She was looking for her cigarettes again.

"I mean, he doesn't know me. I'm a complete—"

"There's a window in his room," she said, ignoring him. "He's up there on the third floor. He—he tried to get out. It sounds . . . it sounds almost funny, but this was—he's *old*, Nick."

"Eighty-four."

Normally his grasp of detail made Barb smile, but this time she just stared, shaking her head.

"An old man," she said, screwing up her eyes, an unlit cigarette between her fingers. "He climbed up, he tried to climb up, screaming—he was just *choking* with terror. I think he hurt himself—his leg."

She fell silent again, and for a long time they just sat there. Nick reached out a hand, but Barb shook her head. She didn't want to be touched. She looked at him, her sad, dark eyes solemnly fixed.

"He's in a rehab facility on Broome Street," she said. "The Delancey-Deere."

3

The Delancey-Deere Volunteer Center was a brown tenement building on the corner of Ludlow and Broome. Chain-link gates covered dirty windows along the first floor. Nick went up steps into a hallway stinking of disinfectant, then followed a backlit Perspex arrow furry with dead bugs toward Reception, which turned out to be four blind walls and a desk buried under dog-eared papers. A soft toy, maybe a Teletubby, was balanced on top of a name plaque that read LUCIA PIREZ, DIRECTOR.

Pirez turned out to be a small Hispanic woman in her mid-forties with signs of a hurried lunch around her mouth. When Nick told her what he was there for, she stiffened up. Jack wasn't doing so well, she said, was in fact recovering from an "episode." Nick asked if the episode had anything to do with Barb's visit, and Pirez started flipping pages in a desk diary.

"Yeah, Seagull," she said, looking up at him. "You know her?"

"She's an art critic. *Was* an art critic. She was close to Jack a long time ago."

"Close, huh? Then I guess there must have been a falling-out somewhere along the way. Going by Jack's reaction, I mean."

"Jack, or Jacob Grossman to give him his proper name, walked out of a clinic twenty-six years ago. He's been missing ever since."

"Jacob Grossman? You're saying that's who this is?"

"That's right. The grandson of Freddy Grossman—the dry-goods millionaire? He made his fortune in Boston in the 1880s. Jack got some of it. Lived it up for a while."

Pirez was shaking her head now.

"Jack comes from money? Are you sure we're talking about the same person?"

"Mr. Grossman, he has these distinctive teeth?"

"Well, that's one way of putting it."

Pirez pushed back from her desk. She said that whoever Jack was, Ms. Segal's visit had really knocked him for a loop. "He had a very bad night. So, I'm kind of reluctant . . ."

"Ms. Pirez, I'd really appreciate the chance to talk to him. And I'd be more than happy for you to sit in. If it looks like Jack is getting upset, we'll stop."

A door banged shut at the end of a landing. Following Pirez's bustling figure over the blue linoleum, Nick absorbed detail, feeling light, weightless almost, energized now that he was back inside the *Life,* all thoughts of home and Linda momentarily forgotten.

They came to a halt in front of a kick-scuffed door. Pirez knocked once, turned a handle, pushed.

Nick took it all in at a glance: the single bed, the pants over the chair back, the blanket folded as a pillow because the real pillow was too dirty, the washbasin with its cake of green soap and cracked wall mirror.

An old man was slumped in a wheelchair facing a painted brick wall. He was wearing a surgical collar. His left leg was encased in plaster.

"Jack?"

The head lifted, wobbled a little.

Pirez walked around in front of him. Then she was leaning forward, smiling, talking to the old guy as though he was a kid.

"Jack, did you rest a little? You have a visitor."

She flipped off some sort of brake with her foot, brought the chair around.

If it hadn't been for the teeth, he could have been anyone, certainly didn't look like any of the versions of Grossman that Nick had ever seen. The mouth that had inspired so many of Spira's paintings hung slackly lopsided, the lips dry and cracked. Silty eyes were shielded by smeared square lenses. A dark seam ran from one eye down to the corner of the mouth, where it became a deep fold. He looked like he'd just gotten out of bed, like he had been sleeping for the last twenty-six years and hadn't reckoned on being disturbed.

It was just the three of them, plus the microcassette turning on a small table spotted with cigarette burns. Beyond the open window a storm was building. Later on, Pirez was going to make a copy of the tape. That was the deal.

Nick started out by talking about the *Life,* tried to make a joke about how long it had taken him to write it, said what a huge break it was to come across Jack like this, to finally meet the person who'd played such an important part in Spira's life. All the time he was talking, Jack fidgeted in his chair—looking across at Pirez, scratching at his beard. It was hard to tell how much he was taking in.

Pirez explained how "the gentleman" had come all the way from England just to see him, just for his book. "We had no idea what a big shot you are, Jack."

Jack covered his eyes with a trembling hand.

"Is it the light?" said Pirez. She stood up and yanked across one of the drapes. Upstairs, a steady yelling started.

"Don't worry about that," she said, giving Nick a look. "That's just Anton."

Nick cleared his throat. "Jack? Barbara Segal told me about yesterday. She's really sorry if she upset you."

Jack kept his eyes on Pirez.

"She told me to tell you that," said Nick. "She wouldn't have upset you for anything in the world. She was just—well, so surprised, so *pleased* to see you after all this time."

Jack started to pick at his face. There were raw-looking marks in a line about an inch below his bottom lip.

"She was telling me how, when you were at the clinic in New Jersey, she used to go visit you."

Jack leaned forward in his chair, mumbled something Nick didn't catch.

"Smoke if you want to," said Pirez gently.

Jack fumbled for his cigarettes, produced a battered Zippo lighter. Nick watched him apply the flame to the tip, doing it with a gentlemanly flourish.

"Nobody knew where you went," said Nick. "Everyone thought

something must have happened to you. And then—well, you just turned up in the street."

The tip of Jack's tongue went out to meet the filter as he brought it to his lips.

"Where did you go, Jack?"

The dirty eyes got a hooded, sly look. Or maybe he was dozing.

"You just up and left," said Nick. "Didn't even put on your shoes."

"This was how long ago?" said Pirez.

Nick sat back in his chair. "Twenty-six years," he said. "Twenty-six years ago, Jack just walked out."

Pirez kept shaking her head. She obviously couldn't get over the idea of someone with Jack's background ending up this way. Jack was fingering his lower lip now, pushing the finger inside against the gums.

"What was he in there for?" said Pirez as though Jack were no longer listening.

"Cocaine—right, Jack? Benzedrine. Alcohol. You were having some health problems at that time."

There was a knock at the door—one of the orderlies, asking for Pirez. She cursed softly, excused herself and left the room, closing the door behind her.

Air stirred the drapes in the open window. Jack was sitting slumped over on his left arm, his eyes fixed on the tape recorder.

"I'm curious about May 1972," said Nick. "What made you run, Jack? What made you leave the clinic like that?"

The tape recorder spooled up a couple of feet of silence.

"Was it—?"

"You. Think. You. Can. Fool. Me?"

It was as if someone else had entered his body. Jack raised his head, fixing Nick with a clamp-jawed stare.

"I'm not trying to fool you, Jack."

Jack pushed his tongue into his bottom lip, making the bristles stand up.

"Why would I be trying to fool you, Jack? Fool you how?"

Jack worked his jaw, chewing at the hidden tongue.

"My only concern," said Nick, "my only desire, is to give you your rightful place in—in the biography. All I'm trying to—"

"You. Think. I. Don't. Have. Eyes?"

The words came out measured and malevolent in a slow unsheathing.

"I'm sero-positive. Did you know that, Mr. Greer? I'm sero-positive, and I bite." He took a breath, then another, pumping himself up.

"Jack, I'm not here to—"

"I'll bite your *fucking face!*"

Nick jolted backwards as Jack lunged.

When he straightened up again, Jack was still in his chair, breathing hard. "So don't *think* you're going to get your hands on it," he spat.

Nick righted the microcassette, checked that it was still working.

"Jack, I don't know what you're talking about."

Pirez came back into the room, and just like that Jack was quiet again, gone again, his eyes following her as she took her seat. It looked like she had broken a thumbnail.

Thunder thumped and rolled in the street.

She asked how it was going, saw the look on Nick's face. "Mr. Greer? You okay?"

Nick realized that he was shaking.

"Yes. We were just—we were just talking about . . ." He looked at Jack, didn't know what the hell they'd been talking about. "Jack?"

"You know," said Jack. "You're the one who came all the way from England."

Nick swallowed and was surprised to feel his ears pop.

Jack turned to face Pirez. "He's here for the picture," he said. "Like Segal. They won't rest until they have it."

Nick came forward in his chair.

"The picture?" said Pirez. "Which picture?"

"Tell her," said Jack. "Tell her about the *Incarnation.*"

Nick swallowed again. His ears felt wadded, stuffed.

"The *Incarnation?*" said Pirez. "What's that? Something this Spira guy painted? Is that what you're talking about, Jack? The picture Spira painted? The picture he painted in Tangier?"

Nick shook his head. "That picture was destroyed," he said.

A look of deep puzzlement came over Jack's face. His tongue came to rest against his lower lip.

"Spira destroyed the picture?" said Pirez.

Nick nodded, shifted in his chair, trying to shut her out.

"Yes. Or do I have that wrong, Jack?"

But Jack had withdrawn again, and, looking at him now, it was hard to believe the vehemence of a moment ago: *don't* think *you're going to get your hands on it.* He was fingering his lower lip again.

"Why'd he destroy it?" said Pirez.

She wouldn't shut up.

"Spira *tried* to work in Tangier," said Nick irritably, his eyes on Jack's, "but it didn't happen—whether because of the light, or his sex life or the drugs; probably because of all those things. The only work to survive that period was a landscape that he painted in 1957, and he *thought* he'd destroyed that. It was in fact retrieved from his garbage can and showed up in London eight years later. Spira came across it in a gallery on Cork Street in May 1965. He bought it for fifty thousand pounds, took it outside and stamped it to pieces on the sidewalk."

"He what?"

"He didn't think it was worthy of him. Tangier was a bad time for him. He touched bottom there."

Jack sniggered. "You know so much," he said.

Nick shrugged. "Six years of digging, Jack. Six years of talking to people. But I'd be the first to admit that Tangier remains—well, maybe you can help me out. You were there, after all."

Pirez turned in her chair. "You were there, Jack? In Africa?"

"Jack went down there in 1960," said Nick. "He moved into Spira's place after this other friend moved out."

At the mention of the other friend, Jack's smile disappeared. He didn't want to hear about Reardon.

"This other person," said Nick, probing now, sensing an opening. "He was what you would call a bad influence. Isn't that right, Jack?"

Jack gripped his armrests. "Suck your *cock* for a pack of Luckies."

"Jack!" Pirez snapped her fingers, suddenly bristling.

"Cocksucking whore!"

"Jack, you know I don't allow that kind of talk."

"Tony Reardon," said Nick. "One way and another he brought the creative process to a halt. Which is why nothing happened in Tangier."

Jack frowned, stared at Nick over the tops of his glasses, but if he disagreed, he wasn't saying anything.

"And the *Incarnation*," said Nick, unable to stop himself now, wanting to roll over Grossman, to sweep him aside, "the painting that has come to be known as the *Incarnation,* was probably actually a Madonna and Child, a large canvas, almost certainly started and then abandoned in October 1957."

"Dates," said Jack softly. "Names. Places."

"Facts," said Nick. "Spira wrote a letter to his dealer, Quentin Blair, dated October seventh, in which he asked Blair to advance him some money in payment for four works he was close to completing, one of which was a large canvas dealing with a religious subject. *None* of which were ever delivered."

Jack was smiling now, smoking his cigarette.

"So he was lying?" said Pirez. "To this dealer?"

Nick kept his eyes on Jack's face. "It wasn't unusual for Spira—especially at this time in his career—to try to get money out of his dealer by promising works he had no intention of delivering. It wasn't the first time that he'd written that sort of letter. A friend of Spira's, Laverne Taubmann, in Tangier at the time, recalls a large canvas that Frank was excited about, a large red painting, two figures in a boxlike space. Maybe this was the Madonna and Child. If it was, it was the only religious work Frank ever attempted."

"And this picture?" said Pirez. "It would be, like, valuable now?"

Nick turned to look at her. "A small Spira portrait sold for just over three million dollars a couple of weeks ago."

Pirez let out a low whistle.

"But of course, it doesn't exist," said Nick, and as soon as the words were out, he knew that he was wrong. Or, if not necessarily wrong, not in a position to be quite so categorical. They had stumbled into an area of the *Life* that was full of holes and gaps and softness. Tangier, a city built on sand, seemed to generate foundationless stories and spurious facts. Despite the warmth of the stuffy room, Nick was suddenly cold. Pirez was saying something to him, but he was thinking about another event from that shadowy time. The burglary of the Rue d'Angleterre apartment. It had happened in January 1960, just before Grossman arrived, and was the reason Reardon had moved out in the first place.

Nick became aware of Jack's contemptuous stare.

"You talk about facts," he said, exhaling smoke. "But what do you know about the *facts?* You're like a . . ." He clutched at the air with his yellow nails. "You're like a guy lost in the woods. A man—lost in

the woods. Yes, yes. Oh my. Oh yes. *Mi retrovai per una selva oscura.*"
He half-sang the words, like a wheedling nursery rhyme.

"Was it the *Incarnation* that was stolen from Spira's apartment?"
said Nick.

"Stolen?"

"Yes."

This was funny, though Nick had no idea why. Jack clamped a
hand against his mouth and snickered. He pressed his eyes shut, trying to contain the laughter.

"*Something* was stolen," said Nick, exasperated. "Something
important."

Jack rocked a little harder.

"I guess Spira decided not to talk to you about it," said Nick.

The rocking stopped. "Frank told me everything."

"Oh, really? Did he tell you he had syphilis?" It just came out.
Nick raised his hands. "I'm sorry, Jack. It's not—I don't know that for
sure—for a fact." He was foundering now, sounding like an idiot.

"Frank didn't—have *syphilisssss,*" said Jack, his eyes blazing.

"Three months before Frank died, he told Martin Marion that he
hadn't been right in his head for the past forty years because of the
Treponema, you know? The pathogen, the bug? Apparently he'd been
following treatment somewhere in Switzerland. Marion wrote about
it in *ARTnews* after Frank's death. He said Frank probably killed himself because he was scared of what the disease was going to do to
him."

Jack looked stunned. "He said that? To Marion?"

"According to Marion, he did. He told him it was Tony Reardon
who gave it to him."

Jack's eyes went wide and dreamy. "But—but how come then . . ."

"How come what?"

"How come I don't have it?"

Nick looked at Pirez, but she returned his gaze with a shrug.
Clearly she had no idea either way.

"Maybe you're lucky," said Nick. "Or maybe . . ." He looked
down at his notes. "I'm not a doctor, Jack, but, well, there are shades
of gray with this thing."

Jack was shaking his head now, not wanting to believe it.

"What's clear is that Reardon had it," said Nick. "And he would have passed it to Frank. The thing about the disease—I don't know if you know it, Jack, but there are different stages. First, you get a kind of ulcer at the site of infection. You might not even notice it. Then around two months later you get fever symptoms, a temperature. You get this distinctive coppery rash. Do you have any recollection . . . ?"

Jack had become very still. "A rash?" he said.

"Tony Reardon told a friend of his, Paul Mann. Mann wrote about it in a letter. Reardon's itching rash. Facts, Jack. Dates and names. Reardon was almost certainly infected by January 1958. This is reconstructing events from a long time ago, but the—the consensus on this is that Reardon may have been stupid enough to get some local treatment for it. Possibly on Spira's recommendation. It seems more than likely that some sort of mercury preparation was used."

"Mercury?"

"Yes."

"Mercury." Jack brought his hands up to his face. "Mercury?" he said softly. "Mercury?"

"Treatment with mercury ointments was still fairly common in Morocco back then. Even after antibiotics started being used in the West."

Jack removed his glasses and covered his eyes with his left hand. The nails were like horn—yellow with big splits along them. He took a long, shuddering breath, then another. "Mercury?" he said. "Reardon was—what? *Taking* mercury?"

Nick looked across at Pirez. "Well, like I say, this is all a long time ago. There are no medical records, none that I could find anyway."

"So how . . . ? How do you know?"

"After the burglary in January 1960—this was just a week before you arrived—Spira and Reardon had an argument in the bar of the Hotel Maniria. Spira blamed Tony for leaving the apartment unlocked, and Tony said if he was losing his mind it wasn't surprising what with all the mercury in his system. That was when the fight started. People had to pull them apart."

Jack let out a low, flat groan. It was as if he'd snagged on something and it had just pulled him open. He leaned forward, then with great difficulty stood up.

"Oh Jesus," he said. "Sweet bleeding Jesus. Oh Jesus."

Pirez rose too. "Jack?"

He clumped over to the washbasin, making a rapid feathery sound with his lips.

"Jack, are you okay?" said Pirez. "You wanna stop?"

Jack looked at his reflection, his lips furiously working. Then he stopped.

"Yes," he said, and leaning way back from the basin, he slammed his face into the mirror.

4

He did what?" said Henry.

Nick was sitting on the bed in the hotel room, looking at his bandaged hand, the telephone pressed to his ear. He was still a little shaken up, despite having walked the length of Broadway in the rain.

"Smashed his face into the mirror."

Saying it, he saw it, heard it—the sound it made, a sickening crack that must have been the bone in Jack's nose. The mirror had come apart in two big chunks. It had happened so fast, had been so jump-cut furious and desperate, that by the time Nick and Pirez got to him, he'd done real damage. Blood spurted from a cut that ran from his hairline down into the flesh between his eyebrows. Nick had gotten both hands inside his surgical collar and pulled, bringing them both down on the floor. For a moment they'd struggled, Pirez screaming, "Leroy! Leroy!" and then Grossman had bitten Nick.

"Smashed his . . . But *why*, for goodness sake?"

Nick shook his head. Henry's "for goodness sake" seemed like a faint transmission from the planet Hampstead. Nick had called him at home, caught him on the way to bed, wanting his agent to know why, with only four weeks to go before the book hit the presses, he had disappeared from the face of the earth.

"I have no idea, Henry. It was completely crazy. We were talking about Reardon. About the syphilis, about the mercury he'd been taking, and Grossman just went—*berserk*. The woman who runs the place called a security guard. I mean, we were literally on the floor. He bit my goddam hand."

He held up the bandage in the gloomy evening light. "Can you imagine that? Jackdaw's gnashers planted in my flesh."

"Are you okay?"

"It hurts. It's a bite. It's not like his teeth met or anything, but . . ."

"But what?"

There was a faint strobing flash. Nick looked across at the window. Lightning was playing tag along the horizon. The sky looked humped and ugly over the park.

"Henry?"

"Yes, I'm still here, old thing."

"Grossman said he was sero-positive."

Henry went quiet.

"I need to call the clinic's director. Maybe she knows if it's true or not."

For the next ten minutes Nick attempted to describe the meeting with Grossman, but it had all been so disjointed and in the end so explosive, he kept getting mixed up, bogged down in the details and their endless goddam implications.

"It's got me . . ." He flopped back on the bed. "It's a disaster, Henry, a complete disaster. The proofs are at home on the kitchen table. Linda's threatening to leave if I don't wrap this thing up, and now there's all this new . . . stuff."

"Leave? She really said that?"

"We had this big fight in the kitchen Saturday morning."

"Well, that's—obviously that's not good. But I think you'll find that she'll cheer up when she hears about New York."

"What about New York?"

"The Crucible Press is looking at the book, Nick. And they seem to like it."

Nick stood up. A New York sale. He'd dreamed about it for as long as he'd been writing the book.

"Why didn't you say anything?"

"I only heard Friday night. Apparently the Guggenheim thing is working in your favor."

A major retrospective of Spira's work was coming up at the end of the month and was then going on to London in the fall. In the panic of getting the book finished, Nick had almost forgotten about it.

"And now this—this incident . . ." Henry cleared his throat. "I mean, I don't want to sound too callous about it, but it could be very useful."

"Useful?"

"For *raising awareness,* dear boy. For getting people interested in what you're doing."

"What I'm doing? Henry, I'm trying to finish this goddam *book.*"

"And you've done it, old boy. A wonderful book."

"That neglects to mention a major Spira executed during his supposedly sterile period in Tangier."

"Nick, just because an old man starts yelling about a picture—"

"You had to see him, Henry—the way he said it: 'Don't think you're going to get your hands on it.' As if I was there to take it from him."

"Bonkers, old thing. Barking. Obviously. You say yourself he may have syphilis. He's probably riddled with it."

"He says not."

"He might not even know."

"Come on, Henry. Grossman's going to know if he's got syphilis or not."

But saying it, he knew it wasn't true. There was syphilis and syphilis. It was an incredible disease; the tiny corkscrew bacteria could creep through a person for years unseen and unfelt, until the final disastrous collapse of the body. Other types manifested themselves only in bizarre behavior, delusions of grandeur, psychosis. And if head-butting a mirror wasn't bizarre, what was? He had to go back. He had to request another interview; he had to ask Grossman to undergo a medical examination.

"The fact remains, you're the only one to have talked to him in— what is it?"

"Twenty-six years," said Nick.

"Which in itself is a feather in your cap . . . hang on a second." There was a muffled crunch as Henry pushed the mouthpiece into his shoulder. He was talking to his wife, Kate. Nick thought of Linda and got a disagreeable shrinking feeling in his stomach. She had left two messages on the answering service. He needed to call her too.

"And what about the *ARTnews* piece?" said Henry, coming back. "Spira's confession?"

"What about it? What if Marion was lying? About what Frank said to him?"

"Why would he lie?"

"*I* don't know. To defend his stupid Faust idea."

"Nick."

"To jack up the prices on Spira's later work. You know how close he is to Nagel."

"*Nick,* you're overwrought. Have a drink from the minibar, for goodness sake. Calm down."

Nick covered his eyes, forced himself to breathe slowly. Henry was right. He needed to stay calm, to think clearly about what exactly was at stake here.

"Henry, Marion has this big idea. The only trouble is, there are no medical records, no doctor who has come forward to say, 'Yes, I treated Francis Spira for neurosyphilis.' No diagnosis, no prognosis, no treatment. And the same goes for Tony Reardon."

"But that's because Spira hated doctors. He led a very irregular life, Nick."

Irregular. A cap with a feather in it. Sometimes Henry's Englishness sounded like a put-on. Nick massaged his eyes.

"I should have gotten this nailed down. I should have nailed this down when I was in Tangier."

He had tried to do just that two years ago, had tried and failed. Tracking down the medical records of a couple of degenerate ex-patriates had been beyond his abilities.

"All you have to do is go back," said Henry. "These people at the clinic—this director woman. Maybe she'll know. Maybe Grossman had a recent checkup."

Nick shook his head. Pirez wouldn't know anything; for her, Grossman was just another street person. But that was what he had to do: go back. Beg for another interview maybe.

"And what about this picture?" he said, talking to himself as much as to Henry. "The *Incarnation*."

"Ask him, old thing. Ask him where he keeps it. Ask him how much he's got it insured for."

5

It was the telephone that awoke him. He'd crashed on top of the bed with all the windows open. He reached for the phone with his bandaged hand and got Linda, his long-suffering wife, calling from work. Linda managed a cinema in the West End, a job that sounded glamorous but actually involved opening the doors when the staff arrived and sitting in a dire windowless room until the credits came up. She wanted to know when he was planning on coming home. He told her the day after tomorrow, said he'd be there in the late afternoon.

"Because we need to talk."

Nick nodded. "You won't believe what happened today," he said.

"I can't believe you did it, Nick. With us being broke. I can't believe you got on the plane."

He closed his eyes. "Baby, can't this wait until I get back?"

"Do you have any idea how many hours I have to sit in this room to pay for your plane ticket?"

There was a scuffling sound on the other side of his door, a sharp knock.

"Do you have any idea how much Visa charges for—"

"Hang on, baby . . . just a second, there's a . . ." He put down the phone and went over to the door. A head bulged darkly in the lens of the fish-eye.

"NYPD Homicide. Could you open up, sir?"

The voice was sober, businesslike, bogus. A voice straight off the TV. Nick half-smiled, scratching his chin, waiting for the punch line, trying to figure out which of his New York friends knew he was in town.

"It'll only take a minute," said the voice.

Nick opened the door on a character in a badly fitting sport coat, breathing through his mouth as though holding up his badge was an effort. He said his name was Lawrence Bittaker, a detective with 9th Precinct Homicide. He had something in his mouth. Nick picked up a sweet smell of caramel and nuts, and over that a smoky burnt odor, as though the guy had just put out a cigarette and was now eating candy to mask the evidence.

"Are you Nicholas Greer?"

He produced a small Ziploc bag containing a business card with Nick's name on it. It was such a bizarre sight, Nick's heart started to knock before he could decide what was wrong. He asked the man to come in, went back to the phone.

"Baby?"

"Nick, I don't want to have to—"

"Sweetheart, there's a police officer here to talk to me. I've got to— I'll call you in an hour."

He hung up, turned. The detective was standing under the ceiling light, staring straight at him. Wiry, unkempt rust-colored hair rose toward the light fixture. He looked solid under his sport coat, a bar-room brawler with orange-peel skin; a guy who'd throw whisky in your face, burn you with his cigarette. There was something wrong with his nose. With the tip of it. Some kind of discoloration of the skin. He was working his tongue around his mouth, cleaning up in there.

He apologized for the intrusion, said it was his understanding that Nick had been down at the Delancey-Deere Volunteer Center earlier that evening. "We picked up one of your cards."

This time when he showed the bag, Nick saw the brownish smudge just above his name and the feeling came back with a rush, the feeling he'd had when Grossman told him about the *Incarnation*; it was like being lifted up. You are in a river, and you are swept away.

"Yes," he said. "I left it . . ." He had left it next to Grossman's bed while Pirez and the attendant were dealing with Grossman on the floor. He'd scribbled his hotel address on the back, a half-assed gesture towards a second meeting. "I was interviewing one of their . . . Detective—what happened?"

"Interviewing?"

The detective picked up the tape which was next to the microcassette, turned it over in his chunky fingers. That was when he noticed the bandage on Nick's hand.

"He bit me," said Nick, and then he was gabbling, trying to explain everything at once: he was a writer, he was writing a book, Frank Spira, Grossman the lover, a millionaire who never got his teeth fixed, Grossman's gnashers, sunk into his flesh.

The cop stared.

"Please," said Nick. "Did something happen?"

It had taken place in Grossman's room. A "blitz attack," the cop called it. They were sitting now, the cop in the armchair, Nick on the bed, taking deep breaths, his hands planted on his knees to stop the shaking.

"They're still working the scene. So we're—as part of our investigation—we're canvassing, talking to anybody who was down there today. Just to build a picture."

Nick nodded, got a flash of Jacob Grossman, aged twenty, sitting at a table, surrounded by laughing people; then Grossman turning in his wheelchair; the absurdly black hair with its yellow roots, the horny nail inside his ragged lower lip. There had been a moment in the struggle—on the floor, Grossman on top of him—when he had grabbed the old man's elbow. It had felt big, corky.

"Mr. Greer?"

Nick came out of it, staring into the cop's pale eyes.

"How well did you know the deceased?"

"Not at all. I mean—not personally. But I've been working on this book for a number of years, so I suppose I know—I mean, what there is to know up to 1972. Pretty much everything."

"Everything, huh? Up to 1972? Well, that just leaves a gap of twenty-six years."

The cop smiled, showing squeezed rodent teeth, but his tone was sarcastic. "Anything you can tell me," he said, "any background information on the victim, would be a big help."

So Nick told the story: the life and sudden disappearance of Jacob Nathaniel Grossman, shaking his head the whole time, unable to take in what had just happened.

When he got to the end, the cop wanted to know if he could think of any reason why anybody would want to do this terrible thing. "Because these people—this Spira circle, it sounds . . ."

"Strange. That's right. Spira attracted a lot of strangeness—a lot of odd people, marginal people, are drawn to his paintings."

The cop looked at the microcassette. "This interview you did. Am I right in thinking you recorded it?" They played the tape. With the volume boosted to maximum, every little sound rumbled through rough-edged, at the limit of coherence. Pirez leaving the room was a series of muffled explosions and then a crash as she closed the door. When they got to Grossman threatening to bite Nick's face, Bittaker stopped the machine.

Nick shrugged. "Mr. Grossman," he said, "he was very—*disturbed.*"

The phone rang. Nick went to pick it up, but Bittaker put his hand on it, smiling, said they weren't going to be much longer. He just wanted to ask his questions and then he would be gone. But when the tape was finished, he went through it again, fast-forwarding here and there, stopping to listen more closely, leaning nearer to the machine as though wanting to catch every little sound. The end of the tape, when Grossman was getting agitated, he listened to four times.

"What's the noise?"

He rewound. Hit PLAY. Nick heard the creak of the wheelchair, Grossman standing up.

Oh Jesus. Sweet bleeding Jesus. Oh Jesus.

There was the thump of his plaster cast on the floor, and the feathery sound he made, a small fricative explosion of teeth against lip. The cop examined the microcassette, a battered old Panasonic with two speed settings. He switched it to the slower speed. Rewound. Hit PLAY.

This time the creak of the wheelchair was an extended metallic groan. Grossman's voice rumbled out of the hissing layered depths.

Oooooh Jeeeesuuuus. Sweeeeet bleeediiing Jeeeesuuuus. Ooooooh Jeeeeesuuuus.

Then there was something else, Grossman, intelligible at the slower speed.

FrankFrankFrankFrankFrankFrankFrankFrankFrankFrankFrank.

Calling out in anguish, maybe, or in reproach.

"And that's when he bit you?"

Nick looked up and met the cop's cold gaze. "Pardon me?"

"There, at the end, when he starts screaming."

"It all got a little—a little crazy. He smashed his face. Into a mirror. I grabbed hold of him and—and that was when he . . ." He looked at his bandaged hand and shuddered.

The cop wanted to know why Grossman would do a thing like that. Nick shook his head.

"Because you'd say there'd have to be a reason."

Nick told him how, when Barbara Segal had called on him a few days ago, Grossman had tried to jump out of the window.

"He was very volatile. Scared. Paranoid, I suppose you'd say."

"Barbara?"

The cop had a pencil stub in his crude red fingers. Nick gave him the full name. Gave him, reluctantly, Barb's number. The cop double-underlined everything he wrote.

"Hell of a thing," he said. "The victim says the word 'mercury' four times. Just before he puts his face in the mirror. What's the signif-icance? We're talking about what? A cure, you say?"

"A cure, yes. For syphilis. I think—for what it's worth, I think maybe Grossman understood that Reardon *did* have syphilis, and that instead of getting it treated properly, went to a local quack. And that—that this meant that Spira was infected and that he too—Grossman—must therefore . . ."

But he couldn't bring himself to finish the phrase. The speculation, the fuzziness of it, was like a bad taste in his mouth.

"Detective, is there any chance of doing a test on the body?"

"A test?" said the cop. "You want to do a test?"

"I'd like to know if Grossman was infected. With syphilis. It's for my book."

The cop stared for a long time, thinking this over, finding bits in his teeth, chewing.

"I doubt that, Mr. Greer."

"It's just that—"

"Let me . . ." The cop put up a hand. He wanted to get through his questions first. That was the priority. "What did he mean about you not getting your hands on it?"

"I don't know."

"What was he talking about? This picture?"

"Maybe. But . . ."

"But?"

"Well, there's a possibility that this business with the painting—that it's just delusional. Neurosyphilis, if he had it, can—"

"You don't think this picture exists?"

"I don't know. I mean, if it existed, if it *still* existed, this picture would be very valuable."

"Yeah?"

"Yes. Even during his lifetime, I mean latterly, towards the end of his life, Spira's paintings were extremely sought after. Nearly all the major paintings are in museums. And here we're talking about what would be his sole religious work. It would come to auction with a reserve of at least six million dollars."

The cop jutted his bottom lip, impressed.

"So you have to wonder why it would be such a big secret," said Nick. "Why it isn't in someone's collection."

"Maybe because Mr. Grossman had it?"

"Where? He's a—he *was* a bum. A street person. He had *nothing*."

Nick stood up, surprised by the sound of his own voice, the desperate edge to it. He wanted to believe in Grossman's delusion, hated the idea that there might be a major Spira out there that he knew nothing about. He walked over to the minibar, offered the cop a drink. The cop shook his head.

"Never drink when I'm stoned," he said.

Nick laughed, but the truth was the cop made him uneasy. There was something about him. An ugliness that went beyond his looks. Nick tossed the drink back, felt it burn all the way down.

"But look at that guy who bumped into Howard Hughes in the desert," said the cop. "He thought Hughes was a bum too. Fact is, this guy's been missing for—what?—twenty-six years. You don't really know who or what he was."

Nick shook his head, found himself laughing. It just seemed to well up out of him—hard, disdainful laughter.

"I'm sorry," he said. "It just . . . none of this really sits with the evidence."

The cop was scratching at his cheek now. His hair twisted upwards towards the light, brittle, red. A frozen flame.

"But wasn't that today's lesson?" he said softly.

"What?"

"That your evidence . . . that it's patchy, incomplete. What was it Mr. Grossman said? That you were lost in the woods?"

"*Mi retrovai per una selva oscura,*" said Nick.

The cop clicked his teeth together—*tic, tic, tic.*

"What he said to me," said Nick. "It's a quote. Dante. From the beginning of the *Inferno.*"

The cop had his head on one side, doing the thing with his teeth again.

"At the beginning of the *Inferno,*" said Nick, "Dante is lost in a wood."

"Yeah?" Nodding appreciatively now, but the eyes cold. "Isn't that great?"

"What?"

"Knowing that kind of stuff. I mean, here you are, and you just know that."

Nick shrugged.

"Is that how you see yourself?" said the cop.

"Pardon me?"

"Lost. Lost in a wood as night begins to fall."

The question hung in the air. Wrong. Weird. Nick didn't know if it was the jet lag, but it seemed to him like a strange thing for a homicide cop to say. The guy was weird.

"So, Nick," he said softly. "Man-to-man. Out here in the woods. Are you telling me you didn't go back up there?"

"Go back?"

"After the—this scuffle? You didn't go back up there? You didn't want to get even? Here's this old guy—bites you on the hand. Fuckin' hurts, famous teeth or not. You didn't go back up there, give vent to your feelings?"

Nick let out a breath. He said he wasn't a murderer, and it sounded like a lie.

6

He didn't sleep more than an hour, too jangled to switch off, the interview with Detective Bittaker, the interview with Grossman, going round and round in his head. He didn't think the cop seriously considered him as a suspect—he'd moved on pretty swiftly after Nick had denied it outright—but just having the finger of the law point momentarily in his direction had been enough to keep him awake until four in the morning, when he called home and got the machine. He tried leaving a message explaining why he'd failed to return Linda's call, but then ran out of tape. With dawn showing streakily red over the park, he sat down at the dressing table and transcribed the Grossman interview into his notebook, feeling a mixture of gloom and euphoria. Not only was the *Life* not finished, somehow he'd gotten inside it. It had bitten him on the hand.

He came to with the sun in his eyes. He'd fallen asleep, slumped over the dressing table, the spiral binder of his notebook digging into his cheek. He called home again and got the machine a second time. Linda was either in the shower or sulking, refusing to answer. He'd hung up on her. At least that was the way she'd see it. He'd hung up on her when she'd wanted to talk.

He went down to the street and bought a paper, read it in a diner right next to the hotel. Between Monicagate and the transatlantic banana war, between Viagra and the World Cup, the *New York Times* carried the story in the "Metro" section.

Millionaire Photographer Dies in LES Hostel
Yesterday evening 7th Precinct detectives were called
to the scene of a brutal killing at the Delancey-Deere
Volunteer Center, a city-funded rehab facility for drug
and alcohol abusers located on the Lower East Side.
Leroy Weller, the facility staff member who found
resident patient Jacob Grossman on the floor of his
room just after 6 P.M., was given counseling by the
New York Police Department and instructed not to
give details regarding the crime scene.

Lucia Pirez, the facility director, said that Mr.
Grossman had entered her care several months earlier
and had been making good progress in his rehabilitation. Grossman was a well-known photographer in the
1930s, and a great-grandson of the dry-goods millionaire Freddy (Flipper) Grossman.

A tight-lipped Detective Eugene Glasco, of 7th
Precinct Homicide, would say only that it was a particularly brutal murder and that the department would
spare no efforts in bringing the killer or killers to justice. Glasco refused to confirm rumors that one of
the inmates of the facility, a white male in his early
twenties being treated for crack addiction, had been
detained for questioning.

Morning light bounced off plate glass on the building opposite,
lighting dusty oblongs in the diner's window. He drank burnt coffee
until his hands were shaking, as he tried to decide what to do. He had
just one more day in Manhattan. He'd given himself two to get the
Grossman interview, hadn't felt he could justify the expense of taking
three, let alone the week he now felt he needed. He had one more day
and a couple of questions he wanted to put to a person he'd probably
never get a chance to see again.

Back in the hotel room he sat down at the desk and flipped open his
address book at the letter T, aware that what he was about to do
broke rules established six years earlier when he'd first started work
on the Life. Eighty-three years of age, and from very old European
money, Laverne Beatrix Scitovsky Taubmann communicated exclusively by letter. Picking up the telephone was not the way you reached

her. Not that she was a reluctant source; Laverne had always been more than happy to help with the *Life,* which she saw as a memorial to her dead husband, the collector Max Taubmann, rather than a biography of Frank Spira, but poor health, and her doctor, didn't always allow it. Laverne employed two nurses on a live-in, full-time basis, a physiotherapist, a spiritual mentor (R.C.), a curator for Max's priceless collection of modern art, a personal assistant, a Hungarian chef, a butler, and a team of domestics, not to mention the standard plutocrat's backup of attorneys, insurance experts, accountants, brokers, fund managers, and bankers. But at the heart of it all was Dr. Adele Gallagher. It was Gallagher rather than the personal assistant who stood between Laverne and the outside world, Gallagher, with her powerful drugs, who stood between Laverne and the next. The guardian of her patron's spectacularly bad health, she had somehow, over the years, also become the guardian of her time. Laverne's daughter, Gael, resented Gallagher's closeness to her mother; it had been the cause of numerous arguments, but nothing Gael could say made any difference. Gallagher was unshakable, and obviously intended to nurse Laverne to her dying breath. She had always treated Nick with suspicion and coldness. As far as he could tell, simply because he was an outsider and so obviously poor.

He took a deep breath and keyed in the numbers.

It was one of Laverne's social people who replied. Nick didn't recognize her, and assumed she was the latest in a long line of personal assistants who sooner or later got on the wrong side of Gallagher. He announced himself and was immediately put on hold. He looked out the window, doodling—circles, spirals, webs—ear to the phone, waiting for Gallagher to come on the line, because that was who it would be, he felt sure of it.

"Mr. Greer?" It was the woman again. "I'm afraid no one can talk to you right now."

"Oh?"

There was a purposeful silence at the other end.

"Can I at least leave a message?"

He heard a sigh, a rustle of papers.

"Go ahead."

"Could you tell Mrs. Taubmann that I spoke to Jacob Grossman yesterday and that he talked to me about Tangier?"

"Tangier?"

"Yes. Actually, could you say 'the *Incarnation*'?"

He could hear the woman's breath against the mouthpiece as she wrote.

"I'm in Manhattan for the day, and I need to see her."

"You're calling today to make an appointment to see her today?"

"I know this isn't the way she likes to do things, but—well, it's an urgent matter. And—"

"I very much doubt whether Mrs. Taubmann will be able to receive you. She had a very bad night, and—"

"Perhaps I should give you my number here."

There was another sigh.

Nick gave her his number and hung up, wondered if Laverne's bad night had anything to do with the news about Grossman.

He checked his watch, then called the Delancey-Deere Volunteer Center and got a busy signal. He called the Office of the Chief Medical Examiner of New York City and talked to a press relations person. He told her about the book. Told her he'd interviewed Jacob Grossman just before he was murdered. She told him they weren't releasing any details to the press.

"I'm not press. I'm a writer. I've been writing this book for—"

"Whatever you are, we're not releasing details."

"The thing is, I have a—what you might call a personal stake in this matter. You see, Mr. Grossman bit me."

"Pardon me?"

"I don't know if you know it, but Mr. Grossman was suffering from paranoid delusions, and—"

"Mr. . . . ?"

"Greer."

"Look, I'm sorry, but I'm going to have to—"

"He told me he was HIV-positive, and I believe he was also infected with syphilis. So my concern is that in biting me he may have—"

"Yes. I see." She put him on hold for a second, dealing with another caller, then came back. "Have you spoken to the director of the facility where Mr. Grossman was a patient?"

"They're not answering."

"Well, I suggest you keep trying them. I daresay the director will have the relevant medical records. If not, I suggest you go see your doctor."

"Can you at least tell me if the autopsy will include—"

"I'm sorry, sir, but I can't help you at this time."

The line went dead.

He called the Delancey-Deere again. Busy. He keyed in a new number.

Barbara Segal picked up almost immediately. She sounded terrible, said she hadn't slept all night. She had been watching New York 1 around midnight when the story started to bleed through—the usual handheld glimpses of red-splashed walls and grim-faced cops trying to go about their business. She didn't think for a second that the killing would turn out to be drug-related.

"They say they're talking to this crack addict, but—Jacob was *scared,* Nick. When I went to see him—when he first saw me—"

"I know. You already told me. Listen, Barb, the reason I'm—"

"No, but I've been thinking about it all night. Nick, he thought I was there to—I don't know, to *hurt* him. He was screaming about knives."

"Knives?" Nick frowned, drew a dagger in his notebook, the tip pointing downwards. "You didn't say anything about that when we talked."

"Well, I thought it was all just part of the general craziness, but since this happened I've been asking myself, just how crazy was he? I mean—did you see the reports? In the press? The *Daily News* is calling it a frenzied attack. Apparently there was blood just *everywhere.*"

For a moment Nick thought he'd lost the signal. Then he heard crying.

"Barb?"

"I'm okay. I'll be okay."

"Barb, have the police been in touch with you?"

"The police, no. Why?"

He told her about the visit he'd received, how he'd been obliged to give up her number.

"How come the cop came to you?" she said, her voice squeezed almost to a whisper.

"I don't know—I was one of the last people to see him alive. This detective was doing a canvass, looking for leads."

"So what did he say? Do they have anything? Did he talk about this crack junkie?"

"No. He didn't talk about the case, really. He was very interested by what Jacob had to say about the *Incarnation.*"

"The what?"

"The *Incarnation*. You know, the painting Frank was supposed to have not done in Tangier."

"You lost me."

"Frank did a painting in Tangier. A Madonna and Child. Then he destroyed it. That's the consensus view anyway."

"And Jacob, he said different?"

"It was freaky. It was . . . He told me I wasn't going to get my hands on it."

"The *Incarnation*?" she said, sounding completely lost now. There was the snap of a lighter, a tight inhale. "Oh Jesus, Nick. This is what I'm saying. This is what I'm talking about. There's something behind this. Something . . ."

Behind, below, somewhere out of sight. Nick scribbled the dagger blade black.

"Barb, the reason I called: I wanted to ask if you told anyone else where Jacob was staying."

She thought about it for a second, blew smoke at the phone.

"Only you," she said.

He watched the hour hand on his watch move around to ten. He was thinking about just walking over to Park Avenue and getting the doorman to press Laverne Taubmann's bell when the phone rang. It was an editor with the *New York Times*. A woman called Miriam Florey, a friend of Henry's. Apparently, Henry had called her the day before and told her Nick was in Manhattan researching the book.

"He said you'd managed to find Jacob Grossman, the lover. That you actually interviewed him."

"Yeah—yes, that's right."

Nick took a seat on the edge of the bed.

"Well, Henry asked if we'd be interested in a piece on Grossman. Unfortunately, we've already commissioned a couple of pieces for the Guggenheim retrospective. So I said to Henry we'd be unlikely to be able to do anything for you."

Nick looked out the window. He hadn't asked for anything, but here he was being refused.

"Did Henry talk to you about this already?" she said.

"No."

"Good. Anyway. Then suddenly this happens."

"What?"

"The murder. What I had in mind was using you as a source for something *I'm* writing—quoting you, if that would be okay, and plugging your book, of course. Henry tells me Crucible is going to be publishing it here.

Nick squeezed the tip of his ear. "I'm not sure they've actually decided," he said.

Florey laughed. "Well, maybe this will decide them."

Nick lay on the bed and for the second time in twenty-four hours launched into the life story of Jacob Grossman. After forty minutes Florey called time. She said she wished she'd known about him when they were commissioning the pieces for the retrospective.

"Who's doing them?" said Nick.

"Martin Marion," she said. "Do you know him?"

As soon as Nick put the phone down, it rang. It was Laverne's assistant.

"Mrs. Taubmann says you should come by at four o'clock," she said. "Present yourself to the doorman. Someone will come down to you."

Nick gaped, so surprised to have been granted an audience without any hassle that he didn't know what to say.

"I hope you're not going to ask me to change that," said the woman. "Because—"

"No, four o'clock's perfect. I'm just . . . Dr. Gallagher okayed this?"

"Doctor Gallagher is *asleep*," said the woman, and it was clear from her tone that Gallagher was not her favorite person. "Mrs. Taubmann herself 'okayed' it. Is that okay?"

7

Detective Eugene Glasco ripped open the fat manila envelope and pulled out the prints. Ninety-six 5 x 7s: four rolls of film, twenty-four frames per roll—400 ISO, color. On the other side of the double desk, Raymond Guthry stopped writing and sipped cold coffee, watching Europe go through the shots. Five feet ten and at least thirty pounds overweight, Eugene had the look of a sourpuss high school teacher as he peered into the envelope in search of the photographic log.

Ringing phones. In the far corner of the big room, Patti Bonner, the catching detective for the day's B&Es, was jive-talking with a guy in the lockup as she processed his paperwork.

But Eugene was oblivious.

He examined each shot, checking it against the log and his own sketch of the scene. He was going to be fifty-three years old in two weeks—a typical Virgo according to Raymond's wife, Karen: cranky, cautious, a perfectionist.

Peering down through his gold-rimmed half-moons, the side of his face lit by a ribbon of sunlight: a sourpuss teacher assessing term papers. From where he was sitting, Raymond could see glossy carnage, red mayhem. A shot of partition wall showed an explosion of arterial crimson. In another, oblique light at floor level illuminated the linoleum beneath the victim's bed. Blood trapped woolly debris, a discarded match, a rubber band—each small thing with its black-red tail of shadow. The surface of a faraway planet.

Eugene looked up and caught Raymond staring. One thing Eugene didn't like about his partner, this tendency to drift. It seemed to him to indicate a lack of purpose. Benign, dreamy, with soft brown hair that he wore a little long, Raymond looked more like a country-and-western singer than a cop.

"Carol Ritt," said Eugene. "Just joined the Brooklyn satellite. Nice job. Did a nice job on my floor."

My floor. Raymond wondered if he even realized he'd said it. Virgo, Karen would say: anal. One of the reasons Valerie left him.

"Scene couldn't be better. From a protection point of view."

Raymond nodded. Protecting the Crime Scene: the creed Eugene lived by.

The officer who'd responded to the 911 had been outside the victim's room when they'd arrived. Like the kid who'd found the body, all he'd done was take a peek inside. A quick glance was all that was needed to see you couldn't do anything for the guy on the floor. A lucky break, since otherwise Eugene would have chewed him out for touching, smearing, moving.

The floor, exactly the way the killer had left it.

The corridor was a different matter. People had been back and forth, tracking in mud and water from the storm. They'd tried the door to the fire escape and found it open.

Eugene worked the stairs with his flashlight, cursing, getting wet, complaining about his back, while they'd waited for the rest of the team to arrive. He'd walked around out back in the storm-blue light, taking a peek in trash cans, checking out likely exit points, windows from which somebody might have seen something. Came back up shaking his head.

Ritt had shot the first pictures through the doorway—walls, floor, ceiling—then from each corner of the small room, moving carefully, following Eugene's instructions. From the general to the particular and finally to the macro.

Finger marks: visible everywhere, particularly on the body.

Ritt shot one-to-ones with Polaroid 665 black-and-white for ten minutes, crouching over the improvised pillow—a picture taped to the wall, a pair of pants. Finger marks everywhere. In one place a full span that suggested a large male. It was going to take forever to exclude facility staff, patients, Grossman himself.

Individual hairs not matching the victim's, scattered over a wide area; fiber—blue, some kind of stretch cotton—snagged on the bed frame.

Their first take on the scene was that it had been a frenzied attack, a blitz. It was something they rarely saw. The 7th Precinct was the smallest in the city, covering just over a square mile. Since the crackdown on narcotics activity in the early nineties, homicides in the area had been reduced to around half a dozen a year. What murders there were tended to result from domestic violence or plain stupidity—vehicle disputes, noisy neighbors.

Raymond canvassed the third floor, making his way along the landing with the facility director, Lucia Pirez, who was clearly upset, and very worried about being closed down. She kept saying how nothing like this had ever happened before. Kept saying that there was nobody in the center crazy enough to do what had been done to Jack. People came to her because they were looking for a solution, she said. They weren't psychotic. The patients opened their doors warily, staring out with scared eyes. Their responses to Raymond's questions were monosyllabic.

Then Raymond had an idea: he asked Pirez if they could set up a command post in the TV room, somewhere the guys working the scene could take a break, have a smoke, a sandwich. She was nice about it. She called a local deli, then went down to the basement to find more Cremora for the Mr. Coffee.

Raymond reworked the landing, starting out with a call on a jumpy Hispanic named Rico he liked the look of. Rico said Jack had been in a brawl with another Delancey-Deere resident, Mr. Spock, earlier in the day. Spock lived in a room with two other guys up on four. Raymond walked up on his own. It took about a third of a second for all the rubberneckers to get back in their rooms. When Raymond asked Spock about the argument with Jack, Spock became very agitated and tried to run. They took him back to the station, but the interview went nowhere and they'd had to release him in the early hours.

"They call the Delancey-Deere 'DD,'" said Raymond. "The Hotel Junky."

Eugene looked up from a picture of Jacob Grossman's face—a painted Halloween mask, dark hair in stiff peaks.

The unbelievable mouth.

"Yeah, but if we were talking PCP or crack or crank or ice or whatever, our perp's gonna stagger off wailing at the moon. We're gonna have smears, footprints. Here what we have is bupkis."

Eugene fingered his mustache when he was worried.

"No blood," he said, dragging slowly upward against the short bristles. "Outside."

He looked down at the stack of prints. "No blood in the corridor, no blood on the fire escape. When he left the room, this guy was clean. He had a routine worked out."

"What about the water?" said Raymond. There had been some water on the bed as if somebody had spilt a glass or cup, but nothing like that had been recovered from the room. The water was annoying. It was like a piece of some childish riddle.

The ringing phones. The guy in lockup, raising his voice.

Eugene looked out the window and gave an irritable shrug.

"The writer," he said. "This character that interviewed Grossman in the afternoon. He's the one I'd like to talk to."

8

Laverne Taubmann was as near as Nick ever got to a real sense of the tidal forces driving the global art market. Valued at $10 billion worldwide, the tide had gone out when Saddam entered Kuwait, but according to the dealers and the collectors, the magazines and the journals, the liquidity was out there beyond the horizon, a glittering tsunami of cash just waiting to come flooding back, and 1998 was the year it was going to happen.

There were plenty of rich Spiraphiles, of course, people Nick had gotten to know over the years of writing the *Life*. Oscar Nagel, the preeminent collector of Spira's work, owned a five-story building in Soho and paintings worth at least $200 million, while Alby Schadt, the other big U.S. collector, was going slowly crazy on a zillion acres of oil land in Texas. But next to Laverne, Schadt was a dirt farmer, Nagel, a guy with a tin cup.

Not that she was spending it anymore. Despite retaining a full-time curator, she'd initiated few changes in Max's collection, which was more or less as he left it when he died in 1975. As far as Nick could tell, the last big check she'd written with her own pleasure in mind had been to Parish-Hadley to have them decorate the twenty-three-room Park Avenue duplex in 1987. It was Gael, her only child, who liked to live it up, Gael who was always having cosmetic surgery, Gael who wore D&G cashmere and Jil Sander suits, Gael who kept a yacht at the Surfside 3 Marina, Gael who wanted to sell Daddy's paintings so that she could *really* start living.

Sitting in the anteroom Laverne reserved for unimportant visitors, Nick tried to pinch creases into the knees of his pants and looked around at the paintings on the walls—none of them from Max's col-

lection, none of them under two hundred years old. A whimsical
Tiepolo. A by-the-yard Canaletto. The real show began once you got
into the depths of the apartment, and then it was like MoMA meets
the Frick. Max was present here, though, represented in a large
monochrome print which showed him standing on the steps of the
New York Public Library, circa 1940. A narrow-faced man with dark
eyes, smiling shyly, glad no doubt to have escaped the Nazis.

Born in Milan, the son of a prosperous banker, he had studied law
at Milan University and then gone on to Budapest to work for an Italian insurance company. It was in Budapest that he met Laverne. They
married soon after and, to the detriment of Max's career in insurance,
spent the next three years on a cultural tour of Europe in one of
Laverne's father's Daimlers. It was during this protracted honeymoon
that Max acquired Spira's undisputed masterpiece, *Cupid,* walking
into the Curzon Street exhibition in London on June 3, 1934, and
paying twenty guineas for it.

Since his death, Max had become a kind of idol for Laverne, and
she wanted him commemorated in the *Life.* Generally speaking, Nick
had been happy to oblige. In the beginning it had seemed like a small
price to pay for what Laverne offered in return, which, simply put,
was credibility. When people had found out that Laverne was talking
to him, they had also opened their doors. But in the last few years her
"collaboration" had come to feel more like a ball and chain. Used to
having her own way in everything, she had a tendency to treat the
book as her own project. She could be evasive too—unreliable, if not
downright dishonest.

It was a matter of record, for example, that Max had affairs in the
late fifties. For Laverne these never happened. Similarly she pooh-
poohed the idea that her selling *Cupid* to Oscar Nagel the year Max
died was in any sense remarkable. But the work had been precious to
Max, the keystone in his collection's great, humanist and essentially
figurative arch. Barb saw the sale as a symbolic castration, Laverne
getting her own back for all Max's philandering. But Nick thought it
more likely that Nagel had paid some kind of nose-bleedingly strato-
spheric price (Nagel had a reputation as an impulsive and sometimes
reckless buyer). There was no knowing either way. Laverne's silence
in this matter was sepulchral, while Nagel would only hint at financial issues better left in the past. *Cupid* was a stone he didn't want the
IRS turning over.

A young woman went by, white moccasins scudding over the price-less Bessarabian carpet. There were people everywhere, coming and going in busy silence. The Louis XVI clock chimed the hour four minutes late.

Nick flipped open his notebook and stared at his scribbled questions for the hundredth time. He drew a line under the word "Tangier," and just like that, characteristically, tuned out of the anteroom and its walnut paneling and began to brood. Tangier was where things went wrong for Laverne, where her life touched bottom.

Spira went out there in 1956, and a year later, Laverne followed—a forty-two-year-old woman, starting to get heavy in the hips but still with her Grace Kelly complexion. She'd been staying in Nice with friends from her Paris days but had decided to go on to Tangier—of all the places she could have gone, of all the places available on her circuit, probably the least prepossessing.

On the two occasions Nick had managed to bully her into talking about it, she'd said she'd been in need of a change of air. She had gone to visit her friends and found that while their Italianate villa was a long way from Manhattan, the table she sat down to at eight o'clock each evening might as well have been in the dining room of an apartment on the Upper East Side, so persistent was the talk of home.

She had decided to go to Tangier to get away from the gossip.

The problem with this version, the thing that had always made Nick uneasy, was that by going to Tangier, by seeking out Frank Spira, someone who fascinated Max, and with whom Max continued to correspond, she had, in a sense, gone round in a circle. She was just as likely to hear news from home, and face questions about Max's infidelity (the circumstance she was fleeing in the first place), in Tangier as in Nice—perhaps even more likely, given Spira's vivisectionist approach to conversation.

Nick frowned, drew another line under the word.

This kind of ambivalence was one of the reasons he found the whole Tangier section of the book so unsatisfactory, so soft, why he had reworked it so often, cementing the cracks, pouring the ballast of circumstantial detail into the shifting foundations. For the same reason, it seemed to him, other commentators, people like Marion, loved the period. With so little to go on, the mythmakers had always had a field day.

He had come to believe that the real point of Laverne's two-week stopover had been to needle Max, to make him jealous. Her friendship and easy affinity with Spira was well-documented fact. That the friendship had provoked jealous outbursts from Max was also a matter of record. But if a desire to get at Max might explain Tangier, Laverne's subsequent journey into the interior, a trek which lasted all of three months, remained unexplained. Laverne's gloss on the matter was typical: tourism—the bone-brown nudity of the Moroccan interior had been too seductive; you couldn't just give it a look and then turn away.

The accepted view, the view promulgated by Martin Marion among others, was that Laverne's Sahara excursion was the culmination of a long slide into depression. There was even speculation that she'd had a nervous breakdown there. The fact that Max sent her off to a clinic on the West Coast when she finally got back to the States seemed like confirmation. But here again details were lacking.

Nick's own contribution to the debate was the discovery of a document which had come to him via the Archive of American Art from the estate of Lee Morgan Lassiter, the anthropologist, a letter in which he described a bizarre encounter with Laverne in the bar of a hotel in Meknes, a city on the edge of the Middle Atlas Mountains, in November 1957. It was the only fragment to have come to light from that empty time in Laverne's life, a little opening in the darkness.

Lassiter had known Laverne in Manhattan in the forties, but since then his work had kept him traveling, mainly in the Far East. He hadn't seen Laverne for over ten years and had been struck by the change in her appearance, describing her as looking "positively cadaverous in the bloated, partially cooked way of cadavers in this climate." She was sitting at a small table sharing a bottle of wine with a "grubby-looking" local who, it turned out, was the driver of the prewar Mercedes in which she was touring the country. Her trademark Charles James dresses had been replaced by a black muslin *haik*, the head-to-foot garment used by the local women to cover themselves in public, but her face, puffy and red, was exposed. She had just come from Erfoud, she told Lassiter, and had been badly burnt in the desert. "She spoke in a monotonous drawl," Lassiter wrote, "struggling to form her words, never quite looking straight at me, or at anything else for that matter. I presume she must have been taking some opiate or other. If I hadn't gone up to her table, I don't think she would have said anything, even though we once knew each other quite well."

Whether it was her failing marriage that had brought her to that low point or something else altogether, something that happened while she was traveling in the desert, Nick had no idea. Laverne's response to Lassiter's observations (Nick wrote to her the day he read the letter in the Smithsonian) was a mixture of fire and smoke. Yes, she did have a vague memory of getting badly burnt in Erfoud, and resorting to kif to deal with the pain, but if anyone was a bloated cadaver it was Lee Lassiter, who, if you'd given him a fly whisk and a tarbush, would have been Sidney Greenstreet *tout craché*.

Nick gazed at the writing on the page, oblivious to the young woman who went by bearing a carafe of water.

Whatever else may have happened in Tangier, he knew that Laverne had seen a painting there, and that the painting was probably the *Incarnation*. The timing was certainly right. Spira had written a letter to his dealer on October 7 in which he mentioned "a large canvas of a religious subject." Since he had never painted anything religious before or since, the *Incarnation* seemed like a good candidate. Laverne had spent the first two weeks of October with Spira and Reardon, almost exclusively in their company, and at least part of the time actually at the Rue d'Angleterre apartment. When Spira did attempt to paint there, it was in an all-purpose space which they called the "loving room." If the painting had been there, Laverne almost certainly would have seen it. In fact, she said as much in a letter written twenty years later.

The year after Max's death, Alby Schadt had apparently written to her (the letter had been lost), asking for confirmation of a rumor that Max had sent a buyer to purchase the *Incarnation* from Tony Reardon in London a couple of months before Reardon's death in 1971, and that Reardon had refused to sell. Laverne penned a categorical reply (Nick had seen it at Schadt's Texas home). Not only had Max never sent a buyer, it was ridiculous to assume that Reardon could have been in possession of such a picture. "Why," she wrote, "would a degenerate pederast like Reardon, whose sole aim in life was to line his own greasy pockets, have refused to part with one of Frank's works, when he had already taken the liberty of selling other pieces of which he was not even the proprietor? The simple fact is Reardon never owned the painting because the painting was almost certainly destroyed in Tangier."

So how had the rumor gotten started? Nick didn't know. When he'd put the question to Schadt, it was clear Schadt had no idea who had told him about the supposed visit. Then again, Schadt wasn't always clear which day it was, and these were events that had taken place a long time ago. Had Reardon been trying to scam somebody? Pretending he had a picture that didn't exist? Why not? It was certainly his style. But if that were the case, the rumor would have been different, wouldn't have hinged on the unlikely idea of Reardon refusing to sell. Unless it was a screw-up: Reardon backing out at the last minute, because whatever it was he'd been trying to pull (selling a copy as the real thing?) hadn't come off.

Nick let out a low groan. This was the trouble with speculation. This was what he hated. Once you started, there was no end to it.

In conclusion to her letter to Schadt, Laverne had pointed out that Spira himself had always maintained there was no *Incarnation*. She then went on to describe a large red canvas that she remembered seeing at the Rue d'Angleterre apartment in October '57, a painting of a mother and baby in a stark boxlike space. "I suspect all the rumors surrounding this religious painting can be traced back to that work," she wrote, " a work that Spira started in October 1957, and which he subsequently destroyed."

Brooding, churning, Nick drew a circle around "Tangier." The painting had existed and then been abandoned. Another of Spira's Tangier discards, like the landscape he had famously stamped to pieces in the street. Except that the *Incarnation* had never been stamped to pieces anywhere, at least not according to the record. And there was another difference: *Desert Landscape 1957* found its way into a gallery on Cork Street for the simple reason that it was worth serious money. How come that hadn't happened to the *Incarnation*? Because it *had* been destroyed, just as Laverne said.

Simple.

But nothing was simple where Tangier was concerned.

The tip of Nick's pen slowed to a halt on the paper as a connection loomed. As he sat there in his wrinkled suit, canted forward, his face no more than a foot from the page, a pattern seemed to condense out of the material, a bizarre pattern. Grossman and Reardon were part of it. Also, the doubtful ownership of a dubious painting. A visit

(Max's putative buyer and yesterday Grossman had certainly thought he'd come on business) and a sudden, brutal death. Reardon hadn't been murdered; he'd killed himself, crashing his car, à la Jackson Pollock. But apart from that . . .

"Nicholas."

He looked up sharply.

Dr. Gallagher had come into the room, approaching with characteristic stealth, and now stood before him, giving off a thin vinegary smell, her upper body swaying slightly as though she were tethered rather than actually standing on the thick black and pink carpet.

Gallagher had a large, imposing head framed by hair raked back into a sharp-toothed headband. Her pale freckled lips were always slightly indrawn, and seemed to be constantly working beneath the gray stillness of her eyes. About to be fifty, she had been with the Taubmanns for nearly the whole of her professional life, having first entered the Park Avenue residence to care for Max when he became ill. Nick had interviewed her only once, and that was at the house Max had given her, a somber, neglected brownstone in the East 90s that she still owned. These days, because of Laverne's fragile health, she occupied rooms on the second floor of the Park Avenue duplex.

"I'm afraid I can't approve of this," she said.

Nick stood up and submitted to Gallagher's hostile scrutiny. It wasn't clear whether she was more appalled by his hair or his suit.

"I understand you want to talk to her about Tangier."

"Hello, Dr. Gallagher. How are you today?"

She registered the sarcasm without the faintest change of expression. "We are *all* very tired. And I'm hoping for some kind of explanation as to why I should allow Mrs. Taubmann to be disturbed."

She was incredible. A total megalomaniac.

"As I explained in my message," said Nick, struggling for a neutral tone, "I spoke to Jacob Grossman yesterday and—"

"Jacob who?"

"Grossman. He was a friend of Mrs. Taubmann's in the old days."

"And this person was in Tangier?"

Nick frowned. Gallagher usually limited herself to being obstructive and left the questioning to her mistress.

"That's right. For a time. Dr. Gallagher, I wouldn't be bothering Mrs. Taubmann unless—"

"Perhaps you could be a little more specific about what it is this Grossman person wants."

"He doesn't *want* anything. Not anymore. He's dead. He was killed yesterday. Murdered. The media picked up on it last night. It's all over the New York press today. Do you happen to know if Mrs. Taubmann is aware of any of this?"

"I don't think you understand, Mr. Greer. Mrs. Taubmann is *sick*."

"Not so sick she couldn't grant me this interview."

He'd taken a stand. A line appeared between Gallagher's pencil-drawn brows.

"Are you going to tell me what this is about?"

"Well—actually it concerns Mrs. Taubmann personally. I'd feel a little uncomfortable airing the matter with a third party."

Gallagher's mouth twisted in a thin smile.

"Such *admirable* discretion," she said, and she turned away from him, muttering. It took him a second to realize he was supposed to follow, and then he was grabbing up his briefcase, hurrying through a door into the heavy gloom of the apartment, catching the end of a phrase, Gallagher saying if Laverne was even able to speak, she'd be very surprised.

For several months now, Laverne had been suffering from acute pulpitis—her teeth (the molars in the lower jaw this time) succumbing, as they did periodically, to years of chronic neglect. The infection had spread through the root canal into the jaw to form two, possibly three, abscesses. The exact number or condition of these lesions, at least one of which drained directly into the old woman's mouth, was not known, because Laverne refused to have anyone other than Gallagher look at them. She had not seen a dentist in forty years. She took antibiotics and heavy-duty painkillers the way other people used aspirin.

There were blinds on the windows, rugs on the rugs. The rugs were for the noise. The blinds were there to protect the pictures and the furniture from the sun, but the effect was stopped-clock funereal.

Apart from the Taubmann and Scitovsky family heirlooms, a collection worthy of the Met itself, Max had left his wife one of the most important collections of modern art in North America. Trying not to trip on the layered floor coverings, Nick barely registered the significant Picassos, Giacomettis, Mondrians, Matisses. Max had bought American too, including some early AbEx and a little Pop, but nearly always with an emphasis on the figure, the representation of the human form. The bigger works, a couple of billboard-sized de Koonings, some early Pollocks, Stills and Rauschenbergs, were out there in orbit, circling slowly around the major museums. The Spiras traveled also, but much less—only seven of them were going to the Guggenheim retrospective—and although they were small enough to hang in the apartment, Laverne never gave them space.

Didn't she like them? She didn't seem to. Yet the fate of the Spiras had been the cause of a rift with her daughter. Gael had wanted to shed a few of the pictures (she made no bones about it: the Spiras gave her the "heebie-jeebies") to help finance the acquisition of a private jet. Tired of suffering the indignity of a time-share Gulfstream for which it was necessary to give six hours' notice, she'd felt that the extra $30 million required to have her very own plane (two hundred hours a year already cost her $7 million) would be money well spent. Laverne, who had always made do with the rigors of first class, had flatly refused. The argument had stopped short of bloodletting or the rewriting of wills, but only just, and the Spiras had stayed where they were.

An antiseptic smell became noticeable through the heavy perfume of lilies. They turned down another corridor, and the light began to fail altogether. Gallagher came to a halt outside a door.

"When did you last see her?" she said, her voice shut down to a whisper.

"A year ago. Thirteen months."

He could barely see Gallagher's expression but felt the pressure of her gaze nevertheless. There was something wrong, something about his visit she found irksome, more than just inconvenient.

"With her lungs the way they are, every breath is a struggle. The carbon dioxide builds up. She suffers symptoms of narcosis—sudden mood changes, confusion. This is something you should bear in mind before you start your scribbling."

Nick frowned. The warning was as bizarre in its own way as the questions of a moment ago. She turned away from him and barely brushed the door with her knuckles.

There was a soft suck of stale air as the door opened like an indrawn breath. Nick moved forward, taking in the brown-red lacquered walls of Laverne's prison. Heavy silk drapes reduced daylight to a crepuscular gloom. Opposite the bed was a smoke-blackened crucifix—Christ dying in agony and despair, thorns, rictus and ribs. Standing next to a carafe on the bedside cabinet was another photo of Max, this one from the early seventies, the old man facing death with a game smile.

Antiseptic. Camphor. A faint metallic smell.

Life-support gadgetry had pushed out the Louis XV: an IPPB ventilator draped with a white plasticized cloth; oxygen bottles linked to nebulizers, in the corner.

Laverne was waiting to be interviewed in what the doctors called the high Fowler's position—of the two positions available that allowed her to draw air into her lungs, the one that came closest to normal posture. The backrest was elevated and she was propped up on three pillows. Over the past couple of years she had gotten used to wearing a nasal cannula to get oxygen, but when receiving her rare visitors, she preferred to make do with ambient air. Her face was a painted mask pierced by dark lusterless eyes.

There was a small silver bell in her left hand, a notebook—battered, much read—under her right. There was no buzzer here because of the oxygen—no cigarettes, matches, synthetic blankets, cellphones.

A frown creased her face as Nick approached the bed. She wasn't angry, just trying to breathe.

"*Nick*-olasss."

Each word she spoke was delivered, gasping, broken-backed, dead.

Nick put down his briefcase and grasped the bony, rock-encrusted hand.

"It's good of you to see me, Mrs. Taubmann. How are you feeling today?"

Knowing it was wrong as soon as he'd said it.

Laverne took a slow, difficult breath, parting her glossy lips so that you could see the moist blackness inside. She was dying, in pain, with abscesses in her mouth, clinging on to what was left of her life by her fiberglass nail extensions—*that* was how she was feeling.

"Tell me. Tell me . . . about Grossman."

He took a seat next to the bed, told her how Barbara Segal had found him.

"This was a few days ago. She was down on Eighteenth Street, saw him going through a garbage can."

A look of profound puzzlement came over her haggard face. Nick nodded.

"Incredible, isn't it? Barbara didn't realize who it was at first, and then—when she did . . . Well, she followed him, went after him."

"Followed?"

There was a soft but distinct click in Laverne's breathing now, a phlegmy click with each gasp. Even from a couple of feet away Nick could almost taste her breath.

"Back to his clinic. He was staying at this clinic on the Lower East Side. Anyway, I went to see him there yesterday."

"Did he say why?"

"Why?"

"Why. Why he—disap*peared?*"

"No. We—it was a difficult interview. He was very agitated." He took the microcassette out of his briefcase and held it up for her to see. "I made a recording."

Gallagher came forward out of the shadows. "Mrs. Taubmann? Are you sure you—"

Laverne's chin jutted. "Get *out!*" she said, the ligaments straining in her neck. Then, gathering all her breath: "*OUT,* god . . . *damn* you!"

She ground her rotten jaws, black eyes fixed on Gallagher as she left the room. Only when she was gone did Laverne collapse back into the pillows.

A machine, some kind of humidifier was Nick's guess, clicked and hissed in the gloom. For a long time all Laverne could do was concentrate on her breathing. Eventually she produced a dark cloth from under the counterpane and put it to her mouth with trembling fingers. When she took it away again, her lipstick was smeared and something glistened on her chin. She stared, furious at being seen this way.

"Play your tape," she said.

Nick pressed the button, heard a rumbling hiss, distant sounds of traffic.

—Jack, I really appreciate your letting me talk to you today. You don't know how often I've thought about this. About what it would mean to get together with you.

Laverne brought her hands together, jiggling the silver bell on the counterpane. She closed her eyes. After a couple of minutes of listening to Nick trying to get Grossman to talk, she opened them again.

"Gross-*man*."

"It's coming," said Nick. "It took him a while to get warmed up."

—Thunder. The creaking of the wheelchair as Jack took out his cigarettes.

—*You were having some health problems at that time.*

Laverne frowned, beginning to get restless.

—A knock on the door, the door opening, Pirez leaving the room.

—*I'm curious about May 1972. What made you run, Jack? What made you leave the clinic like that? Was it—?*

—*You. Think. You. Can. Fool. Me?*

Nick glanced across at Laverne. She was looking straight at him now.

—*I'm not trying to fool you, Jack? Why would I be trying to fool you, Jack? Fool you how? My only concern, my only desire, is to give you your rightful place in—in the biography. All I'm trying to—*

—*You. Think. I. Don't. Have. Eyes?*

—The chair creaking rhythmically, Jack working himself up.

Laverne was shaking her head. Nick hit PAUSE.

"Mrs. Taubmann? What happens next—you might find it offensive."

"Play . . . the tape."

Nick played.

—*I'm sero-positive. Did you know that, Mr. Greer? I'm sero-positive, and I bite.*

—*Jack I'm not here to—*

—*I'll bite your fucking face!*

—Sounds of flurried movement, a hard crack as the microcassette fell over.

—*So don't think you're going to get your hands on it.*

—A long, gasping silence.

—*Jack, I don't know what you are talking about.*

—Pirez coming back into the room.

"This is interesting," said Nick.

—*We were just—we were just talking about . . . Jack?*

—*You know. You're the one who came all the way from England.*

—Jack shifting his weight in the creaky chair.

—*He's here for the picture. Like Segal. They won't rest until they have it.*

—*The picture? Which picture?*

—*Tell her. Tell her about the* Incarnation.

Laverne covered her face with both hands.

Nick hit PAUSE. Laverne was straining to draw breath.

"Mrs. Taubmann?"

It was as if she had forgotten he was there.

"Mrs. Taubmann?"

She removed her hands, fumbled, found Max's notebook and brought it to her chest.

"Mrs. Taubmann, are you okay?"

She nodded, her mouth set in a hard line.

"Play."

"Sure. Of course. But maybe—before I do that, I wanted to ask you . . . That's interesting, don't you think? What Jacob says there. He seemed to be under the impression that I had gone to him to take the *Incarnation*. To 'get my hands' on it."

She reached for her carafe. Nick was up in a second, pouring her water. She drank, rested for a moment.

"Play the *tape*."

Nick stood over her, the carafe in his hand.

"Could you, first—before we go on, I wanted to ask you about this—about Jacob's anxiety. His worry about the painting."

Laverne lifted her bony shoulders and let them drop.

"The *Incarnation*, Mrs. Taubmann. The famous painting we all thought—you have always maintained—"

"Yes, yes, yes . . ." She couldn't breathe. "Nickolass, this . . . *whole* business with the . . . *Incarnation*. I *thought* we had agreed . . . to let it . . . *drop*. I mean"—she clenched her fists and pushed back into the pillows—"why is it so *important* to you?"

"Well, it wasn't really. Until yesterday."

She squinted up at him.

"When Jacob Grossman was murdered," he said.

For a moment she was quite still. Then she pressed her eyes shut, a rattling sound coming from deep in her throat.

The door banged open, and Gallagher burst in, pushing past him, followed by two nurses. Nick stepped backwards, knocking over his chair, details coming through ugly and stark: the pit-stop bustle of the nurses, Gallagher talking steadily against the terrible noise Laverne was making—then the old woman's mouth snapping blackly open, clamping shut as a needle went into her blue-white arm.

9

"Specific Injuries—A through H."
Eugene moved down the third sheet of the autopsy report until he got
to the free histamine tests for confirmation that, with the exception of
the wound inside the left ear, the injuries had been inflicted postmortem. Then he climbed back up, stopping at item F.

He looked across at the windows. They were open because of the
heat, but he felt shivery and his chest was tight. He'd always wondered if there would be a day like this. A day with this kind of case.
The whole thing opening up inside him like a shitty black flower. It
was the kind of case you read about in the papers. It wasn't the kind
of case you wanted to have in your head. What he felt most: that it
had come at the wrong time in his life. He was too old. Probably better at his job now than he was ten years ago, but less settled, less able
to cope with the misery of it.

The desk opposite was empty, Raymond out with Patti Bonner
working Ludlow and Broome—knocking on doors, pulling on the
coats of good civilians, trying to find anybody who might have seen
anything unusual or suspicious the day before. The clinic itself had
tapped out. They'd talked to just about everyone except the writer,
the guy who had come to conduct an interview a couple of hours
before Grossman died. The writer had left a card with Pirez but didn't
say where he was staying in Manhattan or how long he planned to
stick around. They'd called the London number, left a message on the
answering machine.

He forced himself to read on.

None of the excised flesh had been recovered from the scene or
was present with the body. The M.E. speculated: the killer had taken

flesh with him, and in doing so had been seeking to conceal bite evidence.

The phone rang, jolting him back in his chair.

"Glasco."

Traffic. A public phone.

"Eugene. It's me, Ray. I think we got a witness. Mr. Buffy Allen. Patti found him on Broome, but he lives on Orchard. His bathroom looks out back at the Delancey-Deere. This old guy. Says he watches the, quote-unquote, colored sitting out on the stoop smoking, quote-unquote, dope."

"Stoop?"

"Yeah, I think he means the fire escape. So anyway, he's looking out the window at around five P.M. yesterday and he sees a guy walking up and down. Eugene?"

"Yeah, I'm listening."

"This guy is average height, white, stocky build, and he's wearing a jogging suit. Got a little knapsack on his back. He's looking up at a security guard who's on the—on the 'stoop' smoking."

The rubber-glove latents: two three-finger spans, and one full hand. A large male, or a not-so-large male with big hands.

"Did Mr. Allen get a look at his face?"

"Too far away, and this character's got a hood on his jacket that he's wearing up. But Eugene, get this. The guy's jogging suit is light blue."

The thread snagged on the bed frame: sky blue. The lab says a stretch fabric used in leisure wear, jogging suits, etc.

Eugene gave a nod.

"Can you bring the witness in?"

The nurses were so engrossed with the serious business of keeping their employer alive that they forgot about him. Standing in the dark corridor, Nick watched them come and go carrying bowls and bed linen. He could hear Gallagher moving around inside, giving instructions. A young Asian woman came out carrying a rumpled sheet, looked surprised to see him standing there, half-turned to say something to Gallagher but was cut off by a long, strangled moan. She hurried off shaking her head. Nick heard Laverne gasping for breath, weeping.

"You *have* to keep it on," said Gallagher, her voice pinched to a harsh whisper. "Without it, you'll suffocate."

"I don't *care*!" There was a sound of struggle. "I *want* to die. I just want to . . . to *forget*."

Something fell to the floor.

"If that were true, you wouldn't keep reading *this*!"

"I don't . . . I'm not *reading*."

"What are you doing then? *Penance*?"

Nick heard bitter laughter, then a curse. It was getting embarrassing.

He was backing away, clearing his throat, when suddenly Gallagher appeared in the doorway, a bowl of something in her hands. When she was angry, the color fled from her mouth altogether, leaving just the spatter of brownish freckles. She glared at him.

"I hope you're pleased with yourself."

"I'm sorry," Nick managed. "I should have broken it to her more gently."

"*Nicklasss!*"

Gallagher kicked the door shut with her foot.

Laverne called out again, her voice barely audible now.

"You should leave," said Gallagher.

A thin tinkling came from the other side of the door. Laverne's bell. One of the other nurses hurried back along the corridor.

"It's all *right*," said Gallagher, stamping her foot. "I will attend to her."

There was a loud crash, what sounded like breaking glass. Gallagher cursed under her breath and opened the door again.

Nick followed her into the room.

Laverne, wearing the nebulizer mask now, had fallen sideways in the bed. She had managed to knock the carafe from the nightstand. There was broken glass all over the floor.

"Can't you be more careful!" spat Gallagher, squatting down to pick up the bits.

Laverne reached out a hand. "Nick*lasss*."

Gallagher stood up abruptly, turned, saw him standing there.

"*Mr. Greer!*" She was trembling with rage.

"Tell me," gasped Laverne.

"Forgive me, Mrs. Taubmann." Nick went back to his stool. "It was stupid of me. I should have broken it to you more gently."

Her eyes angrily fixed on him, Gallagher pushed Laverne into an upright position. The old woman's breath made an oval bloom of condensation in the plastic mask.

"I want . . . to *know* . . . about Grossman."

"The police were called to the hostel sometime around six. Last night a detective came to ask me what I knew about Jacob. What I knew about the *Incarnation*."

Laverne's left hand came up off the notebook.

"What happened? How . . . did he *die*?"

"I think he was . . ." Nick hesitated, glanced across at Gallagher. "I'm not sure. The papers say it was . . . very violent. The detective called it a blitz attack."

"Blitz?" Laverne frowned, moving her head slowly back and forth, then tried to moisten her lips inside the mask.

Gallagher stepped forward out of the shadows, adjusted the strap over the back of her head, but Laverne jerked herself free.

She fixed Gallagher with a cold look and tried to say something, but the words were lost in a racking cough. Nick watched, increasingly alarmed as the fit continued. Gallagher got behind her and eased her forward, started massaging her back, while Laverne struggled against it, a disgusted look on her face. Finally she was breathing normally again.

She ordered Gallagher from the room.

Nick waited for the door to close behind her.

"I'm sorry if this is upsetting for you," he said, leaning forward. "I mean, I can see it is upsetting, but that too just makes me . . ." He shook his head. He wasn't going to get anywhere by pleading with her to be more open. Something was being kept from him, and he had absolutely no idea why.

"Mrs. Taubmann, Grossman told me I wasn't going to get my hands on the *Incarnation*. Does that surprise you?"

The fixed eyes. Green glass in the wadded pinkness of her flesh. It didn't seem to surprise her at all.

"Is it possible that the *Incarnation*, the painting you saw in Tangier, wasn't destroyed? That somehow Jacob came into possession of it and—"

Laverne laughed. At first he didn't recognize it for what it was. In six years of talking to her, he had never once seen her laugh, but here she was, at death's door, hacking weakly into her plastic beak. Tears filled her eyes.

"It's funny," he said, trying to keep the annoyance out of his voice. "Jacob Grossman laughed too. When I asked him if the painting had been stolen from the apartment."

She raised a hand to her face and slowly adjusted the mask.

"Perhaps I should turn this around," he said. "I mean, here we are. You agreed to see me on very little notice. Why? Was Jacob so important to you? I don't think so."

Any sign of mirth left her eyes now, but her mouth stayed closed.

"I didn't tell you," he said, "but Jacob Grossman attacked me. Bit me, in fact." Holding up his bandaged hand now. "Yesterday, when I went to see him. We were talking about Tangier and—"

She pressed her eyes shut.

"Play the . . . tape," she gasped.

She took a deep, shuddering breath, then another, her face darkening.

"Just play it."

Nick reached into the pocket for the microcassette.

"Sure. I'll let you hear it. The whole thing. I'll even make a copy for you. Just answer one question for me. Did Jacob Grossman die because of this picture?"

Laverne became very still, her face looking more and more congested.

"Mr. . . . *Greer* . . ." she said, setting her rotten jaws, straining to pull in air. "When you first came to me, I said . . . to myself—*here* is a . . . *promising* young man . . . *here* is someone who *understands,* someone who . . . has the *energy,* the *application,* to write a proper life, to get it . . ."

Nick stood up, dropping the tape recorder into his pocket.

"I'm sorry," he said. "I've worked too hard to be shut out."

Laverne groaned, moving her head back and forth on the pillow. Then she raised a hand, beckoned to him. It seemed that whatever she had to say to him needed to be whispered. He came around the bed until he was standing next to her head. Laverne pulled the mask away from her face and grabbed his hand.

"But now . . ." she hissed, "I see . . . that you are just . . . a *hack,* a *hack* . . . grubbing in the dirt, grubbing in the . . ." He tried to draw away, but she held on tight. "And the sad . . . the *sad* thing is . . . despite your scurrying, your *scurrying* . . . you do not begin to . . . understand." Tears rolled down her rouged cheeks. "This picture," she said. "You should . . . *forget.*"

Nick yanked himself free.

"I'm sorry, Mrs. Taubmann. I can't do that."

She stared up at him, and for a second he thought she might laugh again.

"Just tell me," he said. "Is that why Grossman died? Because of this picture?"

She heaved a breath, perspiration showing through the thick layer of cosmetics on her upper lip, beckoned to him again.

She waited until his ear was almost touching her lips.

"Yes," she said. "And so will you."

11

By the time he got back to the hotel, all Nick wanted to do was crash out, but as soon as he closed his eyes, he saw Laverne, the malignant look she gave him when she told him he was going to die. He'd asked her to explain herself, but she'd just waved him from the bed. He'd asked his question and she'd given her answer. So now it was for him to play the tape. He'd put the machine on the nightstand next to Max's photograph and remained standing in the shadows. When they'd come to the passage where Reardon's syphilis was discussed and Grossman said "mercury," she'd started ringing her bell. The meeting was over.

She hadn't so much as looked at him again, and her only words were spoken in stunned introspection: "He didn't know," she said.

The red light was blinking on the phone. He'd been staring at it for maybe five dazed minutes without registering its significance. Then he remembered Linda. He'd let a day go by without getting in touch. She was sitting in the basement worrying about the bills, worrying about him, worrying about them.

He pressed the button with his eyes closed.

10:52: *Nick, Henry. Looks like you're out. I just wanted to say I spoke to Miriam Florey yesterday. She's at the* New York Times. *She's interested in doing a piece on you and the book, which would be great. If she calls, be nice. She's terribly well connected. Toodle-pip.*

4:12: *I always get these things . . . Nick? What did Laverne say? Give me a call. The TV just talks about crack junkies, but—well, I can't believe it. Anyway. Call me. Poor Jacob. I can't . . . Oh—this is me, by the way. Barb. I'm at home. I have something to tell you.*

5:30: Mr. Greer? This is Tod Schaeffer. I'm calling on behalf of Oscar Nagel. Mr. Nagel is organizing a small gathering this evening to introduce the work of Alec Kirkendale. From eight o'clock. Hope you can make it. Thanks.

Somehow no message from Linda was worse than the angry tirade he'd been expecting. He had to call her. He had to explain. He was reaching for the phone when it came to life under his hand. He snatched it up.

"What happened with Laverne?"

It was Barb. She sounded stirred up, drunk.

"Barb? What—"

"Did you tell her about Jacob?"

"Yes. Yes, I did."

"And?"

"She took it badly. Dr. Gallagher had to give her an injection."

Nick caught the sound of a man's voice at the other end of the line.

"Who's that?"

"Just a friend. We've been trying to . . . come to terms with it all."

Just a friend. Nick wondered if she had the speakerphone on.

"Barb? I told Laverne about your idea. That maybe Grossman saw this coming. That maybe he had the painting and that this . . ."

He couldn't bring himself to finish the phrase.

"And? What did she say?"

"Barb?"

"What?"

"We need to talk. I need to talk to you. Can we get together?"

Ice clinked in a glass.

"When are you flying back?" she said.

"Tomorrow morning. First thing."

Barb's friend said something, his voice a bassy rumble.

"Oh, that's right," said Barb. "I have a thing tonight. At Oscar Nagel's."

"The Alec Kirkendale thing?"

"You're invited?"

"There was a message on my machine."

"Oscar must already know," said Barb. "About you getting to Grossman before he was killed."

"What?"

"Why else would he invite you?"

Nick winced. Normally, Barb was more sensitive about the difference between him and them, his life and their life. He talked to the Spiraphiles, but that didn't make him one of them. His conversations with them, though intimate in tone, were actually conducted across a social gap the size of Grand Canyon.

"I guess that's right," he said.

"No. Take my word for it. These things of Oscar's . . ." She seemed to catch up with herself, stopped short of saying how exclusive Oscar's parties were. "He'll be looking to grill you, Nick, get it all from the horse's mouth."

He was a horse now.

"Actually, I was thinking I might pass," said Nick stiffly.

"Oh?"

"I think I'm getting sick."

"You're in shock," said Barb. "It's normal after something like this. After what happened to Jacob. You're bound to feel it."

Nick thought about this for a second. Thought maybe it was right. Like being just missed by a truck. You carry on about your business, but then you have a reaction. He did feel terrible.

"I thought I was okay, but now . . . Anyway, I'm not going."

"I can give you my news there."

"What news?" he said, but she'd already hung up.

12

A couple of hours later Nick was sipping warm white wine and trying to look like he fit in with a crowd of well-dressed, well-connected people in one of the first-floor reception rooms at Oscar Nagel's place.

The space was typical of Nagel's Soho residence, a former pickle factory he'd restored to its original industrial bleakness at the beginning of the nineties. One of the island's first cast-iron structures, when Nagel acquired it, the box frame, windows and floors were about all that was left. Period features like the big steel fire doors had been either ripped out of other buildings or faked by artisans, who'd beaten the patina of one hundred years' pickling into the walls and floors. It made for lots of dramatic space and light, but it wasn't exactly cozy. Nick had read somewhere that it represented an attempt on Nagel's part to get back to the industrial roots his father had put down in the twenties when Nagel's Trucks was an integral part of the New York landscape.

A string quartet was playing dissonant, spiky music somewhere. Hard light washed down over the white tile walls, leaving the middle of the room in shadow. Not one of the portraits on display was less than six feet high.

Nick was talking to a young critic about the pitfalls of overmediation in postmodernism when Barb came out of the crowd followed by an old friend of hers—Anita Broek, a Christie's rainmaker specializing in twentieth-century fine art. She was a middle-aged woman with a long bland face that was like a deliberately understated setting for her eyes, which were almost jewel-like in the intensity of their blue—very sad, and very beautiful.

It was clear that Barb had already talked about his interviewing Grossman just before he was killed, but Broek wanted to hear it again—from the horse's mouth this time. The lovely eyes got wider and wider as Nick told the story, squeezed shut when he got to Grossman putting his face into the mirror.

"And then he was *butchered*," she said, touching a hand to her mouth. "Manhattan's supposed to be safer with zero tolerance and so forth, but it seems to me this kind of thing happens all the time."

She wanted to know if Nick had seen a doctor about the bite. Nick looked at his hand.

"Anita's right," said Barb, leaning heavily on his arm. "You should go and have it checked."

"He hardly . . . look, I mean, he hardly broke the skin."

Nick tried to pull back the bandage.

"They'll have to cut it off above the elbow," boomed a scratchy baritone voice.

They all turned.

The way the light fell, the initial impression was of a blue blazer and gray flannel slacks looming out of the dark. They were trademark clothes, appalling in their way, worn as a kind of Rule Britannia livery. Above the double row of brass buttons, the enormous face was exactly as per the *Tortured Eros* jacket: the heavy tortoiseshell glasses, the boyish abundance of brown hair with its boyish part, the lipless mouth, the soft roll of chin fat pushing down over the silk cravat.

"Bloody Yanks," said Martin Marion, flashing his teeth. "Never happy unless they're making an appointment with some shaman or other."

"Maybe on the West Coast," said Barb stiffly, "but in New York I think you'll find—"

"In New York worse than anywhere," boomed Marion. "Look at Pollock. He was fine until he came here. Isn't that right, Mr. Greer?"

"I thought bourbon was Pollock's medicine," said Broek.

"He was in analysis for a while," said Nick, rallying. "Jungian."

Marion raised a large white hand.

"When he drove his car into that tree, he put an abrupt end to a course of treatment that involved drinking an emulsion of guano and ground beets."

"Guano?" said Broek.

"Yes," said Nick, "he—"

"Poor bugger thought he needed to get the balance of gold and silver in his urine right—yes, *gold* and *silver,* and the guano juice was going to do the job. An organic healer on Park Avenue was helping him with his drink problem. He had Pollock drinking this filth and bathing in a solution of rock salt."

Broek shook her head.

"But as for your hand," said Marion, looking straight at Nick now, "I should get that silly bandage off. You look like you're trying to be excused games. Let the air get to it. That's all it needs, you know."

Nick tried to smile but found that his mouth wouldn't hold the shape. "Well, there's certainly no danger of syphilis," he said.

It was as if they'd hit a bump in the road. There was a moment of readjustment.

"I had an opportunity to talk to Grossman about your idea that Reardon was infected," Nick went on. "That Spira picked it up from him. He asked me how come if Frank had it, *he* didn't."

"How did he *know* he didn't have it?" Marion put his head on one side. "I *do* hope you haven't been airing this rather woolly speculation with the good people at the *New York Times.* You'll be losing your reputation for *rigor.*"

He looked around the circle of faces, making sure they'd gotten his meaning.

"Oh yes," he went on, "Miriam Florey called me this afternoon. I'm covering the retrospective for them, you know. So naturally we've been in touch quite a lot recently. Charming girl. She needed some help with a piece she's writing. She mentioned she talked to you. I was able to put her straight on a few things."

Nick watched the great man swirl ice in his glass. He didn't like to think what the "few things" might have included.

"It is interesting to speculate, though," said Barb. "I mean if Jacob didn't have syphilis, you'd really have to wonder whether Frank ever really did."

Marion gave another swirl to his ice cubes.

"I find it difficult to believe that Frank would lie to me about such a thing," he said.

"Me too," said Barb.

Marion took a moment to savor the implication, then let out a big windy guffaw.

"Perhaps we should do a test on Grossman's body," he said, straining at humor now. "After all, there is such a thing as *asymptomatic* neurosyphilis. Perhaps you weren't aware of that, *Ms.* Segal. It would be a simple matter of checking for abnormalities in the cerebrospinal fluid. And while you're at it, why not dig up Tony Reardon, or Frank himself. After all, we know where the bodies are buried. Get this thing cleared up once and for all."

He turned from them with a dismissive wave of his hand. There was dandruff on his shoulders.

"What an outrageous character," said Broek appreciatively.

"Turkey," said Barb.

"I understand his new book is full of scurrilous details."

"New book?" said Nick.

"I think it's a draft, actually. For some reason he's decided to go out with it early. Anyway, it's being passed around."

Nick looked over at Marion again, wondered if he knew about the *Life* being considered by Crucible. He caught a glimpse of Oscar Nagel then, the old man dapper in a dark suit and open-necked white shirt. He was deep in conversation with Cy Lockhart, the former defense attorney who now handled his legal affairs on an exclusive basis.

The quartet switched into something less dissonant. Broek was drawn away into a huddle by a fellow art expert. Nick saw a passing tray and lunged for a canapé.

"You should be flattered," said Barb.

"How's that?"

"Marion. He just lifted his leg. Marking his territory. He probably heard about you getting to Jacob, getting the interview just before he was killed. People are talking about you, about the bite. He's got this book out there, but they're all talking about you. You're on his turf."

"*My* turf," said Nick. "I've got a book out there too."

"You do?"

"Crucible is looking at the *Life.*"

Barb nodded enthusiastically. "Well, that's great news. I knew it was only a matter of time before it was picked up over here."

Nick looked across the room and saw that Marion had an arm around Nagel's shoulder now. The two men had first met at the Spira retrospective of 1965, by which time Nagel was already well into the second phase of his dealing career. Dismayed by the emergence of AbEx and then by the flowering of artists such as Rauschenberg and

Johns, he'd more or less turned away from paintings to concentrate on furniture from the interwar American Arts and Crafts movement. The meeting with Marion had changed all that.

Both men shared a belief in Spira's importance, and in the importance of figurative art generally. It was in Britain that this seam was being most vigorously worked, and with his London connections and extensive knowledge of the postwar British scene, Marion was able to help Nagel acquire a number of important pieces, including works by Freud, Kossoff, Auerbach, Hockney and Spira.

By the time Nagel opened his fine art gallery in L.A. in 1985, Marion was his right-hand man. If Nagel's Trucks was the basis of Oscar's first fortune, selling paintings to Hollywood celebrities was definitely the second.

"Nick?"

He turned and met Barb's eyes head-on. She was doing her mind-reader stare. Thirty years ago it would have been devastating.

"Did Laverne say something?" she said. "On the phone just now you sounded pretty . . ."

Nick put a hand on her sleeve. He'd been expecting the question, but now that it had been asked didn't know what to say.

"What's wrong?" said Barb.

"This whole thing." He looked around, making sure they weren't overheard. "I asked Laverne if Jacob's death had anything to do with the *Incarnation*."

"And?"

"She said, 'Yes.'"

Barb reached into her purse for her cigarettes and lighter, dipped her wrinkled face to the trembling flame.

"She also said . . . she said that I'd be next. She didn't actually say next, but she said I'd be killed. Because of this painting."

Barb breathed smoke at him, her eyes still points of darkness in the surrounding gloom.

Nick managed a smile.

"She just came out with it. Like some old-time oracle. Warning me more than anything, I think. Telling me to leave it alone."

"And? Will you?"

Nick sipped his drink. He hadn't gotten as far as deciding what he was going to do.

"I mean, I suppose if I really took her seriously, I might, but . . . well, to be honest . . ."

"You don't believe her."

Nick shrugged. He didn't know what he believed. But he didn't see how his asking questions about a painting could get him killed. It didn't seem possible.

Barb leaned in closer.

"But how come Laverne knows about it anyway?" she said, breathing smoke on him.

"That's what I wanted to talk to you about."

"What?"

"Do you remember the interview I did with Marion?"

Barb sucked smoke into her lungs and gave him a long, appraising look.

"The interview he so graciously granted. Sure."

It had happened two years ago and had been deeply unsatisfactory for a number of reasons, one of which, Marion's insistence on everything he said staying off the record. If Nick wanted to quote him or even paraphrase, he could do so only with Marion's okay. Despite this, because of it perhaps, Marion had then gone on to speak very openly, slandering several people, Max Taubmann in particular.

He'd said that Laverne had gone down to Tangier in the fall of '57 because Max had sent her there to make an offer for a painting, and that when Spira had refused to sell, Max had decided on another course of action. When Nick had asked him what that course of action was, Marion had become coy, saying that he should think about the burglary of the Rue d'Angleterre apartment, and ask himself why Spira had been in such a towering rage with Reardon for letting it happen. Whether or not it was the painting that had been stolen, Marion wouldn't say.

Nick had run all this past Barb at the time, showing her his scribbled notes (Marion had refused to be recorded), and she had warned him against taking the matter any further. She looked at him now, a cynical expression on her face.

"What about it?" she said.

"Well, Laverne—when I was talking to her about Jacob, about the *Incarnation* and so forth—she became really upset. Angry with me. I mean she *really* doesn't want this painting talked about. You have to wonder why."

"You think Max stole the picture. That she's trying to cover up these supposedly shameful events of thirty-odd years ago."

Nick nodded, watched the smoke stream from Barb's nostrils.

"Well, I think it's all nonsense," she said. "As I believe I already stated."

"So . . ." Nick was starting to feel uncomfortably warm. "So how does a rumor like that get started?"

"Because *Marion* . . ."

Heads turned at the sound of her voice.

Barb took a drag on her cigarette, blew smoke up into the darkness.

"Because Marion," she went on softly, "twisted asshole that he is, starts them. I seem to remember saying at the time that what it looked like to me was a poisoned chalice. Marion just wanted you to go around asking people if they thought Max was behind the burglary of the Rue d'Angleterre. It would have taken about a day for news to get back to Laverne. Marion would have sent you a good-luck card on the first day of the defamation trial."

Nick nodded. He'd already been through this in his own head a hundred times but couldn't let go of the idea that Laverne was hiding something.

"I'm telling you, Nick, this is Marion's stock-in-trade. Rumors and lies. I hate to think what's in this new book of his." She touched his sleeve. "Nick? Are you okay?"

Nick put a hand to his forehead. It was slick with sweat.

"Don't worry," he said. "It's just a panic attack. All I need is to lie on the floor and scream for a few minutes."

"What's to panic about? As far as I can see, you're doing great. This thing with Crucible, getting to Grossman . . ."

Nick shook his head. His book was about to come out and he was a guy lost in the woods, a B-movie adventurer sinking in quicksand.

"Barb, I'm supposed to be *finished*. The page proofs are on my desk at home. Linda's waiting for me to get them out of the way so that we can get on with our lives, and now there's all this—all this *stuff*."

"The painting, you mean?"

"Yes, and . . ."

"And what?"

"There's something else—something . . ." He shook his head. He hadn't wanted to get into it, but it had been troubling him ever since he left Laverne's. He sucked in a deep, panicky breath.

"You remember what I said about the mirror? About Jacob getting up and . . ."

Barb nodded.

"Well, we were talking about Reardon, about whether or not he'd had syphilis, and—I don't know, something upset him—Jacob, I mean. I've listened to the tape over and over, and it's when I started talking about mercury, about the mercury Reardon may have used to treat the symptoms. Jacob—it was as though he understood something. As though it meant something *particular*. He got up out of his chair, walked across the room, and he . . ."

He went cold, just thinking about it.

Applause broke out on the other side of the room. Cameras were flashing. Nick saw Nagel put his arm around a bald-headed kid in orange overalls. Kirkendale.

"You said 'mercury'? And that set him off?"

"He sort of took it up. Kept saying the word. So I thought, you know, Jacob was not a well man. Who could say what this word might have meant to him? But today . . . I was with Laverne and she wanted to hear the tape I made, okay? She wanted to hear the whole thing. She wanted—I suppose—to know exactly what Grossman had said."

"Why?"

Another troubling question. All he could offer was a shrug.

"Anyway, we reached the moment where Jacob starts the mercury thing, and Laverne . . ." He looked into Barb's eyes. "She told me to stop."

"This was when Jacob—when he . . . ?"

"Before that. We didn't even get as far as the mirror. Jacob said 'mercury,' and suddenly she didn't want to hear any more."

Laverne had become so still, in fact, so quiet, that for a second he thought she'd had some sort of stroke.

"Like it meant something to her too," said Barb.

"Exactly. Meant something. Confirmed something, maybe. Her worst fears. And you know what she said then? 'He didn't know.' Whispered it really, to herself. I asked her what she meant, but it was as if I'd ceased to exist. She didn't say another word. Just rang her little bell. Someone came in. That was it."

Barb was shaking her head.

"'He didn't know'? Didn't know *what*?"

"Didn't know—and this is my piece of speculation for the day, so take it for what it's worth—didn't know that Reardon was taking mercury for the syphilis. Didn't know that Frank *was* infected. Didn't know that he himself had the disease."

Barb frowned, not liking it. Nick didn't like it either. He passed a hand over his face.

"Jesus Christ," he whispered. "I'm flying back to London tomorrow morning. This is all opening up, and I'm leaving."

"But what about Laverne's apartment?"

"What about it?"

Barb looked confused, then her eyebrows jumped into tight arcs. "Of *course,* I didn't give you my news."

The news she hadn't given him on the phone: Gael Taubmann had retained Christie's for the valuation and sale of the art collection.

"Don't talk about this to anyone. Not yet. I wouldn't be telling you, except you have a stake."

"I do?"

"I talked to Anita about getting you into the Park Avenue place when they go in for the inventory. I think Max and Laverne's correspondence is in there somewhere. The stuff was in Newport, but Laverne moved it down to Manhattan when she started to get sick. Anita says one of the rooms is full of boxes. Just papers and junk, according to Gael. But I thought . . . it occurred to me that someone researching a book might take a different view."

Laverne's private papers: a shot at unraveling Tangier, October 1957. Nick put a hand on top of his head.

"Barb, that would be—"

"A kick in the flippers for the Tortured Walrus."

They both laughed. The Tortured Walrus was Barb's nickname for Marion. They looked around the room for him but found instead Oscar Nagel, the old man making his way over, shaking hands as he came, taking a moment to point a finger, letting Nick and Barb know he wanted a word.

Seventy-one years old and no more than five feet eight, Nagel still had the fur-thick hair of his youth, but it was white now and combed back and up into softly rising waves. Despite his age, his face retained a boyish quality, broad across the brow and tapering to an almost pointed chin. His skin had a cured look, was leathery and deeply lined around the dull blue eyes. The last time Nick had met him, three years ago at the Hôtel de Crillon in Paris, they had been separated by twenty feet of Persian carpet and a display of flowers. Nick had been reading from a list of prepared questions, while Nagel smoked a cigar and reminisced, talking about his early life, his decision to cash out of the family business after World War Two, his acquisition of Spira's *Screaming Heads* in 1947. The purchase had marked a turning point for him, had bound him closely to the artist thereafter. He also talked at length about Tangier, where he had spent a month in 1959, alarmed to see what was happening to Spira, alarmed also by Reardon, whom he'd considered psychotic from the very first meeting.

As far as someone so erratic, impulsive and charming could have a mission, Nagel's mission in life had been to promote the figure in art, and he was very proud to have encouraged Spira to paint the human form at a time when everyone else was going abstract.

He took Nick's hand.

"Nick, I'm delighted. So glad you could make it. There's something I want you to see." He started to draw Nick away. "I want to show you the *Heads*. You too, Barbara. The Guggenheim people are coming to crate them up in a week or so. I want Nick to see them here at home. Come."

They moved out of the reception room through huge steel doors into the relative quiet of the lobby, Nagel talking all the way. He said he'd had no idea Nick was in Manhattan until he'd heard about the terrible business with Jacob.

"You are staying, I hope?"

"Staying?"

"In Manhattan. You'll want to be here at the end of the month for the show. Tell him, Barb. He has to be."

Nick beamed, wondering if Nagel even realized that he lived in London and was a pauper.

They came to the elevator.

"Isn't it something?" said Nagel, pulling back the gate and ushering them in. He threw a lever, and the great cage started its shuddering climb up through the building. The bulb in the ceiling shed a sickly yellow light, giving Nagel a mummified look. "Otis," he said. "Nineteenth century. A real museum piece. Exactly the same model as the one they installed at the Haughwout Building—the first elevator in Manhattan."

Nick looked around, pretending to admire it.

"Solid-state electronics," said Nagel. "Silicon chips. Fiber optics. Give *me* physical, give me these old machines anytime."

The elevator stopped with a resounding thunk at the fifth floor.

"Lockhart's been telling me how you interviewed Grossman just before he was killed," said Nagel, yanking back the gate.

"People keep praising me for that as if it were some kind of investigative coup," said Nick, "but it was all thanks to Barb, really."

They pushed through more steel doors and entered a corridor. Here, the cement floor had been covered with woven sisal. There was a smell like stables.

"You got to Grossman because you know people," said Nagel, looking back at Nick over his shoulder. "People trust you, Nick. They know what a serious person you are. Never underestimate that. They know how serious you are about this book of yours."

He stopped at another set of doors and stuck his cigar into the corner of his mouth, smiling. It was a smile that seemed to engage his whole head, drawing his scalp forward and altering the set of his ears. Whenever you saw him in magazines, he was smiling just like this.

"You ready?" he said.

They entered the space that Nagel considered home. The ceiling of the main living room had been raised on cast-iron pillars and lined with pressed tin to give the feel of a classic Soho loft. The main concession to comfort was the terrace at the Grand Street end of the building, where the architect had cropped the building to make an outside space. On the one interior wall, a glimmering field of white-painted brick, spanning at least fifty feet between two monumental steel doors, were four large canvases of screaming heads, the paintings mounted in heavy gold frames under glass.

"Wow."

Nick moved forward, shaking his head. He had only ever seen the paintings in galleries. Here, surrounded by familiar domestic objects—Nagel's battered, clubby furniture and plants, their strangeness, their extremeness, was almost too intense. The pictures dated from Spira's New York period and for many people marked the beginning of his grand manner. The trademark motifs were all here: the steeply raked expressionistic space, the cagelike box with its tortured figure, the arrows and circles borrowed from medical textbooks indicating areas of interest. The paint was applied roughly, looked gritty in some places, glossy in others. In each picture a besuited figure, a businessman or politician perhaps, was bellowing despair, his head opening casketlike to reveal baboon teeth.

"Well?" said Nagel.

Nick glanced across. Nagel was gaping at the works as though seeing them for the first time.

"Extraordinary," said Nick. "And to own them . . . It's almost—"

"Own them! I don't own them. They own me—*hone* me, actually. That's the truth of it. I rub my soul against them every day."

"You bought four out of the seven," said Nick. "Four out of the seven Spiras from that first show. Before he was really known."

"Yes, I did. I got in there ahead of the great Max Taubmann. My very first acquisition. Twenty thousand dollars, I paid. It seemed pretty crazy at the time. I thought my old man was going to write me out of his will."

He chuckled to himself and picked a piece of lint from one of the frames.

"My life changed the day I wrote that check. I was twenty-two years old, Nick. Of course, you know that."

"Nick knows it all," said Barb.

Nagel walked away from them and came back with a bottle of Scotch and some clean glasses. He filled them, raised his glass.

"Here's to you, Nick. To your new book. They say it's a monster." He tossed back the drink. "Footnotes, addenda, bibliography. A friend of mine at Crucible was talking about it the other day."

Nick sipped the whisky and felt the heat rise in his face. It was true. Henry was right. Crucible was going to make an offer.

Barb said she'd heard that Marion had a new book out.

"It's just a draft," said Nick, realizing as he said it that he was showing his contempt.

Nagel's eyes crimped in amusement.

"A draft?" he said. "Well, what do you expect from that old windbag?"

He chuckled and the chuckle became a laugh. Then they were all laughing, Barb throwing back her head to whoop.

"Don't get me wrong," said Nagel when he could speak again. "I love that old fraud. But I wouldn't worry about this book of his, Nick. With Marty it's all very subjective."

He turned to look at the *Heads*.

"But tell me," he said. "What are you going to do with this Grossman interview? It's come kind of late in the day, right?"

Nick told him about Ernest Stanhope, his editor in London. About the prospects for adding new material.

Nagel smiled, shaking his head.

"It's a piece of luck for you," he said. "That's for sure. Finding him in the first place, and just before this terrible thing happened. I mean, you were right there."

"Well—fortunately not *right* there," said Nick.

"But how was he?" said Nagel. "What was he like? He must have changed in thirty years, right? Did he have anything to say about running off like he did?"

"He wouldn't talk about it. He talked about the *Incarnation,* though."

"The what?"

"The painting that Spira was supposed to have—"

Nagel raised a hand. "Yes, yes. Sorry. I'd forgotten. Frank's famous religious work. I thought that went into the trash can."

"Grossman seemed to be under the impression that I'd gone there to take it from him."

Nagel frowned, and sucked at his cigar.

"Really? The *Incarnation?*" He jutted his lower lip. "How extraordinary. Grossman said he had it?"

"Not exactly."

"Nick thinks he might have been killed because of the painting."

Nick shot Barb a look. Only half an hour ago she'd agreed to keep quiet. But then it came to him that Nagel was exactly the kind of person he needed to talk to about it. You never knew what memories might be triggered.

"Because of the painting?" said Nagel, smiling, waiting for the punch line. When nothing came, he touched Nick on the sleeve. "This is a joke, right? Barb's pulling my leg."

"A detective came to my hotel room last night. He didn't think it was a joke."

Nagel looked at Barb, pushing a hand back through his hair.

"I don't know what to say," he said. "I thought the story was, he'd been killed by some junkie."

"Maybe not," said Nick.

Nagel was shaking his head now, looking deeply puzzled.

"And you're going to put this in your book?"

"You obviously don't believe it, Oscar," said Barb.

Nagel ruffled his hair.

"It's not really a question of believing. I'm just saying, if somebody gets killed, it's normal that everybody should want to know who did it. But this is New York, remember. This is Sodom and Gomorrah *plus* crack cocaine and crystal meth. Things don't always happen for a reason."

13

The storm awoke Eugene just after 4 A.M. Distant thunder. Looking up at the ceiling, hearing the rain, all he could see was Grossman—the staring eyes, the matted hair, the clenched, lipless mouth.

This was when he missed Valerie. Waking up in the empty bed. She used to touch him on the shoulder when he was snoring or flopping around, trapped in one of his nightmares. They had been living in Manhattan then. Five minutes from Radio City, Val liked to say. A bed with a mattress that was too soft for him. Probably why his back had gone in the first place.

Valerie. The first time he had seen her.

Think of something else: the last time he saw his father, just before he died, the old guy standing up to hold him in his arms; Kate, his little sister up there in Rhode Island; some kitchen chairs he was thinking of buying; the guy at the garage who said it was going to cost $200 to stop the buckle-up warning light from flashing when he was buckled up. But it was no good: behind the jumbled thoughts his wife was there, a kind of steady blue glow, like one of those Madonnas you saw sometimes, with a lightbulb inside.

Think of procedure. Procedure was soothing. The direction of uniformed personnel at the scene. The teamwork approach. The preliminary interview of the first officer.

Because of what the medical examiner had found, particularly with regard to the possible removal of bite evidence, Eugene had taken the decision to enter the details of the case into the Violent Criminal Apprehension Program. If the Grossman killer had been doing his thing elsewhere—and given the slick way he'd worked it, Eugene figured this was more than likely—there was a possibility VICAP would have a record.

Procedure took your mind off the randomness, the chaos. Searching the scene. Five basic methods. The Strip. The Grid. The Zone. The Wheel. The Spiral. Initiate a crime-scene log. Establish a policy for crime-scene integrity.

A lead or two would be nice, of course, but the whole point of VICAP was permeability, and by entering the system Eugene knew he had effectively sent out an invitation for other agencies to become involved. If the killing turned out to be part of a series crossing state lines, it would be only a matter of time before the FBI came sniffing round.

They had accompanied the VICAP entry with a request for information about offenders using similar MOs, having the physical characteristics of Buffy Allen's man in the blue jogging suit. They had decided that the Jogger probably carried his tools, a change of clothes, and sneakers in the knapsack. There had been too much blood at the scene for him not to get splashed. So it seemed most likely that he'd done his business, and had then changed clothes. The bloody clothes, shoes and stolen flesh would have gone into the bag.

So far, there had been no sightings of the Jogger after 5:30 P.M., the medical examiner's TOD estimate. Buffy had finished in the bathroom and had gone out to buy milk at around 5:15. If the Jogger had come back down the fire escape, the old man wouldn't have seen him.

Eugene listened to the rain intensify, thinking about the knapsack now. He imagined some kid picking it out of a Dumpster or a trash can, opening it up to see what was so heavy.

Once in a secure location, wet evidence, whether packaged in plastic or paper, must be removed and allowed to completely air-dry.

The thunder. Closer now. The front went through like a wave. Eugene heard dripping sounds. A green-leaf smell in the room. One of the reasons he had moved back to Queens.

14

At eight o'clock the next morning, when his wake-up call came through from Reception, Nick was already dressed—stretched out on the bed, feeling the morning slant sharply towards eleven o'clock when a plane was going to lift him out of the *Life* and by doing so make a lot of people happy. Henry and Stanhope would get a book that came out at the same time as the Tate retrospective, and Linda would get her freedom back. As for Laverne, she'd get her "proper life," a life that streamed out behind her like the wake of a luxury liner on a postcard sea.

Nick closed his eyes. He felt the shame of it now. The way he had always more or less played along with Laverne. Because debris rolled in the wake of her leaky ship, he was sure of it. He just hadn't wanted to alienate her by looking too closely. Now that he had glanced backwards, her smiles and cooperation had been replaced by insults and warnings.

He sat up on the bed and looked at his suitcase, already packed, in the middle of the floor. Write up the Grossman incident, he told himself; squeeze a couple of newspaper articles out of it, then get on with your own life again. Think of Linda for once. After all, things were going to be easier now. The Crucible deal was going to take off a little of the financial pressure, and might even open some new doors.

There was a knock at the door.

"NYPD Homicide, Mr. Greer."

He crossed the room and opened up on a stocky red-faced character with half-moon spectacles and a bristling gray mustache. A taller, thinner guy with a mild, dreamy expression was with him. The stocky one held up his shield.

"Detective Eugene Glasco," he said. "This is Detective Raymond Guthry. We'd like to have a word."

Nick stepped back from the door and let them through. It was Glasco who did the talking. Pointing at the suitcase, he asked where Nick was going, and when Nick told him London, Glasco held up a copy of the *Times*.

Nick read the headline: DESTROYING JACOB GROSSMAN: AN EAST SIDE STORY. Florey's name was bylined and scribbled in the right-hand margin along with the telephone number of Nick's hotel.

"We were wondering why it was you didn't come forward," said Glasco. "But I guess you were busy talking to the press about your fascinating encounter."

Nick looked at the dreamy cop, surprised by the tone, the hostility.

"I don't understand."

"Which part?"

"I mean I *did* come forward. I spoke to you guys the day it happened."

The cops exchanged a look then. Bored. Complicit in their boredom.

"Monday evening," said Nick. "Here in the room. Detective Bittaker called by to ask me some questions."

"Detective who?"

"Bittaker. Detective Bittaker."

"NYPD? The guy had a badge?" Glasco flipped out his own badge again, held it up for Nick to see. "Like this?"

Nick squinted, tried to think.

"Yes, he did say NYPD. He knocked on the door and said 'NYPD,' you know, for me to open up."

The dreamy cop walked over to the window and took out his cellphone. He punched in a number.

"So you let him in?" said Glasco.

"Yes and—and he was—he had a card, he had one of my cards. I left a card with Mr. Grossman with my number here at the hotel, just in case he wanted to get in touch."

Glasco brushed his mustache with the tips of his fingers as his partner got through to whomever he was calling, and started asking questions in a low growl.

"He had my card," said Nick. "So he must have been at the—at the crime scene. Right?"

"Tell me about this guy," said Glasco. "What did he look like?"

"Sort of—ugly. An ugly guy with this big nose. Five-ten, five-eleven maybe. Balding."

"White? Black?"

"White. He had frizzy reddish hair. Losing it at the front, but otherwise, you know, unkempt."

"Unkempt?"

"Messy. And he wanted—he asked me questions about Grossman. I made a tape of the interview and he wanted to hear it. So we sat through it, and he asked me questions."

"You made a *tape*?"

Nick rummaged in his briefcase and came up with the cassette recorder.

"For my book," he said, holding up the tape. "For the book I'm writing."

"What time was this?"

"Seven, maybe seven-thirty."

Glasco looked across at his partner.

"Was he carrying anything with him? A bag, a knapsack?"

"Just this little plastic bag with my card in it."

"A plastic bag?"

"Yes, like a—a little Ziploc-type bag; an evidence bag, I thought. It gave me quite a shock, you know, seeing my card in this bag with blood on it."

Glasco touched his mustache again, dragging upwards against the bristle.

"Blood?"

The dreamy cop finished his call.

"Well, I *suppose*," said Nick. "I assumed he'd taken it from the scene. As evidence, you know. Why? Is there—is there anything wrong?"

They drove downtown in the unmarked Crown Victoria. Sitting in the back, Nick said he had a plane to catch. The red-faced cop told him not to worry about it, told him they'd get him on a later flight, then handed him the newspaper to shut him up. It was a struggle to focus on the print.

DESTROYING JACOB GROSSMAN: AN EAST SIDE STORY

Jacob Nathaniel Grossman's life came to a gruesome end two days ago on the floor of a rehabilitation clinic in the Lower East Side. So far, no one from the Rhode Island Grossmans—the nearest surviving relatives—has come forward to claim the body, nor are they expected to in the near future.

Born in 1914 into a wealthy Manhattan family, Grossman led a conventional life until the age of eighteen, when his father discovered him trying on his mother's underwear. Fearing intersibling corruption, he sent Jacob to stay with his uncle, Marcus Grossman, a military man known for his strict discipline and morals.

Grossman's father didn't know that Uncle Marcus was also a pedophile and closet homosexual. Jacob, though never abused by his uncle, who apparently drew the line at incest, was not steered back into the path of sexual orthodoxy. He was also given the run of his guardian's photographic studio, and by 1935, aged only 21, he was already well established as one of the leading chroniclers of Manhattan's slide into depression, his photographs of the demolition of the old Waldorf-Astoria Hotel in 1929 making him famous among what was left of New York's smart set.

But until his murder, he was best known for his amorous association with British painter Frank Spira, who was part of the Tenth Street scene between 1934 and 1956, and whose figurative biomorphs now sell for millions at auction. The turbulent, often violent relationship, described in Martin Marion's seminal work, *Tortured Eros*—

Nick pushed out an irritated sigh and caught the red-faced cop looking at him in the rearview mirror. He hunched back over the page as if the report required all his powers of concentration.

The turbulent, often violent relationship, described in Martin Marion's seminal work, *Tortured Eros,* ended twenty-six years ago when Grossman disappeared. Marion, himself a resident New Yorker since the late sixties, told the *Times* that once Grossman discharged himself from the New Jersey clinic where he was being treated for cocaine addiction in the spring of 1972, he was living on borrowed time. "Jackdaw had a self-destructive streak like a waterslide," says Marion. "The fact that he showed up in this dreadful hole came as no surprise to those of us who followed his meteoric fall from grace."

Writer Nicholas Green, in New York to research a new study of Spira, interviewed Grossman hours before his murder. "He was agitated and fairly confused," says Green, who claims Grossman bit him in a scuffle that erupted in the closing stages of their meeting. The fact that Grossman had sought to change his identity—he was known only as Jack to the staff and had dyed his white hair an unlikely black—fuels speculation that he feared pursuit, and may even have known his killer.

Marion, who knew Grossman personally and was also a close friend of Spira's, was unwilling to speculate about possible motives for the murder but confirmed that it was not beyond the bounds of possibility that the incident was in some way related to the dead artist and his shady world.

"What's the problem?" said the red-faced cop, still watching him in the mirror.

Nick shook his head.

"They got my name wrong."

"Yeah? Hey, I can count on the fingers of one hand the number of times the press has gotten my name *right*. And that's in thirty years on the job."

The 7th Precinct station house was a modern low-rise brown-brick structure facing bleak-looking towers on the other side of Pitt Street.

Nick followed the cops up three flights in a cement stairwell and entered an open-plan area with a gray linoleum floor and light blue walls. Corkboards carried pictures of homicide fugitives, duty rosters, bulletins, articles from newspapers and magazines. Big windows were screened with black roller blinds to keep the sun off desks that ran the length of the room. Heads came up as they entered. Nick felt the eyes on him, cops' eyes—who-the-fuck-are-you serious despite all the joshing going on.

They took his prints, said they wanted to exclude any latents he might have left at the scene. Then they went into an interview room right next to the holding pen. Painted the same swimming-pool blue, the room was bare except for three chairs around a Formica table. Nick got the seat facing a mirror that was set in the wall just above his eye level.

The cops wanted the whole of Monday, from his arrival at the clinic to Bittaker's departure. It took a long time to tell because they kept interrupting to clarify points, asking what exactly Nick was hoping to get out of Grossman, why Grossman had attacked him, why he had run away in 1972, what it was the man was afraid of.

They listened to the tape of the interview once, twice. Around two o'clock they stopped for coffee and hamburgers. A uniformed officer came in and told Glasco that there was a Detective Marie Biedecker with the 70th Precinct, and a Lieutenant Robert Biddaker with the 28th.

After lunch Glasco set up a tape recorder on the table, named everyone present, stated the date and time. It was just after three o'clock.

"So, let's go back to the man who came to see you in your hotel room," he said, getting comfortable. "You think he came to your door at around seven, seven-thirty?"

"That's right. I was on the phone to my wife when he knocked."

Glasco frowned at his notes.

"This is Linda, in London?"

"Correct. I put the phone down and went to the door, and there was this guy. The man I described."

Glasco asked Nick to describe the man for the record.

"Average height, messy reddish hair, frizzy, balding at the front. Funny light gray eyes."

"Funny?"

"Unusual. They were very pale. And this nose. It was . . ." He closed his eyes, trying to think what it was about the man's nose that had struck him.

"Take your time," said Glasco. "These are the kind of things—"

"There was skin at the end that was, like, paler than the rest. Like scar tissue."

"He had a scar?"

"Yeah, maybe it was a scar. It was a different color. Right at the end of the nose."

"Did you notice his hands?"

"Not really."

"Think back. See if you can visualize them."

"They were . . ." He looked up at the mirror for a moment, trying to recall. "They were strong hands. Big. With short nails."

"Any cuts, abrasions, contusions?"

"Not that I remember."

"Clean, dirty?"

"Clean, I think."

"And this man, what was he wearing?"

Nick got a flash of Bittaker standing in the doorway and it brought the hair up on his arms. It hadn't struck him at the time, but there had been something about him, something wrong, something bad.

"Nick?"

"He smelt of cigarettes," said Nick, and he shuddered. Then, seeing the look on Glasco's face: "Sorry, but it just came to me. He stank of cigarettes and he was eating candy. He smoked some of the time he was talking to me."

"Brand?"

"Marlboro, I think. He was wearing a cologne of some kind. Otherwise, jacket and trousers. A badly fitting sport jacket. I noticed the way it stood up off the collar."

"And he came into the room."

"Yes, I let him in. I was so astonished by the card he was holding."

"He was holding the card?" Glasco frowned at his notes.

"Not holding it. He had it in a bag, as though it were evidence. I noticed a brown smudge on the card, and I thought, Blood."

"Blood?"

"Dried blood."

"Have you seen dried blood on paper before?"

"Yes. Yes, I'm pretty sure it was blood."

"Pretty sure?"

"It *looked* like blood."

"And he asked you some questions?"

"Yes, about the Delancey-Deere Volunteer Center. He asked me when I was down there, whether I'd seen anyone unusual, you know."

"Just a second." Guthry leaned forward and switched off the tape. "What about Linda?"

Glasco sighed and flipped back through his notes.

"When the man came to the door," said Guthry, "you were on the phone. What happened? Did you hang up—what?"

"Oh yes," Nick nodded, remembering, "yes, that was funny. I forgot about that. When he came in, I remembered the phone and picked it up. Told my wife I'd call her back. It rang a little while afterwards, and he—he put his hand on it. To stop me from picking up again."

The cops became still.

"Did he touch anything else?" said Glasco.

"No, I don't—oh *yes*. He handled the cassette. He was turning it around in his hand for a while."

They looked at the cassette container on the table. They had been handling it all afternoon. Glasco glanced across at his partner and then stood up. He left the room.

Nick watched Guthry make notes in silence.

It was way too hot.

"Does it always take this long?"

Guthry looked up.

"I mean, do you always go through testimony several times?"

"If it seems important enough," Guthry said. "You want to get it straight."

"Is there a chance—I mean, will you want to call me back? It's just that I live in London."

Guthry stared.

"I wouldn't lose any sleep over it."

A few minutes later Glasco came back in and slumped down, dropping his notebook on the table. Nick noticed what he'd written at the top of the page.

"Oh."

He pointed at the notebook.

"What's up?"

"You got the name wrong. It was Bittaker. B-i-t-t-a-k-e-r."

"Bittaker?"

"That's right, with two *t*'s."

"How do you know?"

"He wrote it down." Nick put a hand to his forehead, only now remembering. "*Damn.* Sorry. It just didn't—I didn't think about it. You've been saying his name, I just assumed . . . When he was leaving, I asked him for a card, and he didn't have one, so he wrote his name in my notebook."

Glasco's face flushed a little darker. Handling it by the edges, Nick put the notebook on the desk. All three looked at it. Black felt-tip scrawled diagonally—"Bittaker 9th Precinct."

"He said just look the number up in the book."

"He got it wrong," said Guthry reflectively. "Not by much. South of East Houston it's the Seventh. Different jurisdiction."

"Got a sense of humor, though," said Glasco under his breath. He stood up and walked to the other end of the room, where he stared at himself in the mirror.

The other cop turned in his chair.

"How's that?"

Glasco came back to the table and pointed at the block capitals he'd just written in his notebook.

"Look," he said, and he drew a vertical line between the two *T*'s.

The Incarnation

15

The cops made a couple of phone calls, got the carrier to put Nick on a different flight. So it wasn't until Thursday morning that he touched down at Heathrow. Riding the Piccadilly Line in from the airport under a sky the color of tin, he prayed Linda would be sleeping when he got back. All he wanted to do was take a shower, slip into the bed next to her and close his eyes.

Opening the front door, the first thing he saw was the sheet of paper. A window was open somewhere at the back of the basement, and the draft pushed it along the hallway. It was a page of the proofs, marked for corrections. He turned it over with trembling fingers, saw Linda's crabbed scrawl filling the page.

> Nick,
>
> This is as much my fault as yours. It takes two to tango and so forth, but I should have walked off the dance floor four years ago when you said you were going to need more time on the book. The music stopped when you said that, and I chose to ignore it. I thought, Nick needs more time, and even though giving you that time was going to mean staying in the basement, and continuing to live like students (not even students because after all I was going to work and certainly not learning anything), despite all that, I said, "Take more time, take another year if you need it," because I remembered the other book and how unhappy it made you to rush it and cut corners and finally to turn in something you knew wasn't finished.

I didn't want to watch you go through that again, and so when the music stopped, I just clung on tight. Then another year went by. Then four. And music or no music I kept on dancing. Even though we didn't have any money and there was no prospect of you making any.

And now you want more time . . . The phone rings in the middle of the night and it's important, it leads to an interview that may open up any number of new avenues . . . I see chapters, appendices, footnotes scrolling away into the distance. But the band's gone home and they've turned off all the lights, and out here in the middle of the dance floor I feel suddenly alone.

Because I realize—I only now realize—that this isn't really about the book, the *Life*, as we have come to call it. It's about you and what you require to get through the day. You're like one of those birds that have to swallow stones

She'd run out of space. Nick flipped the page, but there was just text on the other side. He walked into the living room. Standing there with the note clutched in his left hand, it took him a long staring moment to figure out that his books were all over the floor because Linda had been obliged to dig through them to get to hers. Her screenplay collection, her brick-sized Cinema Guides, her various how-to books had all gone.

The other page was on the table. He took it up and lowered himself into the armchair.

to digest their food. They swallow these big stones and jump up and down and all the thistles and weeds they have to eat get mashed up into something digestible. The biography is your gut stone, Nick. You need it to deal with the rindy scraps and trash that you (we) have to chew through day in and out. And when you're finally done with the *Life* a year from now or maybe two or three, you'll find another stone to swallow and the whole process will start again.

Because it is a process, Nick. A pattern of behavior.

Seriously, and I don't mean this in an accusatory way. I just want you to see it for what it is. I mean, have you ever asked yourself, Why Spira? How it is this painter became so all-important to you? I know you admire his work, and you met him in the street once and you shook his hand and it was a magical moment and so forth, and for goodness sake a biographer has to write about *something*. But is that really the whole story?

You see, I've watched you. I've watched you tunnel and dig. "I want to get under his skin," you say and you do, you get in so far that eventually the day arrives when you open your eyes and they're Spira's eyes—every reference is a Spira reference, every memory is a Spira memory. And we're dancing and I look into those eyes and sometimes (and this is maybe the hardest thing of all) there's a kind of blankness there as if you didn't know me, and I think, of course you *don't*, because Spira never did. We never met.

And maybe it's great for you. I mean, living through this genius, but what about me? What do I get out of it? A dedication. A gut stone with my name on it.

We've always made the big decisions together, and making this one without talking to you feels wrong. I wanted to talk to you on Monday night, but then you had to hang up and I thought maybe it was better that way because there was a chance you might persuade me I was making a big mistake, which maybe I am, but I certainly can't see how. The mistake I think was to wait so long to do what I'm now doing. So this is good-bye, baby. Good luck with your Life.

Linda

When Henry arrived two hours later, wafting into the apartment through the open doorway, he found Nick in the living room filling shelves.

"I'd have got here sooner," he said, then seeing the look on Nick's face, fell silent.

For as long as Nick had known him, Henry had been using ultraviolet light to treat some kind of fungal condition. In the depths of winter, he had a light tan, but in the summer, prescription skin care gave him the nutty sheen of a Greek shipping magnate, an impression underlined by the snowy hair he wore slicked back with gel. Henry had a kind of style, and looked, if you didn't look too hard, like money or good luck. It was one of the things that had drawn Nick to him in the first place.

"Did she say anything?" said Henry. "Leave a note or anything?"

Nick wiped dusty fingers across his mouth and looked around at the living room. Wood-chip wallpaper, crooked light switches with their shadowy aureoles of finger grease. Between them they had never earned enough to redecorate. Or rather *he* had never earned enough.

"She thinks the book's a gut stone," he said and, looking down at the floor, was seized by a sudden drowning panic. He closed his eyes.

"Nick?"

"Is that right, Henry?"

"Is what right, old thing?"

"Is that what you think? That the book is a kind of therapy? A crutch?"

"Of course not."

Nick walked through to the bedroom. There was a pile of clean laundry on the armchair. The bedding plus his clothes. Linda had gone out and done a wash. Thinking of him as always. He picked up a sheet and pressed it to his nose, but all he got was a smell of soap. Then he saw her mismatched bed socks—thick green and red wool things that had gone nubby at the heels. She wore them in bed when it got too cold, which in the basement was most of the time. It looked like she had paired them into a ball ready for packing. He pulled them apart, laid them alongside each other on the bed.

Henry came into the doorway. He said something about the book being a remarkable achievement.

"This is twelve years, Henry. Twelve years."

"She'll be in touch, old thing. You can talk then. After all, you're very nearly finished. With the book, I mean."

"When I met her—when I first met her all those years ago, she was so vibrant. So vital."

Henry returned Nick's gaze with a lost, almost pleading expression.

Another rush of cold despair swept through him, bringing his head forward.

"Well—look, I've got to be getting back," said Henry. "Why don't you give me a call later on? We can talk about the book then."

Nick looked up.

"What about the book?"

"Well, this isn't really the time to . . ."

Nick shook his head, realizing that Henry hadn't come all the way across London to console him. There was business to discuss.

"Is it about New York?" he said.

"New York? No. No, I haven't heard from New York since we spoke. No, what it is . . ." Henry removed his glasses and started to polish them. "I had a call from Stanhope yesterday asking about the galleys, about how close you were to sending back the corrections. I told him you were in Manhattan because Jacob Grossman had reemerged, and naturally he was very interested. We got into a conversation about the changes you might be wanting to make." He put the glasses back on and pushed them up the bridge of his nose. Nick could see by his expression that the conversation hadn't been very satisfactory. "I'm afraid he was rather discouraging."

"What does that mean?"

"He pointed out that there is a schedule here. And a deadline."

Nick walked over to the grimy sash window. A slug was making its way up the glass.

"This really isn't the best time for this discussion," said Henry.

Nick turned.

"But Henry, the book—the book as it currently stands—"

"Don't think I underestimate the importance of the Grossman material. In fact, I think that this is all great. It's just a question of whether or not—"

"I'm not talking about Grossman—not *just* about Grossman, anyway. What I'm saying is things have moved on. This whole thing . . ." He looked down at his bandaged hand. "Yesterday, while you were talking to Stanhope about the galleys, I was being interviewed by a couple of homicide detectives."

Henry's jaw dropped. In other circumstances Nick would have laughed.

"No, I didn't kill anyone," he said. "These detectives wanted to ask me about a visit I received Monday night."

"A visit?"

"Yes. From the murderer of Jacob Grossman."

They went down the road to the café where Nick sometimes ate a lunchtime sandwich. It was a grimy narrow space with a half a dozen tables and a dirty plate-glass window looking onto the street. As a gesture to the idea of a summer, the owner had blocked open the door with a carton of mineral water. Exhaust fumes drifted in on the cold London air.

It took an hour for Nick to tell the whole story. By the time he got to the subject of the killer's sense of humor, the café was filling with people on their lunch break. A tired-looking guy in blue overalls sat down at the next table.

"Bit Taker?" said Henry under his breath.

"The detective, Glasco, he wrote the name in two parts, and the other guy, his partner, got this look." Recalling the moment—Glasco looking up from the notebook to meet his own puzzled stare—Nick felt the hair stir on the back of his neck. "They looked at me, just sat there staring, and then *I* got it. Who this Bittaker really was. I asked them what exactly had happened to Grossman, but they wouldn't say, started talking about the importance of keeping a lid on the investigation."

"So . . . ?" Henry tilted his head, his glasses trapping rounds of light. "I'm still not sure I'm—"

"Mutilation," said Nick, glancing across at the guy in the overalls. "Cannibalism. Whatever. At least that's my guess, because, like I said, they wouldn't give me any details. But 'bit taker'—what else would it mean? This character, whoever the hell he was, was having a little joke."

He shuddered and looked out through the doorway at the ugly street. Then it came to him: Linda had gone. It hit him with all the rawness of the first realization. A truck went past, swirling grit in its wake, and out of nowhere he was remembering a time just before he and Linda had moved into the basement. They were renting a place in Islington, had made arrangements to leave. But then the Elsham Road tenants said they weren't going to move. For two months they stayed at friends' places while the tenants tried to make up their minds.

They'd had to put their furniture into storage: ninety cubic feet in a warehouse full of other people's stuff, all stacked up in cages. All these shelved lives. Every now and then, they would go there to find some essential item—an electric kettle, an alarm clock. Nick remembered standing there, looking at all their things piled up, feeling, weirdly enough, "at home." You could shake up a place like that, break it up, jumble it every which way, but it didn't stop being home.

"Nick?" Henry was sitting forward, his elbows on the table. "Explain something to me—why would this man, this Bit Taker, why would he come to you?"

Nick glanced at the guy in the overalls. He looked Middle Eastern. He was smiling to himself as he ate his sandwich.

"That's what the police wanted to know. We sat there—I mean, this is from yesterday lunchtime until God knows when last night, going over it again and again: Bittaker's questions, his interest in the tape, the tape itself. I could see the cops thought there was a painting behind all this, and that I was withholding information. Here's this . . . this psychopath goes to all that trouble to come and see me, *obviously* I know stuff. Anyway, I told them that as far as the scholarly record was concerned, the *Incarnation* didn't exist. I cited Laverne, I cited Spira. I talked about possible reasons for confusion. They said maybe *I* was the one who was confused. So then I asked them why such a valuable painting would remain a secret."

Henry shoved a piece of bread into his mouth, nodding.

"I didn't tell them what Laverne Taubmann told me."

Henry stopped chewing.

Nick leaned forward until he could see himself reflected in Henry's glasses.

"She told me that Grossman was killed because of this picture. She also told me I should forget all about it. She told me, in fact, that I was going to die too. Because of the picture."

Henry was shaking his head now.

"At the time I thought it was just—I don't know, just talk, but since this visit . . ." He shuddered. "Anyway, when I was talking to the police, I *did* forget about it. I mean, what are they going to do? Bother this sick old lady who's going to deny it all anyway?"

Henry swallowed.

"You withheld information from the police?"

Nick looked away and saw that the Arab guy wasn't smiling after all. There was a scar at the corner of his mouth. It pulled the lip up on one side. Not in a dramatic way. It was a subtle thing.

"I know," said Nick, moving around on his seat. "I don't—I mean, I'm not proud of it, but basically—well, I wanted time to think. This could be really important, Henry. For the book, I mean."

"You believe her? Laverne? You believe what she said?"

"That Grossman died because of the picture? I don't know. But—you had to be there. She *really* didn't want to talk about any of this, and somehow her reluctance makes it all seem more likely."

"But the picture itself. You believe in that. You think it's out there somewhere."

Nick looked at the sandwich on his plate. He'd thought he was hungry.

"I've been thinking about Bittaker," he said. "On the flight over, that was all I could think about. *He's* out there. That's a certainty. I can't stop thinking about him coming to my hotel room. Thinking about what he wanted."

"Information," said Henry. "He's after the picture too."

"That's what the *cops* thought. But I'm not so sure. Grossman gave the impression that whoever he was expecting would be in possession of all the facts. He told me that I wasn't going to get my hands on it—assumed I knew all about it."

"But he was wrong."

"He was wrong about *me*. But it looks like he was right about there being someone who knew he had the painting. Or knew he knew about it. If, as Laverne says, that was the reason he died."

Henry frowned. "So—let me see if I have this right. This Bittaker person, he killed Grossman to—"

"Silence him, maybe."

"He killed him, then came looking for you."

"Something like that."

"But he didn't kill you."

"He came to me because he wanted to find out what *I* knew. He was asking all these questions. At the time I thought it was just a cop trying to develop leads, but afterwards, when I was talking to the other cops, the *real* cops, it came to me, what he wanted to know was what exactly Jacob Grossman had told *me*."

Henry passed a hand back over his hair.

"To see if you were a threat."

"That's right." Nick took a bite of his sandwich. He chewed, swallowed. "He was interested in the mercury," he said under his breath.

"What?"

"It's just something that . . . Grossman got worked up when I started to talk about the mercury Reardon may have taken. Bittaker wanted to know what I thought about that. He wanted my opinion. And when I played the tape to Laverne . . ." He took another bite out of the sandwich. He didn't know what to make of it. Mercury. A toxic metal that used to be employed as a medicine. It was important. "I think Bittaker came to the room to see what I knew, and I've been asking myself what would have happened if I'd said: 'Oh yeah, Grossman told me all about it. The *Incarnation* was painted in Tangier in October 1957 but was then stolen by such-and-such and now it's part of so-and-so's very private collection in wherever.'"

Henry nodded. "You think . . . ?"

"I think he might have—yes, then and there. Killed me. I think he came to the room with that in mind. As it turned out, I didn't know anything. I was just this—this guy lost in the woods."

Henry was wiping his mouth with his napkin.

"You ask me if this painting is out there," said Nick. "Well, I couldn't say, to be honest. But I know someone, or rather I think I just *met* someone, who probably could."

16

Back in the empty basement he read Linda's note again, trying to find some reason for optimism, but all he could see was her honesty and the regret she felt for all the years wasted. She'd given up on him. Just when he was getting somewhere, just when the *Life* was opening up. He had to talk to her. She'd been ready to talk to him on Monday night. So why not now?

He phoned the cinema, but the line was busy. It was only when he hung up that he remembered work. It was Thursday afternoon, and he'd told Bernard Steadman, his boss, that he'd come in for a couple of hours.

He walked into the carpet-smelling bustle of the office just after three o'clock, glad to be there for once. Steadman, a big cable-knit slope of a man who looked out at the world through thick snowstorm glasses, was surly and preoccupied. It was always the same when the IMF issue came around. The high point of the publishing year, the issue was jammed with advertising and special supplements that in turn meant reams of copy, all of which had to pass through the narrow tract of the copyediting department.

Bernard handed him a report on small-cap investment funds in India, and Nick sat down to work, clarifying, punctuating, excising guff and pointless digressions. But it was hard to concentrate. The words of Linda's letter kept coming between him and the text. *The biography is your gut stone, Nick. "I want to get under his skin," you say* . . . Of course he wanted to get under his subject's skin. Any biographer worth a damn did. But to suggest that he was some kind of parasite was ridiculous. Or maybe not ridiculous but wrong.

He squinted at the grubby proofs, had to go back to the beginning of each sentence several times. Linda didn't understand. That was the simple truth of it. She didn't know what it was like to throw yourself at something, to get behind a subject and push. Inevitably it was absorbing. You were absorbed.

As soon as he was finished with the investment funds, Steadman handed him a report on back-office bottlenecks in Bombay. It was over three thousand words long and began with the words "Despite of increased volume . . ."

Nick rubbed at his eyes, squared the papers in the middle of his desk, stood up.

He found Steadman out by the coffee machine.

"What's up?"

"I'm sorry, Bernard, I just can't seem to focus."

Steadman sighed and looked down at him through his thick lenses.

"Focus? What do you need to focus for? Just edit the stuff."

Nick looked at the overflowing garbage pail. Styrofoam and dirty napkins. Spilt coffee and torn sachets.

"The thing is . . ." He shook his head, then didn't know what to say. "This thing came up and I've got to deal with it."

He came up out of the tube into drizzling rain and made his way along Charing Cross Road in the direction of Leicester Square. It was almost six o'clock, and the afternoon show at Linda's cinema was about to come to an end. She generally went across the street to get a sandwich about now, then sat in her windowless office until it was time to open up for the evening. He'd catch her coming out of the main entrance. He'd take her in his arms: *Sweetheart, I didn't know. I had no idea. It's going to be okay now.*

A block short of the cinema building, it occurred to him that she might not like being pounced on, and he crossed the road. He'd give her a chance to see him. She'd see him standing there in the rain.

People were coming up the steps out of the basement theater into the brightly lit foyer. A new print of Maurice Pialat's *A Nos Amours* was showing, and there wasn't much of a crowd. They came out through the big glass doors and looked up at the sky. Umbrellas opened. Nick waited until the woman who collected tickets was putting the velvet rope across the top of the stairs before crossing the street.

She recognized Nick only when he asked for Linda.

"She's not here," she said, scratching at her throat. "She hasn't been in for a few days."

She frowned then, and Nick could see that she was asking herself why he didn't already know this.

He bought a pizza on the way home and got back to the basement just as the rain was easing up. Balancing the warm box on the handlebars of the bike that was propped against the wall, he fumbled for his house keys and opened up. Then it came to him that the bike was Linda's. He couldn't recall if it had been there when he got back from the airport and for a split second thought no—that she had come back and was in the bathroom toweling her hair dry. Then he saw the chain running through the back wheel and around the broken drain-pipe and remembered that she had lost the key several months ago. The bike had been there ever since. It was part of a joint New Year's resolution to get fit and to avoid the daily grind of public transport, a resolution they had made . . . Nick wiped water from the saddle. He couldn't remember. He couldn't remember and suddenly that seemed to justify every word of Linda's note.

The phone was ringing.

He pushed through to the cold darkness on the other side and went into the living room.

"You weren't sleeping, were you?"

It was Henry. And he sounded keyed up.

"Working," said Nick.

"Any news? Of Linda?"

"No."

"Well, listen. This might cheer you up. I just got off the phone to Miriam Florey in New York, told her how great I thought her piece was."

Nick shrugged off his raincoat.

"Great? Henry, she didn't even get my name right."

"And I told her about the police investigation, about how you probably had the murderer in your hotel room, which, naturally enough, she thought was *very* interesting. She wants to do a follow-up piece *and* she wants you to write a couple of thousand words on Frank Spira's lovers. That's the brief: Spira's Lovers. Up to two thousand words. She's going to call you herself, so please be nice to her."

Nick levered off his dripping shoes, then peeled off the socks.

"We're on our way, Nick. This kind of coverage is really going to help things in New York."

"But what about the proofs? I'm supposed to be handing the manuscript back to Ernest Stanhope next week, and this new Grossman material has to go in. Otherwise—"

"Oh, don't worry about that. I think that once Stanhope hears about this, he'll be delighted."

"You're saying he'll give me more time?"

"Well, I haven't spoken to him yet, but this material is sensational, Nick. We're talking about real momentum here."

Nick hung up feeling confused. Then it came to him that he still hadn't told Henry about the Taubmann sale, how Barb was going to get him access to the documents in Laverne's Manhattan residence.

He went through to the kitchen and draped his socks over the water heater, then went back into the living room and picked up the phone. He took a breath, hit number one on the speed dialer. Rebecca Falk.

Rebecca, or "Becks," as she liked to be called, had studied English with Linda at university and was her oldest, most faithful friend. She had gone on to study law and now worked for some tentacular conglomerate in the City where she dealt with compliance. Nick had never really understood what that meant but had no trouble imagining Becks forcing people to comply. She had always disliked him, made no attempt to conceal the fact that she thought he was a loser.

She seemed to pick up the phone the instant it rang and bounced back his timid greeting with a joyful, vindictive *"Nicholas!"* Hearing her voice, he felt suddenly unprepared.

"How was New York?" she said.

"Good. Interesting."

"They say if you can make it there, you can make it *anywhere*."

Her laughter brought the hair up on the back of his neck.

"I expect that the Big Book'll be in all the shops soon."

Nick tried to swallow, couldn't. "Well, it's not exactly that sort of—"

"Of *course* not. Nick, darling, to be honest I've got some friends here at the moment. Was there something you . . . ?"

"I was wondering if you knew where Linda was."

"Of course I do."

"Well—could you—"

"She's staying with me, silly."

Saying it as if it went without saying, pushing that fact into his face. Suddenly it was difficult to draw breath.

"Does she—?"

"She doesn't want to speak to you. And to be honest I don't blame her."

"Oh?" He gripped the phone with both hands. "Oh? Why's that, Becks?"

"Nick, there's really no point in—"

"No, there is a point, *goddammit!*"

The rage came from nowhere, jarred him, shook him through to his bare feet.

"Don't raise your voice to me," said Becks, saying it softly and without the slightest hint of emotion. "Don't you raise your voice."

"I'm not—I'm not raising my voice."

"You Raised Your Voice."

"I'm—I'm just trying to understand what—"

"Well, *that's* something you probably need to discuss with Linda. When she's ready to talk. In the meantime, I will say just one thing."

There was a wadded thunk, Becks pushing the phone into her shoulder. Nick heard muffled talk, couldn't tell if it was Linda or not—then a sharp clunk of metal on metal. A saucepan. They were in the brushed-steel altar of Becks's kitchen.

"Are you still there?"

Nick grunted.

"I just wanted to say that all these years I've watched you control her, and crush her, and hold her back, I've longed for the day she'd wake up and see you for the selfish, abject person you are. And now she has, and I'm glad."

And she hung up on him.

Nick ate the pizza standing by the sink, then went out and bought a bottle of Jamesons, drank whisky sodas until the soda ran out, then drank it neat.

The phone rang: concerned friends, looking for news or wanting to give advice. Word was getting around about the breakup. Nick let the machine take the messages until, at around eleven o'clock, Tyler called. Tyler was a friend from way back, a college drunk who now edited a literary page for a London daily. He had just gotten back from the pub where someone had told him the news. He seemed to be having trouble taking it in.

"I mean, you guys, you're, like, so *stable,*" he said, breathing heavily against the mouthpiece. "So—so harmonious. Never—never fighting ever."

Tyler and his girlfriend had fought all the time until she moved out a couple of years ago. Nick said maybe it would have been better if he and Linda had fought. Maybe then the pressure wouldn't have built up so much.

"Tyler?"

"Yuh?"

"You know how important this book is to me."

"Your book? The *Life*? Sure. Of course."

"Do you think—have you ever thought that maybe it was too important? That I put too much into it?"

Tyler belched. "Can you?" he said. "I mean, is that even possible?"

There was a glugging, slurping noise: Tyler drinking beer in the kitchen that hadn't been cleaned since the day his girlfriend walked out.

"Linda thinks I'm obsessive."

"Me too, Nick. Absolutely. It's what I like about you. You don't know when to stop."

"Thanks. That's really what I need to hear right now."

"Think yourself lucky. Most people, and I include myself in that category, don't know when to start. Or where or how. That's why I'm a fucking journalist. That's why I never . . ." There was some more glugging. "I'm telling you, the road of excess leads to the—"

"Palace of wisdom," said Nick. "Yeah."

He sat in the dark, drinking, listening to the voices.

At three o'clock in the morning, he took the bandage from his hand. The zigzag mark seemed like the strangest thing in the world. He tried to rectify his haircut in the bathroom mirror, feeling around the back of his head for the patches Linda had missed. The scissor blades closed with a crunching sound. He flushed the cuttings down the toilet, then took a seat, sat there for a while, flipping through Linda's alternative medicine books. Ignatia was for depression following the end of a love affair, but also for bereavement. He didn't know what Ignatia was but was sure he could use some, because that was what it felt like sitting there in the cold: someone you'd known forever, who had known you forever, was suddenly gone, suddenly in the ground. Forever. Sliding the points of the scissors into the book, getting the blade as close as he could to the spine, he carefully sheared the page. Of course, Linda hadn't died. She'd left him. She'd left him because he'd left her. He'd disappeared into the *Life*.

He sat there for a long time, the cold metal blades pressed against his mouth, then walked through to the living room, the scissors still on his fingers. He collapsed onto the couch and, staring up at the ceiling, said a few things he thought Linda needed to hear, including the fact that he had always loved her, still did love her, and that if he had neglected her, he was sorry, but she had known what he was like from the beginning. And it was going to be different from now on. The book was finished. Nearly finished, anyway. There were just a couple of things he needed to nail down.

And saying that, he found himself standing again.

Drunk as he was, it took him a while to put his hand on the right notebook. He'd been going through a couple a month for the past six years, using them as a depository for ideas, observations, quotes. They were bundled up in thick rubber bands—each bundle, a year's worth of scribbling.

"May 12–26, 1996" had a plain blue cover. He pulled it out and started fumbling pages. Because Marion had refused to be taped, the best record he had of their exchange was twelve pages of almost indecipherable handwriting, which he'd later annotated. The relevant passage had a big exclamation mark next to it, and the words "Barb says poisoned chalice." Several lines were underscored in black.

> Marion: Tangier—Laverne went there in the fall of 57, because Max sent her to make an offer for a work he knew Spira had completed (chk Max/Spira correspondence 56–57).
>
> —Why no mention in *Tortured Eros*?
>
> Marion: It's a can of worms, Mr. Greer. I'm not partial (to worms). Also, I had no desire to embarrass people I consider my friends.
>
> —What's embarrassing about making an offer for a painting?

Marion: Being refused.

—Spira refused Max Taubmann's offer?

(at this point Marion tapped the side of his nose, rolled his eyes etc., basically saying yes, I think)

—I still don't see any reason for embarrassment.

Marion: You need to stand back. Take a broader view. Cause and effect. Consider the events of January 1960.

—Are you talking about the burglary? The break-in at the Rue d'Angleterre?

Marion: When you stand back, you see all kinds of interesting things.

—Max Taubmann was behind the burglary? Is that what you are saying?

(Marion—stone-faced, the Sphinx with a gin and tonic, but not saying no)

—And it was this picture that was stolen? What proof do you have?

Marion: Ah yes. The proof. The cross you bear. None whatsoever, Mr. Greer. <u>My sources, however, are in a position to know.</u>

Nick scratched at his forehead, swaying a little under the ceiling light. The stuff was *so* Marion: a piece of sensational news wrapped up in nods and winks, unprovable, unrepeatable; Marion unwilling to go on the record because he had to consider his friends' feelings. But looking at it now, considering it in the light of what Laverne had said, he wondered—wondered in spite of everything Barb had said about poisoned chalices. If the picture stolen from the Rue d'Angleterre was the *Incarnation*, and Max was behind it, then Laverne's behavior became, if not comprehensible, at least open to a definite interpretation.

Mi retrovai per una selva oscura.

He wasn't sure what it was that made him decide to decorate the room. The whisky probably, or maybe fear—a desire to fill the emptiness that seemed to be opening up around him. Whatever it was, he applied himself to the task steadily, cutting and sticking, until by seven o'clock the room had become a kind of shrine. Spira's life and work were everywhere—reproductions in hot reds and sticky purples scissored from his books, photographs, some copies of originals, some half-tone prints cut from papers. A copy of the golden mask Roald Meeks made in '62—Spira in his early fifties, serene, hieratic—took pride of place on the mantelpiece. A reproduction of *Cupid* was up over the door that led through to the bedroom.

Linda had always hated the picture, but for him it had a voodoo force, was *the* Spira in fact, seemed to come out of nowhere and everywhere, from Goya and Euripides, from Blake and Picasso—hunched and totemic, a flightless, plinthed penis bird with a humped scrotum body and bandaged eyes.

He loved it—particularly loved it stuck up there over the door, the bird of ill omen, pushing its tooth-crammed leer into your face as you passed beneath. He put the scissors into another page, eyeing a space above the window that was just beyond his reach.

17

Eugene couldn't understand it: the Grossman murder had been running only for five days, but already the case folder had the battered, coffee-stained look of something long unsolved. With the original response report, Kadomato's autopsy, Raymond and Bonner's canvass questionnaires—Raymond neat, Bonner *real* sloppy—VICAP and HIDTA printouts, the report made by the forensics team sent up to the Beacon Hotel to lift latents off the phone, a report which included the bizarre stuff about a fancy wiretap under Greer's bed, a likeness of the perpetrator worked up from Greer's description, a wad of press material—with all this *data,* the folder was getting too fat for its blue rubber band.

And now there were three more sheets to add to the pile: a lead from a rookie officer with the New York City transit police. Responding to a Thursday night complaint about street people in a tunnel off East Broadway, he had discovered a bloody knapsack among the usual rags, spoons and hypodermics. It had felt like a big break but, for the time being anyway, didn't seem to lead anywhere. A budget copy of specialized climbing equipment, the knapsack was empty. No murder weapon, no shoes, no jogging suit, no flesh. It didn't lead anywhere and it didn't make sense. Why would a guy remove bite evidence and then dump it to be found somewhere else? If he knew enough to be cutting chunks out of his victims, he knew enough to know that they could match the material to the body without any trouble at all. Of course, he might have removed any incriminating material from the knapsack before tossing it away, but why bother? Surely the thing to do would be to burn the whole thing. Eugene visualized the guy going down the fire escape steps at the back of the building. Maybe he'd been in a panic; maybe he'd been flustered.

Bob Mellor, the 7th Precinct lieutenant commander, had agreed to authorize a search of the tunnel if the lab came up with a match for Grossman's blood. Eugene just knew there would be more down there and was once again biting his nails, waiting for a call.

"Could mean anything," he said.

Raymond looked up from his desk.

"What could?"

"I'm talking about this knapsack. Turning up in the tunnel. Could mean anything."

"East Broadway. That's the F train, right? Does that go to Coney Island?"

"Yeah. And north to—no, east out to—past Forest Hills. Out that way."

Raymond scratched at his throat. He used the same blade for weeks and then wondered why he got a rash.

"Did you call Mr. Greer yet?"

Eugene shook his head.

The plan was to ask Greer why someone would spend good money to listen in on his conversations. It might or might not have something to do with the case, but it seemed worth a shot. Something was wrong with Nicky Greer, he knew that much.

The phone.

"Glasco."

"I can call later if this isn't a good time."

Suave and sophisticated. A voice that always reminded Eugene of Top Cat, or not Top Cat but the one with the scarf—Fancy Fancy. Detective Lawrence Biondi of the 13th. Eugene leaned back in his chair.

"Hey, Larry."

"Want me to make your day?"

"Do it. I need it."

"I got a witness for you. A Mrs. Ti*tun*ik. That's *T-i* and "tunic" with a *k*. Says she saw your Jogger artwork on the TV. Says she saw the man himself on um . . ." He rustled paper. "Tuesday—no, July thirteenth, *Monday.* Evening. She just walked in off the street. Wants to help the police catch the killer."

Eugene considered telling Larry about the other seventeen sightings he had yet to follow up on, not to mention three calls from the D.A.'s office he hadn't had time to return.

"What time was this?"

"Lady says around six-fifteen, but she can't be sure. She was on her way to her cleaning job at the Bank of . . . New York. Starts work at six-thirty, so . . ."

Six-fifteen. Fifteen minutes after Leroy Weller tried to push open Jacob Grossman's door.

"She gets off the subway at"—Larry rustled paper—"Fourteenth Street, so . . ."

Eugene hitched forward on his chair, holding up a finger to Raymond.

"Say that again, Larry? She's on the subway?"

"That's right."

"What train was she riding?"

Larry let out a sigh.

"Lady's sitting out in the corridor, Eugene. What do you want me to do?"

Mrs. Titunik had very dry black hair, and the red hands of a person who scrubbed a lot of floors. She kept the hands in her lap and looked around at the walls of the interview room like they were going to ask her to clean them and she was planning to refuse. Eugene let Ray tell her what a fine citizen and great sport she was, helping out like this. He took down her details and led her through the preliminary where-and-when questions. She had been riding the F train up to Fourteenth Street when the man in the blue jogging suit had sat down right opposite her.

If this was the guy, he had just finished doing his thing with Grossman.

Raymond asked about the jogger's demeanor.

"Smiling," said Mrs. Titunik. "This man, he was smiling."

She had some kind of accent Eugene couldn't place, but spoke her funny English very distinctly.

"So the car was full?" he said. "There were lots of other people—riding home, riding in to work?"

"Crowded, yes. Hot."

"Did you see the man get into the train? See which station he got on?"

She thought for a moment, then shook her head.

"No. There were people, some people getting off. The seat became free and this man, smiling man, he sat down."

"Smiling—like . . . ?" Raymond shrugged, wanting more, but not wanting to put words in the woman's mouth.

"Like a nice smile?" said Eugene.

"Just happy smile," said Titunik. "Not special. These teeth. Not so good."

"He had bad teeth?"

"Squeezed." She put her fingers into her mouth and squeezed the front teeth together. "Like a rat. And he click them."

"Click."

She clicked her own teeth together—*tic, tic, tic.*

"Okay." Eugene checked his notes. "And did he get off before you? Did you see him get off?"

"No. Not. I get off."

"At Fourteenth Street?"

"Always. For my work."

"Can you describe the man to me?"

A shrug.

"Like the picture. White man. Red hairs. Frizzy, er—curly hairs. No hair here"—she touched her forehead—"but lots of hair. Needs haircut really. Very—eyes with no color," she pointed a raw-looking index finger directly at her iris like she was putting in a lens, "in the *eye.*"

"No color? What, like gray eyes?"

"But very . . ."

"Pale," said Raymond, "light."

"Pale, yes." She hunched her shoulders and made "pale" sound spooky. "*Pale* gray, *pale* yellow-gray. Like—like devil eye. Smiling at me." She shuddered, clearly remembering that look. "So I turn myself away."

"Anything else," said Raymond, "about the man's face. His nose, for example."

"Not. Just not nice nose. Big."

"And this man," said Eugene, "what was he wearing?"

Another shrug. "Blue suit, for running. Sneakers, you know."

"Did you look at the sneakers?"

"I see sneakers, but I'm not looking. Not close up."

If there had been blood, she would have seen it. Everyone would have seen it. The sneakers went in the knapsack, Eugene was sure of it. So where the hell were they? In the tunnel at East Broadway.

"Did you notice anything about the—the jacket, the top?"

"Notice?" She frowned down at her clasped red hands.

"Yeah, you know, the style. You know these—these jackets come in different styles? With some you have, like, a pocket at the front, or maybe a zipper."

"Hat," said Mrs. Titunik, looking up. "It has hat."

"Like a hood?"

Eugene mimed pulling a hood over his head. Titunik pointed, nodded. *"This."*

Eugene leaned forward and put his elbows on the table. He paused before asking the big question.

"And was he carrying anything? Like a bag, anything like that?"

"Bag not," she said simply, looking from one to the other, registering their disappointment. "But," she started to model the air in front of her with her hands, "this."

A cylinder.

"What? What is that?"

"For soup sometimes."

Eugene pointed at the invisible thing. "What? That he's carrying? Like a can of soup?"

She shook her head.

"Not. Not can. Like *hot* bottle, a"—the word hit her with a little jolt, making her smile—"ther*mos*," she said.

Eugene looked at Ray.

"Ther*mos*," said Mrs. Titunik again, nodding, reassuring them that she knew what she was talking about. "Big one—um, Chinese one. Like Chinese. Red."

"A thermos," said Raymond. "Like, for keeping things hot."

18

For Nick, Friday the seventeenth started with the sound of a jackhammer pounding in the street. At midday he squinted his way through to the bathroom and stood under the dribble of lukewarm water delivered by the shower. He called the *Journal,* told Bernard he was coming down with something, not even having to fake a sick employee voice. He was sick. His head felt like it was pumped tight with cold fluid. He made coffee and sat at his makeshift desk, trying to massage the back of his neck, surrounded by the Spiras, encircled by loose-leaf files and ring binders, index cards and document wallets, not wanting to think about Linda or Becks or what a "selfish, abject person" he was, not wanting to think about anything other than Grossman and the painting, because fuck it, and fuck them all.

Florey was going to call. At least that was what Henry had said. So a temptation now loomed: blow everything open in the *New York Times* article, quote Laverne on the reason for Grossman's death, drag in Marion with his story of Max Taubmann and the Rue d'Angleterre burglary.

But even hungover, even firing on one cylinder, he could see this would be pointless. He'd just be scratching where it itched, and the reprisals would be instantaneous. To write what he wanted to write, to finish the *Life,* he needed to go deeper, needed to start by getting back into the Taubmann residence.

He sipped coffee, cupping the mug for warmth, thinking he'd give anything for a couple of days with Laverne's papers. Max was famous for keeping all his correspondence, and never wrote a letter without posterity in mind. If, as Marion claimed, Max had sent Laverne down to Tangier to make an offer for the *Incarnation,* there was a chance there'd be a reference to the work in one of Spira's replies. The problem was, the only way he was going to get back into Laverne's place was over her dead body, at which juncture any pressure that documentary evidence might bring to bear (he saw himself shaking a letter in the old woman's face and demanding that she tell him the truth) would be nullified. Dead dowagers didn't talk.

The jackhammer started up again, but Nick was oblivious, brooding now, turning the material over in his mind. All he had were hints and rumors, and a bunch of dead or about-to-be-dead people who knew, or had known, something about a painting. The only person living who was in a position to tell him anything was Bittaker, and the thought of Bittaker gave him gooseflesh.

Then he had an idea.

He put down his mug and rummaged around for the business card he'd yet to copy onto his Rolodex, a plan taking shape: blow everything open, yes, but not to the press. Tell Detective Eugene Glasco what Laverne had said to him. Tell Detective Eugene Glasco what Marion had said to him in their 1996 interview. Glasco could subpoena the papers at the Taubmann residence. Laverne could be confronted while she was still alive. Glasco wouldn't even have to reveal his suspicions, except to the judge who issued the subpoena. All Laverne would know was that the police investigating Grossman's murder were interested in Max's correspondence. And if they turned up something interesting, something that linked Max and Laverne to the painting, she'd be in no position to point at Nick and cry "defamation"; the evidence would be on his side.

And if they didn't find anything? Then Laverne would be none the wiser. She'd have her suspicions, of course, but since nothing would have been publicly stated . . . And that would still leave Glasco with Marion to squeeze. How did Marion know what he claimed to know about the burglary? Who were the "sources" he referred to? Marion might be tempted to help the police in exchange for favorable treatment. However it turned out, Nick couldn't see Glasco being anything other than grateful to him. It would be only natural for him to reach out for expert help, and who was better placed to expedite the search of Laverne's papers than he himself, the writer of *Francis Spira: A Life*? Glasco might even be persuaded to share information regarding the Bittaker investigation, and if they eventually caught Bittaker . . .

The telephone jolted him out of the daydream.

It was Henry.

"Nick, I've just been talking to Ernest Stanhope, and I think—I *think* he's coming round to our view about the Grossman business. Anyway, he wants to talk to you."

"What does he say about extending the deadline?"

"Well, we didn't really get into that. I focused mainly on the idea of introducing new material. He's pretty much agreed to pick up the tab for changes to the galleys, which, in the circumstances, is very generous."

Changes to the galleys. Nick massaged his neck.

"Henry, what I have in mind goes beyond a couple of alterations."

"Anyway, I was wondering if you could make time to see him this afternoon. Just to get this all cleared up."

Brooding, churning, scheming. He waited until three o'clock U.K. time before calling Glasco, but Glasco still hadn't arrived. So he left a message saying that he'd been thinking about the Grossman case and believed he could be of help.

He was eating a sandwich in the kitchen when the phone rang. He snatched it up, but it was only Florey—Florey sounding contrite and apologetic about the article. Apparently it wasn't what she had written originally.

"The senior editor's an old friend of Marion's. When she saw the piece, she asked me to give him a call. I think I probably mentioned to you that he's writing a couple of features for us."

"You did."

"Well, anyway, the senior editor wanted Marion's input and then one of the copyeditors got hold of it and it was cut and they managed to get your name wrong and—"

"I understand."

He could hear the tapping of keys in the background.

"I don't know if Henry spoke to you about my idea, but—"

"The 'Spira's Lovers' thing."

"Right. This won't be for the Metro section, which means you're going to have a lot of room—if you decide to take it on, that is."

Another silence. Fill it. Nick massaged his forehead, eyes closed. He felt like he was being pulled three ways at once.

"I'd love to."

"What I'm looking for is something personal. Perhaps your interview with Grossman to start the piece—very much in the first person—and then sort of work outwards to Tony Reardon. Did you ever meet him, by the way?"

"I was eight years old when he died." Nick shook his head. There was no point in being snippy here. Florey was just trying to do her job. "But I do have a lot of material on him."

"I had in mind something about the way these two men influenced Spira's life and work. I've been doing a little more reading over the past few days and—well, there are so many interesting symmetries. The fact, for example, that Reardon also died—well, *violently.*"

"Drove his car into a ravine."

"That's right. He had this terrible disease, right?"

She had been reading *Tortured Eros*.

"Debatable," said Nick. "But you were talking about the violence, the symmetries."

"Yes. Grossman, Reardon. These violent deaths. It's like a curse."

"The curse of the Anti-Midas."

"The Anti-Midas?"

"It's a comment Tate Hemmings made. The critic? He said Spira was like King Midas, except that everything Spira touched turned to shit."

"Well, that, that's—the Anti-Midas—I like that. Maybe that's the way to approach the piece—work up the destroyer-creator aspect of it."

"I could try."

"And we have time on this, Nick."

"Well, that's good, because—"

"Four days at least."

"Four *days*?"

The phone wouldn't ring. He considered calling Glasco again, leaving another message. Then told himself to relax, to ride the horse the way that it was going. The "Spira's Lovers" piece was an opportunity, a breakthrough after years of nobody being interested. He needed to get on with it.

The Reardon file was three inches thick, split along the spine and held together with Scotch tape. A photograph fell out as he was opening it, a 3 x 2 black and white: Reardon drinking in a Soho pub, dated

1970. Blurred, overexposed, it wasn't good enough to put into the book, but for Nick it had always been very evocative. It showed a heavy, dark-faced man twisting sideways, his mouth open to yawn or shout. Reardon aged fifty-six. There were other pictures: a much slimmer Reardon with Spira on the Orient Express in '69; Reardon and Spira laughing it up with Billy Elkhorn, aka Billy Flash, in a bar in Tangier—fall of '57.

He worked through the Curlew proofs, tagging the Reardon and Grossman sections with sticky notes. It took him an hour to decide where he was going to introduce the new Grossman material. His plan was to integrate the material first, and then use it as the basis for the article. Two birds with one stone. But it was difficult to keep his mind on the job in hand. Everything he looked at seemed to point towards the *Incarnation*.

Reardon had been there when it was painted. He'd been there, or been around, when it was stolen—*if* it was stolen. In 1971, a couple of months before his death, someone had offered to buy it from him and he'd refused. At least that was the story that had prompted Alby Schadt to write his letter to Laverne.

So had Reardon himself stolen the painting?

Nick pushed the Curlew proofs aside and pulled out another Reardon photograph: 1967, but Reardon looking like a fifties spiv, leaning in the doorway of a Soho shop wearing a camel-hair coat. Another: Reardon standing under a streetlight somewhere in the East End in a herringbone double-breasted, his beringed left hand (Reardon loved jewelry and was never without a fiery garnet on his little finger) splayed, talonlike, on the sleek hood of his Merc.

Tony Spiv-Tony Sadist.

A violent man with gangland connections. Eyes like pinched slits. Unable to read or write. Given to big entrances and exits: staggering out of Spira's life in 1960 after a three-day drink-and-drugs binge that ended with a fight in a bar, then showing up four years later in a Soho restaurant where Frank was having lunch.

Spira's luck had changed after Tangier. He came back from his travels ten pounds lighter, hipper, more cosmopolitan—talking about Tenth Street as though he had been a big hit in Manhattan, talking about Burroughs, talking about Ginsberg. The desert had put some wise lines on his face and Reardon had done something to his soul.

He was less of a painter, perhaps, more of a showman. A showman-painter infected with syphilis. Or not.

The Blenheim Gallery organized a one-man show almost as soon as he got back from Tangier. It was the beginning of recognition and success.

Where Reardon was skulking during this period of renewal was unclear; probably in North Africa, developing his shadowy business interests. Whether he knew about Spira's success before '62 was open to debate, but that year the Tate Gallery included eight Spiras in an exhibition of contemporary British artists, an exhibition which subsequently went on the road, showing in Mannheim, Turin, Zurich and Amsterdam. In October '62, passing through Europe on business, Tony Reardon had checked into the van de Vries Hotel on the Prinsengracht in old Amsterdam, where he had stayed for five nights. Fact. It was Nick who had found the documentary proof.

It was hard to believe that Reardon didn't at some point go down to the Pieterman Gallery on the Rembrandtplein where the Spiras were showing. What was certain was that when he walked through the door of the dining room of Wheelers, Spira's favorite Soho eatery, on the afternoon of July 7, 1964, he was well aware of his former lover's change of fortune.

Nick pulled a page out from the proofs, a hand shading his eyes against the desk lamp: "With Pollock-like panache, Reardon pulled out his famously big member and proceeded to hose the white table-cloth, producing a flurry of movement as people tried to get out of the way. He then dragged the white-faced artist out of his chair—Spira had stayed put to watch the show—overturning the table and sending a £100 lunch of oysters and champagne onto the floor."

Reardon had stabbed Spira in the cheek with a fork—had *known* that was the way to hook him. And a week later, Spira made the first of many cab rides across London to Reardon's Stepney lair.

Everybody knew what was going on because so much of it went on in public. Spira would fight with Grossman—call him names, taunt him for putting on weight, for sulking, for neglecting the housework—then slam out of the house only to return a couple of days later, his face puffy from the latest beating. Far from disrupting the flow of work, this emotional Sturm und Drang was in fact the backdrop for the production of seven big works.

Tony Muse.

Then again, by the spring of 1965, Spira had other reasons for covering canvas, reasons that had nothing to do with his love life. In May of that year the Guggenheim retrospective included a total of sixty-two pieces, four of which were bought by North American museums. In the summer an exhibition in New York organized by the Blenheim, showing twenty recent works, sold out in the first week. Max Taubmann bought six.

Around that time, drinkers in the Colony Room, Spira's principal London watering hole, noticed an improvement in Tony Reardon's dress. The landlady remembered him rolling up at two in the morning in a tailored suit—*He'd have got something down his front or burnt the sleeve, and he'd be wearing these hundred-guinea boots splashed with God knows what.* People wondered why Grossman stuck around.

In the end, he started to ask himself the same question, and in 1969, when Spira took Reardon on what he later referred to as their "*soixante-neuf* junket" across Europe in the Orient Express, leaving the "Blank Yank" at home to oversee the installation of central heating in the studio, Grossman decided he'd had enough. When the painter returned three weeks later, he found the studio empty.

Then came August 1970, a flashpoint, the culmination of ten months' disastrous cohabitation. After Grossman walked out in '69, he was replaced almost immediately by Reardon. Spira was out of control. He could no longer function without the Benzedrine or with it. He wasn't sleeping, had started to suffer nightmare bouts of paranoia. The work suffered. In Tangier that hadn't mattered; he had been happy to pursue other interests, but now it was different. There were dealers to satisfy and, when the Inland Revenue finally caught up with him, outstanding taxes to pay.

So he had to work and, more importantly, had to work in a specific way, had to turn out a specific kind of product. The Spira style was already the subject of critical debate. Spira himself had given interviews defining what he was about, what made him different, special— effectively setting out the terms of a verbal contract with the collectors. Suddenly there were expectations to be met. Just when he seemed to be breaking free of constraint, a whole new maze of obligation sprang up around him. He pleaded with Reardon to move in with him. He wanted to get off the drugs and get back into a regular pattern of work.

But Reardon had no interest in keeping house. Visiting the studio in the spring of 1970, Oscar Nagel was staggered by the filth and squalor. Overflowing ashtrays, moldy food. The refrigerator had been daubed with what looked like blood. There was nothing inside except for a tray of amyl nitrite poppers. In July 1970 Reardon brought back a man from the adjoining cemetery of Brompton Oratory. The guy stayed for a week, eventually running off with Spira's wristwatch and a roll of £5 notes. Spira and Reardon became "Oraltory" habitués. The studio, only three minutes from the cemetery gates, turned into a kind of open house for furtive homosexuals.

Then in August 1970, a party was raided. People present on the night of the raid claimed that the police never would have turned up if Reardon hadn't gone berserk. He'd had words with Frank and then tried to set fire to the house, dousing the mezzanine floor with turpentine. For Martin Marion this "inexplicable" rage was a manifestation of the neurosyphilis Reardon was supposedly suffering from.

The phone. It came to Nick that it had been ringing for a while. He grabbed it up.

"Nicholas?"

A wave went through him: relief, anger, the desire to *be* the right way.

"Nick?"

"Yes."

"It's me."

Her voice seemed to come from far away, muffled by layers of distance, even though she was in the same city. She said she was sorry about the apartment. She said she had to think about the future, about *her.*

"I spoke to the management company. Explained the situation. We're supposed to give three months' notice. You should probably get in touch with them if you—"

"*Linda,*" he laughed, panicking, wanting to hold her back, to slow her down. "Sweetheart, I didn't get back to you, because this—"

"What?"

"Monday night," he said, knowing as he said it that it was all beside the point. "I'm saying, I didn't call you back straightaway because this guy, this homicide detective, this guy who *said* he was a homicide detective came to my hotel room and then—"

"Oh, that doesn't—" An ambulance or a fire truck went past at her end. It sounded like she was down in the street on a public phone. "I'd forgotten about that. A policeman? He was probably the one who called them. There was a message on the answering machine from some policeman in New York. Glasgow? Is that right? Anyway, I didn't call about—"

"But Linda," he cut her off again, then didn't know what to say. He caught the sound of a long, shuddering inhale. She was smoking. She hadn't smoked in three years. She'd put on ten pounds quitting, and had gone through a long period of depression because she'd been unable to wear her old clothes. But she'd stuck to it because she was terrified of lung cancer, the disease that had killed her father.

"You're smoking, sweetheart."

She started to cry.

"Linda."

He could hear her sobs, pictured her standing in a call box somewhere, eyes streaming.

"Linda, this is crazy. Just when I'm getting somewhere with this—with all this . . ." He couldn't finish the phrase, but there was no comeback from her. She was letting him put his case, he realized. Because these were last rites. A certain ritual had to be followed.

"I'm doing a piece for the *New York Times*," he said, and it sounded so empty, so pathetic, his face was suddenly aflame. "Jacob Grossman was murdered. Henry thinks there might be some interest at the Crucible Press in New York. I'm just a couple of months away from the deadline. Linda, once the book's published, I'll—"

"Start looking for it in the remaindered shops," she said, clearing her throat. "Nick, it's *worse* afterwards. How can you have forgotten that? It'll be the same as with the other book. A month after publication and you'll be wondering where it disappeared to."

"But it's different this time."

"It's the same, Nick. Worse in a way. Anyway, that's not really the point anymore."

"Worse?"

"Nick, let's not—"

"Tell me how it's worse. I want to know how it's worse."

"You worked so hard on this, Nick. You worked—"

"That's right. I did. I have. That's why it's a better—"

"Nick, stop. Listen to me." She blew her nose. "For God's sake, listen for once."

He closed his eyes and was seized by a sudden acute need for her, to be next to her. If he could just hold her for a moment.

"I tried to cut my hair last night," he said. "You really—you really butchered it at the back."

But she had nothing to say about this; nothing she wanted to share, anyway.

"Next time I think I'll—"

"Nick. Nick, you need . . . You should talk to someone."

"What?"

"You need to talk to someone. You don't know when to stop."

He tried to laugh. It came out harsh, angry.

"Linda, you don't understand."

"No, I do. I've watched you change. You changed, Nick. This book, it's become—"

"A gut stone," he said. "You already made that point."

"It's all part of the same thing. This endless working and reworking. You pile up all this—all this *stuff* because you think it gets you closer to some sort of, I don't know . . . You think if you know *everything*, you'll end up understanding."

"Understanding? Understanding what?"

"Your painter, Nick. His bloody *art*."

Nick opened his mouth to speak, but a sick, black, angry feeling swept through him, drowning his voice. For a second he could barely see the room.

"Don't you see, Nick? You think you're uncovering something, elucidating something, but what you're really doing is burying it. You buried it, sweetheart. I'm sorry. All the spontaneity, all the chaos. All the insight and luck. Everything that's in the pictures. It's the reason . . . it's why the book's so . . ."

"What?" He was shaking, struggling to catch his breath. "It's why the book's what?"

"I'm sorry, Nick."

"No, come on. Tell me what the book is."

"This can't come from me."

"It's coming from you, isn't it? At last, I might add. After all these years of thinking it, you're finally spelling it—"

"This is why you need to talk to someone."

"I am talking to someone! I'm talking to my fucking wife!"

He blinked, startled by the rage in his voice.

"My loving, supportive wife who complains about how she isn't doing anything with her life because of me when in fact she isn't doing anything, never *has* done anything, because there's nothing she ever wanted to—"

He wasn't sure when exactly she'd hung up. He just knew that one moment she was there and the next he was talking to himself, to the room.

It was raining again, so dark in the basement he had to put on all the lights. He walked through to the kitchen, a hand pressed against his mouth. Then he grabbed his raincoat off the back of a chair. Go to Becks's place. That's what he had to do. But she hadn't called from Becks's place. He didn't know where she was.

And then the phone was ringing again. He turned sharply, hurried back into the living room to pick it up.

"Nicholas. Ernest Stanhope here."

The editor. Nick looked at his watch. They were supposed to have a talk about the rewrite. Stanhope said something about saving him the trouble of coming down to the office, then started in on a long rambling anecdote. Through the jumble of half thoughts and impressions that rained in on him, Nick was vaguely aware of the other man's excitement. Apparently, Curlew had just acquired a big book. There had been a certain amount of celebrating.

"It's all been a bit chaotic," he said, "but I'm here now. We can finally get this situation clear."

For the next five minutes Nick listened to Stanhope, one hand sheltering his eyes. He had a pain high up in his chest, and even as he strained to follow Stanhope's words, Linda's voice kept spiking through—the things she had said to him, and then his own voice, the venom of it, the ugliness.

". . . out of the question."

Nick took away his hand, saw the rain streaming down the window.

"I'm sorry? Ernest?"

"What I'm trying to say is that while I understand your desire to take note of all this Grossman business. I think it's going to be a little difficult for us to accommodate you."

"But—"

"Just a second, Nick." Stanhope put his hand over the phone. Nick heard laughter, another voice. It sounded like someone had come into his office. "Nick, you were saying . . ."

"The thing is, all this new material is—well, *emerging*."

"We're talking about the painting?"

"The *Incarnation*, yes."

"Henry told me about that. All very interesting, I'm sure."

Stanhope paused for a drink.

"So, Nick, when do you think this material will be developed? I mean, at what point will you consider it developed and, er, ready?"

Nick tried to give a time frame. It all depended: on the situation with Laverne, on the Grossman case—how those things panned out.

Stanhope pushed out a sigh.

"Well, this is the thing," he said wearily. "Here at Curlew we rather pride ourselves on our ability to publish young authors; *unknown* authors like yourself. I say that with all due respect. I know you are already published, but I hope you won't mind me saying that not everybody may be aware of that fact."

He let the words hang in the air for a second.

"Now, because of your lack of profile, timing is critical, is in fact of the essence in bringing this book to the market. As you are well aware, the Spira retrospective is going to the Tate after New York and is due to open on November—"

"But the book," said Nick. "It isn't finished."

"Nick, Nick . . ." Stanhope laughed, but he didn't sound amused. "I'm getting—hearing you say that, I'm getting a peculiar feeling of déjà vu." There was a sound of papers being shuffled, a grunt as Stanhope shifted in his chair. "Two years ago, almost to the day, you and I had an interesting discussion about why it was the biography wasn't quite ready."

"That was different. I mean, this is different. The death of Jacob Grossman has—"

"And the year before that in September you said you needed a little more time to work on the Tangier section."

Stanhope got in closer to the phone.

"So let me tell you how I see it," he said, his voice coming through in a soft growl now. "You may or may not turn up interesting new material on this painting. Who knows? It may take you another six months, a year, two years, until you feel happy with the book. In the meantime, the Tate retrospective will have come and gone, interest in Spira will have waned, and you might as well have tossed your book—well, into the Thames."

"But . . ." Nick struggled up out of his chair, pulling the phone to the floor. "It's—from my point of view—it's precisely because I want to avoid—tossing this in the—six years of work, of sacrifices that I—I and my wife have had to make—it's precisely because of this that I know, *I know,* more has to be done. The book—it just isn't finished. It's—"

"Nicholas."

There was a moment of perfect eye-of-the-storm stillness.

"Nick, it is not only finished, it is delivered, bought and paid for. Now, I want to avoid any unpleasantness, but I feel obliged to tell you that we have purchased the right to publish this book according to the terms of the contract—the often *revised* contract, I should say—to which you are a signatory. And that means in November."

19

He stood on the sidewalk, head tilted against the rain, staring blankly along the bleak corridor of the Holland Road. He had no idea what he was doing there or where he intended to go. A truck roared past, throwing water against his legs. He looked down, curious more than anything. The cheap cloth of his pants clung to his ankles like a second skin.

He started walking, humming a tune to himself, conscious only of the clinging wetness and the water coming into his shoes. True dusk was a couple of hours away, but the low cloud made it gloomy as twilight and the air was surprisingly cold. Every few blocks he came to a halt. *You think if you know* everything, *you'll end up understanding . . . It's why the book's so . . .* He shook his head, humming a little louder. The book was complete. That was what it was. That was what it was intended to be.

You buried it, sweetheart.

He entered a busy street. Despite the weather, the shoppers were out in force. He came to a halt next to a bench and stood there wavering, feeling that something was wrong without being able to pin it down. He felt lightheaded, husk-light, confused. A guy in a pinstriped suit swerved past him, giving him a wide berth, and it came to Nick that he was being avoided. People looked away when he met their gaze. He looked down at himself and realized with a jolt that he had come out without his raincoat. Another guy—a short round-faced guy with plump lips—sidestepped neatly, thinking he was a bum probably, with his bummy drenched clothes and butchered hair. All he had to do was stick his hand out, and the picture—the picture they all had of him—would be complete.

He smiled, and out of nowhere a memory came: the first time he met Linda. A friend had introduced them outside a lecture theater. He had taken his hand from his pocket to shake hers and had showered her with loose change. She had often referred to it since, making fun of herself, saying how stupid she had been to see it as propitious—the rich Yank showering her in wealth. Yes, he thought, nodding to himself, that was the American she had wanted to marry.

He walked. He walked the anger and despair out of himself. Let the rain and cold bring him back into the street and the day. He recognized a doorway, took a turn, heading home now but not really wanting to arrive, not wanting to deal with whatever came next. There would be a message from Henry wanting to know what had happened with Stanhope, he was sure of it. Henry would want to patch things up straightaway. It was too easy to picture him groveling, asking Stanhope to go easy: *Nick's not himself at the moment, Ernest—all this Grossman business and now his wife . . .* Stanhope would feel sorry for him, would accept his apology. After all, he was used to dealing with writers, wasn't he? Their megalomania, their impotent rage. Nevertheless, the book would come out on time. By January he'd be looking for it in the remainder shops. *A month after publication and you'll be wondering where it disappeared to.*

He slowed to a halt on the sidewalk, wondered how long Linda had felt that way. It had never occurred to him that she might think the *Life* was anything other than remarkable. *It's why the book is so . . .* So what? Impenetrable? Heavy? Dull?

Lights flickered, striking silvery reflections in the rain-slick sidewalk. It took him a moment to realize where he was.

His split shoe squelched as he walked in through the door of the café. He'd have a drink first. Maybe something to eat. Something warmed in the microwave. The owner, who saw him at least three times a week, stared blankly as he ordered a cappuccino and a sandwich. He took a seat near the window.

Outside, the wind was gusting, throwing rain against the window like handfuls of grit. Nick leaned forward, biting into his sandwich.

"Excuse me—sir?"

Nick looked up. For a second he thought the man was smiling. Then he saw the scar and recognized the character from the day before. The Arab.

"May I?" said the man.

Nick shrugged, chewing, watched him sit down at the table. He was wearing a raincoat today and a snappy waterproof cap. He took out a cellphone and put it on the table.

"This weather," he said, gesturing at the street beyond the window.

Nick nodded, wondering what the hell the guy wanted from him.

"There is a junction box fifty feet from your building," he said, his eyes still on the street.

Nick looked at the guy's face, then back at the owner who was over by the cash register, reading his newspaper.

"That is where they tap your line," the man went on. "A simple thing. Simple to remove. But we won't disturb. We don't want them to know we know." He took a newspaper from his coat pocket and dropped it onto the cellphone. "This phone they can scan," he said, giving the newspaper a tap. "Easier for them than the wiretap. But they are not scanning."

He looked at Nick then, and smiled, a real smile this time.

"Because you do not have a cellphone," he said.

He stood up.

"Go home. Change your clothes."

He walked out of the café.

The whole exchange had taken about a minute.

Nick watched the guy walk past the window, and then everything subsided into banality again. The shitty café and the sound of the rain. But there was a newspaper on the table. And a cellphone underneath it.

Nick pushed the paper aside with a knuckle. The cellphone was in a little plastic case.

The first thing he saw on entering the living room was the red light on the answering machine. He put the cellphone on his desk and went over to the window. He looked up at the street to see if the guy with the scar was out there. Or maybe someone else. Whoever it was who had tapped his phone. It was crazy. Why would anyone want to tap his phone? What did he have to say that could be of any possible interest?

A black cab rolled past at a funereal crawl.

The cellphone started up. Nick turned and stared. The trilling stopped. He picked it up, trying to think, trying to make sense of it all.

It rang again.

He pressed a button.

"Who are they?" said the voice. The same voice. The man had an accent.

"Who are you?" said Nick.

"They are watching you."

"Who is?"

"You have a car, yes?"

"No."

"You drive?"

"Yes."

"There is a rental in the next street. A blue Fiat. Registration RBW 801R. Not locked. The keys are under the seat. You get in the car. You drive. You are careful because they are watching you. If they don't see you get into the car, it will be best. You understand?"

"No. No, I don't."

"You understand. Once you are in the car, it will be harder for you to lose them. So they should not see you get into the car. When you are in the car, you drive out to the orbital motorway. You go anti-clockwise. Just before Junction 9 there is a service station. You go into the restaurant."

"Why? Why would I do that?"

"Because you are looking for a picture."

Nick lowered himself into his swivel chair.

"You go into the restaurant," said the voice. "And you wait. If you are clean, I come and find you at eleven o'clock. If you are not clean, if they are following, you will not see me."

"What picture? Which picture are you talking about?"

"Do not talk of this. Understand? Do not talk on the phone. Or they will know. *I* will know."

"Okay, yes, I understand. But—who are you?"

"I am a friend of Tony Reardon."

He didn't move from the chair. Just sat there shaking his head, trying to come to terms with it all, trying to think how you got into a car without someone—someone professional, presumably—seeing you do it.

He was changing into dry clothes when he got the idea. He'd go across the street and enter the garden of No. 78. The occupants of the garden apartment had moved in three months ago. Friends of friends, they had invited him and Linda over a couple of times for drinks. If they found him sneaking around, he'd pretend he was visiting to ask if they'd had any news of his wife. And if they didn't, he'd go over the back fence, walk south along the railroad tracks to Olympia and then make his way around to the car.

The phone was ringing. He went back through to the living room and picked up.

"Hello?"

"Nick, it's me, Barb."

Nick pressed the phone tight against his ear, imagined a tape turning somewhere in the darkness. He heard the snap of Barb's cigarette lighter.

"Guess what," she said, blowing smoke against the phone. "Laverne died."

20

Somebody was making a big mistake. That was the only way he could make it make sense. He drove west, south, east, on the London orbital, canted forward, hands high on the wheel, tailgating, changing lanes without warning, slowing down as his mind jumped and snagged.

I am a friend of Tony Reardon.

But Reardon had died in 1971, had left Morocco in 1960 when the Arab would have been a young boy. Unless, of course, he was a lot older than he looked. It didn't make sense, none of it did. It was as if all these people—Bittaker, the guy tapping his phone, the Arab— thought he was a player, somehow involved in . . . he didn't even know what it could be. He laughed and slapped the wheel. He was so totally in the dark he couldn't even begin to put together a scenario where he would be of any interest to anybody.

Somebody had it all wrong.

He counted junction numbers after Staines, found the rain again just north of Leatherhead—a heavy, smoking downpour that slowed the light traffic to a crawl. Then he was pulling into the car park of a franchise service station, an ugly seventies-style block that spanned the motorway like a jackknifed truck.

A garbage bag had split somewhere. Styrofoam packaging scraped over wet tarmac. There were only five other cars, none of them a Fiat Punto.

He walked past a bank of vending machines into the warming fug of the restaurant area, where truck drivers were bent over empty plates. An old man chewed on a sandwich. In the far corner of the big space a girl with a shaved head was mopping the floor. There was no sign of the Arab.

He paid for coffee and a slice of lasagna, then chose a table in the middle of the room.

A cigarette machine. Arcade games. On one wall, a mural of birds in flight. A truck driver got up and went out to the phones. He came back a couple of minutes later and said something that made the other guys laugh. Then they all stood up and left.

Somewhere a telephone was ringing. The girl dropped her mop in the bucket and slouched through to the kitchen. It was almost eleven o'clock. He bought himself a Coke from a vending machine and, returning to his seat, saw the old man slowly making his way between the tables.

Nick stood aside to let him through.

"Go ahead."

This old guy, wearing what looked like a hairpiece. Beneath the wig, no eyebrows or lashes—in fact, no facial hair whatsoever. Spooked, filmy eyes did a little dance. A sick old man, confused perhaps.

"Go ahead," said Nick, waving him through.

"Never did learn to read."

Looking at him now. Old, but not confused.

"How about you, Mr. Greer? You read much?"

Someone in the crowd, someone you have never met before, names you. Nick looked around the room, expecting to see the Arab.

"Yeah," he managed. "Yes. Sure, sure I like to read."

A radio started up in the kitchen. Rap, audible through the swing doors.

"Listen . . ." Nick took another look around the room. "I came here—"

"So tell me about this book." The old guy, sitting down now, extending a wrinkled hand, inviting Nick to join him. "This book you're writing."

Crude, blunt fingers unbuttoned the raincoat, revealing a thick roll-neck sweater.

"It's a biography," said Nick, staying where he was. "A life."

"A life," said the stranger. He took out a pack of cigarettes. Fortuna. A Spanish brand. "You never think you're going to die," he said. "Then, one day you're in the—in the supermarket buying your biscuits. You're buying your custard creams, and you see the sell-by date. And you notice because before the biscuits are no good anymore, you'll be dead. It makes you think. I never noticed sell-by dates. Best-before dates. You see things with 2001 printed on them, and you think, Fuck me. You can feel life *rolling* through, away into the future."

Nick nodded, took another look around the room.

"Yeah," said the stranger. "Expiry dates. Renewal dates. I didn't know you was American. Nobody said nothing."

Nuffink. The old guy, this ancient cockney sparrow, with big ugly calluses on the knuckles of both hands. Nick shrugged, sitting down, thinking, Nobody who?

"I'm saying good-bye to everything, Mr. Greer. Went down Stepney yesterday. Drove up and down the Mile End Road. Smithfield Market. Place hasn't half-changed. I mean, the *money.*" He rubbed nicotine-dark fingers, making a papery sound. "Still—bound to in thirty years, isn't it?"

Nick saw the little finger of his left hand, the garnet ring, got a flash of a clawlike hand on the hood of a Mercedes.

Tony Spiv.

He pulled himself bolt upright in his chair. The old man gave him a smile, his chemo-smooth skin wrinkling back like parchment.

"Don't say it," he said.

Nick pointed a finger.

"You're—"

"*Don't* say it."

The smile died.

"You shouldn't believe everything you read, Mr. Greer. You shouldn't believe everything you find in autopsy reports."

Nick knocked over his coffee dipping for his briefcase. He came back up with his tape recorder, fumbled a tape into the slot, watching the old man drag a match into flame, then light his cigarette. He hit RECORD, still shaking his head, his heart pushing up under his ribs as though he were falling through the air.

"How do I know?" he said.

"How do you know what? What you want, stig-fucking-mata?"

The old man laughed silently. Then he was smoking, nodding to himself, sizing Nick up.

"Word is, you're the man," he said, squinting through drifting smoke. "People say you're the bloke what knows."

"Knows?" said Nick. "Knows what?" It was hard to think straight.

"People say Mr. Greer has been joining the dots. Mr. Greer has been filling in the blanks."

"I tried . . ." Nick couldn't stop shaking his head. "I'm beginning to wonder about the blanks, though."

"Got a few gaps, have you? Maybe I can help you there. If you can help me."

Nick frowned.

"There's a person I'm interested in," said the stranger. "A collector."

"Who?"

"That's what I want to know."

"Okay. So—and what—what are you going to tell me?"

The old man extended a yellow finger, smiling, smoke leaking through his teeth.

"I'm going to tell you about the picture he wants to collect."

The soft thump of a rap album. Distant traffic. A mural of seagulls climbing into sulfur-colored cloud. The old man talked in a ragged whisper, biting softly at his knuckles, leaning back to blow smoke at the ceiling tiles. He was interested in a collector, but all his questions were about Grossman and how he'd died. Like Laverne, he seemed to have trouble believing that Barb had found Grossman by accident. He wanted to know who else she had told about it.

"There were others," said Nick. "When I saw her in New York, she said everybody wanted to know about Jacob. So I guess she'd been spreading the word. But I don't think she told anyone where Grossman was living. She kept that to herself."

"She told you." The old man narrowed his eyes to wrinkled slits. The lids were raw-looking, lashless and sprinkled with pale growths. "She told you," he said, "but she didn't tell anyone else."

Saying it as if he didn't believe a word.

"I think she was trying to protect him."

"From what?"

"Grossman was scared. He hurt himself trying to get away from her."

"He was scared of Segal?"

"He was scared, period. I *thought* it was paranoia, but now . . ."

"Now?"

"I think he saw it coming. The violence. His killer. I think if he hadn't hurt his leg, if they hadn't put him on drugs, he'd have been long gone by the time I got there."

The old man said nothing. A long finger of ash curled and dropped from his cigarette.

"Does that make any sense to you?" said Nick. "That Grossman saw this coming? That he expected someone to . . . ?" His voice trailed off to nothing, realization dawning. "This man," he said. "The man who did this to Grossman. This is your collector?"

The stranger blinked his filmy, tumorous eyes.

"He came to my hotel," said Nick.

The stranger became very still. Then seemed to remember the cigarette burning between his fingers. He took a long, hungry pull.

"What did he *look* like?"

Nick described the man who had come to his hotel room, his pale eyes, his brown rodent teeth. For a long time the stranger was quiet, just smoking, staring at the floor.

"You know him?" said Nick.

"We met once. This is going back thirty years. He called me up. Said he was interested in buying one of Frank's pictures. I asked him why he didn't talk to Frank. Or Blair. I told him straight, Blair's Frank's dealer, not me. 'No,' he said, 'I think you're the man I need. I think you're the one who can help me.' There was a particular picture he had in mind."

He looked at Nick over the relish bottles, smiling his ugly smile.

"That's right, Mr. Greer. There was this picture. 'I don't know what you're talking about,' I said. 'Yeah, you do,' he said, 'yeah, you do.' And just so there'd be no misunderstanding, he told me a couple of things about the picture. Specifics. Okay. A year later—this was after that auction in New York."

"The Testori auction?

"That's right. Testori."

"Max Taubmann paid two hundred and forty thousand dollars for Spira's portrait of Alice Gatlin."

The stranger coughed. He took a clump of Kleenex out of his pocket, dragged it across his mouth.

"That summer, every time one of Frank's pictures went for a big price, this bloke called me up. I was on my own at the studio most of the time because Frank was over in Paris, tripping the light fantastic."

Nick nodded, his mind spinning through facts and figures: 1971—the year Spira became an honorary Frenchman. The police raid at the Fig Tree studio in August 1970 had resulted in his being charged with possession of cannabis; he was subsequently released, but the incident got him on the covers of the tabloids. SATANIC SPIRA headlines spiced up a slow week at the *News of the World*. The *Daily Mirror* and the *Sun* followed suit. By the end of September the broadsheets were weighing in with stories that were only slightly less sensational. The campaign of vilification in the British press brought Spira to the attention of the Parisian intellectuals. The art critic Jacques Delaitre, who had known Spira in Tangier, announced to the French nation that Francis Spira was actually a European painter—perhaps the last of the great *symbolistes*. Through the spring of '71, in a series of three radio interviews, Spira talked brilliantly in his rough street French of his love for Delacroix, while discouraging Delaitre's attempts to pigeonhole him. The fact that *les Anglais* considered him dissolute guaranteed credibility in Paris. He was wined and dined, and then, in October '71, ushered into the pantheon of the Republic's *grands hommes,* no less a figure than Georges Pompidou walking with him around the Grand Palais the night before the opening of the retrospective which included 108 of his best-known canvases.

"July," said Reardon. "It was too fuckin' hot. I was sick as a dog. My mouth full of ulcers. I had these big blisters round my arsehole."

"Was this . . . ?" Nick checked the tape was turning. "Mr. Reardon? I'd like to be clear about something. This sickness you were suffering from. What exactly was it?"

Reardon leaned forward and tapped a finger of ash onto the remains of Nick's lasagna.

"The doctor said I was suffering from a chronic social life."

His laughter was weak, silent. Smoke spilled out of his mouth.

"Syphilis?"

The hairless eyebrows contracted.

"Were you suffering from syphilis?" said Nick. "Did you ever suffer from syphilis? In Tangier, for example?"

Reardon shook his head.

"So—this is going to sound"—Nick shrugged—"silly, but the—the *rash,* the rash you complained about in January of 'fifty-eight to Paul Mann. What was that about?"

"What the *fuck* are you talking about? I'm telling you what I'm telling you. We're not talking about fucking *rashes* from forty years ago." He took a couple of drags on his cigarette. Then he was chewing at his knuckle again. "July 1971," he said. "The Yank comes to see me at the studio. Turns up on my doorstep in a suit and tie. Short curly hair. These teeth you're talking about. He's got these X-ray eyes. 'Hello, Tony,' he says, like he knows me. 'Pleased to meet you in the flesh at last.' I should have told him to fuck off then and there."

"But you didn't."

"I wanted to know how he knew so much. How he knew what he knew. So he comes in and we have a chat. He wants to know how Frank is doing. He wants to know about the preparations for the Paris show. He wants to know if I'm going to be involved in any way, *knowing* that I won't be, knowing that because of what happened at the party, because of all the bullshit in the papers, I was persona non grata. So anyway, we sit around drinking.

" 'It's very harsh,' he said, 'the way Frank has treated you.' And all the time I'm thinking, When's he going to get round to it? Because he's building up to something, I can see it."

"To make an offer?"

The offer Laverne Taubmann had dismissed as nonsense in her letter to Schadt. The offer she held up as proof that Reardon had never owned the *Incarnation.*

The old man squinted at him.

"How'd you know about that?" he said.

"Laverne Taubmann wrote a letter to Alby Schadt—this was a month after your 'death.' She wrote in reply to a query about the *Incarnation.* I haven't even been able to track down the original letter from Schadt, but presumably it refers to an offer someone made to you for the painting, because Taubmann said if the painting did exist, and if Reardon, if you, had owned it, why wouldn't you have sold it?"

"Schadt? He knew about this offer?"

"He'd heard something, apparently."

Reardon sat forward, putting his bitten hands flat on the table.

"You see, Mr. Greer? *That's* where you can help me."

"Where?"

"Well, you can start by telling me who told Schadt that someone had made me an offer."

"Schadt doesn't remember. I'm serious. I talked to him last year and—well, he's an old man now. Looking back almost thirty years. When I showed him Laverne's letter, which he had in his *own* library, he vaguely recalled something, but—there was no question of a name coming out of it."

Reardon drew a hand across his face, looking desperate for a moment, wild.

"You were telling me about the Collector," said Nick. "About the offer."

The growth-speckled eyes cut across at him.

"You take," he said softly, "but you don't give."

Nick brought his hands up.

"Maybe—maybe something else will come out. If we keep talking, maybe something will come to me."

Reardon looked at the tape recorder as though he were considering smashing it. He took a breath, relaxed a little.

"Maybe," he said. "Maybe. Where was I?"

"You were saying that the Collector was building up to something."

"Yeah. That's right. This—this shitcunt *collector*, he's talking about Frank, talking about this and that, but his mind's on something else, and he's tense. Like a—like someone who knows something's going to happen. He's got this attaché case. He's sitting there with this attaché case next to him. And I have this moment where I realize what's inside. Call it second sight. Anyway, a funny thing happens. This kid walks out of the bathroom upstairs. It's all open-plan at the studio, and this kid, stark-bollock naked, walks out of the bathroom across the mezzanine and into one of the bedrooms."

"Who—"

"Just this kid. This jock toyboy. Ralph. Used to sell me his arse, but while I was sick, he'd come in with a bit of shopping or just for a chat. Scottish kid. A good boy. So Ralph makes his brief appearance up on the mezzanine. And my Yank's eyes come out like on stalks. He thought I was alone. Anyway . . . 'What's in the case?' I say, because I've had enough by now. 'Your latest offer?' 'That's right,' he says, and he smiles at me, giving me this look. 'A million dollars,' he says. 'It's the best I can do.'"

Nick nodded. The highest prices paid at the Testori auction were not even close to a million. It wasn't until '73 that Sotheby's and Christie's started selling contemporary artists for big bucks, and that was still way below seven figures.

"A lot of money," said Nick.

"That's right. A million. *Then.*"

"Perhaps it was this Ralph who started the rumor about the offer."

Reardon rubbed his hands together slowly, considering.

"If he overheard," Nick added. "Quite a story to tell at the pub. I mean, a million dollars?"

He waited until Reardon was looking at him.

"It must be quite a painting," he said, letting him know he didn't believe it.

The stranger returned his gaze.

"Oh, make no mistake on that score, Mr. Greer."

"And—what did you say? To the American."

"I said no."

Again Nick nodded. He had documentary proof that Tony Reardon had sold at least three Spiras without the artist's permission. Like Spira, he was a compulsive gambler and was always in debt to East End gangsters. Nick just couldn't visualize the moment in which *that* Tony Reardon would turn down a million dollars in cash. Something was being kept from him. A piece was missing.

"You would have been set up for life," he said. "You wouldn't have needed Frank anymore."

Reardon drew on his cigarette.

"Yeah, well. Anyway, the Yank wasn't there to buy."

He dropped the cigarette into Nick's cup, then looked for another. The pack was empty.

"It was only later that it came to me what he really wanted."

"Which was what?"

"To kill me."

He stood up and walked across the room to the vending machines. Got himself a couple of packs of Camels. Nick watched him light one, then go to the window, watched him look out at the parking lot and raise a hand. Everything okay. The Arab would be out there, waiting.

He came back to his seat, settled.

"If it wasn't for that kid walking out of the bathroom, I think I would have found out what was really in that case. And it wouldn't have been money."

"Why? What makes you—?"

"He expected to find me alone and sick, too sick to put up a fight."

Nick shook his head. It didn't make sense to him.

"Why would he want to kill you?"

"Because he knew that was the only way he was going to get it. Over my dead body."

"And this was why you faked your . . . ?"

"Afterwards, when he'd gone, I thought about that little visit, and sick or not, I thought I'd be better off out of it. Then I bumped into Ortiz when I was down with Lionel Murray on his *finca*."

"The coroner, yes. I interviewed him."

"Coroner. Dago bum boy *slag* more like. Probably didn't mention he was also a dealer. He supplied Lionel with coke, acid, heroin, speed—whatever he wanted. Anyway, I scared the shit out of him. Told him I'd blow the gaff on the drug dealing if he didn't help me out. I offered him a thousand quid—good money back then. I don't know what kind of debts he had, what kind of needs—anyway, he was *very* businesslike. There was some poor cunt they'd found on the road who was going to be thrown in a pauper's grave somewhere. It didn't matter that he didn't look like me, because he was going to burn anyway, plus Ortiz was going to be doing the paperwork. We put him in the trunk of my motor and drove him out to this ravine. Doused him with petrol, sent him over the edge with a burning rag in his mouth. Ka*boom*. When Ortiz got back home, he'd already had a call. The *guardias* said they'd found this foreign car at the bottom of a ravine with a bloke dead at the wheel. Ortiz took care of the rest. Anthony Reardon was buried with a little granite headstone what Lionel paid for out of his own pocket. Very touching. I crossed the Strait of Gibraltar the day after the accident."

"You faked your death to get away from this—from the Collector?"

Reardon nodded.

"And—what about Grossman?"

"What about him?"

"Well, a couple of months after your 'death,' he walked out of a clinic in the middle of the night. Disappeared. Do you think the Collector . . . ?"

Reardon shrugged.

"Who knows?"

"But *you* had the *Incarnation,* right?"

"Yeah, but I was dead by then. Maybe the Collector thought Grossman was his best bet."

"For . . . ?"

"To get his *hands* on the picture."

"When I spoke to him, to Jacob Grossman I mean, he told me that I needn't think I was going to get my hands on it."

"Did he?"

"Yes. As if he knew where it was. As if he had access."

Reardon tapped a finger against his temple. Static lifted threads of nylon hair.

"You're saying he was deluded," said Nick.

"If we're talking about the same picture, Jackdaw didn't know nothing about it. Maybe that's why he got cut."

"Cut?"

"Well, that's what happened, right? That's what I read in the papers."

Nick checked the tape on the recorder, put in a fresh cassette.

"What are the police saying?" said Reardon. "About the murder."

Nick sat forward.

"Mr. Reardon. You said you were going to tell me about the painting."

"What d'you wanna know?"

"Everything."

Reardon shook his head, looking exhausted, looking sick.

"*Everything,*" he said, making it sound like an obscenity.

"The circumstances in which it was painted. Why Spira always said it was destroyed. Why everyone seems to want to forget it while this—this *Collector* is ready to . . ." Nick caught his breath. There were so many questions, he didn't know where to start. "I mean, this work, it's obviously special, and yet it comes out of a time when Spira wasn't producing anything."

"Who says?"

"Nothing survives from Tangier. Nothing. The one painting that made it back to Europe, Spira destroyed. And here's this work—"

"He's following you," said Reardon softly. "He's the one tapping your phone."

"Who?"

"Who d'you think?"

Nick felt a chill go through him. Bittaker.

"He thinks you're going to lead him to *me*," said Reardon, nodding. "Sure. Just like you led him to Jackdaw."

"I led him to—"

"How else did it happen? Either Barb told someone where he was or he followed you. I reckon he followed you. Paper said he was killed just after you talked to him."

Reardon smiled, enjoying the look on Nick's face.

"He's been waiting all these years," he said. "Had his ear to the ground all these years."

Nick felt sick now. The crap he'd just eaten was right there at the back of his gullet.

"Please," he said. "I just want—"

"What? What do you want, Mr. Greer? What exactly are your needs?"

"Just tell me about the painting."

Reardon lit a fresh cigarette, took a deep cleansing drag.

"Give me a reason," he said.

Nick shrugged, shaking his head.

"Because you—you said you would."

The silent laughter, filling the air with smoke.

"Because I can help you," said Nick.

Reardon pushed fingers against his tumorous eyelids, gently massaging.

"I'll be honest with you, Mr. Greer, I'm a bit disappointed."

"I can go back to my sources," said Nick. "I'm going back to Manhattan. I'm going back to Laverne Taubmann's place."

Reardon stopped his massaging and stared, hard-eyed.

"Oh yeah? Got your little foot in that door, did you? That's interesting." He pulled hard at his cigarette, sent a jet of smoke across the table into Nick's face. "Wouldn't be surprised if the old cunt wasn't behind the whole thing."

"Behind what?"

"Behind the fucking *Collector*, Mr. Greer. Pushing with her fucking money."

"Laverne Taubmann? You're saying she knows about all this?"

"She was there when Frank did it. Of course she knows. She knows everything."

"So—why did she tell Schadt it didn't exist?"

Reardon smiled.

"You'd have to ask her. Ask her about the burglary while you're at it."

Nick pushed a hand back through his hair. There was just too much. It was all coming at him at once, and nothing was falling into place.

"Mr. Reardon, people say it was the *Incarnation* that was stolen from the apartment. That it was why Frank was so angry with you. Martin Marion—"

"Marion knows nothing."

"So—what was it?"

"What was *what*?"

"What was *taken*? What was stolen?"

"Ask Laverne."

"I can't. She's dead."

The ugly smile went tight, then disappeared altogether.

"Carbon dioxide narcosis," said Nick. "She died at home. Yesterday. I only just heard about it."

Reardon put a knuckle to his mouth and bit down hard.

"But I have access to her papers," said Nick. "All of the correspondence. I'm bound to find something about your man."

"*Bound* to." Reardon was shaking his head now. "You don't know anything about any of it. Bound to. You're like Marion. You haven't got the first fucking clue."

"I can give you this man," said Nick. It just came out. He hadn't thought it through—just knew it was true as he spoke the words. "You said yourself he followed me. He thinks I'm going to lead him to you. To the painting."

Reardon was chewing his knuckle again, dead eyes completely still.

It was past midnight. Nick put in a fresh tape, pushed the machine across the table.

"He was always working," said Reardon. "In Tangier same as everywhere else. But in Tangier everybody was out of their fucking heads on kif. Frank tried it when he first came out, but he blew up like a balloon on account of his asthma. Anyway, he hated the way it made everyone . . . These people, these fucking intellectuals, they were like the fucking lotus eaters. Know what I mean? You'd go round to someone's place and they'd be smoking, and the talk would just like— *die*. Franky, for all his bullshit, he liked a fucking *laugh*. And that's how it was, that's how we got together. Benzedrine. My man Billy had an endless supply."

"Billy Elkhorn?"

"Billy Flash. Pedophile, pimp, bum-bandit and sailor's friend—do you a tattoo of your girl for a packet of fags. Get you into executions. Get you a fake passport. Any drug you wanted. A jack-of-all-trades, a survivor. Anyway, we were speeding and it was great, but Frank, he was on a knife blade all the time. He couldn't handle it, he'd get amped, try and come down with booze, fuck himself up royal. He'd get manic. He'd get *me* manic, and I'd have to . . ."

He sucked his cigarette to a little hot eye.

The beatings.

It was hard to imagine it—this tired old man ripping chunks out of Spira with his belt buckle, beating him until his eyes closed up. Tony Sadist. Strong back then in a bull-necked, round-shouldered way

"But with the *Incarnation* . . . ?" said Nick. "Frank stopped speeding, got it together?"

Reardon considered the tip of his cigarette.

"There was like—a train of events. What you would call a train of events."

"Yes?"

"An accident in the *Petit Socco*. One of the old houses. The lift— the winding ear fucked up and it dropped five floors into the basement. Bang."

"And?"

"Reardon took a drag on his cigarette, held the smoke.

"With a woman and a—a little baby inside," he said, exhaling the words. "Both killed. Franky went round there with Billy Flash. Sick cunt. When he came back, I knew he'd had a look."

"A look?"

"At the bodies. They were in this lift, all smashed up. This little baby, it was . . ." He shook his head. "Franky told me about it later. There was police there and firemen cutting cables, but Billy had friends, 'specially in the police. Frank came back with his look, this look he used to get. Disgusting. Sort of gorged, like a fucking vampire—glassy-eyed. I knew then he was gonna start something."

"What?"

"This picture. But it didn't work. He was all over the place with the bennies. He couldn't hardly get his dick out to take a piss, and he couldn't make the brush marks he wanted, so he scrapped it. Smashed it all up. He was like—you ever seen somebody with the DTs? He was like that. And it wasn't just the Benzedrine, it was his fucking *mind*. Eating him *alive*. He started gutting these medical textbooks he had, putting pictures all over the walls. Books on surgery, books on oral diseases. That's where he found the word."

"The word?"

"Incarnation."

Nick shook his head, not getting it.

"Out of one of the books. A medical term. Elizabethan. For the way a scar grows, the scar tissue in a wound."

"I thought . . ." Nick put a hand to his forehead. "I thought the reference was religious. The *Incarnation*. God in human form."

"It was all bundled up. Like Frank liked it. Blood sacrifice. You know, cut some poor cunt's head off to guarantee the rains. That sort of religion. Wounding and healing. The Golden Bough. Frank's staggering around in his shorts going on about 'flowering of flesh.' He loved it. You couldn't shut him up about it. Christ's wound. God made flesh. The Fisher King. All that bullshit. He had a thing about wounds—wounds and mouths."

The scream of the mother. Dust and debris roaring up the shaft. Spira and Billy Elkhorn looking at the smashed bodies. Nick saw it as a kind of sick diorama, Frank's eye pressed close to a viewing hole, saw it all so vividly, he didn't hear what Reardon said. He became aware of the old man looking at him, a malevolent expression on his withered, hairless face.

"Look at you," he said, his mouth turned downward in disgust.

Nick straightened up in his chair.

"What?"

"You still want to see it? This great work of art?"

"Yes. Absolutely."

Reardon wiped his mouth.

"You think it's all a—like some sort of mystery, like there's this buried treasure somewhere, and you're going to be the one who finds it. You think this is all about art."

"Well, isn't it?"

Reardon shook his head.

"Not at all," he said. "It isn't about art *at all.*"

What was it about then? Money? Love? Nick asked what he meant, standing out in the parking lot in the drizzling rain. But Reardon had nothing else to say. He said he'd be in touch. Told Nick to keep his big intellectual mouth shut.

Driving back, Nick was so tired he took the wrong exit off the motorway and got lost driving through the London suburbs. At two in the morning he was crawling through empty streets, laughing, playing the tape, listening to Reardon tell his story: *It was only later that it came to me what he really wanted. Which was what? To—kill—me.* The *Life* was opening up like a flower, and it was a flowering of flesh. He hadn't buried it. He'd stuck his spade in and hit something. Something big.

He imagined the picture out there somewhere, the real physical thing hanging in some darkened room. Reardon had refused to be drawn on the details but had said that in a few days, if all went well, Nick could be looking at it himself, would be able to come to his own conclusions about how special it was.

It wasn't until he was crossing the river that the fear hit him. He gripped the wheel as though the car were actually sliding out of control, and had to tell himself to stay calm, that the danger, if there was any, wasn't immediate. If Reardon was right, the Collector had followed him to Jacob Grossman and was now trying to get to Reardon himself. But he was following Nick because he wanted the painting. Then again, Bittaker didn't strike Nick as the art-loving type. The guy who had come to the hotel room in New York had looked more like the kind of bruiser who collected debts. But maybe that was what was behind it: somebody was owed. Maybe that was what Reardon had meant about it not being about art. The Collector, the *real* Collector, someone behind Bittaker perhaps, wanted what he'd paid for all those years ago.

But whoever he was, and whatever it was he wanted, there was no getting around the fact that he, Nicholas Greer, biographer and nobody, had just agreed to stand between Bittaker and Reardon. *I can give you this man,* he'd said, and so Reardon had told him some more of the story.

Stopped at a set of lights, Nick checked his rearview mirror, told himself this was how people got killed. Journalists, writers—people like himself. They got into situations without ever really acknowledging to themselves what they were involved in.

He got back in the early hours of Saturday morning and parked the rental near where he'd picked it up. Rain was drifting out of the cloudy sky as he walked along the root-buckled sidewalk, alive to the street's silence and shadows. He entered the garden in front of his building ready to turn, ready to run.

The front door was locked, and there was no sign of forced entry. Of course, there were ways of entering apartments that left no trace. He put his key in the lock, turned it, stood there listening.

A minute later he was walking from room to room turning on lights. There was no sign of anything being out of place. The only thing that was different was the cellphone sitting next to the computer.

The answering machine showed three messages. The first was from Glasco, recorded at 10:42 P.M. The cop sounded terse, said that he'd gotten the message and would appreciate a call back. The second, also from Glasco, recorded at 11:12, was close to hostile: *Mr. Greer. Detective Glasco again. Expecting to hear from you.* The third message, timed at 11:32, was a blank.

Nick sat there listening to muted street noise mixed with a faint sound of breathing. Then the click of the caller hanging up. He told himself it was nothing, nobody, *anybody,* but it was too easy to imagine Bittaker on the other end, Bittaker or some other guy. He punched 171, got the number of the last caller. It was a central London location. He called it, listened to the dial tone, then hung up before anyone answered. He didn't want to know.

He was exhausted, but he couldn't sleep. He jacked the microcassette into the stereo and tried to concentrate on Reardon, but he was jumpy, kept stopping the tape, thinking he'd heard something at the back of the building.

—*It was all bundled up. Like Frank liked it. Blood sacrifice. You know, cut some poor cunt's head off to guarantee the rains. That sort of religion.*

Boosted by the amp, Reardon's ragged voice seemed to be full of harsh whisperings.

—*He's following you.*

And so was the cop. Nick wished he hadn't called Glasco. Laverne was dead, and with Reardon coming forward, everything had changed. If anything, the cop had become a liability. There was a possibility he'd come up with some piece of evidence from the hotel room that would point to some individual already on their books.

Thinking about it, Nick shook his head, softly cursing. It seemed to him only a matter of time before the police came up with a name. And Reardon was probably watching the New York press, tapping in to one of the media Web sites maybe. If the police came up with the name of the Collector, Reardon would no longer need his help.

What exactly are your needs?

He had to hope that Glasco would screw up long enough for him to get a chance to see the painting, and get the story. He awoke slumped over in the armchair with the idea, a conviction that seemed to have formed in his sleep, that Reardon was going to cheat him. With or without the help of the police, all Reardon had to do was sit back and wait. Sooner or later, the Collector would show himself. Nick shook his head, told himself he was being paranoid. Reardon needed him and was going to show him the picture in return for his help. What had happened was the beginning of better luck, the point at which everything turned around.

He wanted to call Linda. He wanted to call Henry. But there was no question of calling anybody. Reardon had been categorical: there was to be no talk of their meeting. If he broke that agreement, allowed anything to slip out, dropped any hints, Reardon would disappear again.

He'd made the tape, of course. That was something. But people, people like Martin Marion, would say he had made it up just to get some attention, people would say he was crazy. And besides, the tape was nothing, the events of that night were nothing compared to what was still out there. Out there somewhere. The *Incarnation,* the real physical thing.

The day had a stalled, suspended feel, even the rain seeming to hang in the air like mist or smoke. He worked on the article for Florey, the words coming easily, fluently. In the end, the article was just under 3,000 words long, and the only hints of the shift in his understanding were a reference, slightly longer than it otherwise would have been, to the offer Reardon was rumored to have received in the summer of 1971, and a query regarding the way that rumor had gotten as far as Alby Schadt. He read it through several times, decided that Reardon couldn't possibly object, spell-checked it and zapped it into the ether.

Glasco called late Saturday night. Nick blustered, apologized for not getting back to him sooner.

"I've been really—"

"Busy, yeah. I can imagine."

"Have there been any developments with the case?"

"Matter of fact, there have. We found the bag he used."

Nick pressed his eyes shut. They were getting closer. They were way ahead of him.

"Oh—oh, that's *great.* You're really closing in. Did you pick up any prints from the hotel room?"

"Couple from the phone. A latent that looks interesting. We're still excluding the hotel staff, cleaners and the like. So . . ." Glasco cleared his throat. "So, Mr. Greer, what was it you wanted to tell me?"

Nick backtracked, hedged, said he thought maybe he'd been too hasty.

"It's silly, really."

"So tell me."

"It's something that Laverne Taubmann said to me. You know, the lady I interviewed on—"

"Yeah, I know who she is."

"*Was,* actually. She died yesterday—"

"Oh?"

"Or the day before. Naturally, I mean. She wasn't killed or anything."

"A lot of people aren't. So she said something to you?"

"Yes."

Nick could hear Glasco breathing against the mouthpiece.

"So, you gonna tell me what it was?"

"Sure, of course." Nick sat down. "Detective Glasco, the reason I hesitate is—well, I think I should put my cards on the table so that you know . . ." He could feel Glasco frowning at the other end. "The thing is, I'm writing this book, and in the course of doing that, I uncover things which, well, I really prefer to keep to myself, so that when the book eventually comes out—"

"People buy it to see what you uncovered."

"Yes. Rather than—"

"Not buying it because they already know. Because they maybe read it in the press. Because maybe a homicide dick leaked it."

His anger, building out of nothing. Glasco, the angry man.

"Don't get me wrong, Detective."

"I'm trying not to, Mr. Greer. I'm trying to balance your needs against the requirements of the judicial process." Glasco paused to take a calming breath. "Just tell me what it was you wanted to share. Your secret is safe with me."

"Laverne Taubmann said Grossman died because of the *Incarnation.*"

There was another silence.

"The picture?"

"Yes."

"That's it?"

"I know it's not much. Which is why I had second thoughts about talking to you. Of course, I thought Mrs. Taubmann was still alive when I called you the first time. I assumed you'd be able to go and talk to her yourself."

"Do you have any reason to believe her? Are you in possession of any concrete evidence?"

"No. No, I'm afraid not."

Once he knew there was nothing to be gained here, Glasco brought the conversation to a close. He told Nick to be in touch if he thought of anything else that might be helpful.

After he'd put the phone down, Nick sat for a long time staring at the Spira mask on the mantelpiece. He told himself that he had not misled or sought to obstruct justice or anything like that, but he knew there was a lot more he could have said. He could have mentioned the papers at the Taubmann residence, and the possibility there might be some trace of the *Incarnation* going back thirty years.

As he brooded on that, another thought came to him, and it brought him up out of the chair, a hand clamped to his forehead: he had said nothing to Reardon about the possibility that Laverne went to Tangier to make an offer for a painting. A key question, and he had failed to ask it. Events had been moving too fast, were still moving too fast. He flipped to a clean page in his notebook and scribbled the question now: *Did Laverne go to Tangier on behalf of Max?* He couldn't believe he hadn't asked it. He stood there for a moment, tapping the pen against his lower lip. Then a second question came to him: *Did Laverne really steal/have stolen something from the Rue d'Angleterre. If so, what???*

The phone wouldn't ring. And when it did ring, it set his nerves on edge. He stood by the answering machine, listening to friends leave messages of concern and support. Tyler called offering to cook him a meal.

"I got some sausages at Lidgates," he said. "We'll have a fry-up."

Nick paced pack and forth, willing Reardon to come back to him. His biggest fear was Glasco coming up with a name and Reardon reading about it in the press. He'd be back on the outside then, schlepping around libraries and trying to decipher the forty-year-old scribbling of so-called primary sources.

Every couple of hours he went to the New York media Web sites to scan for stories. But apart from his "Spira's Lovers" piece in the *Times,* there were no references to Grossman anywhere.

In the end, he couldn't wait anymore. He felt like he had to do something himself, something to make things happen. Late Sunday night he went to a public call box and phoned New York.

"Why this now?" said Barb, coughing into the phone. "This supposed offer to Reardon."

"I just have this feeling. I thought it would be an idea to try to track down this character—this guy who was supposed to have gone to see him in London."

"But I thought that was all bullshit anyway."

"Maybe it is. But I got nowhere with Laverne—trying to make her talk about what was going on in Tangier, but maybe this guy, if I could find him, would be different. *He* obviously thought the picture existed."

"If he even exists."

"If I could get some kind of lead from Schadt, I think I could—"

"Schadt's not going to tell you anything. He's out of his mind."

She told him how, the last time she'd gone down to Schadt's ranch, he had shown her his Hitler watercolors. He had them on the wall with his Renoir.

"We had lobster bisque for breakfast, for goodness sake. Frankly, I'm surprised you're chasing this sort of stuff when things are moving so quickly over here."

"Things?"

"You haven't heard?"

"Heard what?"

"The police found a knapsack in the subway somewhere. The one the killer used. It's only a matter of time before—"

"I *know.*"

There was a stunned silence.

"I'm sorry, Barb, I'm—I'm not feeling so great at the moment."

This was blood in the water. He heard the clack of Barb's bangles as she brought a cigarette to her mouth.

"Anything you want to talk about?"

Nick squeezed the phone until the plastic popped.

"Barb, I'd really like to find out who that guy was. The guy who called on Reardon."

"Well, maybe there'll be something in Max and Laverne's papers."

A truck went past.

"Nick?"

"Yes, I'm still here. It was just a—"

"Are you in the *street*?"

"Yes."

"How come? Don't tell me she threw you out?"

"Of course not. No, it's just . . ." Nick tapped a coin against the grime-covered glass. "What were you saying about the papers?"

"Nothing. But since you mention it, you don't want to leave that situation any later than this week."

"What situation?"

"The Christie's valuation people were in the Manhattan property on Friday. I went along in the afternoon, and Anita showed me the room with the boxes. There's a ton of stuff. I mean literally. Anita says the Smithsonian is thinking of making an offer. I don't think Gael has even thought about it yet, but if the Smithsonian does offer to take it, she may just say yes. It gets it out of her hair, *and* she comes over as public-spirited. Once it's sucked into archive, you won't see it for a long, long time."

Nick looked down at his feet. The split in his shoe was letting in water again. Hanging around for Reardon to call, he was going to miss his chance with Laverne's papers. The whole situation was a mess.

"And there's something else," she said. "Another reason you should be out here."

"What?"

"Someone had been blackmailing Laverne."

"*What?*"

Barb chuckled.

"I had dinner with Anita last night. She gave me the whole story. Sanford Priesack—you know, Laverne's curator? He was going through the Park Avenue residence on Friday afternoon and he noticed that a number of items were missing. Not paintings. Objects, knickknacks. A vase here, a Fabergé egg there—small things, but valuable. Anyway, Priesack sounds the alarm, and there's total panic. Gael gets everyone lined up in the drawing room, because, naturally, she assumes someone's been stealing."

"Right."

"But it turns out that Laverne herself had been *selling* the stuff. Priesack made a few phone calls and learned from one of his art dealer friends that he, the friend, had an arrangement with Laverne going back over several years. These objects were being sold, a steady stream, and always for cash. Now, Laverne, she *had* a bank account. And besides, she wasn't exactly, I mean latterly—she wasn't the world's biggest shopper. The house—all the houses—are run like businesses with proper accounts and so forth. So . . ."

"You think Laverne was paying someone off."

"Anita and I discussed it, and—yes. I mean, what else do you need invisible cash for? It wasn't for drugs, I'll tell you that. With Gallagher coming round daily with the magic medicine cart, you can—"

"My God."

"I know. It's so *bizarre*. I just—laughed actually, could not get my head around the idea of Laverne in compromising photographs or whatever. I mean—doing *what*? She led what you would call a blameless life."

Blameless. Nick was beginning to have doubts about that.

"But then Anita told me something else," said Barb. "You remember that little notebook Laverne had? She had it in her hand all the time."

"The travelogue. The thing Max wrote."

"Well, there was this card, a greeting card, like, marking the page?"

"Which page?"

"No particular page. At least I don't think so. I got this from Anita, remember, so . . . Anyway, the card was in there. This ugly orange card with those seventies-style bubble letters? 'Birthday Greetings,' and a cake with 'sixty' sort of splurged on it in drippy frosting. Six, zero. When Gael found it—Gael was with her when she died, and she took the book out of her hand, right? She saw this card and just assumed it was from Max."

"Assumed."

Barb paused.

"Come on, Nick. This is the kind of thing I expect you to pick up on."

He thought about it.

"Max was dead," he said. "Laverne was sixty in 1975, four months after Max's death."

"Right."

"So . . . ?"

"So the card is from someone else, and Laverne kept it with her for twenty-three years in a notebook recording all the details of her honeymoon tour of Europe."

"Is there anything in it? In the card, I mean. An inscription?"

Barb giggled, clearly delighted by the whole thing.

"Well, yes, there was. In French. And it's very—well, romantic."

Toying with him. Eking it out.

"Barb?"

"*Une nuit avec Vénus.*"

"*Une nuit avec Vénus?*" He leaned back against the phone box. "That's it?"

"One night with Venus. Romantic and flattering. Because, by then, Laverne was, well, more Junoesque." Barb laughed her smoker's raucous laugh. "Well? Aren't you *intrigued*? There was no signature. Just this—"

"Quote."

"What?"

"It's a quote," he said. "It's a quote from Flaubert."

"What makes you say that?"

Nick slid down the wall of the cabin until he was squatting in the trampled fast-food wrappers and filth.

"Nick?"

"Flaubert got syphilis from a prostitute he called Venus," he said, tingling, feeling the pieces come together. "I came across this joke when I was doing my syphilis research. It was something Flaubert wrote to a friend. It's in the second volume of the Pleiade edition of the letters."

"Well?" said Barb. "What's the joke?"

"Une nuit avec Vénus, toute une vie avec Mercure."

"Toute une—"

"A lifetime with mercury."

"Mercury," said Barb. "Your word."

"Yes. Flaubert took mercury to treat the disease."

He drank whisky to knock himself out, but at four o'clock in the morning his eyes snapped open and instantly his mind started up, churning out the same thing over and over—Linda, Curlew, Laverne, Grossman, Reardon, the Collector, everything going round and round until his head was throbbing; and now, on top of everything else, blackmail.

It was hard not to see it all—Tangier, the painting, Laverne's reluctance to discuss either—as somehow related to what Barb had just told him. Especially given the syphilis reference. Because that was what it was, he felt certain: a quote from Flaubert, the first half of a black joke.

One night with Venus, a lifetime with Mercury.

The disease was everywhere. It seemed to stream through the *Life* like an undiagnosed, undiagnosable fact. Lying there in the dark, he recalled standing outside Laverne's room. Something had fallen to the floor. The notebook, he'd assumed at the time. Dr. Gallagher had said if Laverne wanted to forget, why did she deep reading *"this"*? At the time, he'd assumed she was referring to the travelogue—that she had picked it up off the floor and shoved it in Laverne's face, but now he wasn't so sure. Maybe she'd been referring to the card. And Gallagher had said something else. She had asked if Laverne was doing penance. Which made a kind of sense if the card was there to remind Laverne of something she had done. Something bad like going down to Tangier and having a wild time, picking up the disease from Reardon, maybe, or from Frank himself.

A whole scenario opened up like the petals of a black flower, at the heart of which Adele Gallagher was blackmailing Laverne.

Then another thought came to him. Another question. Why was Gallagher the only person Laverne allowed near her mouth? Were there lesions there? Some sign that a qualified physician would recognize immediately as the aftermath of the disease?

The question got him out of bed, and at 6 A.M., when the first light of day was showing in the window, he was still at his desk, scribbling.

First thing Monday morning the cellphone trilled.

It was sunny outside. Through the window he could see the trees green-spangled in a rare moment of summery radiance. He stood there with the phone in his hand, trying to think. Then pressed the button. There was a crackling sound, a sound of kindling licked by flame.

"Greer?"

Greaah. The old-man voice, scratchy, tired, muted by long distance.

"Yes."

Silence. London silence. The steady roar of internal combustion. Nick tried to control his breathing.

"You fly to Tangier. You check into the Hotel Amsterdam. You wait."

"Mr. Reardon?"

"You book the tickets on the phone. Your phone. You reserve the tickets with your credit card."

"But why Tangier?"

There was a rush of static, then the faint scream of a fax. Reardon had already hung up.

Tangier

22

In an air letter to Oscar Nagel, posted two weeks after his arrival, Frank Spira described Tangier as a "fantastic playground," a blue and white city built on scrubby sand hills overlooking the Mediterranean. He was amused by the story of the city's origins, the notion that it had been founded in honor of Antaeus, son of Gaia, goddess of the earth. *"Antaeus made the mistake of getting on the wrong side of Hercules,"* he wrote. *"The musclemen fought, Antaeus lost, and where he was buried, Tangier was built. Bill Burroughs, whom I find quite extraordinary, calls it a city built in honor of a loser, a city built on sand."*

You could get hard drugs over the counter. Kif and hashish were openly consumed. Homosexuality was tolerated despite the widespread belief that passive pederasts, the buggerees, would be severely punished in the next world—obliged to wash their faces in the urine of Jews for eternity. Spira took to it immediately. He moved into a room in Billy Elkhorn's house just next to the Petit Socco, a square that ran downhill, a sink for prostitutes, drug pushers and spies.

The journalist Robert Ruark said of Spira's Tangier, the Tangier of the 1950s, that it was a place containing more thieves, black marketeers, spies, thugs, phonies, beachcombers, expatriates, degenerates, characters, operators, bandits, bums, tramps, politicians and charlatans than any place he had ever seen. As far as Nick was concerned, nothing had really changed since then, except that the operators had elbowed their way to the head of the line. You met them as soon as you got off the bus or out of the taxi. They wanted to be your porter, your guide, your pimp, your whore, your lover, your dealer, your money-changer, your protector, your friend-for-life.

Knowing the score, Nick took a taxi from the airport this time, but even so, stepping out of the car in front of the hotel, he was more or less mugged by a guy who snatched his briefcase, shouting, "I *help* you, I *help* you." The character wanted to carry the bag (not the suitcase, maybe that looked too heavy) inside the hotel. There was a comical moment in which they both considered the four feet of broken asphalt between the curb and the smeary glass doors of the Hotel Amsterdam, then the guy let go of the handle.

The guy behind the reception deck had a mass of curly red hair tied back with an elastic band. His name was Piet, he said. He was from Holland. He didn't own the hotel. The hotel was owned by Mr. El Caabouri. He just ran it. Him and his friend Christophe, who wasn't Dutch but French.

Nick learned all this as he was filling out the passport details.

"How long are you staying?"

Nick shrugged, shook his head.

"Do you need to know exactly?"

Piet looked up from his ledger, swaying slightly. He was as high as a kite in his striped cotton *djellabah,* the hooded, head-to-foot garment favored by the more conservative locals. He scratched at his left nipple.

"Why don't I just put you down for a couple of nights?"

Nick watched him turn and reach, saw keys on hooks and pigeon-holes for mail and telephone messages.

"Did anyone call for me?" he said.

The room was basic but airy, with a high ceiling. A dusty window looked out at the Mohammed V Mosque, which was a little farther up the hill. Above the bed a ceiling fan made a stark cross in the gloom, and beyond its wide black blades the ceiling itself was marked with a small adhesive arrow to show you where east was. You had to pray straight at Mecca, orientate yourself like a satellite dish.

No one had called. So now all he could do was wait.

He sat on the edge of the bed, gave the mattress a couple of bounces. Linda would have insisted they put it on the floor. She couldn't bear a soft bed. Four days had passed since their shouting match on the phone. Nick tried to see the silence as a good thing— four days of water under the bridge. The next time they talked, they would both be cooler, and he would have news for her, lots of news. If things panned out, if the story he thought he had actually came into focus, he couldn't see himself not getting an American deal, and after that . . . He gave the mattress another bounce. As soon as he could, as soon as things were clear, he would go find her. He'd turn up at the cinema with a bunch of flowers, and then they could really talk. Establish priorities, starting with what she needed in order to be happy.

A feeling seized him. It was like falling or flying through the air, out of control. He looked at his hands, tried to ground himself in the here and now, told himself that he was here because Reardon had told him to come, and that made sense only if Reardon was based here. This was what he had decided on the flight over. Reardon was based here, and this was all about him trying to draw the Collector onto his own turf, somewhere he thought he had the best chance of seeing him, and of making his move. His bodyguard, if that was who the guy with the scar was, certainly looked like he could be a local. Then again, he could have been from the East End of London. Nick flopped back on the bed and gazed up at the ceiling fan. The truth: he didn't know what was going on. He closed his eyes.

It was almost dark. He looked at his watch. An hour had passed, but it felt like he had closed his eyes for a second. A noise brought him upright on the bed. Someone was in the room. The noise came again. His door was open. It moved a little, pinching a squeak out of the hinges. He could see the key still in the lock, couldn't remember if he had shut the door when he came in or not, couldn't think why he wouldn't have. He slowly got up off the bed.

Out in the corridor, only two of the ceiling lights were working, making pools of light and shadow on a carpet worn down to its backing. A radio was on somewhere.

He closed the door and turned the key. Then put on the light. He turned to face the room.

A wailing started up, the call to prayer blasting out from the Mohammed V Mosque. Even with the window closed, it was intrusively loud. He crossed the room and gave the bathroom door a push, saw old fittings, a notice taped to a smeary mirror warning not to drink water from the tap. The bidet had a yellow stain like a question mark burned into the crazed enamel. He yanked back the shower curtain, saw cracked tile, a couple of tiles actually missing. Just a creepy hotel, he told himself. He had forgotten to close the door. Nothing more than that.

He went back to the bed and lay down, felt himself drifting off as the ceiling fan turned overhead. At the last moment he pulled back from sleep and sat up. He went across the room and jammed a chair under the door handle.

There were no messages for him on Wednesday morning either. Piet, wearing a T-shirt and jeans, and looking a little hungover, raked irritably at his chest. Scratching where it itched.

Nick ate breakfast by the pool. There were only two other tables occupied. A red-faced German woman was smoking and eating in silence. Tucked away in an alcove, two businessmen in shiny suits were reading newspapers. Nick had the feeling they were watching him.

It was the downdraft from the big ceiling fan that woke him, either that or the call for prayer. Standing at the window, he could see the shadow of a palm tree on a white plaster wall. He didn't know where the real tree was—knew it couldn't be one of the straggly date palms growing around the pool in the courtyard.

From knowing everything to knowing nothing. That was how it felt. The more he knew, the less he knew.

Venus and Mercury.

Mercury meant something. He couldn't let it go, brooding on Laverne's reaction when she'd heard the word—when she'd heard Grossman's reaction to the word on the tape. *He didn't know.*

Beyond the window the city sprawled, metastasized. A million souls. You didn't pay tax on incomplete buildings, so the whole place was a construction site. Different when Frank was here, ten times smaller, *la ville blanche.* He'd arrived in the middle of a heat wave—forty-seven years old but still lean and mean—"without a spare ounce of flesh," as Beaton later wrote. The struggle with paint, the struggle against the tide of abstractionism, had left him drained. The boredom of playing house with Grossman had sharpened his appetite for novelty.

Questions. What was it that Grossman didn't know?

There was a framed drawing of Oujda above the dressing table where the mirror should have been. Nick slotted a photograph into a corner of the frame: Reardon at the piano in the bar of the Maniria in '57. Then another, from the same year—Reardon and Spira in a group which included a mask-faced William Burroughs, everyone standing on a white rooftop terrace in the Medina at sundown. Elkhorn was there. Billy Flash, standing at the extreme right of the group, handing something to somebody out of the frame. An ugly man, with abundant coarse-looking hair. Nick had always dismissed him as one more degenerate in Spira's louche milieu, but knowing what he now knew, knowing particularly about that moment in the smashed elevator, he wondered how important Elkhorn really was.

He needed to confirm the elevator smash. That much he could nail down.

Looking through dusty glass at the Mohammed V Mosque, a square-shouldered rocket aimed at heaven, he tried not to think about the bite, about the virus that might be spreading through his body. He tried not to think about Linda. He thought about sending her a postcard. He wanted to call Miriam Florey to ask what she thought of the "Spira's Lovers" piece. He wanted to put in another call to Barb, to find out if there had been any further developments in the black-mail investigation and to make sure that the Taubmann papers remained open to him. But there was no question of calling anyone. He was to check in to the hotel and wait. And that was what he was doing. Waiting.

The room. The noise of kids playing soccer on the esplanade above the port. The call to Allah at sundown, mingled with the shouts of children.

By Thursday he was beginning to think that Reardon had changed his mind. He drank mint tea and read the French paper, watching the other clients. He saw the same people every day. The German woman sometimes ate her meal with a young man. A different one each day. The Arab men sat in their alcove, rarely speaking. Whenever he saw Piet, the guy was scratching at his chest.

His biggest fear was that Reardon had found the name. Or that Bittaker had indeed come to Tangier and been caught in Reardon's trap.

He would not see either of them again. He was trying to relax in the swimming pool on Thursday afternoon when suddenly he couldn't take any more.

It was hotter outside the hotel. Dirtier, the air filled with car fumes and the razzle of scooter engines. He walked down the hill towards the Grand Socco, conscious of eyes following him as he turned in to the Rue d'Amérique. He couldn't see how Reardon would object to his taking the opportunity to do some research—something at least to justify the price of the plane ticket over.

The museum was just inside the Medina. The last time he'd come here, in 1994, he'd spent a month sitting at a table in the corner of the library, sifting through documents and photographs dating back to the fifties.

He signed the visitors' book, filled out a couple of request slips.

He had gotten to know the librarian quite well the last time he was over. His name was Wolfgang, and he was related in some obscure third-cousin way to the American millionaire who had founded the place. An Austrian-American, Wolfgang had spent his teenage years in Alabama and had first come out to Tangier in the seventies. He was a kind of curator and had been writing a book about three decades of the city's history for the past thirty years. Another slave to the definitive.

"I vaguely remember about this," he said, thumping two ugly plastic ring binders down on the table. "There was a general review of elevator safety regulations in the spring of 'fifty-eight. Some legislation was drafted."

Nick opened the first of the files and started leafing through official-looking documents.

An hour later he was still there, transcribing, quietly making notes. The pickings were slim: dry-as-dust legalese, written in French or, to Nick illegible, Arabic, but they proved that a situation had arisen, that the city authorities had considered it serious enough to introduce some new laws.

He requested newspaper cuttings from October 1957, found an article in *Le Matin* almost immediately—a florid but vague account of the elevator accident in the Petit Socco. Most of the article was taken up with praise for the emergency services, which were described as *héroïque* and *intrépide*. The two victims, locals, a young mother and her baby, were named.

It was exactly as Reardon had described it.

Wolfgang came back in the late afternoon with a table lamp which he set up on the table. He was a small, dry man with a pleasant face. He hung around for a while, organizing the scrapbooks, grumbling about the dust, hoping, it seemed to Nick, for a little break in the monotony of his day.

Nick told him that Billy Elkhorn had taken Frank Spira to look at the elevator smash in the Petit Socco, that it had probably inspired a painting.

"Ah yes." Wolfgang pulled up a chair and sat down. "Billy Elkhorn. Ended up in jail."

"May 'sixty-seven," said Nick. "He exposed himself to some women on the promenade."

"Yes, the daughter of a minister and her French governess," said Wolfgang, always ready to add supplementary detail. He was one of the few people Nick knew who shared his passion for trivia. "His daughter, Betina. . . . She told me he was badly treated. The guards beat him terribly. That thing they do to the soles of your feet. When she went to see him, he came into the visiting room on his knees. The guards were laughing."

"She still lives here? His daughter."

"She still has a home here. Not *here,* but in Asilah, down the coast. One of those houses in the seawall. She came in here about, oh, maybe a year ago. A little *timbrée.* Nutty." He tapped a finger at his temple. "She's in her fifties now. She thinks her father should get more recognition."

"Recognition for what?"

Wolfgang threw up his hands.

"Oh, I don't know. Because he sold drugs to all the best people. She said to me that without her father we would not have *Naked Lunch.*"

He laughed behind his small, wrinkled hand.

"She brought me some things. I said we have so much already, but she insisted I take it. All kinds of junk in these cartons. She has a scrapbook like this." He showed a good three inches between his fingers. "Photos, letters, postcards, menus, this collection of drawings— designs for tattoos."

"Tattoos?"

"Billy had this big album. Perhaps it would be of interest to you."
He pointed a finger. "*That* was something I didn't know."

"What?"

"Billy's nickname. I'd always thought it was because he was . . .
ostentatious or, you know, *flashy.*"

Nick shook his head, not understanding.

"Well, apparently it's not that at all. It's because of this collection.
People knew about his interest in the—the *field,* and sent stuff to him
from all over the world. Flash, I mean. From Mexico, from Japan,
Polynesia, you name it."

"Flash?"

"It's the word for it. If you run one of these parlors, you keep a
book of the designs you can do. The client says he wants an eagle
clutching a snake, and you show him your line in predatory birds.
Come. I'll show you."

Nick followed him into another part of the building, watched him
dig around in a pile of old boxes. Betina's stuff stank. Dust, cured
leather, fruity smells of decay. Finally, Wolfgang came up with an
album. Blotched tracing paper separated the stiff pages.

"Anchors," said Wolfgang, turning a page, "daggers, weeping virgins, naked broads. A little sordid perhaps, but poignant too."

He turned, smiling, forgetting to cover his teeth this time.

23

It was like a crime scene where the journalists had gotten in under the tape and were tracking mud everywhere, destroying evidence in their search for stories.

In the weeks following the Grossman killing, Eugene felt less and less in control as reporters of one sort or another—starting with Nicky Greer—picked up on the "Art Market Murder" angle and ran with it. Airheads from the *Inquirer* and the *Post* called for comments on the Spira connection, making half-assed assumptions about missing pictures and crooked collectors until finally, late Thursday afternoon, District Attorney Walter Hirshorn himself, leaning back in his swivel chair, asked to be filled in on the question of the *Incarnation* and any possible links it might have with the killing.

Eugene and Ray had come up to see Hirshorn just to let him know how things were going—how, on the evidence side, they had fiber from the scene which appeared to implicate Buffy Allen's jogger, a couple of latents lifted from the telephone in Nicky Greer's hotel room—prints which had so far yielded no matches with anything at the scene or on any of the databases—and a knapsack stained with what the lab people had confirmed was the victim's blood.

"And that's it?" said Hirshorn, staring at the fat case file, obviously having trouble believing so little could have come out of so much. "Didn't your lieutenant commander okay a search of the East Broadway subway station?"

"A tunnel *off* East Broadway," said Eugene, "the tunnel where the transit cop picked up the knapsack. Yes, he did. We went through it two days ago. Didn't find anything. Doesn't mean there's nothing down there, of course. But you know how it is, Walter. The rats'll drag stuff for miles, not to mention eat it."

Hirshorn looked at Eugene over his glasses.

"And you have these witnesses," he said.

"We ran four separate canvasses." Eugene planted a hand on the file, making it clear that, whatever else, they had been out there earning their paychecks. "Monday thirteenth, Tuesday fourteenth, and then a week later around the TOD provided by the medical examiner. We did Ludlow and Broome again, plus the F trains."

Riding them out to Coney Island and Forest Hills during the rush-hour squeeze in the hope that somebody else would have seen Titunik's man with the spooky eyes.

"And?"

"We struck out. Until something else turns up, we're looking at Buffy Allen, Anna Titunik and Nicky Greer, the writer."

Hirshorn pushed out his bottom lip and then flipped the elastic band off the file.

For the next twenty minutes he went through the witnesses' signed affidavits, taking them apart the way a defense attorney would: Titunik was responding to artwork put out by the department; given the fact that the subway system carried millions of people every day, there had probably been several pale-eyed, balding men hurtling through its tunnels on July 13. The fact that there were twenty-three other reported sightings of the "murderer" as far afield as Los Angeles and New Orleans only served to undermine her testimony. Likenesses generated likenesses—people who looked like the killer but weren't. It was axiomatic. As for Buffy, he'd seen a man wearing a hood from seventy feet away. Even if he had been looking at the killer, he would never be able to point him out in court. He might as well not have come forward at all.

"Which leaves us with this Greer character," said Hirshorn. He removed his glasses and massaged the bridge of his nose. "Phone taps, missing paintings, a murderer who impersonates a police officer just for the hell of it. Does any of this make sense to you, Eugene?"

In the case file, Greer already occupied a thick wad of closely written pages. There was the transcript of the Greer-Grossman interview, the transcript of the interview carried out two days later at the station house, and then clippings from the *New York Times*, the most recent dating from Sunday, July 6, in which Greer developed the Grossman-

Reardon theme in an article headlined "Frank Spira's Lovers." The piece focused on the principal parties and their sordid history, but Greer also managed to mention his six-year struggle to uncover the truth, his interview with Grossman, their subsequent fight, the bite, Bittaker's visit to his hotel room and NYPD's acute interest in "the *bit taker's* true identity." It was after the *Times* article appeared that the daffy arts journalists had started calling, asking Eugene if he was pursuing the "*Incarnation* angle" and whether or not he had spoken to any of the "Spiraphiles."

A flake called Tony Shearer from Channel 1 News had called reminding him that Oscar Nagel, who lived in SoHo, just a couple of blocks across town from the 7th Precinct, was credited with the biggest collection of Spiras in the United States if not in the world, and must surely be consulted, while a woman from the *New York Post* had asked if he was going to the sale of Laverne Taubmann's pictures, a sale which was bound to include a number of Spira's major works. She also wanted his opinion on Laverne's recent death: was it in any way suspicious, in any way related? The inquiries were all pretty general. It was the kind of stuff that in the usual run of things he passed on to the poor slobs in press relations, but this time he had listened, and in the end had started asking a few art questions of his own.

"All I can see is there are a number of people out there who think that Grossman knew his killer," said Eugene. "The only one who doesn't really buy it is Oscar Nagel."

"How come?"

"He says that Grossman was basically a junkie, and that he ran away from the clinic because that's the kind of thing crazy people do. He also thinks the whole *Incarnation* thing is bullshit."

Eugene reached across to the file and pulled out the notes from the Nagel interview.

"Blah-blah-blah—asked Mr. Nagel if he had never been curious about the *Incarnation,* and he said that there had been a certain amount of speculation back in the seventies around the time Grossman had disappeared. He said that 'they' "—he looked up from the notes— "meaning the collectors of Spira's work, all thought Max had it."

"Max Taubmann."

"That's right. His wife went down to Tangier in 1957, and there was some speculation that maybe she had acquired it for her husband. But"—Eugene refocused on his notes—"Mr. Nagel said that if Max did have it, he'd kept it quiet, and that that wasn't Max's way. Max was always very generous, lending to museums and so forth as well as letting people into his house—scholars, historians, friends. So if he'd had it, we would have known."

Eugene tossed the notes back onto the pile of documents, the corners of his mouth downturned.

Hirshorn tilted his head to one side.

"What's eating you, Eugene?"

"It's this Nagel character," said Raymond.

"He's got this row of paintings on the wall," said Eugene. "*Screaming Heads*. It's like a series. Millions of dollars' worth of paintings. Anyway, we're standing there looking at 'em, and he tells us how he bought them back in 1947, his first big purchase. There were seven paintings in this show, and he got three of the main works plus this one picture which was sold as a study. And you know what he says? We're looking at this study and he says, 'This head is clearly not a study, just another perfect scream.'"

"A perfect scream," said Raymond, shaking his head.

"So I said I wasn't sure what that was. I told him in our line of work we see plenty of screaming, and that I'd never thought of any of it as perfect."

"These people are real sick," said Raymond. "It's kind of: I don't know much about torture, but I know what I like."

Hirshorn nodded, closing the file.

"Yep, it's been a real education," said Eugene. Part of that education had involved a trip to a bookstore on Wednesday afternoon before the start of his shift and spending a couple of hours slumped in an armchair leafing through glossy art books, eventually falling asleep over some smeary fuck pictures which the cognoscenti considered masterpieces. "Sodomy, freaks shooting up on the john, faces that look like they've been through a blender."

Hirshorn twiddled his thumbs.

"So is that what this is going to be about," he said, "art?"

"Art, art theft—money somehow or other at the bottom of it," said Eugene. "I don't know. The fact is, from what I hear, from what I read, this guy Spira lost a number of paintings in his lifetime. His so-called friends took pictures to pay debts. Spira himself sold pictures under the table to avoid paying his dealer, or taxes, paintings he had already received money for. These paintings, if they came to light, would be the subject of litigation. And the stakes are high. A couple of weeks ago a Spira sold in London for three million dollars."

Hirshorn's eyebrows pushed up into thick wrinkles.

"Let's say Grossman knew about a picture," Eugene went on, "knew where it was, knew that the guy who owned it had no right."

"But Eugene, what was done to the body—this guy has to be a psycho, right?"

"Maybe that's what we're supposed to think," said Eugene. "All I'm saying is— Look, there's this one big fucking fact that you just cannot get around: the killer, the guy who must have been the killer, went to see Greer after the murder. A couple of hours after he butchered Grossman, he's in Nicky Greer's room. And what does he want to talk about? He wants to know what Grossman said. You have to ask yourself why."

"I'm thinking about the body," said Hirshorn. He looked across at Raymond. "Seems to me the guy had to take time to do what he did. Maybe ten minutes, maybe longer. Why not just cut his throat and leave? If it was some sort of staging deal, I mean."

"It's a problem," said Eugene. "But let's just say—for the sake of argument—let's say the killer *is* some sort of sociopath. What kind of profile are we talking about? Organized, careful, cool. Incredibly cool. Just walks in there and kills the guy. Has fun with the body. Nobody hears a thing. There's blood everywhere, but he walks out clean. We're talking about someone who's done this before. A profiler's gonna say he's in his mid-thirties, maybe older. Now, there were powerful signature elements in this case, not to mention the distinctive MO. Things that any homicide cop is going to enter on the VICAP forms if he's unlucky enough to catch one of these. So how come we didn't get any hits? How come all the data we fed into HIDTA didn't set off any bells?"

"Maybe he usually hides the body," said Hirshorn. "Maybe his victims haven't been found up to now. Maybe the guy's a foreigner. Like that Austrian, Unterweger, the guy who killed the women in L.A." He gave an irritated shake of his head and turned to Raymond. "What's your take on this, Ray?"

"I'm with Eugene. I think there are problems with the serial-killer idea. I think there's more to this than shows. We're trying to make sense of it without knowing all the facts."

"So—what do we do?"

"I'd like to talk to Greer again. Squeeze him a little harder. He was there that afternoon. Had a fight with Grossman, said so himself. Got his hand bitten. And the weirdest thing in all this? The thing that's hardest to believe? I mean the visit to the hotel room after the murder? That's based purely on Greer's testimony. Nobody in the hotel saw the guy enter or leave. We showed them the sketch. I asked one of the staff if they were busy that night around eight o'clock, the time Greer said Bittaker turned up, and they said it was pretty slow. Now, the lobby of the Beacon is kind of small. I'm not sure you could walk in there without someone seeing you."

"So you think Greer is lying about the visit?"

"I don't know, Walter. I don't know why there was a top-dollar phone tap under the bed either. But I'd sure like to ask him."

24

The bodyguard came for him Friday afternoon. He said they were going to have to drive somewhere.

Tangier was all slant and slope, the Mediterranean, a wall of blue scored crisscross with power lines. They rumbled down the hill towards the port, then back up to the Mohammed V, turning into back streets, mounting the sidewalk, skirting potholes and piles of rubble. Nick perspired into his suit and watched the show: a bald guy with a cart selling churros, a shirtless crazy advancing jerkily through the crowd, a smothered kitten in a plastic bag right there on the sidewalk, nobody caring one way or the other.

Then they were bouncing along the Cap Spartel road—not the pretty road Nick had taken the last time he was here, the road that ran along the coast between pine trees and palaces—this was a no-bullshit route cutting a straight line west out of the city.

They passed the Mohammed V Hospital, the university, the prison. Municipal dumps smoked maybe fifty feet from the road. Even with the windows of the old Mercedes closed, you could smell burning garbage. Black trash bags flecked the parched land. They hung in scrubby trees like broken umbrellas, like dead birds.

Nick wriggled out of his jacket.

"I'm glad you finally decided to get in touch," he said. "I was beginning to wonder, you know. Sitting up there in that room."

The bodyguard adjusted his rearview mirror.

The buildings petered out: apartment blocks, then houses, cement-walled compounds, and then a shack or two and then nothing. The land was lion-colored and smoothly undulating. Away to the north the coast was a rocky crest topped by pine forest.

"So—what, we're going to Reardon now?"

The bodyguard checked the mirror again. He looked keyed up, ready for action. Nick shook his head, pretending to find the man's silence stupid rather than sinister.

"Have it your way," he said to the window.

A bus roared past in the opposite direction. Yellow dust hung in the air. They turned south onto a dusty track which followed a stream bed, dry at this time of the year, but not so dry it couldn't feed the flowering laurel that grew tree-high and thick on either side. The track bent round to the left. A set of gates came into view.

The bodyguard left the engine running when he got out of the car. Nick watched him snap open a padlock and pull a heavy chain through peeling ironwork—none of this reassuring, all of it open to sinister interpretations. He blinked sweat out of his eyes, told himself it was okay, thought of the writers and journalists who never admitted to themselves that they were in danger until it was too late. Then told himself he had nothing to fear. Bittaker was the threat, not Reardon.

But now, watching the bodyguard turn from the gate and make his way, grim-faced, back to the car, he got a different perception, saw Reardon, having rid himself of the Collector, now wanting to get rid of him. After all, who else knew about the *Incarnation*? Laverne was dead. So was Grossman. That left the investigative writer, the guy who filled in blanks. He saw himself getting kicked on the floor while Reardon watched. He saw himself getting shot in the back of the head and pushed into a hole.

The bodyguard opened the door.

"Get out."

Nick climbed out on shaky legs. He walked away from the car, not really knowing where he was going, aware only of the oven heat and the sudden blast of the cicadas. He told himself that a month from now he'd be recounting these details in a restaurant, Linda smiling at him on the other side of the table.

"Hey!"

Nick turned. The bodyguard jabbed a thumb in the direction of a house.

It was a two-story Frenchified villa set in a garden arranged along Darwinian lines. Some kind of vine had taken over the first floor. Nick pretended to appreciate the overblown Côte d'Azure facade, trying to clear his head, trying to think—saw shuttered windows, a cornice shedding plaster. If he had been brought here to die, he needed to give them a reason not to kill him. It was either that or run. He didn't even think about tangling with the bodyguard. Double curved steps wound up to an imposing front door. A scabrous date palm hung bone-colored fronds like a junkie displaying needle tracks. More fronds littered the steps.

They crunched trashily as, climbing now, Nick braced himself for the door opening and whatever came after that. But in the end it was the bodyguard who let them in. They had a little moment on the threshold, looking at each other, Nick refusing to go in first. The bodyguard nodded, seemed to understand. He wasn't there to intimidate anyone.

"I know who he is," said Nick. The words sounded hollow, stupid. "The Collector. I talked to my contacts in New York. I got a name. And I know who's behind him. I'd have told you before, but you've been hard to get hold of."

The bodyguard gazed into his eyes with an expression that was almost intimate.

"Do you understand what I'm saying?" said Nick.

The bodyguard walked inside. Nick looked back at the car, considered running, saw himself being shot in the back halfway down the steps.

It was cooler inside the house. Blue light filtered down from a skylight—something Moorish and ornamental. Nick took in deep ultramarine walls, the paint applied thick and sloppy. An entrance hall. A threadbare kilim on shrunken boards. There was a sour smell. The smell of a house that hadn't been opened for a long time.

He followed the bodyguard through a doorway into a salon, aware of yellow walls, brass lamps, fifties-vintage furniture, rugs, a couple of pictures—a faded watercolor of Marrakech, a sepia print of Fez. No Spiras, nothing modern at all.

The bodyguard opened a window, and the room was filled with the rushing zip of the cicadas. He struggled with a shutter and finally abandoned it half-open. Tangled vegetation grew thickly beyond the window, the leaves pressing against dusty glass, screening out the light. He turned, said something in Arabic, then told Nick to wait.

Nick took a seat, listened to the bodyguard moving around in the other rooms. It was four-thirty. A cellphone trilled. The bodyguard picked up, his Arabic sounding like a stream of curses. After a moment he came into the doorway.

"Wait here."

Then he was gone again.

Nick heard the front door slam. Heard the Mercedes pull away up the drive. As soon as it was quiet, he went to see if he was locked in. The handle turned easily, and the heavy door came open with a wash of warm air. He went out onto the steps. He had been brought here, and he had been left. His panic of a moment ago seemed silly now. He stood there for a long time, finding ways to reassure himself. Then went back into the house.

He took the microcassette from his briefcase.

"July twenty-fourth. West of Tangier, about ten miles along the coast. A house. Probably 1930s. Not abandoned exactly, but very neglected. I don't think anybody lives here anymore. It's not a property I recognize from the research. I'm waiting for Reardon . . . I don't know—I don't know what the fuck is going on, but it all feels very—chancy. I just told a lie."

He walked around the room, picking up framed photographs, dusty knickknacks, papers, junk. His clothes were clinging to him, the sweat beginning to chill. Wiping his face on his shirtsleeve, he realized that he'd left his jacket on the backseat of the car.

"I was brought here by the guy who approached me in London—Reardon's fixer, I think, maybe his bodyguard. A bruiser, a hard man. He came to the hotel room this afternoon about—"

The noise came from the hallway. Nick twisted round, the machine held to his mouth.

"That sounds like a—probably a rat, in fact. Like I said, a *very* neglected house."

His gaze came to rest on a piece of dark furniture. It was a secretary, a reproduction of an Empire piece that had been varnished to a sticky sheen. He crossed the room and pulled open a drawer.

"The bodyguard came to my room at about three-thirty, and brought me here. I just lied to him about the . . ." He stopped the tape and leaned forward. Underneath some old 78s was a stack of yellow cartons. He pulled one out. It was stamped with a Marseille address—23 bis, Rue du Chat—and contained a reel of what looked like 8mm film. Home movies. He put the microcassette on top of the secretary. Frank had brought a camera over from Manhattan in '56, and he and

Reardon had made a number of short films. Nick had seen one at the Pompidou Center in Paris: Frank and Tony choosing fruit at the market, Frank and Tony in the car, Frank and Tony on the beach with local boys who struck muscleman poses for the camera. They were collector's items, and here there were perhaps half a dozen. He took out a reel and examined it, pulled up a strip of celluloid.

The crunch of a dry palm frond brought his head up.

Someone was on the steps.

Fumbling the reel back into the carton, he dropped it, sent it unspooling across the floor.

"Shit."

He scrabbled for it, then froze, listening. He couldn't believe he hadn't heard the car pull up, hadn't heard the slamming of doors. With the tangled celluloid in his hands, he crossed the room to the open window and peered out between the leaves. A guy in a crash helmet was looking up at the house, motionless now. He was in a T-shirt and shorts and was carrying a knapsack. There were insect bites on his pale legs. Something told Nick that this man was bad news. A tighter, harder fear gripped him. He backed away from the window and, dropping the film, went silently out into the hall, then up the stairs.

There were six doors around the second-floor landing. He tried the first. The handle turned with a grinding sound, but the door opened only a couple of inches. He pushed again and it gave a little. Looking down, he saw the thick, tasseled edge of a rug. The front door came open downstairs. Nick threw himself against the door. It gave an inch. Then he was pushing into the gap, frantic, jammed. He struggled in silence, working the door back and forth, pushed through into the darkness on the other side. There was movement everywhere— seething, scurrying sounds. Something brushed his face. He jerked backwards, raising his hands.

Listening. Trying to hold his breath to hear.

Light filtered in through a broken louver. The room was crammed with junk. From floor to ceiling was furniture, trunks, packing cases, cartons. There was an iron bedstead. Rolled carpets. A bicycle. It sounded like the rats had made a home here. The smell he'd picked up downstairs, sour, almost ammoniac, was much sharper here.

He heard the front door close.

He shoved the door again, wanting to close it now, but it wouldn't budge. A rolled carpet sagged against it, its tasseled edge jammed underneath.

He heard footsteps coming up the stairs. Stealthy. Unhurried. He dropped to his knees, got hold of the edge of the rug, his fingers scrabbling for the hard knots in the wool. The footsteps came heavier, whoever it was no longer worried about concealment. Nick yanked the rug clear and threw himself against the door. It closed with a bang.

Silence.

Nick blinked sweat out of his eyes, listening. Then he got both arms around the rolled carpet and pulled it across the door. Then he was pulling frantically, clutching blind, pulling at the junk. A box came down from up near the ceiling, then a small furry body and another. The dark filled with movement as the rats tried to get away from the disturbance. The room was alive with them. But the door was blocked now. He was sure of it. He stood there, heart pounding, both hands over his mouth.

The footsteps came along the landing, squeezing little creaks out of the dry wooden boards.

The door handle jiggled. Slowly turned.

Nick backed away as far as he could into the tumbled junk, blinking perspiration, trying to keep his eyes on the door handle. The handle turned again and this time the door came open, easily, smoothly. Then jammed. Solid. Nick tried to take a breath. He could hear the man on the other side of the door, could hear his steady breathing. Then he heard something else: the rattle of the chain through the gate outside.

Suddenly the man was gone.

A car came round to the front of the house. The engine idled, then died. The doors came open. And closed—one, two.

Footsteps crunched palm fronds coming up the stone steps.

Nick heard the front door come open, then someone call his name. Then. What it sounded like: hands coming together. Not louder than that. Two sharp hand claps. There was a strangled shout. Something fell heavily onto wooden boards.

Two more hand claps. *Crack! Crack!*

Nick covered his mouth. He could see now. Where the baseboard was visible, he could see dark holes. He strained to listen, his pulse throbbing in his throat. He looked around, looking for his way out. Because the killer would be back now, he was sure of it. He clambered over boxes to get to the window. Tried the handle. It turned, but the frame was jammed solid. He was still trying to work it open when he heard the front door again. Steps crunching down the stone staircase.

He didn't know how much time had passed between hearing the gunshots and smelling the smoke. It could have been ten minutes. It could have been twenty. He was standing there in the dark, trying to decide what to do, when he caught the sweet smell of wood smoke. And even then, even when he did smell it and understood what it meant, he couldn't bring himself to move. The thought of Bittaker being down there, or someone like Bittaker, waiting for him outside, made it almost impossible to take a breath.

A soft sighing sound started up. Air was being sucked under the door. The rats started to move again. They were up above him, leaping across what was left of the stacked junk. Nick saw a gaping hole up there. Part of the ceiling had gone, revealing a wormy-looking joist. The rats were getting out that way, sending down a fine rain of plaster. As he was squinting up, one of the dark bodies fell, hitting him on the shoulder. He shrank back, his whole body clenched in disgust.

Air was moving all around him.

He grabbed a wooden box and threw it at the window. Shattered glass rained down onto the floor, and the air flowing under the door started a steady whistling. He pulled a chunk of glass out with his fingers, cut himself, then grabbed a brass pot and worked all the way round the frame, clearing the remaining fragments. He reached through to the iron handle on the shutters. It was rock-solid. The whistling sound increased. He could feel the floor heating under his feet. Smoke was coming up through cracks in the floorboards. Then he was moving, scrabbling, frantic. He righted a tumbled trunk and climbed up onto it. Then put his hands up into the hole the rats had made. Plaster and droppings rained down into his eyes and mouth. He felt around for something up there in the dark to hold on to, found a rough wooden joist, and pulled. The trunk flipped out from under his feet, and he was dangling there. Then he was pulling himself up into the stinking dark, movement all around him. He reached out with trembling fingers, touched something big and solid. It was a beam, thick and rough-hewn. He crept towards it, then got on top. He was on all fours now, moving forward, blind. He came up against a post, moved round it, kept on going. A steady, continuous bass rumble rose out of the depths of the house. He could hear the rats right above him, scurrying over the roof tiles. He reached up and touched wooden slats. He'd reached the other side of the building.

He took a deep breath and kicked down. Plaster and wooden slats split and gave. Hot air and smoke rushed up. He heard a window smash downstairs. Another. He kicked hard, sending down splintered chunks. Then he pulled himself round to look down through the hole he'd made. He jumped, came down on jumbled furniture and mattresses, was on his feet in a second, yanking open the door.

The leaded skylight had gone, and black smoke was funneling through the hole it had left. The heat was intense. He staggered forward, making his way down the stairs to the front door. Grabbing the handle, he turned. Turned again. For a second he couldn't think at all, could barely breathe. He pulled stupidly at the door handle, knowing that the door was locked. Then he got a picture of an open window, of tangled vine leaves. Crouching low, he moved into the heat and smoke of the salon.

Something gave behind him. There was a sound of falling brick and plaster. He turned, saw the bodyguard lying on the floor, saw the startled, angry expression, the lower jaw flaring outward under the left ear. Saw the gun in his hand. He grabbed it, shoved it into the back of his pants. Something burst at the far end of the room, and suddenly the flames jumped, fanning out across the ceiling.

That was when he saw Reardon.

He had pulled himself upright against a chair. His legs were on fire and he was redly smiling through the smoke. It looked like someone had taken a basin of blood and thrown it at him. There was blood everywhere, over his arms and hands, over his chest, all around him on the floor. Nick bent under black smoke, looking, unable to stop himself looking, seeing that the smile was something else.

Where the lips had been were just teeth and gums.

He backed towards the window, horrified, half-blinded by the smoke. There was a sharp crack, then a long, rending groan as part of the ceiling came down. A burning spar fell across Reardon's legs.

The old man's eyes snapped open. He took a breath to scream.

Afterwards, outside, in the garden, leaning against the car, vomiting until he was retching nothing but bitter fluid, Nick had the clearest impression that he had heard the old man's voice raised above the roar and crackle of the blaze. But that was impossible. He looked down at his shoes. He was covered in blood but had no memory of pulling the old man backwards and out through the window. It was as if his mind had been cauterized, burnt clean by the horror of Reardon's eyes—the expression of terror that filled them when he realized what had been done to him.

He had tried to get him into the backseat of the car, but the old man had gone into shock, trembling violently, his limbs jerking puppetlike. In the end, too exhausted to struggle or think, Nick had propped him up against a wheel, then covered his upper body with his jacket. It was only then that he remembered the other guy. Bittaker. Because who else could it be? He pulled the gun out of his waistband and backed away from the body, looking around at the garden, the twisted trees and tangled overgrown bushes lit orange by the blazing fire.

It was Reardon's voice that brought his head round. The jacket had fallen over his legs, and he had raised his hands to his bloody chest. His fleshless jaws parted, and his tongue struggled to form words. But it was the eyes that Nick couldn't bear. He raised the gun and pointed it straight at the old man's head. He couldn't pull the trigger.

It took him over six hours to get back to the hotel, dodging into the scrub every time a car went past, making a detour south of a prison that meant walking through smoking refuse for half a mile. Standing in a doorway, he watched two fire trucks go by, followed by a police car. He tossed the gun into an open drain. On the outskirts of town he came upon a group of kids standing under a streetlight and hid in the bushes until they moved off. He zigzagged up the hill, walking through empty streets, keeping sight of the Mohammed V Mosque, until he finally reached the Amsterdam.

The lobby was brilliantly lit, and there was water on the floor. It was after midnight, and the staff were cleaning. He stood in the shadows on the opposite side of the street, waited there for maybe ten minutes, trying to get up courage to walk in. A blue plastic bucket and mop stood in the middle of the floor, but there was no sign of any movement.

He looked down at himself for maybe the hundredth time. His

jacket wasn't too bad on the outside, but underneath he looked like he'd been in a car crash. Which was about right, given the story he was going to tell if anybody challenged him. He'd witnessed an accident—a kid on a motor scooter hit a dog—and had helped the kid out of the wreckage. The kid wasn't too badly hurt, but the dog was pizza, which was how come his clothes were so messed up. And the smoke smell? The accident had happened next to a burning mound of trash. Whatever. As lies went, he thought it was pretty good. He just had to hope nobody would check up on him, or wonder why there was no mention of it in tomorrow's papers. What there would be, he felt sure, was a report of a burning house at Cap Spartel and a suspected double homicide.

He checked his watch. It was twelve-fifteen, and if he didn't make a move, he was going to collapse right there in the doorway.

He staggered across the street.

The lobby smelt sharply of disinfectant. The door to Mr. El Caabouri's office was open. A TV was on in there. There was no one at the reception desk. Nick walked round the counter and unhooked his key.

Up in the room, he showered, soaping and scrubbing until his skin hurt. He had burnt his hands enough for them to be puffy and red, but he didn't think they needed dressing. He had two quite deep cuts on the index finger of his left hand. His calves were skinned and raw from kicking through the ceiling.

He heard a door open, froze under the stream of water, listening.

Music started up next door. He pulled back the shower curtain and peered through the steam. Craning his neck, he could see the chair jammed under the doorknob in the other room. He was panicking when there was no reason to panic. Bittaker had done what he'd gone to the house to do, done what he had intended to do in the summer of '71.

He saw Reardon's eyes, saw the raw, flayed mouth. For a second he thought he was going to throw up again. He held the shower head in front of his face, letting the water beat against him as though he could wash out the memory that way.

He was panicking and there was no reason to panic.

Nobody had seen him. Nobody had seen him come back. He had been lucky.

"Lucky."

He repeated the word as he leaned back into the jet of water. Then another thought came. He closed the faucet, stood there in the dripping silence. What about when he had left? Somebody must have seen the bodyguard. Somebody would remember the man with the scarred mouth.

Grabbing a towel, drying his arms and chest, he made a decision: get the hell out of Tangier, check out first thing in the morning, have someone phone the airport, see if he could get on a flight.

Breathing the soap smell of the towel, he got a picture of himself at the airport, one of the sullen immigration people asking him to step into the interview room. He could see the hotel staff giving testimony, pointing the finger: "Yes, he left the hotel with the murdered man, the man with the scar, and came back in the early hours, sneaked back, really. He wanted to fly out the next morning." It would look bad, bad enough for him to be held pending trial. Held where? He didn't even want to think about it.

25

He ate breakfast by the pool, thinking if he could just act normal he might get through the day without anybody arresting him. But it wasn't as easy as sitting at a table and eating stale patisserie. The dead men's faces were there, suspended between him and the day, him and the newsprint, him and the blue water with its filmy slicks of other people's sun oil. Shading his eyes against the sun, he forced himself to concentrate on the front page of *Le Matin.*

The news in dictatorships. Accords and developments. *Renforcement des relations bilatérales. Nouvelles perspectives de collaboration.* On an inside page he found a lengthy write-up of a manslaughter case currently being tried in a Tangier court. Right next to it, topped by a grainy photograph of a Berber woman weeping into her ornamented fingers, was a domestic violence story with details going back over several years.

There was nothing about two dead men in a house out by Cap Spartel.

"Morning."

Piet breezed past carrying a bundle of towels.

Nick called him back, asked if there was any chance of someone phoning the airport for him.

"You're leaving us?" Piet stuck out a hip, faking distress. "What a *shaaame*. When do you want to go?"

"There's no real hurry. Today, tomorrow. If there's a flight out later on today, I could take that, I suppose."

Piet said he'd find out about seats and leave a message in Nick's pigeonhole. He flashed his eyes and twirled away across the flagstones, then checked his stride to share a joke with the German sex tourist. Nick watched, alert to anything that might suggest Piet knew what had happened last night. The sex tourist was making solicitous noises. She balanced her burning cigarette in her saucer and leaned forward as Piet pulled down the neck of his T-shirt to show her what was on his chest.

Nick turned right out of the front door and started down the narrow sidewalk toward the Grand Socco. Almost immediately he had a friend. His friend's name was Yusef. He knew where Nick could get a good meal cheap.

"How about a newspaper?" said Nick, easing himself free of Yusef's grip. "How about today's news?"

Yusef frowned. He had a meaty smell of kitchens on his clothes.

"*Mechoui,*" he said, "*pastilla, tagine. Pas cher, muy barato, excellent.*"

"*Journal,*" said Nick, shaking his head.

They crossed the Grand Socco and entered the Medina, Yusef keeping up a stream of questions designed to make Nick more completely his. Coming to a side street, they stopped in front of an old man peeling tangerines on top of a bundle of yesterday's *Herald Tribune*s. The dusty street was dappled with spots from sheets suspended overhead. Yusef said something in Arabic, and the old man spat into the gutter, swept his bundle clean of fruit peel. He snapped out a *Trib* with a little flourish.

"No, no good," said Nick, raising his hands. "I need a local paper. Jesus." He strained for some high school French. "*J'ai besoin journal. Tangier journal.*"

Outside the Medina the streets of the modern town were filled with the noise of cars and scooters. It was a half hour before they found a newsstand, but all the papers were in Arabic. Nick explained to Yusef that he wanted him to translate the papers into French, and Yusef seemed to understand. But after a couple of minutes of picking through headlines, he started to lose interest.

"How about this?" said Nick, pointing at a banner headline in flowing Arabic.

Yusef squinted, scanned, shrugged.

"*Bombe à retardement,*" he said. "*En Algérie. Treize morts.*"

The broadsheet page was crammed with illegible script. It could have been a story about time bombs or babies, and Nick wouldn't have known any different. Yusef was tugging at his arm. He wanted to go to the restaurant.

Nick grabbed him by the shoulders.

"Yesterday two men were killed. *Deux hommes. A Cap Spartel. Vous comprenez?* Tony Reardon. *Un homme s'appelle* Tony Reardon. Killed. *Assassiné?*"

Yusef frowned at the word. Nodded, seemed to understand.

Nick gave him a hundred-dirham bill and they went back to the papers. But it was hopeless. Even with the name, Yusef did no better.

Nick got back to the Amsterdam at lunchtime, walked through to the interior courtyard. The tables around the pool were set, but there was no sign of the German woman, a lunchtime couscous stalwart, or anybody else for that matter. The buffet table was empty.

He strolled into the bar, found Piet with a couple of guys in blue overalls watching TV. Tubing and tools were scattered all over the floor.

Piet apologized, scratching lazily at his eternal itch.

"We sprang a leak in the kitchen, so we had to get the plumbers in. Lunch isn't going to happen, I'm afraid. There's a little Spanish place up the street that's okay, if you want to go there."

The TV was tuned to a local channel, a heavily made-up woman talking Arabic a mile a minute under harsh lights. It occurred to Nick that the TV journalists might be ahead of the print media. He ordered a beer and took a stool next to the plumbers.

"By the way," said Piet, "I checked the flights. Tomorrow looks good, unless you want to fly business."

The anchor was replaced by a picture of what looked like a courthouse.

"Tomorrow's fine," said Nick. "I'll come down to Reception later."

Nick recognized the woman from the domestic violence trial coming down the steps of the courthouse. Something came flying out of the crowd and hit her on the side of the head.

Everybody jolted.

"A stone," said Piet. He was scratching at his chest again.

The network replayed the same footage in slow motion. A smooth-looking white stone looping out of the crowd and hitting the woman flush on the temple. Her eyes shut as her elaborately decorated fingers came up to her face.

Piet said something in Arabic, and then to Nick: "Can you believe that?"

He was scratching again. Nick watched him pull down the neck of his shirt, exposing blotchy red skin. It didn't look like an insect bite. Piet caught his questioning gaze.

"It's nothing," he said. "Just a red reaction."

"What's that?"

"That's what they call it. According to Christophe, anyway."

He lifted his T-shirt, showing taut abs, a pierced navel, and up over his heart a tattoo of a rose. The skin around the motif was blotchy and inflamed. The plumbers all turned to look. Nick frowned.

"A red reaction?"

"From the mercury," said Piet.

"Mercury?"

"Yeah, they used to make the red pigment with mercury, apparently, and sailors and so forth would get this reaction. They're not supposed to use it anymore, but in this town you never know . . ."

He said something about Christophe, something about deciding to have a tattoo to mark their fifth anniversary of being together, but Nick was no longer listening, felt in fact like he was being lowered through the floor. He reached out a hand to steady himself against the bar.

Everyone was pointing at the screen.

"They're all stirred up about these killings out at the cape."

Nick turned to look at the flickering screen, saw jerky video, a picture of a hospital, police cars parked zigzag outside glass doors.

"Duc de Tovar," said Piet. "Where they've taken the bodies."

A reporter's face filled the screen. Then Reardon: a photograph from at least ten years ago on a piece of charred ID. Another jerky cut, sun flaring into the lens.

"Here we go." Piet raked at his rose with practiced fingers. "They keep showing this."

The track leading to the house. Blue sky, dawn glaring white through flowering laurel. Nick saw without seeing, impressions jolting him in rapid succession: flash from Billy Elkhorn's collection, weeping virgins, daggers, naked broads. Tattoos and mercury. *Incar-*

nation. Flowering of flesh. It was like putting a foot through rotten boards and dropping into the dark.

The camera jolted and panned, picked out the smoking ruin of the house. Then the corpse in the driveway. People walking in and out of shot. A hand came up to the lens.

"They think it was some gangster from Marseille," said Piet. "Hey, are you okay?"

Like dropping into darkness but being able to see for the first time, detail rushing up to meet him like the floor of an elevator shaft. It was grotesque, almost funny. It was sick. *Incarnation.* A tattoo. Lesion as line. A picture. On a man.

"The reporters are pretty confused. First of all they said it was some character called Wegman. But now we learn that Wegman was killed in Marrakech about twenty years ago. So it's probably somebody else. Say, are you sure you're okay?"

He pounded on the door of the museum until his hand hurt. Eventually, Wolfgang opened up, looked startled as Nick bundled him back inside, Nick realizing he was talking too fast but unable to slow down. *I was wondering—what you said about Billy Flash's daughter—been preying on my mind.* Wolfgang led him through to the back of the building, shooting puzzled looks over his shoulder, wanting to know what it was he was looking for.

Then they were in the stuffy, junk-filled room. Nick squatted down, pulled back the flaps of the first carton, aware of his crazily shaking hands. He started pulling things out, tossing them onto the floor.

"Sorry to seem so . . . Something happened, you see, and—something weird that I need to . . ."

And then he had it. Jumbled up in a box that was full of jars and rags. It was heavy, about the size of a flashlight. There was a length of coiled electric cord and a broken Bakelite plug.

"What is it?" said Wolfgang.

Nick sat back on the floor, the ugly brown thing in his hands.

"A pen," he said.

"A pen?"

Nick became aware of Wolfgang leaning over him.

"Yes," he said. "A pen for drawing on people."

· · ·

The Duc de Tovar Hospital was a modern low-rise block located in the residential area surrounding the Spanish consulate. Nick left the taxi driver at the front gate and walked towards the main entrance, aware of turning heads, of people coming to a halt.

Inside the big glass doors some kind of argument was going on. People were standing three deep at the counter and shouting. Nick looked up at a plan of the hospital on the wall, saw the names of the various wards and departments written in French and Arabic.

He turned and went back out, took a right and went down a concrete ramp, trying to look purposeful, like a man with business to attend to, but feeling like a sleepwalker, seeing everything but at the same time not seeing. The one thing that had never made any sense to him now making sense—an ugly, stupid kind of sense.

There was a door at the bottom of the ramp. He knocked, went in, found himself looking at off-white walls decorated with calendars. Lots of calendars. There were filing cabinets too. A big metal desk stood at the far end of the room. There was a black leather-bound ledger. A big white telephone. Behind the desk, up on the wall, a yellowing chart with handwritten mortality statistics. Moroccans sorted by religion: Jews, Muslims, Christians. French bundled together.

A man entered through a doorway to his left. He was slim and neatly dressed. He frowned, said something in Arabic.

Nick shook his head, replied in his stilted French.

The man touched a mole on his lip, examined the tip of his finger as though expecting to see blood. His shirt had epaulets.

"You are American."

"Yes. I'm sorry to—to walk in here like this, but . . ."

And then he didn't know what to say. Beyond the basic idea of coming here to see Reardon's body, he had no particular plan, and no strategy for getting past officials. He had a pocketful of cash, had taken the money with the vague idea that he might be able to bribe someone, but looking at the man, he realized he had no idea how to go about it.

"But?"

The man waiting for an explanation.

"Well, I won't waste your time, Dr.———?"

The man. Touching his lip again, staring.

"A body was brought in here today," said Nick. "A European."

The man looked down at Nick's wrinkled pants and scuffed shoes.

"I saw it reported on the news," said Nick.

"It is regretful, but next of kin obviously require a *rendezvous*, *Monsieur*."

"Oh." Nick looked at the doorway on the left, saw a strip of light blue wall, a cement floor. The colors swam a little before his eyes. "But I'm not next of kin," he said.

"Well, concerning that . . ." The man shrugged. "Also we are closed."

"I think I can help you."

The man pointed at himself.

"You," said Nick, "the police, I don't know. I think I know who this man is."

"You are journalist?"

"A writer."

The man sat down behind the big metal desk.

"I understand the police are having trouble identifying the body," said Nick.

There were three big chairs along a wall. The man gestured for him to take a seat.

"I saw it on the news this afternoon," said Nick. "Apparently there is now some doubt about who he really is."

"Unfortunately, Dr. Yacoubi, the *responsable* for this—for this *morgue*—is that your word?"

"Yes."

"Unfortunately, he is not here." The man opened a drawer and took out a piece of candy, unwrapped it, put it in his mouth.

"But you work here."

The man shrugged, chewing.

"So, you know what is going on," Nick insisted.

"The police do not talk to me, Mr.————?"

"Nicholas Greer."

"They talk to Dr. Yacoubi."

He put the candy wrapper into his breast pocket, and it came to Nick that this was Dr. Yacoubi's office, and that the man in the chair was his assistant.

"And Dr. Yacoubi?" he said. "Where is he?"

"But I think you may be right," said the man, ignoring the ques-

tion. "I think there may be a problem with the foreigner, yes. The
other man . . ." He gestured towards the open door. "There were two
men. He was known to the authorities."

"Really?"

"Yes, really."

"So—who is he? Was he?"

The man shrugged again, joined his hands on top of the ledger.

"This is all—for the authorities, Mr.—*Green*? But in what concerns this—information, if you have information, perhaps you should
be talking to the police."

"I wanted to be sure I was right. That's why I came out here. I saw
the pictures of the body on the television, the ID card they flashed up,
and I recognized him, at least I thought I did, but I wanted to be
sure."

"And . . ." the man separated his hands with a little open-sesame
smile.

"I believe it's a man called Anthony Reardon. I've been doing
research on a book that deals—it's partly about Mr. Reardon's life."

Nick looked down at the ledger, wondering what he could safely
say. When he looked up, he was surprised to see the man smiling, a
complicated smile, not friendly, but intimate somehow, complicit.

"This is very *irrégulier,*" he said.

He kept on smiling for as long as it took for Nick to understand.
He just wanted to be paid.

There were three rooms—the first, empty, the second containing a
glass cabinet displaying steel instruments and a tiny hand basin.
There were two autopsy tables in some sort of marble-chip compos-
ite. The third room—down a step—housed the main autopsy suite
and was furnished with another of the tables, another hand basin and
twelve cold cabinets.

Natural light came from windows set above head height along one
wall. Cobweb-furred striplights buzzed overhead. A stretcher propped
up against a wall in the second room was smeared with dried blood.

Nick followed the assistant through, breathing tainted air, his
stomach fluttering. There was a smell like the smell of garbage cans
but without the generalized fruitiness of household waste. Only one
thing was decaying here, and it smelt sour, like raw chicken gone bad.

The autopsy tables had a channel cut around the edge like a platter for carving a roast. There was no other visible drainage.

The assistant, richer now by twenty dollars, reached for the handle on one of the cold compartments. He gave Nick a sharp look.

"You have seen this before?"

Nick shook his head.

"What we say to people is to look somewhere, to look away, and then slowly let the *cadavre,* the dead person, to come into your eye."

Nick focused on a crack in the wall, wondering if he was going to throw up.

Hearing the pop of the metal catch and the door coming open. The smoke smell, rising from the body.

"Okay?"

Nick blinked, looked at the assistant's face. He was smiling again, showing gold in the dark of his mouth. The corpse loomed at the bottom of his field of vision.

"Okay, Mr. Green?"

Nick let out the breath he'd been holding, looked down.

Lesion as Line

26

Monday morning, Eugene started in on how the evidence from the Hotel Junkie wasn't taking them anywhere.

"When did it ever?" said Ray, meaning it as an encouragement, like—don't worry about it; there's more than one way to skin a cat, etc.—but as soon as the words were out, he knew Eugene was going to take it the wrong way. Backpedaling, trying to make some kind of useful sense, he said that evidence was what you used to put pressure on criminals to make them talk; it was what you used to convince a jury to convict. It wasn't about establishing what exactly happened.

"So what are you saying?" said Eugene. "That the evidence doesn't matter?"

"It's not that. It's just . . . Look, you can have hair, you can have semen. You can have skin under the victim's fingernails. And it'll get you nowhere. Then, ten years later, some asshole trying to cop a plea talks to his attorney and suddenly . . ." He put up his hands: that was life.

"Yeah, well. That isn't the way this one's gonna work."

"How's that?"

"I'm saying there isn't gonna be any plea-bargaining shitheel coming forward. This one's buried *deep,* Ray. Perfect fucking scream. I tell you, talking to all these people, these *Spiraphiles*—it's like some kind of cult."

Eugene took a sip of coffee, watched his partner return to his paperwork.

"So what are you saying?" He waited until Ray looked up. "All we gotta do is man the phones? The skells will give it up?"

Ray shrugged, ready to drop it now.

"It's about people, Eugene. That's all I'm saying. It's about people, not things. Not little bits of fiber and fluff."

Eugene smiled, shaking his head.

"What the hell are you talking about, Ray?"

"I'm saying to do it well, you have to be a people person."

Ray ducked back into his case forms. He hadn't wanted the discussion to become personal, and now it had. There was a long silence.

Eugene looked at the part in Raymond's hair. You could see pale scalp where the hair was beginning to thin.

"I'm not a people person?" he said. "Is that it?"

Ray shifted on his seat.

"I'm talking about permeability, Eugene. There has to be a kind of permeability between us—between law enforcement and the bad guys. I mean, how many times have you been able to get a conviction because of what scumbag A was ready to say about scumbag B? Because that's how it works. Either you catch the killer with the gun in his hand, or better, you *see* him shoot the victim, or else somebody else sees it and for one reason or another—"

The phone rang.

Eugene picked up, heard the voice at the other end, then sent his coffee flying, grabbing for a pen. He got to his feet, stabbing at the other phone, mouthing, "Line three, line three." Ray grabbed the receiver, hit a button in time to catch Nicholas Greer say he thought he could help them with the Grossman murder.

"Yeah?" Eugene returned Ray's astonished stare. "Well, that's—it's great that you're calling us."

"The murderer was in Tangier last week."

"Tangier?"

"In Morocco."

"Tangier." Eugene sat back down, squaring his notebook in the middle of his desk. "That's—that's very interesting. What makes you say that?"

"I was down there interviewing someone. A man called Tony Reardon."

Eugene scribbled the name.

"Oh—yeah, right, this is one of Spira's—"

"He was killed last week, last Friday."

Eugene raised a hand to his mustache, saw coffee running along his shirtsleeve.

"Reardon was? But . . . Help me out here, Nick: I thought you said in your report that Reardon died, like, thirty years ago. Do I have that—"

"He faked his death. He was killed last week. With his bodyguard."

Eugene shook his head. Faked death, bodyguard, assassination. The can of worms getting bigger and deeper.

"And you think the murder—that this murder was in some way related to the Grossman killing?"

"Well, yes, I do, but—well, to be sure, I need . . ."

"What do you need, Nick? Tell me."

"I need a favor."

Eugene looked across at Ray again.

"I need to see Jacob Grossman's body."

"Need?"

"For me to understand what happened here."

"Right," said Eugene. "And this'll be for your book."

"Correct."

"Gee, Nick. That sounds so—so cool, so detached. I mean, we're talking about a—"

"Reardon was mutilated, Detective Glasco."

Eugene watched Ray scribble the word on his pad.

"I had a feeling that would be of interest," said Greer. "The body was disfigured in a specific kind of way."

"Specific?"

"I say this so that you know I'm on the level. So that you know I want to help."

"When you say 'specific,' what do you mean? Are we talking about some kind of signature thing?"

"Signature?"

"Yeah, you got your MO and your signature. The MO is how the guy organizes things, the signature's what he can't help doing. Like that sick fuck Bundy biting people on the ass. It's how we catch these animals."

Greer was silent for a long time.

"Nick? You still there?"

"Reardon's mouth was disfigured. The lips, they were cut off."

Ray thought Eugene was going to shit. Blotches of red appeared high up on his cheekbones.

"Detective?"

"Nick?" Eugene tugged at his collar. "Does anybody else know about this? I mean, are the police involved?"

"Yeah."

"This is the Tangier police?"

"Yes."

"So, what—they gave a conference, an interview?"

"I don't know. There was some coverage on local TV."

"And they reported how this man, this Tony Reardon, was killed, how he was mutilated?"

"No. No, they just showed the house where he was killed."

"So . . . Look, I'm probably being stupid." Eugene looked up, met Ray's eyes again. "I'm just trying to understand—how do you know about the mouth?"

"I saw it."

"You saw the body?"

"Yes."

Eugene watched Ray write: "WHERE?" They had gotten in so deep so fast, he felt tumbled over, turned around.

"Where was this, Nick?"

For a second all he could hear was a soft razzle of static.

"Nicky? You still there?"

"Yes."

"Where did you see the body?"

"Detective Glasco? I get the feeling that you are trying to implicate me somehow."

"I'm just trying to get the story straight. We're just having a conversation."

"You see, this picture, it's much bigger, much more complicated, than perhaps you realize."

"You know what? It's interesting you should say that. I talked to some of your New York sources, and I got the same feeling."

"I know. Barbara Segal left a message on my machine. She wasn't very pleased. She said you gave her the impression that I recommended you speak to her."

"She did?"

"Detective Glasco. Understand. I felt I had to talk to you. I felt that there was an obligation."

"Like a moral obligation?"

"I think that what is happening is very wrong. And I want to help you catch the person responsible."

"Well, that's good. I'm glad you feel that way about it."

"It was in the morgue in Tangier."

"Say again?"

"You asked me where I saw the body. Well, that was where."

"You went to the *morgue*?"

Raymond scribbled, "WHEN?"

"I'm telling you this so that you don't waste any time at your end. I saw the murder reported on TV, Saturday, and I went to the hospital where the body was taken."

"Why'd you do that?"

Another silence, then Greer's voice, Greer coming through withdrawn, muffled, as though he'd had to go deeper inside himself for the answer.

"I needed to see it."

"Needed?" said Eugene. "There's that word again. You felt like—what?—a compulsion?"

Eugene heard tired laughter.

"The thing is, like I said, this is all part of a bigger picture, which I am very close to putting together, but I need your help."

Eugene nodded.

"Yeah," he said, "you still haven't explained that part."

27

There was crap all over the floor. Pizza boxes, KFC Express cartons, newspapers, bank statements, bills, junk mail. Mixed in with the garbage: the Spira pictures. *You felt like—what?—a compulsion?* Glasco talking to him as though he were the sick one. Nick tried to laugh, but it came out sounding fake. The cop didn't like him. That was the bottom line. He sat in the armchair brooding, the telephone in his lap. The handset felt moist under his palm. This was new. Sweating palms. Also, the nerve tweaking in the corner of his eye. Lack of sleep, he told himself. Or too much sleep, maybe. He was still wearing the clothes he'd worn on the plane; he hadn't gotten back until late Sunday afternoon, when he'd crashed out almost immediately. He'd slept a solid fifteen hours on the unmade bed.

He stirred in the chair, snagging a piece of letterhead stationery with his foot. It was from his bank manager, the guy "wishing to remind" him of the overdraft agreement they had come to two months ago. He wanted to know when he could "expect funds" to be transferred to his current account. Nick drew a hand across his face. Any liquidity coming his way was already earmarked for minimum payments on his credit cards. The Tangier trip would hit his Visa account over the next few days; he wasn't clear about the numbers but had a feeling it might take him to the brink of cardlessness, and without credit he was sunk. There was a way to reverse the trend, of course: stop spending money and put in a couple of months at the *Journal.*

He kicked the letter away and scuffed up another, half-buried under a pizza box. It had been scrunched up and then flattened out again so that you could see the property manager's logo and some scribbled words: "Are the pictures absolutely necessary?"

When he'd gotten back from the airport, he'd found the note from the property manager on his desk. Linda had left another, angrier message on the machine. Apparently the manager had called her Wednesday with a warning that they were in danger of losing their deposit if they didn't get the basement cleaned up before they moved out. In a second message, recorded a couple of days later, she informed him that the owner of the apartment was back from abroad and intended to redecorate. He was ready to start immediately. In other words, they didn't have to worry about the notice period. She wanted to know when he could move his stuff out.

Hearing her recorded voice, her *tone,* Nick had been seized by panic, then blind, seething anger. He'd snatched up the phone and keyed in the property manager's number, wanting to let the guy know that he had no right to come into the apartment without notice, and that he, the tenant, would put whatever he felt like on the walls of his own home. A machine had answered, blandly informing him that the office wasn't open Sundays, and, standing there with the phone in his hand, Nick had a moment of understanding: it didn't matter what anyone else said—he himself could no longer live with Spira's work around him. It was too close to what he had seen at the house in Cap Spartel.

When he'd finished tearing the pictures down, he'd called Rebecca Falk's number. But Becks wasn't open Sundays either. He'd left two messages but hadn't heard back.

The blank walls. Here and there pins snagged scraps of red. There was just one piece of Spiraphilia left. Standing on the mantelpiece where the golden mask used to be, it looked like a big brown dildo or forties-vintage vibrator. A piece of history. Wolfgang had let him have it for nothing. Looking at it now, Nick got a flash of the fresh-drawn tender rose on Piet's burning chest. Then he saw Reardon's face staring up at him in the morgue. And all he could think about was having been so close. He'd known what to look for, had known from the moment Piet rolled up his T-shirt in the bar of the Amsterdam, but by the time he'd worked himself up to confronting the horror of Reardon's body, Dr. Yacoubi, the guy who ran the morgue, had returned, bringing the visit to an abrupt end. It was only when the assistant pulled the sheet up over Reardon's ragged smile that Nick had realized there was someone else in the room.

I knew he'd had a look.

Another image that wouldn't leave him: Spira picking his way through the wreckage to take a good look at the smashed elevator's contents. The way Nick imagined it: the artist had sucked up that detail, and when he'd tried to respond, starting the big Madonna and Child, he'd found that canvas was wrong. Three months later Tony Reardon had gone to Paul Mann complaining about a rash. Something like that. Something along those lines.

Grotesque. It was grotesque. It wasn't about art at all.

Of course, he had known from way back that Spira was a regular visitor at the house on the Petit Socco, but he had always focused on William Burroughs, the celebrity junkie on the top floor. Now, knowing what he knew, the dealing that must have gone on in Billy Elkhorn's rooms four floors below took on a kind of radiant darkness. He imagined Spira and Elkhorn talking about the old days, Spira swapping stories of London during the blitz for Elkhorn's tales of "Old Amsterdam" and how he had made his living there. Billy Flash, the sailor's friend. He imagined Elkhorn guiding Spira's hand, showing him how to run the machine over the skin as the needle stitched through to the deeper tissue—seeing this as clearly as if he had been there.

Seeing it but still not quite able to believe it. Another moment in the morgue, and he would have known for sure. But he was getting somewhere now. That was the way it felt, anyway, the idea of the *Incarnation* spreading like an infection through the body of the *Life,* tainting the most neutral of statements. Laverne's response to the news of Grossman's death, for example—her "How did he die?" At the time, it had seemed like the tying up of a loose end in the somber business of obituary, but now a deeper significance seemed to well up between the words, just as it had welled out of Grossman's terror, his fear of attack, his fear, specifically expressed to Barb, of knives. And it welled out of Detective Glasco's stunned silence when Nick had told him what had happened to Reardon's mouth. Because what had happened to Reardon had happened to Grossman. Nick would have bet money on it. And the *Incarnation* wasn't one work but two.

He'd nail that down in New York on Tuesday morning. Glasco had said if he could help them with the case, they would show him the

Grossman autopsy. There was no question of going into the morgue and looking at the body (there was a limit to what Glasco would do for him), but they would show him the autopsy report and then he would know.

He picked up the phone and dialed Barb's number for the fifth time. It was early morning in New York, but she was already out or just not answering. The machine cut in and he hung up. He worried that she was angry with him and refusing to take his call. The message she had left on his machine had been playful but tart: "The next time you put the cops on to me, maybe you could let me know about it so that I can prepare my alibi."

If she was turning her back on him, he was in trouble. Without Barb, he didn't get access to Laverne's papers, and no access meant no chance of examining the card Laverne had received for her sixtieth birthday. *Une nuit avec Vénus* . . . and a lifetime with mercury. He knew what mercury referred to now, and it had nothing to do with syphilis. What he didn't know was why someone would send a card making a joke about it. A look at the handwriting might at least reveal who that someone was. After years of poring over letters and diaries, he was pretty confident that if the card was penned by one of the known Spiraphiles, he'd recognize the writing.

He went through to the kitchen and opened the freezer compartment. Icy smoke drifted over a sealed Tupperware tub containing unidentifiable chunks suspended in brown ice. Vegetable soup. They'd made it a month ago—he and Linda finding a use for leftovers as part of their waste-not, want-not campaign. They'd prepared it standing side by side—chopping vegetables, talking about their day. For a moment he stood there, held by this vision of domestic happiness. Of course, they hadn't been happy. Linda would have been asking herself where she had gone wrong, while he—what would he have been thinking? He'd have been thinking about the *Life,* about the brilliance of his concluding chapters. The refrigerator shuddered as the compressor came on. Icy air drifted against his face.

Linda had left him—still, it felt new and raw when he allowed himself to know it.

He ran hot water into a bowl and dropped in the frozen container, then stood there staring at his reflection in the kitchen window, thinking about Grossman, thinking about Reardon. Thinking about Laverne.

Mi retrovai per una selva oscura.

He was a guy lost in the woods. But he had a compass now. He had a needle.

The phone jolted him. The machine kicked in, and then Henry was talking. He had been leaving messages all week, each one a notch higher on the scale of recrimination.

"Nick? Look, I hope you're picking these up. I wanted to talk to you about the situation at Crucible. The waters have been muddied slightly. Did you hear about this new book by Martin Marion when you were over there?"

Nick walked into the living room and stood over the answering machine, debating whether or not to pick up. Henry rambled on. Apparently the Crucible editor who had first expressed an interest in the *Life* was under pressure from the sales division to go with this other book submitted by Marion. The editor hated the Marion book but had to take account of the salespeople's position.

"We need to talk about the possibility of your making some cuts, Nick. All you have to do is show a willingness to work with them."

Henry had said he'd send Nick an e-mail just in case he wasn't picking up the phone messages. He was about to put the phone down, then paused. He cleared his throat.

"Oh—yes. Regarding the Curlew situation, I'm afraid Stanhope has decided to go ahead with his plan to publish the book as is. I know this is going to come as a big disappointment to you, but—well, to be frank, your disappearance hasn't exactly helped. I do wish you could have said something before just . . ." There was a weary sigh. "Anyway, for what it's worth, Stanhope says any supplementary material can go into the paperback edition in the form of an appendix. So. So that's where we are. Look, I hope—I hope everything's okay. Do give me a call, when you get a chance."

Nick went back into the kitchen and filled a glass with cold water, drank it standing at the sink. The Walrus had muddied the waters at Crucible. Stanhope had vetoed further changes. Everything was turning to shit.

The phone rang again—his mom this time, calling from the States. He hadn't spoken to her since the day he'd gotten the proofs back from Curlew. That was two murders ago, and it seemed like a lifetime. She had been so happy to hear that he'd finally finished the book. He listened to her voice, one hand holding the frozen soup underwater, shaking his head. Her accent had changed over the years, from the clipped English he remembered from childhood to something much closer to his father's rather nasal Bostonian. More recently, more disturbingly, she had started to sound old. Dad was fine, she said. Skipper, their golden retriever, was fine. She said a friend had sent her a cutting from the *Times*. His article on Frank Spira's lovers. She said how proud she and his father were. She wanted to know if he had any news about publication in the States. She asked him to give their love to Linda.

Nick winced when she said good-bye. He would call her when everything was straightened out. He'd carry on with his life when everything was clear. He pulled the tub out of the water and prized off the lid, dropped the brick of soup into a saucepan.

Back in the living room, he picked up the phone and punched in the number of the cinema, asked if he could speak to Linda. A guy he'd never heard before said she'd left a week ago.

"What?"

"I'm replacing her, actually."

"When did she—"

Whoever it was put his hand over the mouthpiece. Nick heard muffled questions, became aware of his palms again—how wet they were.

"Apparently, she didn't come in on Friday," said the voice. "I mean Friday week. Then she called to say that she—well, that she was resigning, basically."

Nick thanked the guy and hung up. Friday was the last time they had spoken. The day of their argument. He called Becks at work.

"Nick."

He took a breath: "Rebecca, hi. I just—"

"I was out all day yesterday and this morning was a bit chaotic. So . . ."

He was so stunned by her tone—not friendly exactly, but bordering on the amenable—that for a second he couldn't find his words. He told her that he'd just called the cinema and learned that Linda had quit her job. She said she knew, and from her tone of voice it was clear something was wrong.

"She hasn't been in touch with you?" she said.

"She left messages, but I've been away all week."

"That's too bad."

"Why? What's going on?"

"I'm a little concerned, to be honest."

Nick listened in appalled silence as Becks told him how strangely Linda had been behaving. At first Becks had thought it was because of the situation. But it was more than that. Linda had been withdrawn, uncharacteristically secretive. Last week they'd had an argument.

"She told me she was going to quit her job and go abroad for a while. And I—well, I don't think she should. I mean, she's not a student anymore."

"She's going abroad? She didn't say anything to me about that."

"Well, I—look, I hate to point out the obvious, but it's you she's going away from. Anyway, she left. Just packed her stuff. Don't ask me where she's gone, because I don't know."

The soup smell hung in the cold air. Nick called the people who'd be most likely to know where Linda was. Nobody did. Then he remembered the property manager. Linda had been talking to him. He called the main number and got some kind of secretary. She told him the manager, Guy, was showing another flat. She took his number. Guy would get back to him.

He ate the soup from the saucepan, standing under the kitchen light, telling himself that Linda would be in touch. She'd be bound to call again. And this time he would insist on a meeting. They could finally talk things through. Properly.

He took a shower. Shaved. Put on clean clothes. For an hour he just paced, his mind unable to fix on any one thing long enough to make sense. He called Barb again, left a message this time, saying that whatever impression Detective Eugene Glasco may have given, he had never suggested that she might be able to help in the Grossman investigation. He said he was ready to come out to New York as soon as she gave him the okay.

"I'm obviously very keen to get into Laverne's place and—well, give me a call."

Once again, he was waiting for the phone to ring.

He pulled the Tangier file out from the bottom of a teetering stack. Photocopies, faxes, six years' worth of notes scribbled on every kind of paper. He dumped the whole bundle on the table and pulled out the original typescript of the Tangier section, plus the edited Curlew proofs—all 883 pages.

He'd lost the tape recorder and briefcase in the fire, but there was no detail of the Tangier trip that he was going to forget. He wrote "Billy Flash" at the top of a page. Then "Billy Flash and his box of tricks," wondering who had known about it, who had known about Frank's visits to the house on the Petit Socco and what had gone on there.

Next to the mass of detail that he'd accreted over the years, the new material looked thin, fanciful. Apart from the press reports of the elevator smash that he had found at the museum, there was no documentary corroboration of the story Reardon had told him, no extracts from journals, letters, official papers. There were no eyewitness accounts or photographs. All he had was Betina Elkhorn's junk-filled box and a theory. What he needed was to go back to Tangier, to talk to Betina. What he needed was to talk to Dr. Yacoubi at the morgue, see if he could get his hands on a copy of the autopsy report. Someone had to tell him exactly what had happened to the bodies. He needed to know.

Just after six o'clock the phone rang. He snatched it up.

"Nick, I hope I'm not catching you at a bad time."

He didn't recognize the voice at first. It was a beautiful elder-statesman, radio-broadcaster voice, edged tonight with tiredness.

"Mr. Nagel?"

Mr. Nagel wanted to be called Oscar. He said he was in London. He hadn't planned on being in London, but here he was. He was staying at the Savoy, needed Nick's help, a small matter of authentication. There were a couple of paintings he wanted him to look at.

"Spiras," he said. "Early. I think you'd get a kick out of seeing them."

Two early Spiras. Nick got a little frisson, wondered if the late fifties counted as early.

"What—which paintings are we talking about?"

Oscar didn't want to get into it on the phone. He said he wouldn't be calling if it weren't a matter of some urgency.

"Can you come over? I'd really appreciate your help on this. And I'd pay you for the consultation, of course."

Forty minutes later, Nick was knocking on the door of a suite on the fourth floor of the Savoy. It was Nagel who opened up, a cellphone to his ear. He was in a T-shirt and black jeans and, despite the smile, looked tired, preoccupied. There was a slight swelling on the side of his mouth as though he'd had a shot of Novocain, and he kept dabbing at it with a handkerchief. He ushered Nick through to a reception room.

"Yeah, that's him," he said into the phone. "The person I was telling you about. Yes . . . we shouldn't be too long."

Cigar smoke hung in the air, sweetened by the perfume of lilies. Nagel pointed Nick in the direction of two small portraits propped up on a couch.

"Okay," he said. "Talk to you later, sweetheart."

He tossed the phone onto a chair.

"I'm drinking wine," he said. "Can I offer you a glass?"

"Sure. That'd be great."

"I'm sorry to drag you out like this. It's just that this situation arose." He handed Nick the wine. "Margaux," he said. "The 'seventy-eight. Did you lose a few pounds?"

Nick looked at his midsection.

"You should watch that," said Nagel. "Not eating properly. The body can be very unforgiving. Especially in the later years." He touched Nick's glass with his own and explained the situation. A month or so earlier he had acquired a couple of pictures.

"Marion acquired them, in fact. He paid for them out of the Beverly Hills account."

"For your gallery?"

"In the name of the gallery. Yes. The purchase goes through the gallery's accounts. But these—"

His cellphone trilled. He held out a hand, inviting Nick to take a look at the pictures while he took the call.

Nick crossed the room. Two portraits. Side by side on the couch. Whenever he'd seen Spiras outside of museums, they'd always been behind glass and in heavy frames. Spira liked glass, liked the way it brought the paintings together, but he had started making systematic use of it only in the sixties, originally as a way of stabilizing his notoriously fragile surfaces. Many of the collectors put even the presixties works behind glass, referring to Spira's often expressed preference, but to Nick it seemed to have more to do with the transformation of the works into a commodity. If you paid a million dollars for your ruby, you wanted it in a proper setting.

But these pictures were naked. Raw. Exactly as they would have been when the artist put aside his brush. Painted on canvas board, they even had pinholes in the corners, where Spira had probably fixed them to his studio wall. Nick turned. Nagel was deep in conversation now. He caught Nick's look and put the phone against his shoulder.

"Go ahead. Be my guest."

Nick picked up the first and felt an immediate tingle of connection, the same feeling he'd had when he took Spira's hand in the street all those years ago.

"I'm going to have to go, sweetheart. Yes—we'll go on to the Ivy later. Sure they will. Sweetheart, they'd hold the table for you until dawn if you asked them."

He finished the call.

"You see, the gallery's a kind of showcase for us," he said, picking up where they'd left off. "Somewhere people can go to look at extraordinary things, but actually most of the dealing goes on outside. Pictures, pictures like these, won't go anywhere near L.A., let alone the gallery. In this case the client is buying them for her Notting Hill house. At least, I hope she is. That end of the deal isn't tied up yet."

Nick nodded.

"She tells me she brought in an expert," said Nagel. "Stewart McQueen. Used to be at the Tate. Prewar British art. Tweeds, pipe. Old-school faggot. Anyway, I'm going up to see her and this McQueen later on tonight, and I wanted a word with you before I did that." He smiled at Nick's expression. "That's right," he said. "I'm on a very tight schedule."

He touched the work in Nick's hands.

"Marion tells me they're early Spira's, probably executed before 1934. I felt my client would take something like that. So I told Marion to go ahead and write the check."

Nagel sucked at his cigar, tired eyes exploring the portrait.

"But now you have doubts?" said Nick.

"Just tell me what you think."

"What . . . ? Whether I think they're from that time? Whether I think they're genuine?"

Nagel backed away to the other side of the room.

"Describe, express. Tell me what you have in your hands."

Nick focused on the picture.

"Fifteen inches by eleven," he said. "Give or take. Oil on canvas board."

He glanced across at Nagel, who was lowering himself into a chair. Nagel nodded, waved him on.

"Good condition," said Nick. "Pinholes in the corners. The 'S' signature as opposed to the spiral monogram."

"I wondered about that."

"Spira didn't start using the spiral monogram—the coil, as he called it—systematically until late 'thirty-three."

"So in an early work like this—"

"You might expect to see the 'S.' Yes."

He held it out at arm's length, turning it to catch the light. A red and purple face. It showed the influence of Picasso's primitive manner, also not unusual for the period. It was hotter and stiffer than a Picasso, though. There was none of the master's playful lyricism. This was crude, violent. Again, Nick looked at Nagel.

"Where did Marion . . . ?"

"I couldn't tell you. All I know is he found it in the north of England and that it was a gift from the artist to the previous owner. So what do you think? About the date."

"I think 1934 is stretching it. In my opinion it's unlikely to be any later than 1930. *Cupid*, as you know, dates from 1934, and by then the artist had developed his grand manner. This is slightly derivative, stilted."

"Ouch. Nick, I can hear the zeros dropping off the price."

"Transitional, anyway."

"'Transitional.' I must say I prefer that to 'derivative.'"

"The really early work, the proto-Spiras, tend to stand in the shadow of their influences, tend also to be at the cooler end of the emotional spectrum. This is hot, almost priapic. The paint has an annealed quality. The drawing is—well, it's more than bold. These slicing marks"—he drew a finger along the jaw—"are, for me anyway, particularly interesting. By the time he gets to *Cupid*, the drawing all but disappears in favor of a more hazardous process of mark-making. And these lines are cuts, but they are not yet openings. It's as though one were looking at a later-period work but with everything still glued down."

He glanced back at Nagel. The old man was watching him, the cigar held just in front of his swollen mouth.

"Go on."

"It's also, I mean, if it's genuine, it is also very rare. There are, to my knowledge, only fourteen Spiras in existence that predate 1934. These two would be fifteen and sixteen. If I had to take a guess, I'd say 1930."

"You would? Why?"

"Spira gave an exhibition at his studio in November of that year. There were a number of self-portraits listed, many of which disappeared subsequently. Spira claimed he'd destroyed at least six of those works. Perhaps this one got past the Stanley knife."

"You're saying this is from that exhibition?"

"No." Nick put the picture down. "Without proof of provenance or proper analysis—I mean chemical analysis, spectrographic, X-ray, etc., I wouldn't like to say what it is. But assuming it is a Spira, if I were trying to find out about it, I'd probably start with that exhibition in November 1930. Assuming I couldn't go the other way, that is."

"The other way?"

"From the last owner backwards. The simplest way, after all, to establish provenance. Presumably, Mr. Marion knows who he bought it from."

"How about the other one?" said Nagel, pointing his cigar.

The second work was another head, but much more disturbing. The first thing that came to mind was late Goya. It was almost black, the features drawn in dry white streaks. The effect was somewhere between an X ray and a cartoon. The best that could be said for it was that the scumbled line on a black background anticipated the idiom of the famous scream pictures. Beyond that, anyone buying it would be doing so principally for the name—to say they owned a Spira. Nick put the picture back on the couch.

"Thank you, Nicholas."

Nagel rose and went over to the desk where he flipped open a leather document wallet. He took out a clean wad of bills, still held together with the paper band. Hundred-dollar bills. Nick watched him peel off twenty.

"We didn't discuss your fee," he said, holding out the cash. "I hope this is going to compensate for me dragging you out of your house."

Nick looked at the money, then at Nagel's tired blue eyes. He shook his head, smiling.

"For thirty minutes' work?"

"Think of it as a retainer. I may come back to you on that chain-of-provenance question. Anyway, I'm not paying you for the half hour. I'm paying you for the six years that led up to it."

"But what did I tell you that you didn't already know?"

"About this exhibition. I didn't know about that. You forget. What I know about Frank is what I know personally. Remember, I only met him in 'forty-seven. And anyway, that's not the . . . It was interesting hearing you talk about the work. Very interesting: priapic. Cuts that aren't yet openings. You gave me your opinion," he said finally. "You gave me your honest opinion."

He held out the money again, and this time Nick took it.

"Now," said Nagel. "Can I give you a ride?"

He was going Nick's way. Across town to Notting Hill. Nick rode in the back of the limousine, breathing Nagel's cigar, the taste of the Château Margaux in his mouth, conscious of the stiff bills in his pocket. The paintings were in an ostrich-hide portfolio on the seat opposite.

Gazing out through the rain-streaked window, Nagel talked about London—how much he liked it, the restaurants and the galleries. He was very interested in some of the contemporaries, particularly Marc Quinn. He'd seen Quinn's *Self* at the Saatchi Gallery, a sculpture of the artist's head made from his own blood. There was a conceptual element, but it was above all a thing, and a very sensual thing. He said he usually stayed for at least a month, came over when it got too hot in New York. But this time it was purely business.

Nick nodded.

"I'd have thought Marion would handle this sort of thing for you."

"Yes, well, Martin, as you know, is always very much in demand. And he's writing some piece in anticipation of the Guggenheim show. I can't just snap my fingers."

They lapsed into silence as the driver negotiated the free-for-all at Hyde Park Corner.

"By the way," said Nagel, "I had a visit from a Detective Glasco last week."

Nick pulled upright in his seat. He had completely forgotten about it.

"It's okay," said Nagel. "I realize the man has to do his job."

"As long as you understand I didn't put him on to you."

"Of course. No, no, it was actually very interesting. We had an interesting discussion about art. Very interesting. I'm afraid he's not a big fan of Frank's work."

"No."

"I invited him to the opening on Friday." There was a glint in his eye as he said this, and Nick could see that he'd been having a little fun at Glasco's expense. "I thought perhaps seeing it all—the oeuvre, I mean—he might change his mind."

They turned off the Bayswater Road and headed uphill. Tall white houses were all but hidden by thick foliage. The driver made a left and rolled into a broader street where London plane trees draped greenery down almost to the garden walls. Enormous properties loomed, screened by wisteria and honeysuckle.

"Look at this," said Nagel. "I don't know why she bought here. It's not like she's going to be throwing any parties."

He asked Nick if he'd seen her latest film. People said she'd probably be nominated this year. But Nagel didn't think the film was so great. He preferred her in romantic comedies. Not that she was an airhead, he said. Nick should make no mistake about that. To be at the top for so long was proof of that, as was the quality of her art collection. She had acquired some beautiful things over the years.

The car drifted to a halt. Nagel turned and shook Nick's hand.

"Thanks again, Nick. It's been a great help."

Nick saw the front door of the house open. A woman came out wearing rubber boots and wrapped in some kind of shawl. She was holding a pocket umbrella over her head. Nick glimpsed the red-gold hair, the huge smile.

"Look at that," said Nagel. "Twenty million per film, and she runs around with a five-dollar umbrella."

He grabbed up the portfolio and clambered out of the car, laughing.

"Sweetheart, go back inside. I'll be fine."

"It's not you I'm worried about," said the woman in that big joyful voice. "It's my pictures."

Nagel slammed the door, and the car pulled away from the curb. Nick turned, saw the old man walk up the front path, saw the woman bend to kiss him.

Nick opened the front door and for a blank minute just stood there looking at the entrance hall. When he and Linda had moved in, they'd thought they were going to be closer to the center of things. It was a basement, sure, but it was only a ten-minute walk from Holland Park and the beginning of the West End. But looking at it now, at the peeling wood-chip wallpaper and the naked lightbulb hanging from a ceiling that hadn't been painted in thirty years, it seemed to him about as far away from the center of things as you could ever possibly be.

At four o'clock in the morning Barb finally got back to him. She had spent the evening with her "friend," the person who was going to be buying Laverne's big de Kooning. Nick sat huddled in the duvet, looking at the hundred-dollar bills scattered on the floor, listening to her talk about how she had gone to her friend's suite in the Plaza. Money was in the air like pheromone.

"Around six o'clock he says, 'How about a bottle of wine?' We started with a Château Pétrus. 'Sixty-one, I think. This sommelier comes up to the room with the bottle on a tray. Nick, my friend put it on the room. Five thousand eight hundred dollars."

Nick made an astonished sound, hoped it sounded sincere.

"Look, Barb, I want it to be absolutely clear, I had nothing to do with Detective Glasco calling you. He called everyone. Just pulled the names out of the piece I wrote."

"How's Linda?"

Not listening. Either that or she was too disgusted with him to get into it.

"Linda? Fine. Fine, I guess."

"What do you mean, you guess?"

"Barb?"

"Is she giving you a hard time?"

She stifled a belch.

"Barb, the reason I called—I wanted to try to organize a time to visit Laverne's place."

"Ah."

"I'm going to try to get a flight tomorrow, so . . ."

Silence.

"We're still on for that, right?"

"Actually—actually that's all a little screwed up at this point in time."

"Screwed *up*?"

"Nick, I did warn you."

"How is it screwed up?"

"The Smithsonian people, the Archive of American Art, actually—they're pretty much *entrenched,* if you know what I mean. There's this character, George Addison, who's—"

"George? I know George. He's helped me out before. I'm sure he wouldn't—"

"Unfortunately, he's not working alone." Barb paused for a drink. "You're not going to believe this, Nick."

28

Barb was right: he didn't believe it. While Oscar Nagel had been dealing with business in London, the "in demand" Martin Marion had been going through the papers at Laverne's place, and this despite the fact that Gael had never forgiven him for representing her mother as a pampered drunk in the pages of *Tortured Eros*. George Addison, a curator at the Archive of American Art, had called Gael a few days before to inform her that the great Walrus would be accompanying him. "Didn't ask," said Barb, sounding outraged at the other end of the line, "didn't say, 'Would that be all right?' Just *informed* her." Someone had been pulling strings.

It was startling, bad, untimely news. It meant that getting into Laverne's was going to be even harder than Nick had thought.

"What's Marion doing in there, anyway?" he said.

Barb had no idea but said that whatever it was, there was no reason for him to keep other scholars from getting at the documents. She said that, despite the circumstances, she thought she might be able to work something out, and on Wednesday afternoon, having crossed the Atlantic for the third time in a fortnight, Nick found himself in a French restaurant on East 82nd watching Anita Broek fork salad into her severely downturned mouth.

It was Barb who had invited him to lunch, saying that he'd have to go through Broek to stand any chance of getting into the Park Avenue residence, but, sitting at the table, fingering the embroidered edge of a heavy napkin, he got the feeling that it was Broek who'd organized this meeting and for reasons of her own. Reasons that became clear when she turned to him to ask what exactly Barb had said to him about Laverne selling valuables for cash.

Barb returned Nick's questioning look with a nervous smile as she tried to straighten a wayward shoulder pad in her jacket.

"I insist on being told," said Broek.

Nick dabbed at his mouth with his napkin.

"All I know is there was some speculation that maybe Laverne was being blackmailed."

Ugly marks appeared on either side of Broek's mouth.

"Nicholas," she said softly. "You mustn't think I am trying to stand in your way or prevent you from getting material. But you have to understand that Christie's is investing a great deal of time and money in the sale of the Taubmann collection. I can't tell you how unhelpful it would be if you were to start publishing hearsay and gossip in the *Times.* Particularly"—she shot Barb a look—"if you were to *cite your sources.*"

"I have absolutely no intention of spreading gossip," said Nick. "And if I'd wanted to go to the *Times,* I'd have done it yesterday. My only interest here is in Laverne's papers. In any letters Mrs. Taubmann might have written or received while she was in Tangier. And during her stay in Santa Monica in the spring of 'fifty-eight."

Broek shook her head.

"You seem to be under the impression that these papers—that the Newport material is in some sort of order."

"I did tell him, Anita." Barb shook her head. "It's just boxes full of papers, Nick. Cartons and boxes up to the ceiling. You could be digging for days."

"And unfortunately George Addison has a prior claim to the shovel," said Broek firmly.

"And then there's the travelogue," said Nick as though only now remembering it. "The notebook Laverne had with her when—"

Broek flushed. The color rose on her throat so that you could see where her makeup started. It was an abrupt chameleon change that stopped Nick mid-sentence.

A waiter came forward and whispered something into Broek's ear. A call had come through to her on the restaurant phone.

Nick watched her walk away between the tables.

"My God. What did I say?"

Barb was dabbing at her mouth.

"There's some kind of problem with the Smithsonian people," she said in an undertone. "So Anita's a little on edge." She put a hand on his sleeve. "Things have gotten a little—I shouldn't really have spoken to you so—well, *openly*. About the blackmail business, I mean."

"Why did you have to tell her you spoke to me at all?"

Barb frowned, shrugged. They were both watching Broek now. She was using the phone on the bar, smiling, nodding.

"I told her all about the book," said Barb, "about how serious you are, and she seems—you know, well disposed. I think she's going to swing it for you if she can. Getting in, I mean. All you have to do is promise not to spread any rumors about this—this *business*."

Barb emptied her glass, and it was immediately refilled. Nick saw Broek put down the phone, then pick it up again, punching numbers.

"What exactly is the problem?" he said. "With the Smithsonian people?"

"It's probably Marion," said Barb. "Stirring things up as usual."

"That's why Nagel was in London," said Nick.

Barb glanced across at him.

"He was in London a couple of days ago," said Nick. "He called me. Wanted me to look at some paintings. I thought at the time it was more of a job for Marion, but obviously the Walrus had other business to attend to."

Barb frowned and took another sip of her wine.

"Did Oscar seem all right?"

Nick shrugged.

"Sure. I guess. Why?"

"The word is he's ill."

Broek came back to the table.

"Everything okay?" said Barb, offering up a weak smile.

Broek nodded sternly, but something had changed with the phone call. It looked like a burden had been lifted.

She reapplied herself to her lunch and, as they moved on to coffee, seemed to relax a little.

"This travelogue," she said, turning to Nick, "is it of *great* scholarly significance?"

"She let me look at it once," he said. "It has a certain literary quality. For a time she had plans to publish it as a sort of deluxe limited edition, but—well, I guess she changed her mind. Why do you ask?"

Broek examined her fingernails.

"Well," she said, "on the understanding that this, like *that other matter,* stays off the record."

"Of course," said Nick.

Broek settled back in her chair. All the time she was telling the story, she caressed the tablecloth with her pale, tapered fingers.

The Archive of American Art had come to an arrangement with the Taubmann estate for the purchase of the personal correspondence, diaries and so forth, left by Max Taubmann. Everything had been going smoothly until a week ago, when arrangements were being made with the undertakers.

"Laverne died with the travelogue in her hands. It was obviously very important to her. And, quite naturally, Gael wanted it to go into the casket. But—and this is the crux of the matter—the Archive, George Addison in fact, requested and then subsequently, not in so many words, but perfectly clearly, *demanded* that the travelogue be handed over as part of the Smithsonian's booty. Under the terms of the agreement, you understand. Which I think was—well, 'insensitive' would be understating it."

"Golly." Barb pushed at her shoulder pad. "That doesn't sound like George Addison at all."

"I know."

"So what did Gael say?" said Nick.

"Gael decided—I think she probably had no choice—to abide by the agreement."

"So Laverne went into the ground empty-handed," said Barb.

"And the travelogue went to the Archive." Broek smiled and drained her cup. "So, I'm afraid you're going to have to get in line to consult that particular document."

She asked for the check, and while they were waiting, the talk turned to the Spira retrospective, Broek saying that she had received a copy of the catalogue, and that the foreword by Martin Marion was rather overblown. But Nick was no longer listening, wondering now if the travelogue had actually been removed from the Taubmann residence or whether it had just been put aside for collection; wondering also if Marion had gotten his foot in the door solely for the sake of the travelogue (for the greeting card it contained) or whether there might be other items of interest. Because that was how it looked to him. In fact, it was hard to see it any other way. Marion knew. He'd somehow heard about the greeting card and, using his connections, had gotten in there first. But how? Why? What did the Flaubert quote mean to *him*? It was all deeply unsettling.

"Do you think Oscar Nagel's going to be there?" said Barb. "Nick?"

"Pardon me?"

"Did he say anything about the Spira show when he was in London?"

"He did. He said he'd invited Detective Glasco." Nick registered Barb's astonishment. "I think he was being provocative."

"He invited a policeman?" said Broek. "Goodness. Well, I hope the gentleman realizes his good fortune. People are fighting over invitations at the office. All those Hollywood collectors in one room . . ."

"Who says these Hollywood people are going to show?" said Barb.

"I understand Mr. Nagel has been making a lot of personal calls. Julius Spiegelman will be there. I can tell you that much."

Spiegelman was a twenty-five-year-old dot-com multimillionaire. Every dollar he made went into paintings.

"He flew over to woo Gael," Broek went on. "He really had his heart set on the Cubist pieces."

"The Picassos?" said Barb.

"A Picasso and a *Braque*," Broek corrected. "From 1908. They were painted when the artists were standing side by side in the same studio. Julius was terribly disappointed."

Barb saw Nick's puzzled expression. "Of *course*, you don't know about the will," she said. "The division of the spoils."

Laverne had gone into the ground on Friday afternoon. While Nick was crawling around the attic of the Cap Spartel house, the Taubmann family had been gathering together in the cemetery at Swan Point, Providence. On Monday morning Laverne's last will and testament had been read out in the main drawing room of the Newport house.

"Pretty swift, huh?" said Barb. "I think Gael, crippling grief aside, wanted to move things along. Anyway, guess who got the Picasso?"

"And the Braque," said Broek.

"*And* the Braque."

The check arrived. Broek tucked in her card without looking.

"The lady with the lamp," said Barb. "Laverne's faithful supplier.

Dr. Adele Gallagher. Can you believe it? I mean, we're talking fifty million dollars."

"There would have been a reserve of at least thirty million dollars on the Picasso," said Broek. "The pictures would almost certainly have been sold back-to-back. So who knows how high the bidding might have gone."

Nick could hardly believe it. The last time he had seen Adele Gallagher, she had been in Laverne's room, massaging the old woman's back. He wondered where she was now. Probably talking to a financial consultant somewhere.

"It just goes to show you," said Barb. "How wrong you can be about a person. I thought Laverne hated Adele. I mean—and this is going to show my age—but I remember when Max brought Adele home the first time. This would have been back in—"

"'Seventy-two," said Nick, not even having to think. "March."

"When Max was first getting sick. Everybody was talking about it; how Max was up to his old tricks again. Did you know that Laverne insisted Adele live outside?"

"Max set her up in a town house," said Nick.

"Like a concubine. And when he died, he left her the house, so . . . One way and another, she's done pretty well out of the Taubmanns. Of course, these—paintings, they—"

"But how did she end up caring for Laverne?" said Broek. "If there was all this bad feeling, I mean."

"Adele understood her needs," said Nick. "When Laverne got sick at the beginning of the nineties, she hired a team of caregivers through a Boston-based agency. Experienced people used to the ultrarich and their peculiarities. They stayed with her for three weeks. Couldn't take the tantrums and abuse. After that it got worse. By the summer of 'ninety-one, she was going through health-care people at a rate of—well, in one instance, she had two different doctors in one week. And when she started having problems with her teeth, it made her worse."

"What Laverne wanted was a dealer," said Barb. "A supplier."

"Painkillers," said Nick, "antibiotics, antidepressants. What she *really* needed was a local anesthetic and for someone to deal with the abscesses in her jaw, but she'd never let people touch her mouth."

"Except for Adele," said Barb.

"That's right," said Nick. "Except for . . ."

And it was like a door opening. Mouths. Barb was still talking, but they might as well have been underwater for all Nick could hear. He felt sick. His hands were moist in his lap.

"There's a mark," he said to himself, and became aware of Barb squeezing his hand. He focused on her plump, dry lips and shuddered.

"Nick?"

"I'll be fine," he said. "It's a blood sugar thing. Nothing at all."

"So Laverne took her back," said Broek. "But there must have been plenty of people out there, I mean shady health-care types."

Barb hitched herself forward, putting her elbows on the table.

"Are you sure you're okay, Nick?"

Nick smiled, laughed. His hands were shaking.

"Laverne called Adele back because, however much bad blood there was, they understood each other. There was an understanding."

Nick looked at Broek's narrow, powdered face, looked at her finely curved mouth. The gloss from her lower lip had gone with all the eating and wiping. He got a flash of Jack's room in the Delancey-Deere, remembering Jack as he stomped around, a finger pushed into his lip.

They were marked. In the mouth. Grossman. Reardon. Laverne.

Bittaker had removed the evidence. Not of his own handiwork, but of Spira's.

29

Tell a lie to get to the truth. He made the phone call in the street, standing there with a finger in his ear to block out the noise of the traffic crawling south on Fifth Avenue. Gallagher's machine came on.

"Dr. Gallagher, this is Nicholas Greer. The last time we spoke, you warned me about taking what Mrs. Taubmann said at face value. Well, she did say something in that last interview, and it concerns you, actually. She said something about her mouth. It's been worrying me, worrying me a lot. So, if—"

"Nicholas?"

Gallagher. She was there after all. It sounded like she'd had to run to the phone. There was a hammering noise, the sound of a drill.

"I'm sorry to bother you at what must be a difficult time," said Nick, "but I didn't want to go ahead and publish without talking to you first."

"Publish?"

"Dr. Gallagher, perhaps I could come by and talk to you?"

That was going to be impossible, she said. She had a dinner engagement, had to leave the house at seven. There were a thousand things to do between now and then. She had workmen in, had to watch them like a hawk to make sure they didn't bring the ceilings down. Nick leaned forward, touching his forehead against the scratched plastic bubble of the phone booth. He needed this to happen, needed her to see him.

"That's too bad, because—well, I think you have a right to know what she said."

"A right to know?" Gallagher's laugh sounded fake. "What are we talking about here?"

"I'd rather not get into it on the phone."

The drilling sounds got louder. Gallagher cursed.

"Four o'clock," she said.

He thought about this for a second. It wouldn't do.

"I have meetings all afternoon," he lied. "How about six?"

"That won't leave me enough—"

"I'll come to you. It'll only take a half hour. Maybe less."

After he'd hung up, he stood there with one hand on the phone, trying to catch up with himself. Then he called the operator, got the number of a local cab company, ordered a car for 68 East 92nd Street for 6:30 P.M.

Coming out of the booth, he walked slap into Barb.

She had followed him from the restaurant. She wanted to know what was going on.

"I bend over backwards to set up this meeting with Anita. She says she can get you into the apartment, and then you say don't have the time?"

"I said I didn't have time *today*. I'm here until Sunday night, remember?"

"Come on, Nick." Barb made a little give-it-up gesture with her hands. "What is it about this goddam travelogue?"

Nick took a breath and looked down at his shoes. Tell another lie. Keep the lies coming.

"I think Laverne *was* having an affair," he said. "I think the greeting card was written by the lover. I think Marion knows about this and, somehow or other, pulling whatever strings he had to pull, made sure he got to it first."

Barb's eyes were dancing, searching his face for telltale signs.

"Who was the lover?"

"I don't know. I'd need to see the card. But somehow I don't think I'm going to get a chance."

Barb was shaking her head now.

"You think Marion is really interested in all this?"

"Don't you see? I come out with my masterwork, and Marion hits it below the waterline, *kapow*! Revelations about Laverne's love life. 'The sensational story Nick Greer missed.' Or maybe it's to do with his book." She frowned. For a second he thought she was going to see the lie for what it was. "Barb, there's no point in going to Laverne's apartment. Marion's already been there."

This at least was true.

"And the blackmail?" she said.

"Probably had something to do with this—affair." Nick held up a hand. "Barb, when I know, when I have the complete—the definitive picture, I'll tell you all about it."

"Who were you talking to?" she said, pointing at the phone.

Nick looked deep into her eyes, decided she'd probably been listening anyway.

"Gallagher."

"Was she the one? The blackmailer?"

"That's what I want to ask her."

"But—if that were true, why would Laverne leave her these paintings?"

Nick shrugged.

"A final payoff, maybe."

"But Laverne's dead. Why should she care what Gallagher says about her?"

"Posterity."

He wandered aimlessly for a couple of hours, unable to sit down and rest, his mind churning through the *Life* and its detail, unable to come to any conclusion other than the one he'd reached at lunch. Laverne was marked in the mouth. Just like Grossman. Just like Reardon. And somehow Gallagher knew. She didn't have the full picture. When he'd shown up at Laverne's two weeks ago, it had been clear that she didn't even know who Grossman was. But she knew other stuff, he was sure of it. *I understand you want to talk to her about Tangier.* It was the first thing she had said.

He got to her place at six-twenty. Her brownstone looked run-down compared to the other properties on the street. He had been there three years before to interview her and had been struck then by the relative squalor of the place. At the Taubmann residence she lived in luxury, but her own home looked like it hadn't been touched since Max bought it at the beginning of the seventies. The drapes and wallpaper certainly dated from that period, and the few pieces of furniture scattered through the gloomy rooms of the first floor recalled the dusty neglect of a secondhand store.

He rang the bell and stood back, crunching grit underfoot. There was stone dust and debris all over the stoop. He looked up, saw the ugly red alarm housing over the door.

"Shit."

A lock turned, then another. Bolts were shot back. Finally, Gallagher appeared. She barely acknowledged his apology for being late, looking past him at the street as she pulled off the chain.

"Is everything okay?" he said, stepping inside.

Gallagher kicked at a chunk of masonry and grumbled about the mess as she relocked the door. She was wearing makeup, her freckled lips painted a dull brown. She had pulled her hair back into a tight knot. A shirt in heavy burgundy silk hung loose over black pants. In the six years he had known her, Nick had never seen her out of her work clothes. The last time he was here, she'd been wearing her usual no-color polyester smock-dress.

"I had a break-in last night," she said, leading him along the gloomy hallway to the back of the building. "Attempted, anyway. About two in the morning I heard this noise downstairs. They tried to come in through the basement at the back of the house."

They walked into the living room. It was exactly as he remembered it except for the stacked fabric samples, and catalogues on the floor in the corner. Gallagher was obviously planning on spending some of her money. A tall sash window looked onto a yard which had been turned into a garden years ago. All the adjoining properties were the same. Nick stood next to her for a moment, looking out through the glass.

"How did they get in?" he said. "There's no *access* from the street, right?"

Gallagher pointed to the Lexington Avenue end of the block.

"The police say they probably came in through the service entrance of that apartment building. Got over the wall at the back. Once they're in the yards, they can move around. The kids pull boards out of the fences. It's basically a private park out there. The residents encourage it."

She turned from the window, sighed rank breath into his face. If she was concerned about what he was doing there, she didn't show it.

"It's the second time in a week," she said.

"That someone has tried to break in?"

"Last Friday the next-door neighbor disturbed this character who was supposedly talking to me on the intercom. The only thing was, I wasn't here, which my neighbor knew perfectly well. I think he was maybe messing with the lock. Anyway, the police told me to install an alarm. So"—she gestured in the direction of the front door—"I called a local company, and they put that hideous thing up over the door. Leave chunks of stone for me to break an ankle on. This man said he'd clean up when the job was finished."

"He's coming back?"

Her mouth twisted in an ironic smile.

"You don't think they can do a job like this in one afternoon? Tomorrow morning. Eight o'clock, he said, though of course it'll probably be more like ten."

She pointed Nick to a fat swivel chair.

"But all these flashing lights, and codes to remember and keys," she said. "To protect *what*?"

"Paintings, maybe?"

Nick blushed. He had meant it to sound archly playful, but it came out insinuating, tacky. He watched Gallagher walk over to the ceramic-tile fireplace and pick up a pack of cigarettes. She shook one out, struck a jumbo kitchen match.

"I'm sorry," he said. "I didn't mean to . . ."

Gallagher took a piece of the geometric-pattern wallpaper where it was opening up along a seam and pulled. A long, thin strip came away from the wall.

"You know, that's one of many things I'm not going to miss about working for Mrs. Taubmann. The gossip. Everybody knowing everybody else's business. Working in a place like that, it is quite remarkable. Who said what to whom. What the cook had for breakfast."

She considered the strip of paper she was holding.

"Congratulations anyway," said Nick, trying to rally.

She looked at him, frowning, the cigarette held in front of her mouth.

"On the paintings," he added.

"Ah yes." She seemed to reflect for a moment, her lower jaw pushed sideways. "The burglar couldn't have been looking for the pictures anyway. I didn't know about that until Monday. So . . ."

She peeled another strip away. Stained ocher plaster showed underneath.

"It must be gratifying," said Nick, trying to move them forward, "being rewarded for all your years of hard work, your commitment to—"

"Nicholas?" She examined the second strip of wallpaper in her hands. "Wasn't there something you wanted to say to me?"

She remained like that, contemplatively peeling wallpaper and smoking as he took her through the lie. Basically what it was: he had been asking Laverne why she never allowed anyone to touch her mouth, and Laverne had said that she, Adele, was allowed because she understood.

"I asked her what it was you understood, and she said that you understood about Tangier. About what had happened to her there."

Gallagher stopped peeling.

"In Tangier?"

"That's right. I asked her what Tangier had to do with her mouth, and she said—"

The doorbell rang. Gallagher continued to stare at him, her wide-set mascara-spidery eyes fixed and unblinking. The bell rang a second time. Frowning, she left the room.

Nick rose and crossed to the window. He unscrewed the lock blocking the sashes, then went back to his chair, heart pounding. He could hear Gallagher talking. Then the taxi driver, angry, struggling to state the case in broken English. Nick looked up at the ceiling. A motion detector gleamed in one of the grimy corners. But there would be no alarm this evening.

Gallagher came back into the room, touching at her hair. Apparently the driver had been under the impression that she'd ordered a cab for six-thirty. It was very odd.

"So Nick," she said, "you were saying."

Nick made a stir in the leather chair.

"This is going to sound a little crazy. That's why I wanted to talk to you first. I remembered you said to me—"

"We've been over this already. Can you get to the point?"

"She said Frank had put a mark on her."

Gallagher lowered herself into a chair.

"A mark?"

"Inside her mouth."

Gallagher stared.

"A tattoo," Nick added.

"*Inside* her mouth?"

"Yes."

"This is . . ." She shook her head, touched at the knot of her hair. "Did she—did she *show* it to you?"

"No."

The tension went out of her. There was a moment of slow unclenching.

"And this—this was supposed to be something that I knew about?"

"That's what she said."

Gallagher tried to smile. Did smile, touching at her throat.

"I'm sorry, but I'm rather, this is rather . . . You're saying that Frank Spira, the artist, *tattooed* Mrs. Taubmann? It's—it's bizarre, barbaric. It's grotesque." She drew hard on her cigarette, then stood up to tamp it out on the mantelpiece. "Obviously, Laverne was raving."

Nick came to a halt in the middle of the sidewalk and asked himself exactly how much he wanted to do this. Exactly what he thought there was to gain. He crossed Third Avenue, barely aware of traffic waiting at the lights, telling himself that even if there was something, something Gallagher had used to keep Laverne under her thumb and paying all those years, she would have destroyed it by now. Or if it were that important, she wouldn't keep it in the house. It would be in a strongbox in a bank somewhere.

Then he saw what he was doing, and it made him pull up short before he reached the curb. He wanted to pare down his chances of success to something he could walk away from. But it was hopeless. The chance, however small, was nevertheless real, and the potential reward was . . . This was harder to express. But it came down to knowing. Knowing everything. Beyond that, they, whoever *they* were, thought there was something worth breaking in for. Maybe Marion, if Marion was indeed part of it, hadn't found what he'd been looking for at the Taubmann residence.

A driver touched his horn, jolting Nick out of his thoughts. He stepped up onto the sidewalk as a group went past, two middle-aged women with big hair and a man in a blazer and jeans who looked like Linda's father, the way he had looked before he'd gotten sick.

Linda. He didn't even know where she was. He had left London without trying to track her down. A wave of confused feeling washed through him—shame and resentment and self-disgust. Their last conversation came back to him. *You should talk to someone.* She thought he needed help.

He found that he was moving again, almost despite himself. Above the terrace of brownstones the last dirty streaks of daylight were draining out of the sky. Gallagher's windows were black all the way up to the top floor.

He walked on as far as Lexington, saw the apartment building Gallagher had pointed out to him. The service entrance was no more than thirty feet from the brightly lit lobby, and it was open. A trash can had been placed against one of the doors. Inside, a strip of twitchy neon picked out curling plaster on a damp-streaked wall. He moved into the warm stink of refuse, heard a mop knock in a metal bucket. There was a sigh, a low, grumbling voice. The super was around somewhere. Nick kept walking—walked past the neon and into the shadows at the back of the building.

The wall loomed above him, ten feet high, featureless, dark, topped with barbed wire. Looking around for something to stand on, he saw more trash cans, a broken armchair, some wooden palettes on which oily machine parts glistened. He grabbed the wire handles of a plastic trash can and tipped it onto its rim. It was full, the handles greasy. He rolled it to the base of the wall.

The barbed wire looked like it had been there forever. It was rusty, and fixed to crude metal stanchions cemented into the top of the wall. Taking hold of the wire between two barbs, he pulled.

The super came into the yard.

He was still grumbling, dragging something over the ground. Nick froze, his forehead touching the wall, waiting for the guy to start yelling.

It didn't happen.

The guy hawked and spat. Footsteps receded. Then it was quiet again. Nick opened his eyes, blinking perspiration now, looked up at the coils of wire, black against the sky. He pulled off his jacket and, hanging on to the collar, flipped it up and over the top. Then pulled.

There was a tearing sound, but the jacket held. He pulled harder. It was snagged fast now. Squatting down, he let the jacket take his full weight. Then, looking around at the yard, he got a toe in the brick-work and pulled himself up.

The yards at the back of the buildings ran like a patchwork all the way over to the Third Avenue end of the block. Long-established trees and bushes made it look like a park. Barbs spiked up through the jacket, pricking his legs as he edged along the wall. Ripping his jacket free, he jumped down into the darkness.

For maybe a minute he lay there in the grass, breathing country smells of dirt and plants. He had cut himself. There was a sharp sting-ing sensation at the back of his right thigh. But he couldn't feel blood or even find the rip in his pants. He rolled over, looked around. There were lights on in the basement of the property he'd landed in. He could see an elderly woman sitting at a table in front of an electric fan. She was leaning back in the chair, a hand held to her forehead.

Doubled up in a crouch, he moved across to the next fence, hoping to see a gap. Sure enough, a couple of boards had been taken out near the corner of the property. He squeezed through and moved on.

It was easy enough to find the back of Gallagher's place. A red alarm housing, exactly like the one over the front door, had been fit-ted above the first-floor window. A waste pipe snaked up the wall maybe three feet to the left of the window ledge.

At the foot of Gallagher's property, he pressed himself back against the warm brown stone, breathing hard. There were more buildings on the other side of the block, more back windows, some with lights in them now—more potential witnesses. He closed his eyes, turned, put his hands on the waste pipe. Like the stone, it was warm, and years of painting had left it smoothly ridged. A bracket, three feet up the wall, gave him his first toehold.

An anecdote came to him: Spira shinning up a drainpipe in Monte Carlo in July '63. He had gone down there with Grossman and a group of friends to gamble at the casino. After just two nights every-one was cleaned out, and so Spira had decided to break into the room of a rich American acquaintance who was staying in the hotel next door. He stole £300 and spent the rest of the evening drinking cham-pagne in the casino bar and winning at the tables. Later he went back up the drainpipe and replaced the money.

He had reached the window. He stretched out his right foot and, getting a firm grip on the sash, pulled himself onto the window ledge. It was narrower than he'd expected, and he had to keep both feet turned sideways. Below him the yard was a dark pit. He worked his fingers under the sash and pushed the lower window up a couple of inches, squatted down, got hold of the bottom of the frame, pulled.

The room smelt of cigarettes. Distant traffic sounds filtered through the pounding of the blood in his head. He looked at his watch, figured he had maybe two hours.

There were two rooms on the first floor: the living room, where he'd had his talk with Gallagher, and the parlor that looked onto 92nd Street. He decided that the best place to start was the study; somewhere Gallagher might keep papers. He didn't know what he was looking for but figured it had to be something like that. A letter. A photograph. Something Laverne wanted kept secret. Something Gallagher had at some point acquired.

He stumbled against a stack of phone books, reached out for a light switch. Thought better of it.

He needed a candle. Maybe a flashlight.

The kitchen was in the basement. He walked to the head of the stairs and made his way down.

A big cast-iron gas range stood in the dark, its blue pilot light burning steadily amid the ironwork of the burners. He moved around looking for cabinets or drawers, eventually coming up with a flashlight under the sink. The feeble beam lit a bookshelf, grease-spattered cookbooks dating back sixty years, other heavier volumes with roman numerals on the spines.

The study was on the top floor, a cramped room with a cast-iron fireplace. There were more books here. Books and papers, bundles of magazines. Under the dormer window, a large desk. He sat in a creaky metal chair and started to sift through papers. Bills, junk mail, a letter from a consumer guide. He tried the central drawer.

Locked.

For the next ten minutes he cleared bookshelves, riffling pages, dumping Gallagher's heavy medical books on the floor, searching in the dusty spaces behind. Then he trained the light on the locked drawer again, saw a steel letter opener in a cup.

Working the point in between the drawer and the frame, he jiggled and twisted, pressed down. The lock gave with a sharp crack.

It was only when he saw the damage that the criminality of what he was doing came home to him. He had to keep moving. He'd come too far to just back away. Yanking open the drawer, he pulled out more papers, a wristwatch, a couple of pens. The papers were what Linda called bumph: insurance, banking, tax—business documents going back twenty years.

It was almost nine o'clock. He had to get out.

That was when he saw the rug in the middle of the study. It was an ugly needlepoint thing, half-buried now under the jumble of medical books. He squatted down and, pushing books aside, pulled it back. The floorboards were almost a foot wide. They had the dark burnished look of things that had been around forever.

It was hopeless. He was reckless. Stupid. He needed to talk to someone. He needed help.

Getting to his feet, he kicked a book. It flipped open, exposing the torn title page: *Geriatric Medicine: Managing Senescent Change*. The book had a green spine. It was marked with a roman numeral: XII. He hunted for XI, couldn't find it. Couldn't find anything lower.

They weren't here. But he had just seen them. He was sure of it.

Then he was moving again, almost falling as he clattered back down the stairs, the flashlight jerking crazily over the walls.

Back in the basement, he went straight to the bookshelves, trained the flashlight on the ugly green spines. Volume XI covered *Integumentary Systems*. He pulled it off the shelf. Then X, then IX. *Respiratory Disorders. Bowel Dysfunction*. There was a cupboard hidden behind them. He swept the other books to the floor. He opened the cupboard door.

He didn't stop walking until he had reached the other side of the park. Only then did it occur to him that he should have taken a cab, should have gotten off the street as soon as he'd left Gallagher's building. He wasn't thinking straight, his mind jangling with thoughts of Tangier, of Laverne, of the *Life*.

He walked into a bar on West 86th Street, went to pay for a beer, then saw the battered yellow carton in his hand. He had crossed the city holding the film in plain view. He put it into his jacket pocket now, looking around the bar. Franchise neon and a TV blaring sports. It was empty apart from the guys playing an arcade game near the door. Everything was fine.

The burglary had left him buzzing, despite the walk.

Standing in the basement kitchen, shining the flashlight into Gallagher's cupboard, recollection had come to him in a series of flashes: louvered shutters and the sound of cicadas; Art Deco moldings on a high ceiling; a crudely varnished secretary standing dark against a yellow wall. There had been a whole drawer full of similar cartons, all printed with the Rue du Chat address.

Those films and this film. Scenes of Tangier life.

Despite himself, despite the other people in the bar, he took out the box and furtively removed the film. Brown celluloid wound no more than a couple of inches deep on a scratched plastic spool. A short film, whatever it was. His idea: a record of Laverne's visit to Tangier in the second week of October 1957. A record of something shameful, something that either Laverne or Max or perhaps both had paid to have stolen in January 1960. Sometime later Gallagher had acquired it, and the pumping, the *sucking,* had started.

He took a long pull at his beer, laughing softly, sounding even to himself a little cracked. The guy behind the bar looked away when he met his gaze. He had beaten Marion to it; he had stolen from Gallagher what Gallagher had stolen from Laverne.

His fingerprints were all over the house, but he had a feeling that Gallagher would not go to the police.

The carton was in his hands like some magical gift that could not be put aside. It was velvety from years of handling, the label barely legible.

Getting to his feet, he went through to the bathroom.

The face in the mirror surprised him. There were marks under his eyes so dark they looked like bruises. The eyes themselves were red-rimmed and sore-looking. His jacket had a rusty tear on the left shoulder, and an oily dark stain bloomed over his heart. He looked like someone who had lost control of his life and was just now beginning to sleep in the street.

He bent forward to the curved faucet and splashed cold water on his face. Then he reached up and unscrewed the bug-filled light shade.

He held a strip of film to the naked bulb.

Sprocket holes running along one edge. Spidery marks in the colored celluloid rectangles.

He found the store at the corner of Broadway and 78th. It was one of those bulk-purchase-discount-camera-world emporia, a two-hundred-watt cave ablaze with Day-Glo sale stickers and boxed merchandise.

A photocopier was running somewhere, and there was a smell like chicken soup. Nick shuffled in, tripping some kind of Yankee-Doodle chime. A Chinese-looking old guy in a plaid shirt came up from behind the counter, a cigarette holder between his teeth. He insisted on handling the film as they discussed Nick's needs. He said that transfer to video would cost only $40.

"I don't want to transfer. I just want to view it. I want to see what's on it."

The guy removed his cigarette holder and said something in Chinese which brought a kid in a Brian Eno T-shirt out of a back room.

"It's old," said the old guy, squinting at a length of film.

"It's Super 8," said Nick. "From the fifties. Late fifties."

The old guy handed it to the kid in the T-shirt.

"Fifties, yeah? Who say so?"

"No one. It's just a guess."

"Yeah, well, Kodak didn't make Super 8 until later."

"'Sixty-five," said the kid, pulling out a couple of feet.

"'Sixty-five," said Nick, starting to feel sick. "Are you sure?"

"'Bout Super 8? Sure, sure." The kid sounded bored, tired. "But this not Super 8. What you got here is about four hundred feet Regular 8. Regular 8, before Super 8. Sixteen mil sliced down the middle. So, maybe from the fifties, like you think."

Nick watched him hold a strip up to the light.

"Can I view it? Do you have somewhere I can sit and watch it? Some kind of room. I'm ready to pay."

They looked at him then, a brisk, low-pressure scan, checking out his hands, his clothes, his face. Getting detail for when they might have to talk to the police. Or maybe he was just being paranoid.

"Don't have no *room*," said the old guy. "Anyway, you put this through projector, it likely come to pieces. Thing this old and in this condition, tricky. You should transfer."

Nick put out a hand. They weren't going to help him.

"What is it?" said the kid, still squinting at the film. "Like a home movie?"

"I'm not sure."

Again they looked at him. This white guy. Skinny. Look like shit. Like a street person.

30

Get the witness to relax and talk about himself. Offer coffee. A cigarette.

"So I said I thought art should be something beautiful. You know what I'm saying? A woman. Some flowers, maybe."

The windowless interview room. Deep-end blue. Nick touched at the film in his pocket and looked around, hoping he'd made the right decision in coming. It *felt* chancy. He'd always thought of cops as functionaries, blank-faced agents of the law, but watching Glasco flip off the thick elastic band that was holding the covers of the case file together, he was struck by how personal he made everything.

"Or is that a stupid way to look at it?" he said now, flashing Nick a challenging look over his bifocals.

Nick blinked, straightened up in the chair.

"I'm sorry, I'm a little jet-lagged. Catch me at four in the morning and I'm great but . . ."

The truth was, he'd barely slept. Returning to the hotel just after eleven, he'd decided it was no longer safe to sleep there. With his hand on the polished brass handle of the street door, he'd gotten a sudden vivid picture of Bittaker waiting for him in the room. *"Where's the film, Nicky?"* Bittaker or maybe someone else. He'd asked himself why that wouldn't happen, and had been unable to come up with an answer. So he'd ridden down to Times Square and checked in at an Art Deco hive called the Edison, where he'd spent the night lying on top of the bed fully clothed, listening to the cables thump inside an elevator shaft.

Glasco looked across at his partner and snapped out a list. He checked an item, riffled through documents until he found the transcript of their last telephone conversation.

"Of course, Mr. Nagel knows more about it than I do," Glasco said. "He knows enough to have pictures of people screaming on his living room wall."

"The *Screaming Heads,*" said Nick.

"That's right." Glasco tucked his thumbs inside his belt, giving Nick a look. "Tell me," he said. "Honestly. What do you think?"

"Of the heads?"

"Of the heads."

"They're—they're remarkable."

Glasco looked at his partner, smiling.

"See? I knew it. I knew Nicky'd go for 'em."

Personal.

Nick held up his hands.

"Hey, don't get me wrong. I have a lot of respect for . . ."

But Glasco was no longer listening, leaning forward now, talking into the mike, recording the day and date, and giving his and Guthry's name and rank. When he was finished, he leaned backward and set his hands on the table as though presenting an invisible package.

"The deal," he said. "On the autopsy: I talked to the lieutenant commander, and he okayed you lookin' at it on the basis it's for your book. But he doesn't want to see any slick articles in this weekend's *Times.*"

Nick asked for coffee. Three cups later he was beginning to see straight. Glasco wanted to know exactly what he brought to the case.

"I thought I made that clear on the phone."

"Just run it by me again. For the record."

Nick ran it by him, emphasizing the links between the two homicides. Glasco nodded as Nick talked, his eyes moving from Nick's mouth to his hair to his hands. When it was over, he held up a chunky finger.

"You keep talking about these links, these connections, but so far . . ."

"Well, that's what I bring to the table. I'll tell you all I know when you show me the autopsy report."

Nick watched Glasco remove his glasses and give them a little polish with his tie.

"I'm not"—Nick hitched himself ahead in the plastic chair—"I'm not playing games, Detective. I just don't know—I mean, how do I know you'll show me the autopsy if I start out by giving you all you need?"

"You could try trusting me, Nick."

"How about you trusting me? I'm the one who called you. I'm the one who set this up."

"Okay." Glasco scratched at his mustache. "Just so you know where *I'm* coming from. I called Tangier Monday, after your call, but I guess they'd all gone home or whatever. The time difference and so forth. Anyway, they don't answer the number I'm calling, right? So I try again Tuesday, and I get lucky. They pass me around a little, everyone wants my ID, my date of birth, my shoe size. I fax some details with an NYPD letterhead. I call again, and finally I'm talking to this guy who seems to understand me. I say I'm looking to get some information about a Mr. Tony Reardon. Victim of a homicide. Possible postmortem mutilation. And he's like, 'Who?' This is all in English, you understand, and I'm not sure the guy is catching the detail. So I say it again. Tony Reardon. Guy was killed with his bodyguard in Tangier couple of days ago. It was on the TV. And the guy, the guy I'm talking to, says you must mean the person we found out at"—Glasco squinted at his notebook—"Cap Spartel, Saturday morning."

"They don't know who it is," said Nick. "They thought it was someone else. Josef something. Wakeman."

"Wegman. That's right. The guy said they thought it was this Wegman because the vic was carrying Josef Wegman's papers."

Glasco leaned forward, giving Nick the full benefit of his bloodshot stare.

"So I guess my question, my question to you, is, how can you be so sure it's Reardon? I mean, you never met him before, right?"

"No. I mean, no, that's not right. A couple of weeks ago I met Mr. Reardon in London."

They wanted detail: dates, times, descriptions—verifiable facts. It seemed to Nick that they were looking for inconsistencies, ambiguities, wrinkles in his story that might betray hidden lies. They were treating him as if he had something to hide, was somehow implicated.

He talked about the first meeting in the café.

"It wasn't as if this guy even looked that much like Reardon. I

mean the Reardon I knew from the photographs. Towards the end—
late sixties, early seventies—Reardon got kind of big, kind of bloated-
looking, and this guy was really skinny. But he told me things. Things
that no one else knew or could have known."

"What things?" said Glasco.

"Things about the *Incarnation*."

Glasco nodded, waiting for more. When nothing came, he removed
his glasses, massaged the bridge of his nose.

"So, Nicky," he said into the silence, "are you going to explain that?"

"I thought we had a deal, Detective."

"I want to be clear about something," said Guthry. "You say Reardon told you stuff that nobody else could have known? But how were
you able to verify that? If nobody else could have known, how come
you knew?"

Nick had to think about this for a moment.

"At the time—when we were speaking—I didn't understand the
full importance of what I was being told. In fact, the truth is he talked
around the subject. It was only in Tangier that I put the whole thing
together."

Glasco shook his head, starting to lose patience.

"Can we just . . ." He drew a hand across his mouth, picked up his
pen. "Okay. Did Reardon say why he faked his death? Maybe you
can just first of all explain why Reardon faked his own death. Because
he was dead before, right? You said so in your article in the *Times*."

Nick told them the story as Reardon had told it to him, starting
with the Collector's phone calls in 1970, the visit in July the following
year, the moment in which the male hooker came out of the bathroom.
The moment, later on, when Reardon realized what the Collector had
really come for. Glasco sat through the whole thing stone-faced,
stone-eyed.

"So you're saying this collector was there to kill him?"

"Reardon thought so, yes."

"But why? I mean, it doesn't make sense. If he wanted this painting
so much, why not just steal it?"

It was the question Nick had always asked himself. If you didn't
know the truth about the *Incarnation*, it could not be answered.

"Nicky?"

"Let me see the report," said Nick. "Then we'll talk about that."

Glasco gave a tight nod, looked down at his notes.

"Before we get to that, I want to be sure I'm understanding this. When Reardon realized that his life was in danger, he decided to disappear—to fake his death, in fact."

"That's right."

"So how come he came out of hiding? How come he decided to contact you? He was taking a big risk, right?"

"He wanted my help."

"Yeah? He thought you would be in a position to help?"

"He heard about Grossman's death. When I told him Bittaker had been to see me at the hotel, he was very—I could see how important it was to him. He was very interested in Bittaker."

"Interested?"

"He thought Bittaker might be the Collector."

"The same *guy*?" said Guthry. "The guy that came to him in 'seventy-one? We're talking about—this is a thirty-year interval."

Nick shrugged.

"The Collector is single-minded."

"So—I don't get it," said Glasco. "The Collector, he killed Grossman for what?"

"The *Incarnation*."

"But I thought Reardon had the *Incarnation*."

"Yes. Also. That's right. He did." Nick put up his hands. "Look, you're not being fair. I'm not going to explain any more of this until we get to the report."

Glasco leaned back in his plastic chair. Not holding all the cards was killing him. Nick could see it.

"I'm ready to work with you on that, Nick, but you have to give me a little room here."

Nick asked for a drink of water. Glasco stopped the tape. They all had a drink of water.

It was warm in the room despite the air-conditioning. The cops took off their jackets. Glasco suggested Nick do the same. Nick hung his over the back of the chair, conscious of the film, a visible bulge in the left pocket.

The tape was turning.

"You said Reardon wanted your help," said Glasco. "What kind of help?"

Nick had thought about this, took the view that any mention of the real deal between him and Reardon—he had been the bait that drew the Collector out into the open—might take him down a very rocky road at the end of which lay a conspiracy-to-murder charge.

"He wanted me to tell him who the Collector was," he said. "He thought with all my research, with all my contacts, I'd be able to give him a name."

"And did you?"

"No."

"Why did he want the name?"

"I don't know. Maybe he thought he could apply some pressure if he knew who was after the picture."

"Apply pressure?"

"Take some action. He didn't share his thoughts on that."

"But, Nick—Reardon, he faked his own death. He was dead. What made him think he was a target?"

"*I* thought he was dead. Maybe the Collector wasn't so naïve. Maybe Reardon thought the Collector was closing in on him. Maybe Grossman's death spurred him to act. I just don't know, Detective." Nick took a drink of water, pushed the empty cup into the middle of the table. "Can I see the report now?"

Glasco held up his hands.

"Well—just hang on a second, Nicky. This is interesting to me. This is all very interesting." He drew his fingers back through his hair. "Again, just so that it's clear in my mind: Reardon wanted you to give him a name, in exchange for what? I mean, what was the deal here, exactly?"

Nick wiped his hands on his pants. Even without his jacket he was beginning to sweat.

"He was going to show me the *Incarnation*."

"Oh man, this picture," said Guthry, sitting back. "This has got be one very special picture. All these people running around."

"In Tangier?" said Glasco.

"Pardon me?"

"He was going to show you the *Incarnation* in Tangier?"

"Yes. I think so."

"So you *did* give him a name?"

Nick frowned, puzzled. Glasco tilted his head to one side.

"Well, that was the deal, right? He sets up a—what's the word I'm looking for? A viewing? He sets up a viewing if you give him a name."

"I didn't give him any names."

"So how come you were down there?"

Nick shook his head, trying to think. He snatched up his cup, but it was empty now.

"He asked me to come."

"Why?"

"I don't know." Nick looked at the tape. "I never got to ask him. He told me to go to this hotel and wait. That's what I did. Then—then I saw him on the TV. Dead."

Glasco was frowning again, pushing his fingers up under his glasses to rub at his eyes.

"So this guy, Reardon—you see him on the TV. You've been waiting for him to be in touch, sitting in your hotel room for three days, and you see his photograph on the fake ID and you think, Gee, I just gotta go see his dead body at the morgue."

"I believed something had happened to him, something had been done to him. I wanted to be sure about that."

"Something had been done to him?"

"Yes."

"By the Collector?"

Nick nodded.

"I thought that was a possibility."

"So he doesn't just collect," said Glasco. "He doesn't just kill you and take your pictures." Saying it like it was silly, like he didn't really believe it.

"And had it?" said Guthry.

"Had it what?"

"Been done to him? The thing you expected?"

"Yes. The same thing as was done to Jacob Grossman."

The cops sat back in their chairs. Guthry lifted a shoe onto his knee, gave a little tug to his sock, his eyes on Nick the whole time.

"And what was that?" said Glasco.

"You tell me," said Nick. "You're the ones with the autopsy report."

"Tell us what you *think* was done to him," said Glasco, cracking a thin smile.

Nick stared.

"Well, let's stick with Reardon then," said Glasco. "Let's talk about what was done to him."

"He was shot. The killer tried to burn the body. The—"

"No, no, I'm talking about what was *done* to the body, Nick. What do you know about that?"

"Things were done to his mouth."

The only sound in the room was the hum of the tape recorder.

"Things?"

"That's right. Like I said on the phone, but I'm not going to talk about this until—"

"This is the guy in the morgue who told you?"

"That's right."

"Whose name was?"

"I don't know. I didn't get his name. He was some kind of assistant."

"Like a diener, a prosector?"

"I'm sorry, I don't know what those words mean."

"They're kinds of assistant," said Guthry.

"I don't know what he was."

"And this guy," said Glasco, "this assistant, he let you see the body. You just walked in there, said, 'Hi, I want to see a body,' and this assistant said, 'Step right this way, sir. This is where the bodies are kept.'"

"No. Not exactly."

"So," Glasco shrugged, "exactly—"

"We talked first. I told him I knew who it was. They were beginning to doubt their initial identification of the victim as Wegman, and I think he was intrigued."

Glasco checked the tape.

"Intrigued," he said, making it sound like a phony word. "You intrigued him, and he let you see the body."

"I also gave him some money."

"Oh? A bribe? You bribed him?"

"Yes."

"How much did you pay?"

Nick sighed. They were getting sidetracked now, getting away from the real issues.

"What's the difference?" he said. "I needed to see the body, and the only way I could think of to do that was to pay this guy. I could see that was what he wanted."

"He wanted you to bribe him?"

"They call it baksheesh in the Arab world. A gift. You bring a gift for the host. He was ready to show me the body, but he wanted a gift."

"Do you have a lot of experience of gift-giving, Nick?"

Nick looked down at his hands. His fingers had made greasy marks on the Formica.

"So, how much did it cost you? Just for the record."

"I gave him twenty dollars."

Glasco pushed out his bottom lip, nodded.

"And you don't remember his name?"

"No. I'm not even sure he told me."

"And what time would this have been?"

"That I bribed him?" said Nick, irritated, sick of it now. "That I paid the bribe?"

"That you showed up at the morgue."

"I'm not sure. Sometime after lunch. The guy who runs the unit wasn't there. Maybe if he had been, I wouldn't have gotten in so easily."

"After lunch. Like two, three?"

"I don't know. Look, why is all this—what does it matter? The fact is, I saw the body, I saw what had been done to the body, and I think Bittaker did it. If you let me see—"

Glasco raised his hands: stop, yield, slow-the-fuck-down—directing traffic.

"We'll get to that, Nicky. We'll get to the man you call Bittaker. But—"

"The man I *call* Bittaker?"

The blue walls moved in a little closer. Nick brought his hands together under the table. That Bittaker's existence might be open to question was entirely new to him. He had a bad moment seeing it all from the cops' point of view, having only his word for things. He tried to think back, to seize on something that proved Bittaker was real, but Glasco was already moving on.

"Bittaker," said Glasco, flapping a hand, "whatever. What we're trying to do here is reconstruct events, so that later on we can refer back and there's no confusion about what happened when. You say you went to the morgue at the Duc de Tovar Hospital in Tangier on

Saturday, July 25, sometime around two P.M., and bribed a man whose name you don't remember—"

"Whose name I never knew."

"Whose name you never knew. You bribed him to let you see the body of the shooting victim who you believed was Tony Reardon. Do I have that right so far?"

"Yes."

Glasco leaned back in his chair, eased a thumb inside his waistband.

"Okay," he said, putting a little steel into it now. "So here's the problem I have with this. When you called Monday, you said more or less what you just said, that you saw the body at the morgue in Tangier. So, naturally, when I was talking to my man Ahmed, I asked if he wouldn't mind checking with the Duc de Tovar to see if the morgue received any visits from next of kin or friends or whatever of the John Doe over the weekend, which I have to say Ahmed thought was very unlikely, given that nobody knew who this guy was. So anyway, yesterday Ahmed faxed me saying, 'No,' nobody went to the morgue to see the John Doe. They had a family in over the weekend to identify the victim of a motorcycle accident, but that was it."

Nick scratched at his throat.

"So they're wrong."

"He was pretty sure about it."

"Look, the guy, the assistant I bribed to see the body, he's not going to say anything, is he? He's not going to say, 'Oh yeah, I let this character in while the boss was out.'"

Glasco hunkered down in his chair and stared, unblinking, pushing his fingers against the short bristle of his mustache.

"What are you saying?" said Nick. "Are you saying I never went? That I'm making this up?"

"For me, the interesting thing is that the details of injuries you describe didn't appear in any of the press or TV coverage of the case. Ahmed tells me the Tangier homicide people didn't talk about it. So, the question arises: if you didn't read about it in the paper, and you didn't see it on the TV, how did you know?"

"Because I went to the morgue," said Nick.

Glasco nodded, frowned at his notes, then turned a page. He shifted in his chair, moving on to the next thing.

"Let's go back to July twenty-fourth," he said. "Friday. Friday afternoon."

Nick felt his scalp go tight, and it came to him that he should stop it right there, should ask if he was a suspect in the killing of Tony Reardon, should ask for a lawyer. But he couldn't do it, felt that if he refused to cooperate, his one chance of seeing the Jacob Grossman autopsy, of finding out what had *really* happened to him, would be snatched away.

Glasco leaned forward, getting into his face now.

"What's wrong, Nick? Is it too hot in here for you?"

"I want to see the report. I've been more than patient."

"Just tell me what you did Friday."

"I was at the hotel, waiting."

"All day?"

"I may have gone out for a while, just to get some air and to buy a paper."

"This was"—Glasco looked back through his notes—"at the Hotel Amsterdam?"

"That's right."

"So if I call the Hotel Amsterdam and ask the owners if Mr. Greer was in his room on Friday afternoon, they're going to be able to confirm that?"

Nick shrugged.

Glasco stared at him for a long time. Then he leaned back and pulled a document out of the file. Nick could see "Office of Chief Medical Examiner, City of New York" typed at the top.

"Ad Kadomato did a great job on this," said Glasco, flipping through a couple of pages, pretending to read. He looked at Guthry. "Thing about a medical examiner like Kadomato is that he's seen it all. Isn't that right, Ray?"

"Absolutely."

"I've seen him peel the skin off a drowned woman's hand, put it on his own hand like a glove—this is the truth, Nick—put it on his *own hand* just to get some decent prints. That's the kind of guy he is."

He pushed the report into the middle of the table, keeping his hand on it.

"We're going to take a little break," he said. "So you can do whatever you need to do with that, and then maybe you'll let us in on the big fucking secret."

31

He read the report once, twice, three times, chalk-mouthed, unblinking, looking for the essential detail, the one important artifact. After Reardon, he thought he was ready for anything, but there were elements here that opened up a new subbasement of brutality. He kept getting flashes of Grossman sitting in his wheelchair—an eighty-four-year-old man with swollen ankles. It was hard to believe that these things could have been done to that man.

Mi retrovai per una selva oscura.

Someone was in the room.

"So, Nicky."

He looked up, saw the skinny cop, Guthry, watched him sit down opposite, smiling.

"You having a good time?"

Like it was a day out for him, a big adventure.

Guthry pulled the autopsy report across to his side of the table, and refreshed his memory, though Nick had a feeling he knew the contents pretty well.

"Surprising, isn't it? I mean, I don't know about you, but I think of art collectors as kind of sophisticated, civilized. Still, I guess that shows how much I know about the art world, right?"

"The report—it talks about histamine levels."

Guthry nodded.

"If you cut yourself, if someone else cuts you, you get what's called a vital reaction. Swelling, redness. Itching. Histamine and serotonin are what makes that happen. You cut a dead body, it doesn't flare up the same way. You have to be careful because with old people—with a very old man like Mr. Grossman—the levels can be different. But in this case it seems pretty clear: the head injury came first."

"Why?"

"Nobody heard anything. According to our canvass, there was nobody on that floor of the clinic when the killer came in. Even so—any of these other injuries—if the victim'd been alive, there would have been some screaming."

Guthry paused, letting this sink in. He was different from the other cop. Cooler, impersonal. He had the kind of eyes that didn't have to be looking to see stuff.

"Someone would have heard," he said. "No, we think our man walked in there, grabbed Grossman, stuck him in the ear, then did his thing."

His thing.

"Maybe the . . ."

"What's that?"

"Maybe the semen was put there," said Nick. "To make you think it was something it wasn't. To hide the real motive, I mean."

"The real motive? Which in this case would be . . . ?"

Watching him now. A steady, patient gaze. Nick looked down at his hands.

"Yeah, staging," said Guthry, still watching him. "Interesting. All I can say is he went to an awful lot of trouble. I mean, it's not just semen. There's also the bite evidence to consider."

"*Bite* evidence?" Nick said, heard himself say it, his voice sounding unfamiliar, small.

Guthry's eyes never left his face.

"The flesh removed from the thighs," he said. "From the inside of the thighs. Bites, probably."

Nick looked at the report again. The paper fluttered in his fingers.

"It says those wounds were made with a knife."

"That's right." Guthry sat forward, putting a hand on the table. "The way it works is, the guy gets excited, bites, then he cuts out the bite mark. Remember Ted Bundy? Asshole they put in the chair in Florida about ten years ago? Serial killer. Mr. Devious. Worked out disposal sites, cut off victims' hands and heads to beat the forensics people. They caught him through some bite marks he left on a young woman. Since then all these guys, the organized ones—if they bite?—

they remove the evidence. We think our man was probably cutting out the bite marks. Same with the mouth. Same with the shoulders. You read Item F?"

Item F detailed the excision of the victim's lower lip with a sharp instrument, possibly a scalpel.

Nick nodded.

"So we figure our man bit him on the mouth. Then cleaned up with the scalpel." Guthry smiled again. "Bittaker," he said. "Bite-taker. Your guy couldn't have had a better name if you'd invented it."

Nick met his gaze, held it.

"I didn't make him up, Detective."

"Then he's got a killer sense of humor."

"And—the shoulders?" Nick looked down at the report. "The back?" The autopsy referred to a series of ragged, gouging cuts across the shoulders, to extensive acid burns.

"You want to see pictures?"

"No." Nick was having trouble breathing. He needed to see the pictures. He didn't know what he wanted. He wanted out of there. "Yes."

"Yes? No?"

Guthry was looking at him, one hand on the file.

"Show me."

He watched the cop take an envelope from the back of the file. Watched him pull out a stack of large color prints on stiff paper. He slid the first one across the table, then another, kept the images coming, his eyes on Nick's face the whole time.

The body stripped naked: the white belly like a cantaloupe, the bruise-color root of Grossman's sex lolling in its gray ruff of hair. Three big wounds on the inner thighs. Slice marks across the abdomen. Glossy stuff peeped through. Blue-gray. Nick clamped a hand to his mouth.

"You want me to stop?"

Nick shook his head.

"You sure? This stuff fucks with your mind if you're not used to it."

Another picture.

Grossman's face. The mouth. Reardon's, except that here only the lower lip had gone. Nick shook his head again.

"You wanna stop?"

"No."

Another print. The body on a steel table. Grossman facedown. The injury to his head visible inside his left ear. It looked like a bullet wound, though the report said a screwdriver or possibly an ice pick. Tufts of dyed hair on the back of the scalp, which was splashed with grayish-green blotches Nick thought at first were paint. Gouges across the shoulders—deep, erratic. The rest of the back raw and blotchy like the scalp. It looked like coins or petals had been thrown over the wounds.

"Battery acid," said Guthry. "We think. Kadomato says sulfuric acid. We think this guy uses acid either to disfigure or to cover his tracks. Probably carries it to the scene in a thermos flask. Then, when he's done, he carries the bits away. Cooks them up, maybe. Eats them in front of the ball game."

The cop trying to get a reaction of some kind. Nick stared.

"If you're gonna barf, you tell me, okay?"

"A thermos?" said Nick.

"Yeah. Hey, Nicky. You wanna drink?"

Nick shuddered.

"It's a lot to take in," he said. He was finding it hard to concentrate, going back over what he knew, fact by fact, like knots in a cord.

Guthry pulled the prints back across the table.

"Must be hard. Seeing this stuff. Knowing you're responsible."

He gave it a few seconds, let the idea cook all the way through.

"Sure," he said. "Like one of those dogs."

"Dogs?"

"What are they called? Pointers? Think about it, Nick. You come to New York. Talk to Grossman. Grossman is murdered. You go to Morocco. Talk to Reardon. Reardon is murdered."

"I didn't talk to Reardon in Morocco."

"You sure about that?"

"Absolutely."

"You didn't go out to that house on the cape? What's it called? Cap Spartel?"

Nick looked at the photographs.

"Remember last time you were here?" said Guthry. "We searched your hotel room? We came up with this very interesting surveillance gizmo. Under your bed. Sophisticated. Top-dollar. Somebody wanted to know who you were talking to. What you were saying. What you knew. There was stuff already recorded. We checked with AT&T, matched a call to a number."

Guthry shook his head.

"The machine picked up an interesting conversation. You and Barbara Segal, talking about the interview you did with Laverne Taubmann. Looks like the device was put in your room the day after Grossman's murder. Didn't make much sense to me. I had to ask myself, What did that tape recorder make you? A *player*? Someone on the inside? Until you started talking about Reardon just now, I couldn't work it out. You know, how he came to you asking for help, thinking maybe you could tell him who this—this *collector* was."

There was a long silence. Nick finally looked up.

Guthry was smiling at him—a closed-mouth smile.

"That's right. Yeah, you were talking about Reardon and it kind of fell into place. I thought, What if Bittaker got to hear about Grossman? Segal was talking about it, after all. Everybody knew. They knew, but nobody except Segal knew where the old guy *was*. But then you show up. The guy who always gets his man. The man everyone talks to. So Bittaker's thinking: All I got to do is stay close. He follows you to Segal's place, he follows you down to the Delancey-Deere."

Nick was shaking his head.

"Why not? While you're in there getting the skinny, he's out back looking for a point of entry. He waited until you were gone, then came up the fire escape with his screwdriver and a hard-on like you wouldn't believe."

Guthry lit a cigarette, blew smoke sideways at the wall.

"You go back to London. He follows you there. He knows Grossman didn't tell you anything significant about the *Incarnation*—he already *talked* to you about that. But now he's thinking maybe Reardon—who he knows is *not* dead—will be in touch."

"Why? Why would he think that?"

Guthry took a long drag on the cigarette.

"What is it links these two old guys together? The painting, right? You already told me that. The Collector killed Grossman for the painting, you said. Reardon also. For the painting. You said it. So, let's say Reardon heard about Grossman's death. He wants to know what happened there. He wants to know if the police have come up with a killer. Something like that. Who's he going to approach? Who's going to know? He hears, he *reads*, you talked to Grossman just before he died."

Nick closed his eyes.

"Reardon approaches you in London. But he's clever about it. Bittaker misses his chance. But he's listening to your phone now. Put a tap on, down in the street. Nothing easier. He's checking your credit card transactions. He finds out you're going to Morocco. He follows you there. Out there to the cape where the bodies were found."

"I didn't go to the cape."

"You didn't?"

Guthry leaned back, an expression on his face: disappointment. He shook his head, took another drag and then tamped out his cigarette.

The door opened.

"So, Nicky. Whaddaya say?"

Nick looked up, watched Glasco come back to his chair. He had a book in his hands. Not a book. A catalogue. The catalogue for the Spira retrospective.

"I know why he cuts off the lips," said Nick. "It's got nothing to do with sex. All this stuff about bites, about bite evidence—it's wrong."

Another silence. The longest yet.

"So you gonna put us straight?" said Glasco eventually. "You gonna put us out of our misery now?" He was smiling. "We played ball with you, Nicky. Don't say we didn't play ball."

"I need to see the body."

Glasco's smile got tight and ugly.

"The coroner," said Nick. "He missed something."

32

Eugene riffled through the pages of the catalogue. He had an idea: leave Greer in the interview room for a couple of hours. Turn the AC off and let him take a sauna in the cheap suit he was wearing. Start with that.

Raymond came out of the locker room wiping his hands on a scrap of paper towel.

"This guy."

"He's screwing us around," said Eugene.

Raymond took the catalogue from him, opened it at the front. There was a scrawled inscription from Oscar Nagel: "Hope you can make it, Detective!"

"What is this?"

"Came in the mail," said Eugene. "Old fart jerking my chain."

Raymond went over to the window and peeped out past the blind.

"He was there," he said.

"What?"

"Greer. He was out there at the cape. I'd bet money on it. You see the way he looked when I got him onto that subject?"

Eugene nodded, chewing at a cuticle. He'd seen it through the mirror: Greer's face going deadpan like a bad poker player's—*I didn't go to the cape.* "We should put in a call to Tangier," he said. "See if my man Ahmed can put Greer at the cape Friday afternoon."

"Doing what, though? I still can't see him as a killer."

Still chewing, Eugene ripped skin, so now his thumb was bleeding. He didn't see Greer as a killer either. But he kept thinking back to the conversation they'd had on the phone: Greer saying he preferred to keep things to himself so that there'd be no leaks before his book came out. He could see him withholding information. He could see him obstructing justice if he thought their investigation spoiled his plans to become a celebrity author.

"You think he was out there looking for this painting?" said Ray.

"Doesn't make sense. The deal was Greer got to see the picture if he came up with a name."

"Maybe he did. Maybe he knows who the Collector is, but he just isn't saying."

"You know, I had an idea. When you were talking about him being a bird dog—leading the Collector to Grossman, then to Reardon."

"You think there's something in that?"

"Maybe. It kind of unties a knot. When I asked him how come Reardon invited him down to Tangier, he said he didn't know. But what if Reardon thought he was a bird dog too?"

Ray pointed a finger.

"He invites Greer down to Tangier thinking the Collector's not going to be far behind."

"He invites Greer out to this house in Cap Spartel . . ."

"A trap."

"Why not?"

"Maybe Greer was in on it. Like maybe he agreed to bring the Collector out in the open?"

"In return for a look at this picture."

"That'd be conspiracy."

"Only if you could prove he knew what Reardon had in mind."

Eugene walked into the little room behind the mirror, chewing on his thumb. Greer had his head tilted all the way back as though he'd fallen asleep. Ray came and stood next to him.

"So what do you want to do?" he said.

"I'd like to kick his intellectual ass."

"We gonna call Kadomato? Set something up at the morgue?"

Eugene pulled at his collar, straining upwards, trying to free himself from its grip.

"He's just jerkin' us around, Ray. What's he gonna see at the morgue?"

"A body."

"Exactly. That's all this is. A cheap fucking thrill. Something he can put in his book."

"He says Kadomato missed something."

"Yeah, right. One of the city's most experienced forensic patholo-gists."

Ray put his head against the glass.

"But he's talking, Eugene. Maybe he'll talk himself into a corner."

Eugene pushed his glasses up and massaged his eyelids. His back was killing him, but there was nothing he could do about that. Ray was right, of course. Greer was still talking. And he'd promised them more. Maybe a trip to the morgue would be all it'd take to get him to open up.

The reception area of the Office of the Chief Medical Examiner had a kind of airport feel: gray sectional furniture seemed to float just above the gray carpet. Someone had put black-and-white photographs around the gray walls in an attempt to pin things down, but the general feeling was unanchored, notional.

The morgue's PR lady looked thin inside her gabardine suit. She had a sad face framed by perm-damaged hair that was greasily dark at the roots. Kadomato had referred Eugene's request to her, since she was the one who'd have to deal with the PR implications if Greer decided he wanted to write something about what he saw.

Nick found it hard to follow what she was saying—something about their duty of respect. Then she was telling them about a family who was there to identify a young African-American man. The cops weren't going to be able to use the viewing room.

"They keep the bodies downstairs," said Glasco, giving Nick a nudge as if they were old drinking buddies. "Send 'em up for identifi-cation."

"If people request it," said the PR lady. "We advise identification from a photograph. But sometimes people want to see the deceased in the flesh. We used to take next of kin and so forth downstairs, but it was upsetting."

Nick got a straight look from the woman and realized that he had been warned.

"Oh, Nicky knows all about morgues," said Glasco, patting him on the shoulder. "I don't think we have to worry about him losing it down there."

She led them out of the waiting area, through double doors and into a corridor where she had to duck into an office to answer the phone.

"I'm sorry," she said, waving them on, "I have to take this."

They passed through another set of double doors and then started down a flight of steps. It got chilly, then meat-locker cold, as they pushed through more doors into a brightly lit basement. The center was taken up by a block of cold cabinets, the square doors marked with cheap adhesive numbers of the kind you found on mailboxes in low-rent suburbia. Nick registered blue ceramic tile that looked like it had been applied to the walls forty years ago. The floor was wet. A lemony smell of cleaning products didn't quite mask the cadaver smell. Two battered gurneys had been parked in a corner. It looked like business was over for the day.

Rounding the central island of cabinets, they found Kadomato, the doctor, perspiring despite the chilled air. Glasco did the introductions, said Nick was helping them with their investigations. All the time he was talking, Kadomato kept his eyes on Nick's face. He was straining for something like professional coolness, but it was clear he was very unhappy.

"It's not every day a member of the public questions my work," he said.

Nick shrugged, unable to speak, already preparing himself for what came next.

The body came out on a sliding rack.

Nick told himself he had already done this, took a breath, forced himself to look down, saw—in quick succession, his gaze unable to settle at first—a puffy, half-closed, lusterless eye, the other tight shut, bared bloody teeth, tobacco-stained, twisted, in brown, blotchy gums. The lower jaw had sunk a little, changing the shape of the face. The chin and the cheeks were sprinkled with stubble, silvery under the neon. Along the Y incision, postexamination stitching had snagged the flesh into a puckered welt, pulling the left nipple across towards the sternum.

Then Nick saw the wounds between the thighs, and suddenly it was all too much. A sourness flooded his mouth, and he thought he was going to throw up. He closed his eyes, swaying slightly. When he opened them again, he met Glasco's stare head-on.

"Gettin' you hard yet, Nicky?"

Nick opened his mouth, but the words stuck in his throat.

Glasco bumped the rack with his groin.

"So?"

Nick stepped back from the body and took a breath.

"I need you to turn it over."

Daylight filtered in through frosted glass windows lighting eight steel tables, each equipped with a set of scales and a body block. With the help of an assistant, Kadomato laid Grossman's body out face-down.

Shadows moved past the windows high up in the wall. There was a muffled sound of feet pounding the sidewalk.

Kadomato flipped on a light.

Grossman's back was puckered and blotched with acid burns, ripped in places so that dark muscle tissue showed through. Seeing him laid out there, Nick was surprised by a sudden rush of pity as he recalled the pictures from *Life* magazine, the smiling young man with the thick blond hair. Grossman had been twenty-one years old when he first met Spira.

The body had been washed. With so much to look at—gouging, tearing, burning—it wasn't surprising that Kadomato had missed the important detail. Either that or the important detail, the thing Nick had crossed the Atlantic to see, wasn't there.

Kadomato took up a position on the other side of the table, alertly watchful as though he thought Nick might cheat somehow, might do something to the body that would then justify his ridiculous claims.

Nick bent farther forward, a hand over his mouth and nose.

"See anything you like, Nicky?"

Glasco again, standing behind him.

Nick walked around the table. Nobody said a word as he bent forward frowning, trying to follow an imaginary line down from the right shoulder in an area he would expect to find the cut. He moved slowly, examining the tortured flesh inch by inch—a gouged wound so deep a rib was visible, a flap of skin that curled like a breaking wave, a gray area of burnt flesh.

Then he saw it, thought he saw it, lost it again, *saw it*, reached.

Kadomato grabbed his hand.

Nick looked up. Kadomato was staring down at the area Nick had been examining, the flesh between his brows bunched in an angry frown. He was looking, but he still couldn't see it, and he couldn't see it because he didn't know what he was looking for.

Glasco came forward into the light.

Nick pulled free of Kadomato's grip and walked away from the table, euphoria rising through him like a soft, slow flame. It was true. He was right. About everything.

"What is it?" said Glasco.

Nick turned to face him.

"You'd better talk now, Nicky."

"There's a cut."

Glasco brought his hands together in front of him.

"There are cuts everywhere."

Nick came back across the room and looked into the cop's tired red eyes.

"A different kind of cut," he said.

He pointed at the spot where the incision was just visible in the sub-cutaneous tissue. A straight line ran parallel to the spine. He followed it with his finger to where it disappeared in a burn. Then followed an imaginary line until he reached another incision, a continuation of the same incision, in fact.

Kadomato pushed him away and leaned forward, spreading the stiff puttylike flesh with his fingers. The cut was arrow-straight, not deep, but regular.

"He was hiding something," said Nick. "Not bite marks. Incisions."

33

At three o'clock in the morning Eugene was still sitting at his desk, the Guggenheim catalogue open in front of him, too tired to move or think, too stirred up to contemplate sleep. He flipped pages as he ran the tape. They'd printed the thing on thick creamy paper, had done something clever with a grainy laminate to get Spira's spiral monogram to loom through Frank Lloyd Wright's coiling ramp. It was all very classy, down to the moody black and whites of the artist standing outside the Guggenheim back in 1965.

Greer had talked for hours, had taken them through thirty years of detail, from the collapse of the elevator through every twist and turn. The story of the *Incarnation*.

So, Nick. What are you saying? Bittaker is the Collector? Or just some kind of enforcer?

Greer laughing then, the laugh sounding to Eugene just a little forced.

That's what I'm trying to tell you: I have no idea.

For three hours they'd questioned him. Most people would have complained. But not Greer. Greer was too slick for that. He knew when to roll. The fact was he'd had a very good day. He'd gotten what he'd come for. He'd gotten his proof.

There were more photographs, many taken by Jacob Grossman. They showed Spira at different stages in his career. This little guy with glassy, hypnotic eyes. Even in old black and whites, you felt their pull.

The color plates ran chronologically. A whole lifetime of daubing on canvas. Some of the pictures had a weird boxlike quality. These boxes in which crimes of one sort or another were being perpetrated.

There was a picture of a guy dying on the john with a spike in his arm. A masterpiece, according to the commentary, but Eugene couldn't see it. He stared, blinking eyes that were raw from lack of sleep, but saw nothing more than a sick, smeary daub. A guy on a john in a room with no carpet. Evidence littered the floor. Discarded clothing, a syringe.

Ray came out of the bathroom drying his hands.

"You planning on going home?"

Eugene stopped the tape. He watched Ray put on his jacket.

"Do you believe him?" he said.

Ray paused, one arm caught in his sleeve.

"You should go home, Eugene. You're not going to listen to the whole thing again."

"You didn't answer my question."

Ray shrugged himself into his jacket and went over to the water cooler.

"The skin thing kind of fits," he said. "The Titunik testimony. If this turns out to be some kind of Edward Gein deal—if the guy is harvesting skin, I mean—then I guess he's keeping it cold. He cuts it, rolls it up, puts it in this thermos."

"You salt a skin," said Eugene, rubbing at his eyes. "You kill a deer and take the hide off, you salt it."

"You can freeze it too. One or the other. Depending on what's easiest. And if you don't salt it, you don't have to spend time getting the salt out of the skin afterwards."

"Anyway, that's not—that wasn't my question. I was asking you whether you believe Greer. Whether you think he's—"

"Shooting straight?" Ray crumpled his cup and dropped it into the trash. "What difference does it make? Whether I believe him or not. It doesn't get us any closer to Bittaker."

He turned, on his way home now.

"Get some sleep, Eugene."

"I'm gonna fax his fingerprints to Ahmed. See if he was lying to us about being out at Cap Spartel."

Ray pulled up short. He looked at his watch and sighed.

"What time is it in Tangier?" he said.

34

The day of the Guggenheim opening, Nick was on the phone first thing calling Manhattan-based companies offering 8mm-to-video transfer services. There were more than a dozen listed in the Yellow Pages, but, one after another, they turned him down. The fact that he just wanted to sit and watch a film made people uneasy. Then he got lucky. This character down in the West Village who didn't seem to care one way or the other.

"So you don't actually want a transfer at all?"

"All I need is a projector, a screen and some privacy."

"What are we talking about, like a snuff movie?" The guy did a kind of Beavis and Butthead snigger.

"It's tied up with something I'm doing for a client. Hence the need for privacy."

"Hence—what are you, some kind of cop? A private dick?"

"Kind of." There was a pause, and for a second Nick thought he'd blown it. "There's about four hundred feet of film," he said. "I don't suppose it'll take too long."

"Twenty minutes. Give or take."

The guy told him to bring it down to his place. They could talk about money there. Nick figured he wanted to see what kind of degenerate he was dealing with. He said he'd be there in an hour, hung up, then redialed.

It took the woman at the Smithsonian five minutes to locate George Addison's name on a list, but then he was through, talking a mile a minute. Once Addison remembered who he was, he relaxed, became the friendly old guy Nick remembered. He wanted to know how the book was going, who was going to be publishing Nick in the States. Nick said that was yet to be decided.

"Mr. Addison, I'm calling about the material you recently acquired from the Taubmann estate."

"Oh, you heard about that."

"I know you only just got hold of the stuff, but—well, I'm particularly interested in the travelogue that Laverne Taubmann had in her hands when she died."

There was a long silence. Nick heard Addison clear his throat, then softly, and very mildly, curse.

"It's always the same when we acquire something."

"Pardon me?"

"There's this sudden explosion of interest, and then, once it's in the catalogue, everything goes quiet."

"It's a little niggling thing."

"Do you know how many separate items we have at the Archive of American Art? Thirteen million. Documents, diaries, material like this that doesn't get consulted from one decade to the next. But as soon as we show an interest in something, people come out of the woodwork."

"People? Anyone in particular?"

"No, no. I'm just saying—they think that if we think it's important enough to buy, it's important enough to study. Word gets around like you wouldn't believe. We have graduates, doctorates, professors—all these text-starved academics looking for something to annotate."

"It would only take a second. The thing is, I'm very close to publication with my book, and there's a blank I need to fill in."

"A blank."

"All I'm asking is for you to turn to the last page. Do you have the travelogue with you?"

It sounded like Addison had dropped the phone.

"Mr. Addison?"

With all the street noise coming in through the open window, it was difficult to tell what was going on at the other end. Then the old man was back, breathing into the mouthpiece.

"I'll have to call you back."

Nick stood at the window looking west onto back lots and blind brick walls. Low cloud hung like smoke over the city, but the air was tropically warm.

The phone rang.

"So—what is it you're looking for?"

"I want you to turn to the last page. The last entry, I mean. I think it probably dates back to 1975."

He could hear pages turning. There was another soft curse.

"Mr. Addison?"

"Yes, yes, forgive me. What did you want to know?"

"Is there something wrong?"

"No—well, it's just that there's a—there was a card here. I can't seem to . . ."

Nick nodded to himself. The greeting card. It had doubtless fallen into Marion's pocket.

"Is something missing?" he said.

"A greeting card. It's probably not important, but it was there and now it isn't. Now, what is it you wanted to know?"

Nick asked a bogus question about the date and nature of the last entry in the travelogue.

"Are you turning up any gems?" said Nick when they were done.

"Gems? Oh, I don't know. This travelogue looks interesting. But at this stage we're producing an inventory. That's all. The significance of any given document won't become apparent until later. Once people like you start in with the scholarship."

"If we're not too late by then."

"Pardon me?"

"Well, I'll be honest with you. I can't help feeling a little miffed that Martin Marion's going to get first look. Seems a little unfair on us mere mortals."

Addison grumbled something incoherent about friends in high places. He didn't sound too happy about the situation either.

"High places?" said Nick.

"Nick, I don't want to get into any kind of internecine gossip."

"Sure. I understand." The man was on the brink of an indiscretion. Nick could hear the dissatisfaction in his voice. He just needed a push. "Still," he said, "with all the rumors going around, you can't help wondering."

"Rumors?"

Tell a lie. Improvise.

"I was at a dinner party last week, and someone—well, they were saying that money had changed hands. That Marion had—"

"That's—that's *utter* nonsense!"

"Well, I'm glad to hear you say that. Because for people like me, and there are plenty of us, that would be pretty discouraging."

"I can assure you there was nothing of that sort. At least not to my knowledge. There may have been a certain amount of string pulling, but—"

"Strings were pulled? Who by?"

Addison sighed into the mouthpiece.

"Look at the Board of Regents," he said. "Take a wild guess."

And he hung up.

Nick sat on the bed looking at the phone in his hand. The Board of Regents sat at the top of the Smithsonian hierarchy. Someone on the board had gotten Marion in through the front door despite Gael Taubmann's well-publicized hostility.

He took a cab down to the West Village, where the film guy conducted business out of a converted produce store. Nick had to push packages out of the way with his foot just to get the street door open. The place was a fire hazard, every inch of wall space covered by peeling posters, the blocky, jagged titles peeking out between stacked film canisters, cameras, projectors, editing equipment.

The guy came out from behind the counter followed by a poodle.

"I called earlier," said Nick.

"Right, yeah." The guy gave a short, dipping nod, checking Nick out, his dark eyes working under a tight leather beret that compressed the skin of his forehead. He wore a fanny pack that was all zips and flaps. It bristled with keys, tools, cellphone and pager. "So . . . ?" He pointed at the film Nick was holding.

"Like I say, it's about four hundred feet of Regular 8."

"Yeah?"

"It was filmed in France in the late fifties."

The guy checking him out, still nodding. Film that old, how bad could it be?

"My dog's French," he said, apparently for something to say. "Monsieur Tooks. He's a terrible snob." Then the nodding stopped. "I got a room back through here. But it's gonna cost ya."

Nick followed him into the back of the shop, trying not to step on the dog. There were more canisters, more posters—*The Invisible Man*, *Plan 9 from Outer Space*, *The Mighty Gorga*.

"Posters," said the guy over his shoulder. "That's my partner's thing. Me, I collect film. Eight mil, sixteen mil."

"You have quite a collection."

"Started in the seventies. I have *King Kong* on eight-millimeter. I have *Journey to the Center of Time*, *The Iron Maiden*. Eight-reelers."

He opened the door of what looked like a storeroom. A wire-glass window set high in the wall had been painted over. There was a couch and a coffee table. Pieces of garden furniture. A couple of projectors were set up in front of a small screen. Bits of another projector were spread out on a plastic sheet in the corner.

"Fifty dollars," said the guy.

Nick pulled out five bills, then added another. "I may need to watch it a couple of times."

"I'll give you an hour."

Nick watched him thread film through the gate and clip it into a second empty reel.

"When you switch it on, give this reel a turn with your hand. Make sure the film's feeding through. You gotta be careful it doesn't come off the sprocket, get stuck in the gate. That happens, the lamp's gonna burn your film. Other than that, it's pretty straightforward."

A thumping sound started up. The whole building shook.

"The train," said the guy. "Nothing to worry about."

It was quiet with the door closed. Nick pulled one of the aluminum garden chairs into the middle of the room, then switched on the projector.

35

Raymond didn't get to work until after ten and, walking into the office, half-expected to find Eugene already at his desk. But apart from Patti Bonner, buried as usual in a mountain of paperwork, the room was empty.

Bonner looked up as he came in through the door.

"He's in with the lieutenant," she said before Ray could even open his mouth. "There's been some kind of break in the Grossman case."

Ray slipped out of his jacket and walked on through, found Bob Mellor's door half open and Eugene sitting with a stack of papers on his lap. He was unshaven and bleary-eyed, had obviously been up all night.

"Ahmed found a match for the prints I sent him," he said as Ray came into the room.

"Greer's prints?"

"That's right. On the car."

Ray took a seat.

"Which car?"

"The car at the scene, Ray. The car out at Cap Spartel."

Eugene turned back to face Mellor—the lieutenant very sharp this morning in the lightweight wool suit he wore for court appearances. His shirt cuffs looked tight on his wrists.

"Clean matches," said Eugene. "Bloody prints. Reardon's blood and hair. Inside the car. Outside the car. All over."

Mellor nodded, looking unimpressed though.

"I know what D.A. Hirshorn is going to say," he said wearily. "He's going to say Tangier is in Morocco."

Eugene shot Ray a so-help-me look and raked at chin bristle.

"Okay," said Mellor, squeezing up his shoulders like someone trying to get through a gap in a fence. "Let's say you find out what Greer was doing in Tangier."

"At Cap Spartel."

"You find out what he was doing at this Cap Spartel, which is probably not murder, right? You don't think Greer's the killer?"

"No." Eugene tugged at his collar. "Accessory, possibly. I think he—"

"You find out about his movements in Tangier." Mellor tilted his head to one side. "How does that concern this jurisdiction?"

"I think we can make a good case for these murders being related," said Eugene. "And if we can link Grossman to—"

"Related? Based on . . . ?"

"On what was done to the bodies. On the shared history of the victims. On the story of this . . ." Eugene puckered his lips, staring. He still hadn't found an easy way to describe the thing itself, the *work*.

Mellor sighed. He leaned forward, putting his face in his hands.

"Correct me if I'm wrong, Eugene, but this is a story that goes back maybe thirty years, a story that is—Jesus, *complicated* doesn't really cover it. This is a story that has only come to light because of Mr. Greer's research." He peeped at Eugene through his fingers. "I mean, what are you telling me? You're planning on calling the accused as an expert witness in support of the prosecution's case?"

He pushed back from the desk, shaking his head.

"We can put pressure on him now," said Raymond. "He lied to us."

Mellor shook his head.

"He's just going to clam up."

"We read him his rights," said Eugene. "Tell him we're arresting him as an accessory to murder. Tell him the Moroccans have instituted extradition proceedings. We tell him that if he helps us out at this early stage, it'll look good for him. If he thinks he's in deep enough, if he thinks he's getting the shitty end of the stick, maybe he'll talk. Maybe he'll point the finger, tell us what's really going on, starting with what the fuck he was doing at the crime scene in Tangier."

Eugene took a breath and sat back in his chair.

For a moment nobody spoke.

"Don't think I don't sympathize," said Mellor.

"So we sit on this?" said Eugene, looking at the papers in his lap.

Mellor came forward in his chair, putting his elbows on the desk.

"Eugene," he said. "Bottom line. Short of finding this—this *work*, I don't see you going anywhere with this thing."

36

The film went through with a stitching sound. Then Nick was looking at scratchy nothing—a slow pan of rooftops, TV antennae, washing on a line, a palm tree. Pink dawn light flared in the camera.

He backed towards the door and slapped off the lights.

Laverne Taubmann at the wheel of a car, in her early forties, maybe—still a good-looking woman, a pale green scarf ripping out behind her. The camera jolted, panned, found a group of women by the roadside, lost them in a cloud of dust. A red road disappearing in a cloud of red dust.

Jump cut: Laverne again, driving slowly now, just cruising along, a slow pan across to the person in the seat next to her. Nick recognized the hair—pomaded, slicked back in a DA like a forties hoodlum. A white shirt. Spira. Franky, taking a spin in a rented Merc.

Nick wanted to rewind, to rerun the first images, but this was film, he remembered. There was no way back.

The building started to shake as a train rumbled through.

Jump: a room somewhere. A patch of light on a rug.

Jump: a street scene. The Rue d'Angleterre? Yes. A shot of the inside of the apartment. A slow pan, underexposed. Things on a wall. Pictures.

A close-up out of focus, then in focus. A picture. A young girl.

Nick jolted in the lawn chair, saw what looked like the head of a baby coming out from between a young woman's legs. No hair, no ears. Dark, cantaloupe-smooth. Not a baby. Something else.

Sun on a rug. A slow pan—Frank reading a heavy book, sitting next to the window. Saying something to the camera, standing up.

The camera followed him across the room. He squatted down in front of a wooden box on the floor and took out a flashlight. Not a flashlight. He held the thing on his groin, holding it like a dildo.

Nick put a hand to his mouth.

Laverne in a chair. From behind. Reardon holding her head and Spira frowning, concentrating, doing something to her face that Nick couldn't see. Her head jerking, Spira shouting silently.

Hurting her.

The building shuddered with the rhythmic thump of the train.

Laverne's face filled the screen. Puffy. Glass eyes. Nobody home. Bringing a reefer to her lips. No, someone putting the reefer to her lips. A man's grimy fingers. She sucked the pinched end. The paper coming away bloody. Laughing smoke into the air, something wrong with her mouth.

The camera jerked away. Back.

Bloodshot eyes adrift, fixing on the lens. She put a finger into her lip.

Nick swallowed, dry-mouthed.

Jump cut: lens flare, white to black, then Laverne on a bed, naked on her hands and knees. Reardon behind, his dick, long, dark, tapered like a bull's, fucking her *hard*, his chest covered with marks, like welts from a beating. Not welts, a design. A drawing.

Laverne asleep, pink drool coming from her closed mouth.

Jump: Laverne sucking a cock, blood on her chin.

Jump: Laverne looking into the lens, her mouth puffy, discolored. Exhaling smoke, putting a finger into her lip, pulling down.

Inside out, the lip flared pink in the white face.

Through the smoke Nick saw what was marked there.

Fifth Avenue pointed uptown, funneling fumes and people. Nick was up around 42nd, following the flow on rubbery legs, dazed, poisoned by gassy air, by the heat. Above the buildings, the sky was darkly condensed, but the sun was burning somewhere, flaming in windows and glazed brick, striking fiery lines in brass and bronze. Street sounds came through muffled, like noise from the surface of whatever it was he was drowning in. The film was back in his pocket—all that misery and humiliation wound tightly in its little yellow box, wound tightly like the mark inside Laverne Taubmann's mouth.

He knew what had driven her into the desert now. The woman Lee

Lassiter had found in the bar in Meknes was stunned with pain, branded like a steer. She had gone to Spira, vulnerable and confused, and had come away . . . It was hard to give a word to what Spira had done to her. He had broken her and made her into something else.

Nick came to a halt in the middle of the sidewalk. Someone cursed him, brushing past. It was exactly what Tate Hemmings had said. Exactly that. Spira. The Anti-Midas. The sorcerer king inverted. He had touched Laverne and, lo, she was excrement. He had made her and, as with all his works, had marked her with his coil. Nick brought a hand to his mouth, tugged at his lip, stalled there in the street, imbecilic, picturing Grossman, standing in the middle of the room at the Delancey-Deere, and Reardon, dead on the table in Tangier. It was the monogram the Collector had wanted, the monogram he had taken. Because, after all, what value was a Spira without his mark?

37

Murray Hill rippled above massed traffic, the apartment buildings stacked like kiln bricks in the blank light. Crawling towards the Queens Midtown Tunnel, Eugene blinked sweat out of his eyes, cursing under his breath. He was sick of it, sick to death of it all. Big Bob Mellor had suggested he might usefully spend the next few days helping Ray prepare his trip to Portland, Oregon, which was scheduled for next Wednesday. A scumbag currently residing in Attica State wanted to share his thoughts on the murder of a twelve-year-old Chinese-American girl they'd pulled out of the East River ten years ago. Mellor's message had been clear: the Sally Wong murder might be old business, but it was business they could finish.

Meanwhile the Spiraphiles could throw their party and get on with whatever fucked-up games they felt like. Eugene grabbed the catalogue and opened it on his lap. It seemed he couldn't stop touching the damned thing. He'd had it in the car only a couple of days, but already it was splashed and stained. He flipped through images, lifting his foot off the brake from time to time to gain another few yards.

A rap on the window brought his head up. A kid with a bundle of the *Daily News* under his arm was staring in at him. Eugene was about to wave him on when he saw a headline: MAYOR SLAMS SICK ART. He lowered the window, letting in a blast of superheated air.

"Do you know that's illegal?" he said.

The kid squinted at him in the heat. There was something wrong with his left eye. It was streaming and the bottom lid looked raw.

"What are you, a cop?"

"Yeah."

Eugene shook his head, then pushed a dollar bill into the kid's grimy hand, told him to keep the change.

The article was short and shrill. The gist of it: that while attending some fancy fund-raiser, the mayor had asked someone how it was that public funds were used to support exhibitions that the public found offensive. Asked if he had any particular exhibition in mind, he'd named the Spira show.

"Damn right," said Eugene.

There were some figures on an inside page—a breakdown of individual and corporate sponsorship, ticket sales versus government funds.

A horn sounded close behind. *Faaaaaaaaaarp.* Eugene looked up. The car ahead of him had rolled forward another ten feet. The driver behind leaned on his horn again. *Faaaaaaaaarp-faaaaaarp.* The guy didn't want any spaces. Spaces were slowing him down. Eugene took his foot off the brake, then looked back at the report, but he'd lost his place now. Then he saw a subheading in bold type: "Guggenheim Patron Has Cancer." He frowned, leaning forward against his seat belt, saw Oscar Nagel's name.

> Oscar Nagel, probably the foremost collector of Spira's works, confirmed rumors of his illness Thursday, saying that it was time to end speculation that had been growing in recent days. "This will probably be my last public appearance," he said. "I started with Spira and I can think of no better way to finish." He also said that in addition to *Cupid,* and four major works from the *Screaming Heads* series, he will be contributing two as yet unexhibited drawings from the artist's difficult Tangier period. Executed in colored ink on vellum, the drawings are said to recall the spirit of the much earlier *Cupid* painting, for many people Spira's masterpiece.

The horn was sounding again. Eugene looked in his rearview mirror, saw the guy talking into his cellphone, talking and laughing, his other hand pumping rhythmically at the wheel. A big guy with epaulets on his shirt.

"All right already!"

Eugene lifted his foot and inched forward into the space ahead of him. Then put the newspaper on the passenger seat and opened the catalogue, flipping through the color plates to 1957.

"Tangier," he said under his breath. "Tangier." He had no recollection of drawings. On vellum or otherwise.

There was only one entry: *Figure of Man on a Mountain Road.* No reference to any drawings. Eugene dabbed at his forehead with his sleeve, turning pages, seeing more reproductions, then a detailed chronology with illustrations—source material recovered from the Fig Tree studio, photographs, bits of text.

He reached the last page.

Faaaarp-faaarp-faaaaaaaaaarp.

The unbound folio came away in his hand.

It was on the same heavy stock, the pages printed exactly as per the catalogue, each page showing a color plate. Marked at the top of the page: "Addendum to page 233" and below that, "Study I, 1957, ink on vellum, 18" x 13" (private collection)." On the opposite page: "Study II, ink on vellum, 15" x 12" (private collection)."

Faaaaaaaaaaaaaaaaaaaaaaaarp.

Eugene took his cellphone, eyes in his mirror. He punched buttons, saw the guy wind down his window to lean out—the guy yelling now, letting him have it.

Eugene's phone was dead.

He got out of the car.

The street was surprising: the heat, the noise. The people behind the crazy guy were also honking on their horns now. A wave of noise. This much rage and frustration for what must have been twenty feet of space.

Eugene tucked in his chin, seeing the guy open his door, seeing a foot come out. The guy ready to get into it, to mix it up right there. A big guy in some kind of security guard outfit.

Eugene showed him his badge.

"Sir?" he said.

The guy sat back in his seat, his mouth coming open.

"Detective Eugene Glasco. I noticed you were using your cellphone while driving the car."

The guy swallowed.

Eugene put out his hand.

"Can I look at it for a second?"

The guy handed him the phone. Eugene walked away from the car. He called Ray, listened to the dial tone with a finger in his ear.

Ray's voice was barely audible.

"Ray, it's me, Eugene."

"What's going on? Sounds like an air raid."

Eugene looked back along the street at the traffic.

"What do you know about vellum?" he said.

38

Someone had set fire to a trash can in Central Park. The drifting haze gave the Guggenheim the look of a docked cruise ship in the early evening gloom and smudged the taillights of the limos swooping in to drop people off. Standing on the other side of the street, breathing tainted air, Nick watched the collectors arrive, saw black doors flare like lustrous wings, saw a bodyguard emerge, closely followed by the bodies themselves in a soft blooming of linen and silk. Some publicist had been spinning his Rolodex. It was more like a premiere than the opening night of a retrospective. Flashguns glittered, strobing a Hollywood princess and her mogul husband, freezing a dot-com zillionaire with his sitcom-star girlfriend. Some faces Nick recognized—the older people for the most part, some of them outright seniors bent with age. They were the venerable Spiraphiles. He knew their homes and their lifestyles, their pets and their illnesses; knew everything from his years of working the *Life.*

Crossing the street, he wondered what they'd say if they knew about the *Incarnation,* about what Frank had done to Laverne, wondered if they'd be here anyway, smiling their complicit smiles as they funneled into the stacked hive of light.

One night with Venus. He knew who'd written it now. Thought he did, anyway.

The air was full of perfume and greetings. Everyone knew everyone. Everyone was delighted. A guy with a wire in his ear eyed Nick's invitation, then pointed him in the direction of the massed bodies cramming the entrance.

He felt a pressure against his chest.

"Nicholas Greer?"

A small, gingery woman with pleading eyes was looking up at him, a crooked smile on her face.

"Miriam Florey?" she said. "The *New York Times?*" She pointed back past herself at the crowd on the sidewalk, explaining something, laughing. Nick nodded, understanding nothing. All around him people were grinning, excited by the comedy of having so much money and being crushed like shoppers at a sale. Someone grabbed his hand, asked him when they could expect to see the book in the stores.

"I guess it's all the celebs," said Florey, sticking close as they worked through into the light.

Above the crowd a black-and-white photograph blown up to grainy indistinctness hung like a banner. Nick recognized it immediately: Spira and Grossman sitting in the shade of a date palm. The last time he'd seen it, the image had been in Linda's hand.

Linda. Only a few weeks ago they'd been living together in the basement. Nick found himself holding a glass of champagne, took a sip, then drained the rest in one gulp. It made no difference. His mouth felt like it was lined with ashes. And now that he was here, he didn't know why he had come. To confront Nagel? To ask him why he'd written the card? Florey's mouth worked darkly in her pale, perspiring face. She was saying something about some drawings.

"Martin Marion says they're of immense importance."

"Nick!"

A perfumed cheek bumped his. Then Barb swam into focus, staring at him through her brows like some vaudeville mind-reader.

"I've been calling you," she shouted, the sinews in her neck jumping tight with each word. "I left messages at your hotel."

Nick tried to say something, but there was a surge in the noise, a sudden tidal roar. He looked around him at the other shouting people, then up at the tiered, winding gallery. Spots sizzled on his retina, and he thought he was going to black out.

"In *New York* magazine," said Florey. "Of course, it's terribly self-promoting. So-and-so admitted to me in the strictest confidence, etc. There's an extract from his new book."

"What I don't understand is why Oscar kept them secret all these years," said Barb.

"Kept what secret?" said Florey.

"These drawings."

"There are some legal issues, apparently."

"Which drawings?" said Nick.

Florey squinted up at him.

"From Tangier. Don't say you haven't heard?"

"Where on earth have you been these past few days?" said Barb. "It's all anyone's talking about. That and the Walrus's new book."

"Nagel purchased them when he was down there in 'fifty-eight," Florey went on. "Apparently there's some question as to whether or not the Cork Street gallery already owned them. Frank had been paid an advance, you see."

"Drawings," said Nick.

"Yes," said Florey. "Some people are making comparisons with *Cupid*. They're extraordinarily powerful."

"You've seen them?" said Barb.

"The Guggenheim people showed us around earlier. The press, I mean. We're running some color photos in this weekend's *Times*." Florey pointed a finger at one of the upper tiers where a crowd had gathered. "They're up there."

Nick tilted back, slower this time, taking in the great expanding, light-filled funnel. Faces showed dark against the blinding white, people waved.

"Apparently Martin Marion dug up some documents at Laverne Taubmann's residence," said Florey. "Letters from Spira to Max in which he wrote about Nagel acquiring these works. Anyway, Marion confronted Nagel, and Nagel decided to come clean, decided in fact that it was time to show them. If not now, when, right? Of course, the Guggenheim people were delighted to make room."

Barb said something about the Cork Street gallery and Quentin Blair, but Nick found it impossible to follow. Florey was pulling at his arm again.

"So, Nick, I just wanted your comment."

"My comment."

"You see, I can't help feeling that Spira's use of vellum was a response to the—to the sensuality of that time and place. All that casual nudity. In the hamams, on the beaches. I think it must have opened something up in him. Because otherwise—ink on vellum? Which is what I wanted to—oh, could you just . . ."

She turned from him, then moved away, heading for a tight knot of people that had formed on the other side of the room. Nick passed a hand over his face, saw Marion, the great man towering over the crowd in a rumpled linen suit. There was a woman with him: elderly, elegant. Lyn Mortenson. Marion's agent.

"He sold his book?" said Nick.

Barb shook her head, a disgusted look on her face.

"There was an auction," she said. "Lots of hype. Of course, this news about the drawings just *happened* to break as Mortenson went into the market."

"Who bought it?" he said.

"Crucible, I think. High six figures, supposedly. But they always inflate things for the press." Barb narrowed her eyes. "So, Nick? Where *have* you been? The last time I saw you, you were on your way to beat the truth out of Gallagher."

Nick raised his eyes to the upper tiers again, saw a feather come floating down, a feather or a piece of paper. A business card, perhaps. Crucible had bought Marion's book. Did that mean he was without a buyer? Another card came spinning down. Nick blinked, struggling to focus, aware of Barb's voice close by. There were drawings up there. Ink on vellum. Drawings on vellum that Nagel had acquired in Tangier.

"Drawings," he said under his breath.

"So?" said Barb. "Did she say anything? About the greeting card? About Laverne's thing with Nagel? The dangerous liaison."

Une nuit avec Vénus . . .

"In 'fifty-eight?" he said.

"What?"

"That was when Nagel bought these drawings?"

"There's no point in trying to keep it a secret," said Barb, flashing him a conspiratorial look. "You see, I've been doing a little research on my own."

Nick looked up again, blinked, swayed. He couldn't quite bring himself to believe what had happened—what was happening. Another card came sailing down. Barb was an insistent pressure on his arm.

"Is this your blood sugar thing again? You need to eat. Cold cuts are floating around somewhere."

Cold cuts. Nick's gut twitched. He swallowed ashes.

"Look, Nick. I know how Marion got into Laverne's apartment. Nick?"

He turned and looked into her filmy eyes.

"I mean into that whole situation," she said. "I know who's been pulling strings at the Smithsonian."

"Cy Lockhart," he said.

Barb leaned away from him, her mouth dropping open.

"You know? You knew?"

"Uh-huh."

At some point in the middle of the afternoon's dazed stumble through the city, he'd walked into an Internet café and surfed his way to the Smithsonian Web site. *Look at the Board of Regents,* Addison had said, and that was exactly what he had done. Lockhart's name had jumped right off the screen.

Barb was saying something about proof, her face in his face, shaking her head in disbelief.

"What proof of what?" he said, looking away. The gallery's spiral ramp coiled up from the ground floor, but there was a crowd at the bottom. You'd have to fight your way through.

"Proof that Nagel's involved," said Barb.

A tray appeared. A platter. Sushi. Sashimi. Nick grabbed a piece and pushed it into his mouth.

"That Nagel was the one who wrote the 'One night with Venus' thing," said Barb, cramming something pink and glossy between her lips.

Nick shook his head, grabbed another piece, lost the rice, saw it fall, saw it roll. It was trampled underfoot. The problem was that Lockhart's being on the Board of Regents didn't *prove* anything. It suggested a link between Marion's appearance at the Taubmann residence and Nagel, perhaps, but it didn't tie anything down. You would need the card for that. The card itself. Physical evidence, with Nagel's handwriting on it. And even then, the card would prove only that Nagel sent Laverne a card on her sixtieth birthday. It didn't prove that he knew what had happened to her in Tangier.

On the other side of the gallery a line was forming by the elevator. People were riding up to the top of the spiral ramp, then walking down through Frank's life and work. Helter-skelter. Barb moved in closer, too close, her whispered words coming in a wash of gassy breath.

"Let's say Nagel got wind of this blackmail business, guessed that it had to do with him and Laverne—with their liaison. He hears about the card Laverne keeps in Max's travelogue and, realizing that the Smithsonian people are going to get first bite at the cherry, he calls

Lockhart and asks him if maybe Marion could go in with Addison and, you know, destroy the evidence." She increased the pressure on his arm. "I mean, Marion with all his scholarly clout, and his—his interests, could be expected to want to get his foot in the—"

Nick pushed away from her, pushed her harder than he meant to. He saw her startled face, held up a hand in apology as he moved away.

Even with the top button undone, Eugene felt like he was suffocating. The Crown Vic's AC was on the fritz, blowing hot like a goddam hair dryer.

Ray was looking at the warrant.

"All I'm saying is, if you're wrong about this—"

"I'm not wrong." Eugene tightened his grip on the wheel. "I'm telling you. You look at these so-called drawings, and . . ."

"And what?"

"You *know*." Eugene looked out at the free-for-all of Times Square. You knew. He knew. He hadn't known to start with, but then he'd made a couple of phone calls, found out a little about vellum, how it was made. After that he'd found it was impossible to look at the pictures and *not* see. "And they're the right size," he said. "The bigger one is anyway."

The catalogue said 18" x 13". Ad Kadomato estimated that the section of skin removed from Jacob Grossman's back was closer to 15" x 10", but the skin was stretched. You pegged it on a frame as part of the curing process. Everyone knew that. Eugene had sent a fax to Tangier, asking the coroner there to take another look at Reardon's body, see if he could make out anything like the rectangle found on Grossman. So far he hadn't heard back.

"Plus, Spira didn't work on vellum," said Eugene, twisting his hands on the wheel. "None of those guys did. That was monks in the Middle Ages."

"So, what, you're an art expert now?"

"I've read the literature, Ray. I know the work."

"But Nagel, he'd have to be crazy. He'd have to be out of his mind."

Eugene looked across at him, tugging at his collar.

"Sure. Why not? You telling me it's normal behavior to have screaming fucking heads on your wall? He thinks he's above the law,

Ray. He thinks we're all down here in the dirt fucking and fighting for his amusement. *Nostalgie de la boue,* they call it."

"Nostal-what?"

"It's in the catalogue. It's French. We long for the mud we crawled out of."

Ray just stared.

"Then there's this whole cancer situation to consider." Eugene made a sharp turn, pinching a squeak out of the tires. "It's in the *New York Daily News*. Oral cancer. Fucker's already dead. What does he care? Or maybe it went to his brain, so he doesn't even realize."

"But why not wait until tomorrow?" said Ray. "I mean, the pictures are still gonna be there. We could wait until there's no one around. Go in after hours, for chrissake. Do this thing quietly. Leave ourselves a way out."

Eugene grabbed the warrant and stuffed it into his pocket.

"That's what Big Bob said."

"Well?"

"Ray, this is dead guys' skins on a wall. This is the sickest fucking thing—the sickest *homicide* I've seen in over thirty years on the job. A double homicide. For the sake of some pictures."

"So Bob okayed it?"

"He said it was my call."

Eugene tucked his chin in tight.

"So we are making arrests, and we are seizing those pictures, and if Oscar Nagel or Cy Lockhart or Nicky fucking Greer don't like it, they can—well, they can scream." He laughed then, seeing it, loving the idea of it. "Yeah, that's right. They can all scream together. Hey, maybe it'll be perfect."

Nick backed into the elevator, pushed sideways in the polite crush, thinking that one thing was clear: he had to go take a look. Before he did anything else—called the cops, called Henry, put a word down on paper—he had to be sure. Because maybe he was wrong. Maybe this was just a couple of drawings. He'd take a look and he'd know. Because it would be clear, wouldn't it? And then he'd call Glasco. And after that?

The elevator began its climb.

He'd lose the story.

That was what would happen. It would slip away from him—the whys, the wherefores, how it had all come about. If Nagel chose to talk, his confession would be a matter of police record. From there it would percolate through to the national media. He'd be back on the outside, picking through secondary sources, gleaning.

"Nicholas, congratulations."

Nick stiffened up, saw a meaty hand come out to grab his, saw Marion.

"You've written a remarkable book," he said.

People shifted, turning to look. Nick saw Lyn Mortenson. She was smiling at him, eyeing his butchered hair and wrinkled clothes.

"It's an extraordinary book," she said. "Exhaustive, really. I do hope you find a publisher for it."

Marion smiled, flesh pushing up against his lenses.

Nick felt the heat rise in his face. The New York deal was dead.

"I love the opening quote," said Mortenson.

"'The road of excess leads to the palace of wisdom,'" said Nick, at a loss for anything else to say.

His stomach lifted as the elevator slowed, and he thought he was going to throw up right there. The sushi had left his mouth greasily lined. He stumbled out into the heat and intense light just under the roof, watched the others make their way down the gently sloping ramp. Every few feet Marion stopped to shake someone's hand.

The fat fraud. The documents he'd supposedly found at Laverne's place would turn out to be fakes; Nick was sure of it. The whole story of the Tangier drawings was bullshit. It had to be. And if Nagel turned out to have been complicit, then he was covering up. And he was covering up because he was guilty. He was the Collector. And Bittaker was his instrument.

Nick touched his face. It was burning. He was burning up. Just take a look, he said to himself. He'd take a look and he'd know. And once he knew, once he was certain . . .

"Don't get ahead of yourself," he mumbled as he moved forward, keeping one hand on the balustrade. "Go take a look."

He made his way down the ramp, barely aware of the paintings on the outer curving wall. A buzzing rose out of the building's deep well.

A couple of turns lower, all movement had stopped.

He came to the outer fringes of the crowd. People were rubbernecking, hands held to their faces, trying to get a look at the extraordinary new discoveries. Marion's fruity baritone cut through the ambient buzz: ". . . a growing tendency to focus on the life—on the meat and-potatoes aspect of the artist's day-to-day existence, to cover everything, if you will. In the face of works such as these, works that came out of a time when Spira was supposedly idle, supposedly confused and lost, this wall-to-wall approach to commentary is revealed for what it is: an exercise in appropriation, an attempt to occupy the terrain."

Cameras flashed. It looked like Marion was getting his picture taken in front of the drawings. Nick started to push. "Frank had a saying. It was a quotation, actually. From Blake. 'The road of excess leads to the palace of wisdom.'" Nick wedged himself into a gap and pushed harder. Someone pushed him back. People were turning, their heads snapping round to see who could be so rude. "Let us hope that neither the road nor the palace are ever carpeted." The camera flashed again and there was laughter, a ripple of applause.

"Excuse me." Nick kept pushing, head down, his face aflame. "I'm sorry, I need to—I have to come through here."

Bodies yielded reluctantly; he had to work his shoulder into gaps.

Nagel was speaking now, his voice barely audible: ". . . and if Martin hadn't come to me, hadn't confronted me with the evidence, maybe I'd have left the drawings where they were. For which I hope you'll forgive me. But understand, my biggest fear was litigation, the prospect of these wonderful creations being locked away in a vault while the lawyers argued the toss."

And suddenly Nick was through—out into the open at the front of the crowd, nothing between him and the works hanging there on the wall.

Eugene shoved in through the front door holding up his shield like a cross, thinking as he did it that this was probably the finest moment in his career, the peak in a career that he'd never even thought of as having high points. Ray and the two uniformed cops they'd picked up on Fifth Avenue were right behind him, frowning, trying not to look amazed at all the famous faces turning their way.

Ink on vellum. The smaller of the two with a noticeable yellowish cast. After the first shock of seeing, Nick looked around him at the rapt faces. A woman was doing her best not to weep, touching the tears away from her eyes with discreet dabs of her sleeve. An old man in a dinner jacket, a pillar of the New York art-critical establishment, was reaching out a manicured finger to touch the smaller of the two pictures.

"... one knows not where, on an unknown vessel, an absolute struggle with the elements of the real."

"Motherwell!" said a woman with cropped white hair. "You're quoting Motherwell. Spira will be spinning in his grave. You might as well say the Lord's prayer backwards."

Nagel turned away from Nick, doing his best to laugh, but he too had tears in his eyes. This was his moment. This was what he had dreamed of all these years.

"Intermittent, softly feathered, softly bursting at the tip where the pigment diffuses into the support," said the critic, following another line. "Quite exquisite."

Nick pressed a hand to his mouth, not wanting to look, seeing the hunched figure of a crone perched on a table. Thalidomide flipper limbs held something out of sight as she ducked her coiffured head trying to get a better view of the undepicted, unimaginable disaster.

It was extraordinary. Somehow Spira had tapped in to the *Cupid* and come up with the purest representation of evil Nick had ever seen.

"Extraordinary," he whispered.

Scratchy rising marks followed what would have been Jackdaw's spine, opening out on what would have been his shoulders. There was a perfectly round hole which had been patched almost invisibly with vellum.

"*Exquisite,*" said the white-haired woman in a disgusted tone. She looked smaller than she did on TV. Her silk blouse was stained darkly under the arms. Chains dangled from her tortoiseshell glasses. "There's nothing exquisite about it. It's the boldness. The boldness of it."

"Yes, the boldness," echoed Marion. "Of both."

"Of both. Of the ensemble. To take a gothic motif, this crone figure—who is she? *La tricoteuse*? A Fury? One of the Fates? Atropos, perhaps, the smallest and most terrible—to incorporate the phallic, thrusting head of Cupid, place her, place *it* upon a table, but—but a gothic figure for all that."

"Gothic?" said the critic, rolling his eyes.

"You think gothic?" said Marion.

"To take the gothic, a minor, for me, *minor* subromantic genre, and anneal something so hard, so intense, to re-create it, actually . . ." The woman stepped forward, licking her lips, touching the glass mount on the second picture. "And here again, the thrusting head, the thrusting mouth on a creature that springs bristling out of this African scrub, this odd pudendum growth. It's—it's . . ."

"Exquisite."

"*Bold*. Brilliant. Audacious."

"But classical, surely," said Marion. "Not gothic."

"Gothic in its treatment of a classical subject," said the woman, with a sharp jerk of her head. "These creatures are gargoyles. Devastating, beautiful gargoyles!"

Nick blinked, reds and blacks and grays swimming before his eyes. The image was the one he had seen on Reardon's chest. The vellum support was missing its top two corners where the nipples had been removed.

"They're hanging in the wrong order," he said.

Faces turned in his direction.

"Ah, Nick," said Nagel as though seeing him for the first time.

Marion tilted his head, all pretense of bonhomie gone now.

"Mr. Greer," he said mockingly. "The *expert*."

"We need your opinion on a little matter of genre," said the critic.

"Is he right about the order?" said the white-haired pundit.

"Vellum," said a voice. "Is that the same as parchment?"

"We are now committed to an unqualified act . . . ," said the critic, looking at the pictures, quoting again.

"Made from skin, anyway," said another voice. "Goatskin or calfskin."

"Sometimes unborn calfskin," said Nagel. "Isn't that right, Martin?"

Nick looked past Nagel's head at the smaller picture, at the bottom right-hand corner where the spiral monogram showed, an odd, elongated patch or stripe of added material. Spira's coil.

"Uterine vellum," said Nagel, getting in closer. "If you get it out of the amniotic fluid, it's even finer."

Nick pressed his teeth together, his gorge rising.

"Is that what this is?"

"Skin of some sort."

"You wash it to get the grease out," said Nagel, his voice hardening against the tumult rising from below. People were turning, shuffling backwards. There was an angry shout. "Then you soak it in an alkaline solution for a couple of weeks until the hair starts to slip."

Nick closed his eyes as the bitterness flooded his mouth, and then it flushed out of him, squirting between the fingers of his clamped hands. A woman screamed as he blundered forward, fell against a body that softly gave, then found himself up against the sloping balustrade, convulsed, retching, bringing up what he felt must be his entrails as he roared again, choking, spraying chunks of flesh out into the pristine air.

Below him people were screaming, pulling backwards, stumbling, covering their heads and faces.

Then everything slipped sideways. An elbow hit him in the mouth, and he turned, saw everything at once: the jump-cut ugliness of clutching hands and flailing, twisted limbs. He lost his grip, fell heavily to the floor and for a vivid second knew that he was no longer breathing, and the feeling of detachment that followed was so powerful that he thought he must be dead—shot or stabbed or simply dead. A voice was calling to him from far away. Glasco's voice. At first it sounded like a condemnation, a judgment, but he knew it was too soon for that. Someone was reading him his rights. He tried to call out, but his mouth was full of blood and bits of what he guessed must be enamel, and it was this broken grit that brought him back into the moment, facedown on the sloping floor.

"It's over, Nicky."

He twisted, trying to get his head round to see the pictures, as the handcuffs pinched his wrists, but all he could see was Nagel, the old man being cuffed against the wall. A uniformed cop was talking directly into his swollen face, but still Nagel was calmly explaining.

"You scrape it clean with a blunt blade. If you do it right, it can last thousands of years."

I lost the story. That was the thought that came to Nick as he relaxed under the weight that pinned him down. Blood ran from the side of his mouth, mixing with the vomit.

"They're in the wrong order," he said, saying it to himself this time, laughing weakly, seeing the lunacy of it now, the crazy pedantic wrongness. They had hung them in the wrong order, and it didn't matter at all.

39

Of all the surreal events that Friday evening, Cy Lockhart's handing him his business card was probably the strangest. He didn't say anything, just pressed the thing into Nick's hand as he was being led away, trying to be discreet about it. Glasco saw it anyway.

"See that, Ray?" he shouted, his face suffusing darkly. Guthry, a couple of steps ahead, one hand on Oscar Nagel's shoulder, the other pushing back members of the public, half-turned to look. "Tricky Nicky's already lawyered up."

Nick glanced across at Nagel, wondering if this had all been thought out beforehand, but the old man seemed oblivious, shuffling forward, head down, as though already in the exercise yard. They were taking him away. In front of his friends he was being humiliated. Lockhart had gone around to the other side of him and was giving what looked like much-needed support. All the way down the ramp, across the ground floor and out through the exit, he kept up a steady monologue about his client's medical requirements. Mr. Nagel was a very sick man. He, Cy Lockhart, would be holding them personally liable for any negligence. Then Nick was in the back of the car with Glasco. A uniformed cop drove. As soon as they were rolling, Glasco lowered the window.

"You stink, you know that?"

Nick turned the card over in his hands, trying to understand what it meant. First and most obvious, if it wasn't some sort of sick joke, Lockhart had just made himself available to him. Second, Nagel was in some way reaching out.

"So what happened?" said Glasco. "You didn't like the canapés?"

He shifted his bulk, getting a fruity squeak out of the vinyl. "Or is it Spira's work does that to you? Because there I could understand."

Already the card was bent out of shape. There was an embossed logo—the scales of justice or some such. A phone number. An e-mail address. Nick straightened out a crease. Lockhart had given him the card because Nagel had told him to. Because why else? Somewhere on the other side of these simple facts a conversation loomed. A conversation with Nagel.

"Your prints are all over the car, Nick."

Nick surged back into the moment, froze, turned.

"We know you were out there," said Glasco. "We know you lied."

He leaned in closer.

"In a way I feel sorry for you," he said. "Because—well, to be honest, I don't think you're going to get a fair shake over there in Tangier."

"Tangier?" said Nick, and just like that he saw Laverne in the Mercedes, the scarf ripping out behind her. Forty-some years ago a wealthy woman goes to visit her bohemian friend. Another image came to him: the spiral in the bottom right-hand corner of the Grossman picture. A patch of different-colored tissue. Why had Spira put his coil in Laverne's mouth? Was she also marked with an image? Marked on the body?

"The detective running the investigation, he doesn't strike me as a very democratic kind of guy," Glasco was saying. "In fact, he seems to me the kind of guy who comes up with a theory and then goes looking for the facts that fit."

Glasco shifted his weight again, pushing so close Nick could feel his breath.

"*He* thinks you went down there to help the Collector nail Reardon. He thinks—and this is the kicker—you were probably involved in the actual skinning."

He nodded, letting this sink in.

"Which, knowing what a chickenshit voyeuristic bookworm you are, I know is probably not true, but Ahmed, my friend in Tangier, he's got this whole other perspective, not to mention a skinned body in the morgue and your fingerprints in the victim's blood."

"I was trying to help," said Nick.

Glasco sat back against the seat. He turned to the driver.

"Pull over."

They rolled to a stop under a streetlight.

Nick saw chain-link fence and scraps of cardboard, bits of some street person's home.

For a long time they sat there in silence.

"He'll be waiting for you when we get there," said Glasco eventually. "Lockhart. He'll tell you not to talk. He'll tell you to keep your mouth shut. Hide behind the Fifth Amendment. But remember, he's Oscar Nagel's lawyer. Not yours. He doesn't give a damn what happens to you."

Nick nodded, waited, looked out at the street, trying to think, trying to decide what was best, what he should do. He saw himself getting off the plane in Tangier and shuddered. Then another image came: Nagel sitting in a darkened room, waiting for him, waiting to talk. Maybe he wanted the film. Maybe that was it. But surely things had moved on now. The cops had the so-called drawings. They'd taken them right off the wall.

"It can all change right now, Nick."

Glasco shifted again, coming back in close.

"I believe in giving people a second chance," he said. "You say you were at the house in Cap Spartel to help and I believe you. I believe you now despite all your lies because I think you want to make things right."

There was a tap on the roof. Then another. Like someone tapping with a finger. Summer rain. A fat greasy droplet ran down the windshield, cutting a track in the dust.

"Nick?"

Nick turned, met Glasco's cold cop stare.

"I want to talk to a lawyer," he said.

It seemed to take forever for Lockhart to arrive at the station house. He'd been making sure Nagel was comfortable for the night. Almost immediately after they'd gotten into the squad car, the old man had started to complain of chest pains. He was okay now, though. Or at least he was okay for someone as old and sick as he was. They had him in a hospital bed, a cop standing guard at the door.

"All this has been a terrible strain," said Lockhart, pulling out a legal pad and a microcassette. "And I have to say, it's difficult not to see some sort of animus here, some desire on Detective Glasco's part to deliberately humiliate."

Nick watched from the other side of the table, waiting for the wink or nod that would let him know they were in on this together, that this was all an elaborate charade to throw the cops off the scent. The wink never came.

Lockhart talked about the bewildering events of the past few weeks as though he knew nothing of the *Incarnation,* didn't begin to appreciate the seriousness of what had happened at the Guggenheim.

"In over forty years in practice I've never seen anything quite like this," he said. "The warrant served on you and Mr. Nagel—well . . ."

He shook his head.

"What exactly is the charge?" said Nick.

"Conspiracy," said Lockhart. "Conspiracy to murder Jacob Grossman."

Nick brought his hands up to his face. The police thought he was part of it. It was Guthry who had talked about his leading the killer to the victims. Did they think it was deliberate?

"The exact nature of the complaint, its basis in fact, will become clearer at the arraignment," said Lockhart, still keeping up his lawyerly bewilderment.

"Arraignment?"

"The law enforcement official states the exact nature of the complaint before a judge, who, if he considers the case suitable for trial, then sets a date. In the state of New York they're obliged to bring you before the court for arraignment within twenty-four hours. So hopefully sometime tomorrow. In the meantime, for tonight, they will hold you here and will probably try to put pressure on you to talk."

Nick nodded.

"They already did. Glasco tried to get me to talk on the way down here. He said the Tangier police think I skinned Tony Reardon."

"Skinned?"

Lockhart withdrew Nick's hands. For a moment he was absolutely still, his startled eyes lost in the shadow of his prominent brow. Then he pushed a hand back over his thinning hair. Lockhart the stunned lawyer. If he was acting, he was very good.

Nick looked past him at the observation mirror set in the wall. "Yes, skinned. You see—"

Lockhart's hand came up.

"Nicholas." He cleared his throat, settled. "Nicholas, I may at some point ask you for information. In the meantime, I'd appreciate it if you'd try to focus on the issues."

Nick choked.

"The issues?" he gasped. "What about me being extradited to Tangier? Isn't that an issue?"

"Extradition?"

"Yes. Glasco said that—"

Again Lockhart's hand came up.

"Nicholas. Whatever charges the Tangier authorities may have brought, I'm sure they're insufficient to—"

"They have my fingerprints at the murder scene. *In* the victim's blood."

Lockhart frowned, made a movement with his mouth. He'd been given another detail he hadn't requested, and now he had to chew it over.

"There's an explanation for this," he said after a moment, putting it as a statement of fact rather than a question.

"Yes."

"An innocent explanation."

"Yes."

"Then you won't be going to Tangier. The United States of America doesn't just hand over its citizens."

Nick gave the two-way mirror a straight look, hoped Glasco was hiding behind it so that he could see what Nick thought of him.

"Detective Glasco was just playing a little game with you," said Lockhart. "Trying to get you to say something." He frowned, brought his hands back onto the table. "You didn't, did you?"

"Yes." Nick hesitated. "I said I was trying to help the victim of the—of the . . ."

Lockhart shook his head. He didn't want to know.

"Nicholas," he said. "Listen to me. For some reason or other the police set great store in the drawings they seized tonight. They appear to believe that they have a bearing on the Grossman case. They appear to believe that they have acquired an important proof. Of what I don't know, and I don't wish to know. Suffice it to say that Mr. Nagel believes he does know, and believes also that they are making a terrible mistake."

Ornament

40

The media coverage started that night with a local cable TV crew arriving at the Guggenheim just as the collectors were starting to leave. A young woman in a blue linen suit frowned to the camera, talking of the arrests and the dramatic seizure of valuable art works by "controversial artist" Frank Spira. Startled Spiraphiles squinted into powerful lights as they came out through the main entrance, some of them stopping to talk about the heavy-handedness of the police and the impeccable character of Oscar Nagel, a man they had known for forty years or more.

At around ten o'clock news broke that the pictures, ink drawings on vellum, had been sent for analysis at an NYPD laboratory. By that time three different cable stations were competing for space in front of the museum, and the fact that Detective Glasco was also running the Jacob Grossman homicide case had become a salient issue. Speculation veered towards art-fraud-and-murder scenarios. Sometime later—no one was sure exactly when or how word had gotten out—it emerged that DNA derived from the vellum of at least one of the drawings was being analyzed. At that point the story exploded onto the national networks with everyone asking the same question: was the vellum in fact of human origin?

Lying awake in his filthy clothes, stunned by the simple fact of being in custody, acutely aware of every sight, sound and smell, Nick knew nothing of what was going on outside. He couldn't think straight, couldn't switch off, his mind jumping from the pending arraignment to Lockhart and his business card, to the look on Nagel's face as the cop read him his rights, to Laverne's swollen mouth leaking smoke, to Reardon banging into her, and behind everything—

beyond everything—the pictures themselves swimming up in front of him like flesh-colored balloons.

He was still awake when a guard came to give him his food on Saturday morning: this bored-looking kid with acne scars who shoved a copy of the *New York Post* at him through the bars of his cell and said congratulations, he'd made the front page.

GUGGENHEIM SNUFF ART SEIZED

Last night NYPD detective Eugene Glasgow seized million-dollar art works thought to be made of human skin from the Guggenheim Museum. The "drawings," originally thought to have been executed on vellum by deceased artist Frank Spira in the late fifties, were taken directly from the gallery walls to a forensic laboratory in lower Manhattan where DNA tests are to establish whether or not the vellum was in fact removed from the body of recently slain Jacob Grossman, Frank Spira's former lover.

Detective Glasgow, who has been investigating the Grossman murder for the past three weeks, also arrested art dealer Oscar Nagel and writer Nicholas Greer in what Guggenheim bystanders described as a "heavy-handed snatch."

Nagel, 72, the owner of the "drawings," was hospitalized shortly after his arrest, while Nicholas Greer, 35, was held pending arraignment at the 7th Precinct station house. None of the parties involved has so far made any comment. ("Spira's Sick Art," page 23.)

Nick read the article with his head in his hands, read it three times trying to get the words to register. It wasn't that he was surprised by the news, but after what Lockhart had said in the interview room, he'd been nurturing a tiny hope that things would turn out differently. But whatever "terrible mistake" the police were supposed to have made, it wasn't reported in the *Post*.

He spent the rest of the morning trying to find out more about what was going on but couldn't even get near a radio. Repeated requests for a telephone were ignored. The guards said he'd had his phone call, even though he hadn't. He had to sit tight and sweat it out in his filthy clothes, wait until he was called for the arraignment.

And then they let him go.

It happened in the late afternoon. The guard who came for him refused to talk, just took him to a windowless room where a guy got him to sign some forms before giving him back his personal belongings.

Walking out into the heat and humidity of the street, he found himself staring into a lens.

"Mr. Greer, what do you have to say about your treatment?"

A microphone came up in front of his face. A shout went up. People started to run.

"There he is!"

They came out from between a line of parked cars and vans. Someone tripped, sending a camera flying.

"Mr. Greer?"

"Sir! Will you be suing the city?"

"How do you explain the actions of Detective Glasco, Mr. Greer?"

There were maybe a dozen of them. They jostled and pushed, got in so close he had to back up against a fence.

"Tell us about Jacob Grossman!"

"What happened to him, Mr. Greer?"

Nick tried to push past, did push past, then saw Lockhart, ashen-faced, buttoning his jacket as he barged into the back of the crowd.

"They told me you were being released at four," he shouted, coming up against Nick in the crush. Nick smelled sweat and all-night-coffee breath, saw stubble and bloodshot eyes. "Then I got caught up across town. The whole thing's gotten completely out of hand."

Lockhart pulled him through the crowd, then zapped the locks on his SUV. The shouting turned desperate.

"Hey! Who the hell—"

"We were here first, buddy."

Nick pushed microphones aside, strained against unyielding bodies.

"How about a comment, Mr. Greer?"

"What can you tell us about the Grossman connection?"

"Mr. Greer has nothing to say at this time," boomed Lockhart.

"Who says so?"

"It's the lawyer! Nagel's lawyer."

Everyone started shouting at once then.

"Hey, Lockhart, give us a break, you asshole!"

Nick climbed into the SUV and watched Lockhart pull the door closed. The shouting shut down to muffled yelps. Faces strained close to the glass. Cameras flashed. Nick put up a hand.

"What's happening?" he said as Lockhart got in alongside him. "What the hell is going on?"

Hands slapped the windshield as the car eased forward.

Then they were pulling out into traffic.

"What did they mean about Glasco's actions?" said Nick. "They wanted to know how I explained his actions."

Lockhart negotiated traffic at a junction. He kept rubbing at his eyes, shaking his head as though he too couldn't quite believe it.

"It's what I told you last night," he said. "About the mistake they were making."

"So? What was the mistake?"

"The drawings. You know they were taken to a lab."

"Yeah, I read about it."

"Well, the results came back a couple of hours ago." Lockhart glanced in his mirror and cursed.

Nick looked over his shoulder. A TV van was about five cars back.

"Someone at the lab must have leaked the results to the press," said Lockhart, making a smooth turn into a side street. Two blocks farther on he rolled down a ramp into an underground parking garage. He flashed a card and the barrier came up.

They drove across to the other side of the building and took an exit back up to the street.

"How much do you know about using gene probes to match DNA?"

"Nothing."

Lockhart glanced across at him. "It's a delicate process. Defense lawyers always raise the contamination issue." He checked the rear-view mirror again. The street behind them was clear. "But in this case the effectiveness of the probes was hampered by the fact that the material retrieved from the drawings came from a goat."

He marked a pause, then allowed himself a dry little laugh.

"Goatskin. That's what the drawings are made of. All this other business—about human DNA and what have you—it's some kind of bizarre misconstruction."

Nick sat back in his seat. He didn't get it. It didn't make any sense.

He considered the possibility that he was still on the prison bunk, dreaming.

"I know," said Lockhart, shaking his head, getting back to his lawyerly manner. "It's outrageous. I'm going to recommend that Mr. Nagel seek Glasco's dismissal."

At the mention of Nagel, Nick was suddenly aware of the situation, of their movement through the city, of the headlong flow of things. Everything was happening way too fast.

"Where are we going?" he said.

Lockhart gave him a puzzled look.

"That's up to you. Mr. Nagel asked me to pick you up, that's all. He wanted to save you from the press."

"Why? What does it matter to him?"

Lockhart checked the mirror again.

"Pull over," said Nick.

"What?"

"Pull over. I'm getting out here."

Lockhart slowed to a halt.

They were a few blocks north of Houston. A couple of miles or so from Times Square and the hotel. Nick looked out at the street.

"I expected you to be relieved," said Lockhart.

His look of fatigued bewilderment was perfect. Either that or he really didn't know what was going on.

Nick shook his head.

"I'm having a little trouble understanding all this."

He opened the door. Hot air rushed in with a stink of drains.

"I think Mr. Nagel was worried about the press getting to you," said Lockhart. "He was worried that there might be further confusion."

Nick got out and stood there looking back in at him. Lockhart's face was shiny with sweat. An ugly man in elegant clothes.

"He thinks perhaps it might have been something that you said to Detective Glasco that led to last night's debacle."

Nick put his head on one side.

"Oh, really?"

"Something to do with your book."

Lockhart smiled then, and Nick had an uncomfortable moment of looking back at everything he had done and wondering if he had been mistaken. The *Incarnation* was made of goatskin. The murders had nothing to do with it.

"He'd like to talk to you," said Lockhart.

"Really? Why?"

"To clear up any misunderstandings. I think, as much as anything else, he's curious. Puzzled by all this. As you seem to be."

Nick looked down at the gutter.

"Should I give him a message?" said Lockhart. "A contact number, maybe. Are you still at the Beacon Hotel?"

"Thanks for the ride," said Nick, and stepping back, he slammed the door. Lockhart called out, but the words were inaudible and Nick was already turning away, moving along the street.

He started to run, then pulled up short, looking back along the street, telling himself to slow down, to cool down, to *think*. Think in a straight line for once, starting with the fact that whatever threat he had been to Nagel was now nullified. Wasn't it? The old man had seen him coming way, way back, had anticipated all his moves. Anything he now said to the police, anything he wanted to write, would lack all credibility. The *Incarnation* was made of goatskin, and the rest was an elaborate theory.

The pictures came back to him—the smaller one particularly, with its odd yellowish tinge. It had seemed so real—*was* real, goddammit, but if the pictures were real, how had the results come back skewed? Had Nagel bribed a lab technician? He was rich enough to do it, but somehow it didn't ring true. Bribery was too elaborate, too risky. And it required time. You couldn't just call up an official and offer a wad of cash.

He reached the other end of the street and came out onto Broadway. The air rippled with heat and fumes. He saw a dozen SUVs that could have been Lockhart's. Lockhart couldn't possibly have made his way around the block so quickly. The traffic wouldn't allow it. But what if someone else had been following? Someone Lockhart had picked up when he came out of the parking garage, for example? Someone Lockhart was now talking to on his cellphone? Nick blinked sweat out of his eyes, breathing tight and hard, looking at traffic—all of it suddenly sinister.

He ran again, cutting through department stores and markets, ran down into a subway tunnel, then doubled back, arrived in the lobby of the Edison, panting and streaming with sweat.

He made his way over to the elevators and punched the up button, pretending not to notice the stares of the other clients.

Are you still at the Beacon Hotel?

Standing there, watching the numbers tumble, he remembered Lockhart's question, and it seemed sinister. How did Lockhart know he was staying at the Beacon? The only person who knew he was there was Barb. Of course, Barb might have mentioned it, might have told Nagel or Lockhart or anybody that she'd been trying to reach him at the Beacon. Why not? There was nothing sinister about it, really. He was just being crazy.

But even as he thought this, he got the exposed feeling again. He looked sharply around at the lobby, saw nothing but tourists and a few staff.

The doors slid open and he stepped inside. There was no danger, he told himself. There was no danger because he wasn't a threat. He raked at his greasy hair as the elevator started to climb, tuning out, working his way back into his groove, thinking that if he was right about the *Incarnation,* and the police were right about the goatskin, then the pictures in the Guggenheim were copies. Nagel had gotten someone to copy the original—in a matter of days he'd had the Reardon picture reproduced in every detail, down to the patched-lip spiral monogram and the excised nipples. But why? You didn't put feathers on a decoy. You didn't have to because with context and the right noises the geese just flew right in. Like he had. Like the police had.

He got it then.

The elevator slowed to a halt and the doors slid open.

Nick stared down at the stained carpet, oblivious, seeing it all at once—understanding that the pictures had to look real, because when all the fuss was over, when the police had finished tripping over their own feet and making their apologies, it was the real thing that would be going back to the Guggenheim.

The elevator was climbing again, but Nick stayed in his corner, staring at nothing, seeing how it would now play out. It was Grossman and Reardon's skins that would make the trip to London when the Guggenheim show was finished. It was the dead men's skins that would travel on to Amsterdam and Berlin and Tokyo. The *Incarnation*—grafted onto the artist's oeuvre, part of all future shows.

He had to go back to Glasco. He at least had to try to share his thoughts. And he had the film. The film showed Reardon, and what was marked on Reardon's chest. And maybe that still didn't make goatskin human, but it would give weight to his story—to the true story of the *Incarnation*. Glasco could demand a second test on the pictures. Maybe he'd have to get support from higher up, but with backing he could demand a second test, and the second test would be conclusive. Unless Nagel had foreseen that possibility too—planned to keep the fakes out there for a few years until everybody had finished burning their fingers.

Nick laughed behind his hand, soft, appalled, admiring laughter. Then another thought came to him that killed the laughter dead: he could go to Glasco, and the pictures might be seized and they might turn out to be real—all those dominoes might fall, but he would never get the real story. He would never tell the full story.

He got out of the elevator two floors late and walked back down to twenty. Putting the card into his door, he got a chill. There was someone waiting on the other side. Bittaker was sitting there in the gloom. He knew it.

Footsteps brought his head around.

One of the maintenance staff was coming along the corridor, this young guy with a startled look on his face. Nick said it was lucky he'd come along, that he was having trouble with the air-conditioning unit. Five minutes later the maintenance man, puzzled, suspicious, left the room and Nick leaned back against the closed door, listening to the roar of the AC unit.

He had to do something. He had to make something happen.

He went into the bathroom and saw the face in the mirror. It brought him up short. In a few weeks he'd aged ten years, looked now like one of the stinky addicts he'd seen down at the station house, with their burned-out-socket eyes and scraps of beard. He grew still, really looked—looked at this new self as though actually looking into the future, at the person he was going to become.

"You don't know when to stop," he whispered.

The words were Linda's. It was what she'd said to him the last time they'd talked on the phone. He wondered what she'd say if she could see him now. She'd probably think she'd been proven right. The person in the mirror shook his head. Linda was wrong. He did know when to stop. You stopped when you were finished. You stopped when you were done.

He pulled back the plastic curtain and unscrewed the shower head. The key dropped into his hand. A small round-headed key stamped with a number. It opened a locker in Grand Central Terminal.

. . .

He called the Beacon, told them to charge the room to his card and toss his stuff. Just put it all in a box and throw it out. The woman on the other end cleared her throat.

"Actually, sir, I'm glad you got in touch. You had the room until this morning. Since we hadn't heard from you for a couple of days, we went ahead and charged the room to your card. The payment was refused."

"Really?"

"Oh yeah, really."

Nick sat down on the bed, realizing that the reason he'd taken the room only until that morning was because his flight back to London had been scheduled for that afternoon. He'd forgotten all about it.

"Look, I'm coming straight up there," he blustered. "I'm coming straight there and I'm going to pay you in cash."

"I hope so, sir. Because otherwise we're going to have to—"

He slammed the phone down, held it there as though it might spring back up. He didn't want to hear what they were going to have to do. He'd missed his flight. His credit card was dead. Everything was falling apart. He felt in his pants pocket. He still had some of the money that Nagel had paid him. He'd go and settle with the Beacon as soon as he was done.

In the meantime, he had to get out of there.

He went downstairs and checked out, using cash. Then blew a hundred dollars on jeans and a sweatshirt, and threw his dirty clothes into a trash can. He walked into a bar on 43rd Street and ordered a hamburger. The TV was tuned to New York 1, but thumping music drowned out the sound.

He was drinking his second beer, trying to think, planning his next move, when the screen jumped to the 7th Precinct station house and Detective Eugene Glasco coming down the steps.

Glasco's face was the color of ground beef. Cameras flashed as he read from a piece of paper. Another man stood beside him, nodding soberly. Not Guthry. Someone else. The camera jumped in close and a caption came up: DETECTIVE EUGENE GLASCO: NYPD. Glasco was shaking his head and frowning at his statement. Then it was the other guy's turn. Nick saw sad eyes, grizzled hair that was black as shoe polish. The caption changed: DISTRICT ATTORNEY WALTER HIRSHORN. The D.A. didn't need notes. He looked like he'd done this before.

. . .

Nick made the call standing in the street. The woman who answered said that Mr. Nagel was resting and could not be disturbed. Nick told her that Mr. Nagel would be really upset if he found out that she had stopped him from getting through.

He was put on hold, then there was a clunk and the sound of breathing. Nagel said he was glad he'd gotten in touch.

Nick nodded, eyes on the street.

"In a public place," he said. "I'll meet you in a public place."

Nagel weakly laughed.

"Nick. I don't think you understand. My health—"

"You looked okay in London."

Nagel sighed.

"A lot has happened since then. These last few days—detectives, doctors, *writers.*"

A guy in baggy jeans was making his way along the sidewalk, a mean look on his face. Nick tensed up, watched as the guy went past. It came to him that this was how it had been for Grossman. This constant fear.

"Nick, there are people here. Staff. This nurse who is driving me crazy."

"I know what you did, Oscar. I know everything."

There was laughter then. It took Nagel awhile to come back at him.

"Really," he said. "Then why are you calling?"

41

Standing in the street outside Nagel's riveted steel door, Nick told himself that it was all going to work out, that what he was doing made perfect sense. But entering the building, following one of the gloomy staff through the ground floor to the rickety Otis elevator, then riding it up to the fourth-floor landing, he couldn't shake the feeling that he'd made a mistake, that Linda was right, that he didn't know when to stop.

A woman in a dark blue smock was waiting for him in the gloom. She had the sour, flustered expression of someone who'd just had an argument. Without saying a word, she turned away and led him along a corridor. She knocked on a door, opened it, then stepped back to let him through.

A lamp was on somewhere. In the feeble light Nick saw what looked like a library. There were books all over the floor. Some neatly stacked, others pushed into piles.

"Mr. Nagel." The woman's voice rose in a recriminatory whine. "I won't take responsibility for—"

"No one's asking you to take responsibility," snapped a scratchy voice. There was a sound of someone moving around, grumbling. Nick heard a bottle touch glass. "Now leave us alone."

The woman gave Nick a hard stare, then walked away.

Nick turned, his eyes beginning to adjust to the gloom now, seeing scattered furniture—battered armchairs and couches, low tables. Floor-to-ceiling shelves. There was a space on one of the walls where a picture had been removed.

"*Cupid*," said the voice.

Nick turned sharply, saw a shadow move on the wall.

"Up at the Guggenheim. Without it, the room's empty."

Nick crunched broken porcelain, then stepped on something soft.

"You know," said the voice, "Frank once said to me, this was a few years before he died. He said that *Cupid* and the drawings, these drawings we're all so interested in, that they should hang together. Three figures for the base of a crucifixion. Not that he had any plans for a crucifixion per se. It was the figures that interested him, and the idea of this—this emblematic event that we all know so well, with its paraphernalia of thorns and nails and wounds, happening just out of frame. Such a simple, dramatic idea. Frank wanted you to stand beneath the crucified Christ and be unable to look up. He wanted you to see only this world, and know it was the devil's creation."

Nagel walked out from behind a bookcase, a cigar in his left hand.

"The Manichean heresy," he said softly, dabbing at his lips with a handkerchief. "Did you know Aquinas was a Manichean for a while? In Carthage. At a time when they still practiced human sacrifice there."

Nick cleared his throat.

"Mr. Nagel."

"Of course, Mani himself came to a bad end." Nagel went over to the window and looked out at the lights of Midtown. "Do you know what they did? To Mani? They flayed him. They skinned him and cut off his head. Which, you have to admit, is one up on crucifixion."

He pulled on his cigar.

"Mani thought he was an incarnation of the Holy Spirit. Followed the Buddha around India for a while. Was also a great admirer of Christ's. In Islam he is thought of as an artist rather than . . ." He sighed then, considered the tip of his cigar. "What do *you* think, Nick?"

"About Mani?"

"No. I mean, given the choice, would you go for the skinning or being nailed up? Or—and again I'm saying, given the choice, would you take the skinning, the nailing or having part of your jaw removed, the floor of your mouth and a chunk of your tongue—walking around like that for a while, unable to swallow properly, unable to speak properly, your mucosal tissues turning to a kind of parchment and then dying slowly and in pain anyway?"

He smiled his face-changing smile.

"They want to turn me into one of Frank's portraits, Nick. How about that? You're a writer. You can probably see the irony."

"How long have you known?" said Nick. "About the cancer."

Nagel shook his head.

"These things come at you in a rush," he said. "First the problem, and then, my God, the *solution*. These last few days I've been asking myself—I've been wondering if this is perhaps Reardon getting at me from the other side. Or Jackdaw. Or maybe . . ."

He lapsed into silence.

"Laverne," said Nick.

Nagel turned. He was still for a moment, then crossed the space between them, put a hand against Nick's chest.

"There's no wire, Mr. Nagel."

Nagel nodded, looking up into Nick's eyes. He searched anyway, rummaged, probed, dead-eyed, his mouth set slightly askew.

When he was finished, he turned away and walked over to a cabinet where he poured two drinks.

"You know, you don't *look* that interesting," he said, sitting down. "I can't tell you how let down I felt the first time I met you. I'd heard from Marion about this character who was writing a 'definitive' work of Frank's life, and I thought, *Definitive?* I wondered what kind of person would want to do that. What kind of interesting person would be so drawn to Frank. And then *you* walked into that room in Paris with your eyes everywhere like . . ." He massaged his own eyes, grimacing. "Like a Coney Island rube. But then you do something like the other night"—he gestured towards the window—"sneaking around like some kind of cat burglar, and—well, you surprise me."

He took a drink.

"And then—you come here. Tonight. Knowing what you know, you come."

Nick shrugged.

"No, Nick. It took real courage. Then again, maybe it's just pride. There's this fucking book and so forth, but beyond that, I wonder if you really know what it is that drives you."

"I'm here to make you a proposition," said Nick.

Nagel took a moment to clean the end of his cigar. He rolled the moisture-blackened tip between his lips.

"Where's the film?" he said.

"Safe."

"I can't tell you how unhappy I'd be if that film got into the wrong hands."

"What about Gallagher's hands? It was with her all those years."

Nagel leaned back, massaging his eyes.

"Yes, well, things didn't turn out quite the way I expected. Who'd have guessed that Laverne would hang on to it in the first place?" Nagel took away his hand and fixed Nick with his tired eyes. "Did you watch it, by the way?"

The pale misshapen lips twisted in a smile.

"Of course you did. You had to. You have to see everything, don't you?"

"I'm writing a book."

"Of course. The book. Your book. The definitive work."

There was a soft knock at the door.

"Go to hell," said Nagel.

The woman mumbled something about medication. Nagel cursed her, told her to leave him in peace, listened to her footfalls move away.

"Can't you sit down?" he said.

"The burglary," said Nick, finding a chair. "Tangier in 1960. It was the film that was stolen?"

Nagel's eyes crimped in amusement.

"There you go. This was what I was saying before. You just can't help yourself. You're like a . . . Do you know what I thought? About you, I mean. I thought you were a kind of stalker; with your lists, and your index cards, and your picture-covered walls." He smiled. "I thought you were one of these no-life people jerking off in their basement room, yearning for some kind of connection with the world, wanting to fill your life with Frank's life."

"I'm a biographer."

"That's why you're alone now, you know." Nagel gave a slow nod. "That's why your wife walked out on you."

Nick's throat went tight.

"And you know what?" Nagel shook his head. "It was the best thing that could have happened. To you, I mean. It took you to another level."

There was something in this that made him smile. He drifted off, grim-faced again, feeling absently at his jaw, his lips, the meat of his cheek—conducting an inventory.

"Did he show you the body in the end?" he said. "Your policeman friend? When you called him from London the other day, I got the feeling he was of two minds."

Spelling it out for him: We listen, Nick. We know. Everything. The argument with Linda. The insults.

"Yes, I saw the body."

Nagel pushed his lip out, shaking his head.

"They're picky at the morgue. They don't let just anyone walk in. Your friends must feel you have something to contribute to their investigation."

"They *know* I do. We already talked about it."

Nagel's head rolled forward.

"You didn't show *them* the film, did you, Nick?"

Nick looked down at the drink in his hand.

"No, I didn't think so," said Nagel. "You'd want to keep all that to yourself. You wouldn't want Glasco 'leaking' things."

He shifted in his chair, settled.

"So," he said. "How much do you want? For the film." He drew smoke into his lungs and sent it up into the darkness. "A million dollars? Would that cover it? Would that meet your needs?"

"What Bittaker offered Reardon."

Nagel was watching him, smiling his smile.

"Get you out of that basement," he said. "Get you out of your dirty little husk of a life."

Nick nodded. It was true. It would. It would change his life completely. It would put him on a different road. He took a breath.

"I want the story," he said. "I want the story of the *Incarnation*."

Nagel's mouth came open. He started to say something, but then he was laughing.

"This is what I'm saying," he said, dabbing at his eyes. "This is how it is with you."

"You give me the story, and I give you the film."

Nagel became still then.

"But . . ." He brushed at ash on the leg of his pants. "Forgive me, Nick. Perhaps I'm missing something. Wouldn't that incriminate me? I mean, speaking in all modesty, I have a considerable role in the creation and—*preservation* of this work. A curative role, you might say."

Nick shook his head.

"I could never name you," he said. "Without the film, I'd have no proof. You could—in the courts—you would destroy me. Any publisher I approached would know that. No publisher would ever touch the manuscript."

Nagel smoked in silence for a while, then stood up. He walked over to the window. Away to the northeast the Empire State Building was a green-lit spike pushing up into low cloud.

"But what's in it for you?" he said softly.

"I'd get the story. The story of how two men were marked by a great artist, then murdered by a collector. I don't know what happened to the works that were taken from the bodies of the men. And I have no idea who the Collector is. But I know everything else."

"How?"

"Because the Collector called me."

Nagel turned.

"Why did he do that?"

Nick sat forward.

"He admires me," he said. "For what I have achieved. He admires me for going out to the house at Cap Spartel. He thinks it was a ballsy thing to do. And he thinks it's time that the world knew about the *Incarnation*."

Nagel turned away again, blowing smoke against the glass. For a long time he said nothing. Beyond the window, away to the north, a summer storm was flickering along the horizon.

Nick stood up.

"He explains that the Tangier drawings, the works you acquired in 'fifty-eight—these controversial works on vellum—were preliminary studies, preparation for the great work, the extraordinary work he had in mind. He explains how, when I, when you, when anyone looks at the Tangier drawings, they're effectively looking at the *Incarnation*."

Nagel turned from the window and looked into Nick's eyes.

"It would explain all this confusion with Detective Glasco," said Nick.

Nagel shook his head. He went over to the liquor cabinet and refilled his glass.

"And you would be ready to tell this story?" he said. "Even though it's a lie."

"A lie grafted onto the truth," said Nick.

Nagel offered him the bottle, but Nick shook his head.

"You'd never do it," said Nagel.

"What choice do I have?"

Nagel eyed him coolly.

"There's always a choice, Nick."

"I've worked too hard. I've come too far. I've sacrificed too much."

Nagel nodded.

"How do I know you haven't made copies of the film?" he said.

"What difference does it make? The film just proves my story."

Nagel tapped a finger against his lips, nodding.

"Even so," he said. "I'd want the film."

Nick took out the key. Held it up for Nagel to see.

"Tell me the story," he said.

It had started with a phone call. Frank dialing collect from Tangier in the fall of '57. He had been there for a year, doing nothing in particular. Then an accident happened. An elevator collapsed in an old building.

"I know about the elevator," said Nick.

"You do?"

"From Reardon."

"It got Frank stirred up. Anyway, he called me. He wanted my opinion, wanted to know if I thought there would be a market for this kind of thing."

"For what kind of thing?"

"For the work he had planned."

The idea had been to execute this work. To do this thing, to bring about this happening, then use it to generate other material. Frank had been planning paintings, photographs, a film.

"It was performance before Rauschenberg," said Nagel, "'happening' before Kaprow. At the heart of it was"—he held the tip of the cigar in front of his face—"a magical wounding."

Reardon had agreed to do it for money. This was the other reason for the telephone call, of course. Frank wanting to know if Nagel would fund the project. He needed materials, film. Nagel would have an option on whatever he produced.

"He'd been reading this architect. Loos? Yes, 'Ornament and Crime.' In this essay Loos said body painting was the root of ornament, that ornament was primitive, unacceptable in a civilized society. He said that the modern man who tattooed himself was either a criminal or a degenerate. Of course, for Frank this was like some kind of manifesto. 'Criminal or degenerate.' Frank thought of himself as both. He told me about Billy Flash. About what he had been up to at this character's house."

"With the tattoo pen."

Nagel reached for his whisky, sipped, a hand held over his eyes. "Reardon told you?"

"I worked it out."

"You worked it out."

"A drawing made of wounds," said Nick. "Lesion as line."

Nagel took away the hand.

"So Reardon, he didn't—*show* you?" he said. "The work, I mean."

Nick looked down at his glass, shaking his head.

"You never actually saw it?" said Nagel. "You never have seen it?"

"Well—last night—"

"Last night was nothing. Last night was not the same thing at all."

Nick kept his eyes on the glass, his stomach twitching queasily.

"Would you like to see it, Nick? Do you think that would—*help* you?"

Nagel sighed, smoked, nodding to himself. Then he was talking again, telling the story. The fact that the project had been in such bad taste was, for him, like a guarantee of its importance. And he had known all along that Frank was going to be the one to take them all forward.

"Frank was out there in the desert—at least that was how I pictured it then—and where everyone else, especially here, where they were trying to empty art—to pump *out* the content, to remove the significance, to remove even the significance of *line,* Frank was—"

"Planning a snuff painting."

Nagel smiled.

"Reardon said he'd do it for a thousand pounds. I wired him the money. This makes it sound . . . But it wasn't just a business thing. Reardon wanted to be paid, but that was just the—the *whore* in him. The work, its execution, was bound up with their mutual . . ." Nagel shrugged. "They left marks on each other all the time. Frank wanted to work in that—let's call it *idiom.*"

"So—Reardon, he *was* the work?"

"No. As I said before. There were going to be spin-offs. The film was going to be part of it. But things changed. Laverne changed things."

Nick got a flash of Laverne again—the broken eyes. He saw her as Lassiter had seen her in the bar in Meknes, wearing the haik, her sun-ravaged face void of expression. Burned. Burning.

"What happened to Laverne, it just *happened*," said Nagel. "It wasn't part of the plan. Afterwards, Frank was scared Laverne would talk to Max. That the whole thing would come out, that he would be finished. The following year I went across to Tangier, spent a week in the city. Frank had lost a lot of weight. He had this bandaged hand. He blamed Reardon for what had happened with Laverne. He was thinking of destroying the film."

"He showed it to you?"

"No. He was remorseful. Ashamed, I think. He didn't want to talk about it. He wanted news from Manhattan. What was going on, whether or not he had been forgotten. I asked him what had happened to his hand, and he told me that Reardon had broken two of his fingers. It all came flooding out then. Reardon was out of control. He'd stormed out a couple of days earlier. Frank didn't know when or even if he was going to come back. I decided not to hang around to find out. I spent a month traveling, taking in the sights, thinking about this film, making some useful friends." Nagel pointed the cigar. "You met one of them, actually. He grabbed your bag when you were checking in at the hotel, put a beacon on you, a little surveillance toy. Made it easier to follow you out to the house."

Nick shook his head, refusing to believe, then remembered, remembered it vividly. The cop had been right: he had led the killer to his victims.

"When I got back to Manhattan, I thought about the film the whole time. Then, when I finally saw it—"

"*You* had it? But I thought it was Laverne who'd gotten somebody to steal it from the apartment."

Nagel chuckled, rubbing papery hands together.

"I thought you knew everything, Nick. I thought you had every little piece nailed to the floor."

He leaned back in his chair again.

"Understand. I was worried Frank was going to follow through. Burn the film, perhaps. I knew, the same as I knew the first time I saw the *Screaming Heads* at the Egan gallery, that this work was *significant*. That something important had happened."

"But you hadn't seen the film. How could you judge?"

Nagel returned his gaze, and was for a moment silent.

There was murk here. Softness. Nick recognized the signs only too well. Some soft elision was taking place, a blurring of events into something convenient.

"Call it a dealer's instinct," said Nagel, moving on. "I followed my nose. I acquired the film."

"You got someone to break into the apartment?"

Nagel nodded.

"After that—well, you know the sequence of events," he said. "The emotional origami. Reardon folded out. Jackdaw folded in. Frank called Jacob 'Mrs. Mop,' laughed about how big he was getting in the rear, ridiculed him for changing the sheets every week. But despite all that, I could tell he was doing better. And if his life was less—interesting, that was good too. It pushed him back to image-making. Two months after Reardon left, Frank was working on a cast he'd made of Jacob's teeth. A new departure, he said. A new departure."

He fell silent. Down in the street a car alarm was wailing.

"I wondered about this need Frank had to strike out in a new direction. It seemed to me—and subsequent developments proved me right—that what he was doing was pretending that Reardon, and Laverne—the *Incarnation*—had never happened. It was out of sight and out of mind. Of course, for me that wasn't the case. I had the film, for one thing, and I was still seeing Laverne socially. She had changed. She wore too much makeup, sat like this high priestess among the throw cushions. Some of these gatherings were pretty wild, despite Max's attempts to maintain decorum, and I'd get back home with no idea what had happened, what had been said to me or what I had said. You see, I was the only one who knew what was hidden inside Laverne's smile, and I have to say—I *have* to say . . ."

He didn't say, didn't need to say. He had found the idea stimulating. Nick watched him turn the cigar between his lips, savoring, remembering.

"Max didn't know?" said Nick.

"Not then."

"Later? When?"

"One thing at a time, Nick." Nagel blew smoke at the lamp.

"Frank moved back to London. It was the start of the good times. The Blenheim did the one-man show. I went over to London in 'sixty-two to see the Contemporary British Artists' show at the Tate. Frank was beginning to believe in his prospects, and he was more anxious than ever about Laverne and the film. That was when I told him that I thought it was probably Laverne who had organized the burglary, that the film was probably destroyed by then and that he shouldn't worry about it anymore. I asked him if he ever thought about the *Incarnation,* and he was—*evasive.* I asked him if he'd ever considered doing the same thing with Jackdaw."

"What did he say?"

" 'No.' " Nagel brushed at his pants. "Two years later Reardon was back in the frame, and this is—this is where." He looked at the stub of the cigar, tamped it out on a plate. "Frank called me late in the summer of 'sixty-four to make a proposition. Reardon was prepared to sign a contract."

Nick sat forward in the armchair and put his drink down.

"For the picture? It was Reardon's idea?"

"I thought maybe it was something he and Frank had cooked up together. Frank was selling paintings by then, but living like he did—*gambling* like he did—cash flow was always a problem. All I can say is, Frank was the only one who knew about my interest in the piece. It seemed unlikely to me that Reardon just came up with the idea of the sale on his own."

"But Reardon—when I spoke to him, it was clear he had no idea who else knew about the—about this picture."

"Then Frank presumably didn't mention my name. Perhaps he told Reardon that he knew of a collector who would be interested in doing a deal like that. Anyway, I said yes, I was interested."

"In buying his skin?"

Nagel leaned forward until his knees were pushing against the low table.

"The state does it all the time, Nick. I mean, what are they if not a contract with the state giving them the right to remove tissue from your body after your death?"

Nick shook his head.

"What are what?"

"Donor cards," said Nagel, deadly serious. "The only difference is the state doesn't have to pay a penny, and here I was ready to pay twenty thousand dollars up front for something I might never get to own."

"Twenty thousand. So you did the deal?"

"Not on those terms. I told him that there was no way I would be putting my name to that particular contract." He looked down at his hands, seemed annoyed to see them empty. He stood up and went across to a heavy wooden humidor, selected a fresh cigar. "The *Incarnation* was way too—too *evocative,* too close to Treblinka lampshades for me to do that. A lot of my new clients in New York had actually gone through the camps, for chrissakes. I made a suggestion of my own: that Frank sign a contract with Reardon for the purchase of the *Incarnation,* and that I sign another with Frank for any and all works executed during his period in Tangier."

"And?"

"Frank didn't like the idea. I asked him what the problem was. After all, it wasn't as though he had done anything else down there." He cut the tip off the cigar. "And that was when I knew."

Nick watched him strike a match.

"That there was this other piece," said Nagel, shaking the match dead. "I was already pretty convinced. Frank's behavior just confirmed it. I asked him why he was being so—so secretive. I mean, it hurt me, you know? After all, I was the one who suggested going back to that particular source. So then he said that what had happened with Jackdaw was different." He drew on the cigar, then held it away from him admiringly. "I said I understood perfectly. I said Jacob and Tony were very different people. He said that Jackdaw—"

"Did it for love."

Nagel chuckled again, then laughed outright, bending forward slightly, touching the handkerchief to his lips.

"For love," he said finally. "Yes. Love. Stupid Cupid. He didn't even know about Reardon, about the other picture."

Nick nodded, tingling, seeing it all come together. Grossman hadn't known about the marks on Reardon until that moment in the Delancey-Deere when they had started talking about mercury. He'd thought he was the only one.

"Did Reardon know?" said Nick. "About Jackdaw?"

"Sure. He and Frank thought it was a great joke. Grossman was endlessly entertaining to them, a supreme gonzo. But—and here's an interesting thing—despite that, despite the way Jacob was, because of it probably, Frank was moved too, and protective. No doubt about it. He told me Grossman wanted to die with the thing on his back."

Nick narrowed his eyes.

"But you couldn't let that happen."

Nagel batted away smoke.

"Of course not. I asked Frank to explain to me the point of letting this work rot with Grossman in the grave. I said—I believed, still *do* believe—that the *Incarnation* would be his greatest work. I told him that even if it hadn't been conceived as a diptych, that was what it was. He told me I was wrong."

"Wrong?"

"About the work. He said that it was a triptych. In his head and in his heart. He said that when I'd talked to him, when I'd suggested he work on Grossman, he'd seen the possibilities right away. The *Incarnation* and *Cupid*. Three studies."

He passed a hand over his face.

"And if I hadn't suggested he do it—well, it simply wouldn't exist. This beautiful thing. No more than . . ." He drew rectangles in the space in front of him. "And the colors," he said. "The subtlety. And beyond that—well, as you can imagine, the force, the significance— quite unlike the thing you saw in the Guggenheim."

There was a knock at the door. Insistent this time.

Nagel cursed under his breath and got to his feet.

42

After he had sent the woman from the room, Nagel stood for a long time in front of the mirror rubbing at the place where the needle had gone in. It was hard to look at his face now without seeing the other face, the one the surgeon was planning, but he looked anyway and saw a person standing at the end of his life—this person on his own, standing there in a rumpled suit, like a guy standing on a platform maybe, looking away from the station's lights into the outer darkness. And he found that he had only one regret: that the story of the *Incarnation* would never be told. He'd never even considered the possibility, but now that it was out there, now that Greer had raised it, he found the idea almost irresistible. *When you are looking at the Tangier drawings, you are effectively looking at the* Incarnation. It was a brilliant idea, and almost certainly workable. All it needed was for him to trust Greer to put it into effect.

He reached for the phone next to the bed. He punched in the number. The ringing gave place to a rush that could have been the wind in the trees.

"I'm calling from home," he said into the silence.

They had rules about calling each other. The phone was for making arrangements only, and only in the most guarded language. When they talked details, it was face-to-face. They had rules for lots of things, rules they had agreed on many years ago, rules he had recently broken.

"I know you've been calling," Nagel went on. "I haven't been able to get back to you until now. Things have been—well, I guess you probably saw the reports on TV."

He could hear breathing now, and in the distance, the muffled thump of music. He wasn't at the house, then. Sitting in the truck, maybe. Sitting outside, a titty bar on the outskirts of Kingston, just east of the Catskills. Nagel wondered if the payment he'd made to the Cayman Islands account—the funds were wired the day he'd returned from Tangier—would bring about a change in the other man's lifestyle, and thought probably not.

"With the police and my health problems, this is the first time I've had a chance to—"

"I'm out here in the dark."

Hearing the voice, Nagel got a familiar tingle: except for the accent, and the fact that this man was at least thirty years his junior, it was his father speaking. There was the same anger held in check, the same thick-tongued delivery. And it was not only the same voice, but seemed—Nagel had never been able to understand quite how—to come from the same place. It almost made you believe in reincarnation.

"I'm in the dark here. Where you left me."

Nagel swallowed, found that his mouth was dry.

"But that's why I'm calling," he said. "To explain."

Whomp, whomp, whomp. A titty bar. The truck parked away from the lights. There was a clicking sound close to the mouthpiece—*tic, tic, tic.*

"Listen to me," said Nagel. "I'm going to bring someone to the house."

Nick turned at the sound of the door. For a moment Nagel stood there on the threshold, the cigar still smoldering in his hand.

"What is it?" said Nick.

"You ever get the feeling Frank is near you? With you?"

Nick shook his head.

"Never? In all these years of writing your book?"

"No."

"Sometimes—I'm here with the *Cupid* . . ." Nagel pointed at the blank place on the wall. "I'm here alone and I can—I *know* he's with me. More recently with all this—bringing this long struggle to a successful conclusion—I've felt it more than ever."

Nick watched him cross the room.

"You didn't finish the story," he said. "You were telling me how Frank wouldn't do a deal."

Nagel shook his head, too tired to laugh.

"Jesus, Nick."

"I thought that was what we agreed. You tell me the story. I give you the film."

Nagel talked, slumped forward in the chair, one hand supporting his head. He talked on into midnight and beyond, reluctant under Nick's persistent questioning at first, but then going with it, enjoying it, listening to his own voice, fascinated to hear what he had to say on a matter he'd never discussed with anyone.

"In the end, I decided to go ahead on the basis of the initial agreement with Frank," he said. "Worry about Jackdaw later."

Contracts were drawn up and signed. Frank sent him a copy of his separate contract with Reardon and got another twenty thousand dollars.

The following year the Guggenheim retrospective happened. Sixty-two works, including the *Heads* and *Cupid*. Marion did his piece for *Time* magazine. The figurative tradition—a cultural artery flowing back through Renaissance humanism to classical antiquity, and beyond that to the roots of ritual, totem, magic.

"It was wonderful," said Nagel. "'Sixty-five was a great year. It felt like we had driven a stake through the heart of Abstract Expressionism, killed its trivial undead soul. The value of Frank's work started to climb. He came back to me twice in 'sixty-six, and once each year for the next four years. Each time with the same story: Tony felt that he was being cheated, was threatening to talk to the press about the burden he carried."

"I've wondered about that," said Nick. "How it was nobody ever talked. Not Reardon. Not Grossman."

Nagel pushed out his bottom lip.

"After Laverne," he said, "Frank didn't want anyone talking about it. He really thought it would finish him as an artist as far as selling pictures went."

"But that wouldn't have stopped Reardon, would it? I can't see him not bragging about it. Showing it to a lover, whatever."

Nagel shrugged.

"Well, this is—this goes right into the swamp of it. What Frank knew about Reardon, what Reardon knew about Frank. What could be said and what could not. It's a shame none of them are around anymore to ask. Anyway . . ." He drew on his cigar. "At that time—the time I'm talking about, late sixties—*I* didn't want anyone talking, because I knew nobody, the general public, would understand. So—Frank called me up. Tony was unhappy, twenty thousand wasn't nearly enough, especially given the nature of the deal and the uniqueness of the work. I became a kind of checking account for Frank to draw on when he had debts that needed urgent attention. Over that period I paid out just over one hundred thousand dollars. Then, in 1970, around then, I began to think that maybe Frank was lying."

"Why?"

"Call it a moment of clairvoyance. I began to think that maybe Reardon knew nothing about the extra payments I was making. And once I'd begun to think along those lines, I wondered if Reardon had *ever* known anything about the deal—whether the whole thing hadn't been cooked up by Frank as a way of making a little extra cash. Don't get me wrong. This—this deceit just—it made the whole thing richer for me. I was used to Frank and his ways. But I realized that I needed to deal with Reardon directly."

"You called him."

"I called him. Didn't tell him who I was. He was very wary at first—denied all knowledge of the work. Then, when I made it clear that I knew *exactly* what I was talking about, that I had seen some interesting film recording its creation, he didn't say, 'Too late. It's already sold. Frank's already agreed to buy it,' or 'Frank's got a buyer.' He just said he'd think about my offer. So then I knew."

"That Frank was cheating you? That he'd never said anything to Reardon?"

"Either that or Reardon was ready to cheat Frank. Their relationship was well into its final, fatal downswing—there was all that stuff in the press."

"The party. The SATANIC SPIRA headlines."

"Divorce was in the air. A split. I was over a hundred thousand dollars out of pocket. The money didn't matter, but I really didn't want to lose the *Incarnation*. I guess I'd always thought that Reardon was more or less in agreement about what was going to happen once he died. But in the aftermath of the tabloid campaign against Frank, and the problems that was creating in his personal life, I was faced with the prospect of another Tony Reardon disappearing act. And given the state of his health . . . As far as I was concerned, Reardon was on his last legs. I couldn't sleep at night. I'd lie awake thinking about Reardon keeling over in some alleyway, imagining the *Incarnation* rotting in some cheap pine box. Lost. Gone."

"So you hired a hit man."

Nagel took a moment to refold his handkerchief.

"Nick, I'm an art dealer, not a drug dealer." He dabbed at his swollen mouth. "No, finding a killer—I'm told it's not that hard, but it's not really my sort of—no . . ."

"So?"

Nagel shook his head.

"I was lost. What can I tell you? And then—well, call it serendipity. I had this conversation. Someone told me about this person who was in very serious trouble with the police."

He settled deeper into his chair.

"This was back in 1970. I read about the murders in the paper. The naked hookers in the woods. Some bodies had been found in the area of Eagle Lake, up in northern Maine. They'd been stalked like game, killed with a hunting rifle. Everyone was talking about it. The local police were under tremendous pressure to find the killer, had brought in the FBI later than some people would have liked. Anyway, a friend of mine, a judge, told me that an arrest had been made based on the FBI profiler saying that the killer was probably disfigured. Bowyer was a perfect fit."

"Bowyer?"

Nagel frowned, then nodded, understanding.

"Detective Bittaker," he said, smiling now. "That was his idea, the name. When I read it in the press . . ." He chuckled, coughed, laughed.

"Bow," he said eventually. "He prefers to be called Bow. Bow lived in the woods on his own, scraped a living selling services of one kind or another to local hunters. He was a keen hunter himself, had several rifles and had been arrested the year before for assaulting a prostitute in Millinocket. He also . . ." Nagel put a hand to his face. "He had this nose. It was separated at the tip by this growth. An extraordinary thing. Like a piece of coral, really. Anyway, my judge friend told me the case against Bowyer was very flimsy, but that he'd more than likely go to prison anyway. So—now I'm sort of interested, but just, you know, riding the horse the way it was going. Nothing more than that. I pulled strings. I went to see this character in prison."

He paused to suck smoke into his lungs.

"This ugly-looking kid," he said, exhaling. "Barely twenty years old, but with this voice—this voice that seemed familiar to me. And all he wanted to do was to go back to his cabin in the woods and get on with mounting trophies and selling salt. Anyway, to make a long story short, I found him an attorney, and the FBI case fell apart before the grand jury. Didn't even go to trial.

"The day he got out, we drove back to his place, sat there talking until the light came up outside. He was more than grateful for what I'd done, but he was wary too, didn't understand why I'd go to all that trouble. I told him I had a problem, and that he could help me with it. I didn't say what it involved. All I said was there was half a million dollars in cash waiting for him if he decided to do it. I told him to think about what he'd be ready to do for that kind of money. He called me a week later."

"He agreed to go along?"

"He was much younger then and, like a lot of these woodsman-hunter types, a *deeply* conservative, not to say homophobic, person. It wasn't hard to see which buttons to press. So I painted a picture I knew he'd respond to: two degenerate, faggot, freeloader junkies were trying to rip me off. And then there was the money to consider. All Bow wanted to do was live his life, look for spore in the woods, shoot things. I offered him that life on a plate. I offered to do something about his face too."

"You paid for surgery."

"It was expensive. And all he had to do in exchange was recover some property of mine. So we made a little pact. Like you and me." He smiled, his lips shrinking back from the cigar. "Of course, the whole thing took a lot longer than I thought. I *paid* a lot more than I'd intended to, but . . ."

Nagel paused, pointed a finger.

"You should be taking notes, Nick." He drew the cigar to a hot eye. "But there'll be plenty of time for that," he said. "I probably have a little time left to me. Enough to get this stuff nailed down." He sat forward in his chair and touched Nick on the knee. "I'm grateful, Nick. I want you to understand that. This idea of yours . . ."

He rolled the tip of his cigar on the brim of his empty glass.

"Do you never get the feeling that there's a flow to things?" he said. "A pattern? I look back at my life and I can see patterns. All the way through. Chance meetings, people's lives braiding into mine. Like you and Frank, for example."

He nodded, the lids of his eyes coming down so that the light went out of them.

"That's right, Nick. Without you, where would I have gone with this? And without me, how would you ever have gotten to see the pictures?"

He settled then, his lower jaw pushed sideways. Something fluttered in the gloom overhead. A bug had gotten into the room. A moth.

"You do want to see them, don't you?" said Nagel.

Nick looked up, trying to see whatever was making the noise.

"Nick?"

Nagel was watching him, his lifeless eyes fixed in the sockets.

"I mean, having come this far," he said.

Nick opened his mouth, but nothing came out. He took a breath, shrugged.

Nagel smiled. Nodded. He eased himself back into shadows, leaving a drifting tongue of smoke.

"That's what I thought," he said.

43

Nick had a moment standing on the sidewalk out in front of Grand Central. A moment of doubt, of fear.

It was just after one o'clock in the morning and the air was changing, a discernible freshness seeping in from the East River as though the city itself were drawing a breath. He'd left Nagel's place on his own, making sure that people saw him go. Nagel was worried about police surveillance, thought that Glasco himself might be crazy enough to camp outside. And where they were going, they certainly didn't want anyone following. As for Nagel, he had his own way of coming and going unnoticed, had cars he could use that did not have to come out of the basement garage.

Standing there with the film in his hand, watching a plastic bag drift towards him along the sidewalk, Nick felt suddenly lost. The feeling came with a sudden upwelling of sadness that was almost grief. He looked at the film, and for a moment considered walking back into the station. Whatever else he'd done, what he was about to do now was wrong, and not just wrong but disgusting. It meant men's skins on a gallery wall—on a series of gallery walls stretching away into the future, and all because he wanted to tell the story, because he wanted to sell a book.

He looked down at his scuffed, filthy shoes. He'd wandered from the path. That was how it seemed to him: a straying from the path he'd set out along all those years ago. Somehow he had gotten onto a track that led straight into the heart of things only to reach a place where the definitive statement he had always wanted to make was impossible.

The Daimler rolled to a halt at the curb—this great black thing gleaming coffinlike under the lights. Nick saw the driver's door come open, saw Nagel get out. Nagel was in a dark suit. He looked stricken, his face gray next to the white of the handkerchief he held. Nagel saw the yellow box in Nick's hand, then registered the look on his face.

"What's wrong?" he said.

Nick went to say something, then saw that Nagel was holding the film, realized that he had allowed him to take it because this was what he wanted, that this was the path he was following now.

"You drive," said Nagel. "I'm too fucking tired."

He got in on the passenger side and looked up at Nick.

"Listen, Nick," he said. "You don't have to do this."

Nick wavered, then went around to the other side and got in behind the wheel.

Nagel turned in his seat.

"This is second thoughts," he said. "This is you getting me to spill my guts and then not liking the mess."

Nick adjusted the rearview mirror.

"I was just thinking—I was thinking about how hard I worked."

"It's amazing what you did."

Nick turned to look at Nagel's face. The old man was sweating. His pupils were tiny dots.

"I know now," said Nick.

Nagel frowned.

"Yes, you do."

"I know, but I can't talk about it."

He tried to smile.

"That's how initiation works," said Nagel.

Nick frowned.

"You were outside, and now you're inside," said Nagel, looking ahead through the windshield. "You're frustrated. I understand. But from now on everything you say, everything you write about Frank, will come from real knowledge. Especially after tonight."

They crossed the Hudson on the George Washington Bridge, then followed the Palisades Parkway north, Nagel talking all the way. He'd taken something to get him through the night. Nick could see it in the

way his hands fluttered and jerked in his lap. And whether it was the
drugs or reacquiring the film or the release that came with disclosure,
the floodgates now opened. It seemed that there was no end to what
he had to say—about his youth, the suppression of his early dreams to
be a painter himself, the brutality of his immigrant father.

"Did you know Nagel means 'nail' in German?" he said. "No? In
the neighborhood everyone called my father Cash Nagel, and he was
as hard as nails, harder, a driven man, a driven nail."

Nick listened, peering ahead into the darkness, spaced out with
fatigue and the whisky, telling himself that everything was fine. He
had spent six years crawling towards the edge of what now seemed
like a kind of abyss. He wasn't about to *not* look down.

"You know the architect's name, Nick?"

Nagel's eyebrows pushed up into deep wrinkles. For a while now
he had been talking about patrons of the arts through history, their
influence and power: the Borgias, the Medicis, Pope Julius II, Ludwig
of Bavaria. Now he was on to Shah Jahan, fifth Mughal emperor, the
man who'd built the Taj Mahal.

"Of course not," said Nagel. "Who does? Everyone knows about
the prince. The prince whose wife died. It's a great story—very
romantic if you leave out the details, like the woman died giving birth
to their fourteenth child, but people never tell it to the end. You know
the ending?"

"What made you steal the film?" said Nick. "In 'sixty-one?"

Nagel looked out at the Hudson, a wide black ribbon sliding under
the moon.

"Jesus, Nick. Do you ever let up?"

Nick nodded. *You're like a dripping fucking faucet.* It was what
Barb had said to him. Barb. Another outsider. Another person who
knew nothing.

"I'm writing a book," he said. "I'm trying to—"

"Stop selling it, Nick. Christ, I'm already buying." Nagel took out
a cigar and clipped the end. "I already bought. The book, you as the
writer of the book, the whole package. You made a believer of me. I
think this idea of yours is brilliant, visionary—and what you did, the
way you picked up those scraps, the freaking rash, the mercury talk in

the bar. The way you never believed the syphilis thing, unlike Marion, and despite what Marion said. You've got these eyes, Nick. Road to Damascus eyes. You see a guy in a bar with a tattoo, and *kapow*."

Nick blushed. Heat suffused to his face.

Nagel put a match to his cigar, and the air filled with smoke.

"And once you've gotten it written down, there's no one in New York who won't be begging you to let them publish. Marion's going to be twisting in the wind."

"How much does Marion know?"

"About this? Nothing."

The car swooped into a dip. Nick tightened his grip on the wheel. He was going way too fast. It was the car—all that power under a hood polished like a mirror—it made you want to fly.

"But—when he went to Laverne's place the other day?"

"He was doing as he was told," said Nagel. "He had a vague notion I was trying to cover something up. Marion—he's not like you, Nick. He'll listen to anything if he thinks it comes from the horse's mouth. And he's not one to get bogged down in little inconsistencies."

"And the documents?" said Nick. "The letters he supposedly found?"

"They're very good," said Nagel. "I went to a great deal of trouble to get hold of the period paper."

"Does Marion know they're fakes?"

"It was Marion who planted them."

"So—"

"Nick, as far as Marion is concerned, the drawings are genuine. He thinks I'm trying to cover myself in case there's an ownership dispute."

Nick pushed back into the plump upholstery, thinking of Marion knowing nothing, imagining a meeting in which Marion floundered in his ignorance. Marion, the outsider. They turned off the interstate and headed west up into the Catskills, following the Sawkill River. Suddenly the air was raining bugs. Nick sprayed washer fluid, watched the wipers beat clean half-moons.

The question came back to him. A little niggling thing.

"What I was going to ask you before . . ."

"Nick . . ."

"You said you were worried Frank was going to destroy the film. And that that was why you had the house broken into."

Nagel rubbed at his face, cursing softly.

"But—you didn't even see it," Nick went on. "You didn't even know what was on it until you got it back to New York. And Frank—he told you about it in 'fifty-eight, right? The burglary happened in 'sixty. If you were so worried he'd destroy it, why did you wait so long to go get it? Maybe something happened in between? Something you forgot."

"I didn't *forget* anything."

"Then—"

"Then nothing. Anyway, what does this have to do with the *Incarnation*? With the fact that this is Frank's most—"

"It has everything to do with it. It has to do with the circumstances in which you acquired the film. The circumstances in which you first saw what was marked on Reardon's body."

Nagel strained against his seat belt.

"Well, it's a long time ago."

"But you just said—"

"I *know* what I just said."

Nick took his foot off the gas. The car rolled to a halt.

A smell of washer fluid drifted in through the air-conditioning. They were out in the country now, well away from any highways or traffic. Trees hung close to the windshield. Nick lowered his window, heard the steady chirping of crickets.

"What's this, you're going to throw me out now?"

Nagel—trying to make a joke of it, but his eyes were like steel bearings.

"How much did you pay for the *Cupid*?" said Nick.

There was a movement in the air. It ruffled the dry leaves of the oaks.

"You never paid a cent, did you?" said Nick.

Nagel sucked on his cigar.

"That was how the film ended up with Laverne," Nick went on. "You blackmailed her. For the *Cupid*. You didn't acquire the film because of the *Incarnation*."

Nagel gave a tight nod of recognition. A vein had come up in his forehead.

"It is a long time ago," he said quietly.

Nick waited, his hands on the steering wheel.

"Don't tell me you can't remember, because—"

"He used to get people together to discuss the importance of the figure," said Nagel. "I'm talking about Max. Trying to establish some kind of salon, something to counter the thing Rockefeller was promoting over at MoMA."

Nick glanced across.

"I wrote a book about this, Oscar."

"Yes. Yes, of course. You wrote the book. Yeah, well, I was there, Nick. A twenty-one-year-old kid with truck grease under my nails. I'm exaggerating, but just a little. Max threw this big party for Frank after the Egan exhibition."

"July 'forty-seven. You'd just acquired the *Heads*."

"He wanted to get a look at me. This know-nothing kid. The son of Cash Nagel. Clement Greenberg had written something about me being a prime example of the kind of American who *would* buy such worthless kitsch. Anyway, Max—well, he made no attempt to disguise his feelings. He was angry with me, I think."

"For buying the pictures?"

"For getting in there ahead of him, yes."

Nagel looked out at the dark.

"Why are we sitting here? I thought we had a date with destiny."

Nick started the car.

"That night," said Nagel once they were moving again, "the night of the party, *Cupid* was up on display. Max wanted to show everyone that maybe Spira was new in New York, but that *he* had been collecting the work since the thirties. He'd invited some nutty Republicans—Congressman Dondero, some other characters who hated the whole AbEx thing. They thought the country was going down the drain. Things got out of hand. Some character claimed that Pollock's paintings were actually maps, that he was passing secrets to the commies about key military installations. Serious cold-war lunacy. Frank started talking about what a great guy Joe Stalin was. One of the Republicans called him a commie sodomite. Punches were thrown."

Nagel shook his head.

"I mean, you have to imagine—when I got the invitation. I was thinking: do I wear a tux? Then I'm in this salon, and there are people, artists in paint-spattered clothing, drinking whisky by the tumbler, Max's Jew intellectual friends, Max trying to keep things civilized. But the point I'm trying to make: all this was going on, I mean an actual fistfight in that beautiful room, but I only learned about it later. Someone had to tell me."

He turned, making sure Nick understood.

"Because once I'd seen the picture—*Cupid*—it was like all I could see was this—this thing up on the wall. You see, I didn't come at it through years of art. All I knew was trucks. It sounds corny, but it was true. Trucks, tarps, grease guns, the business, my father—this brutal man. And I saw the picture and knew instantly where it came from. Because it came from inside *me*."

He thumped his chest—a single hard rap.

"And Frank was right there in the room. Frank, Nick. The man you met in the street. But younger then, raw and beautiful. Not as young as I was, but with this utterly"—he clutched at the air, looking for the right word—"*unfettered* look in his eye. He thanked me for buying the *Heads*. *Thanked* me. This man who had just changed my life. I wanted to throw myself at his feet. I tried to tell him something about what it was I felt, but I didn't know how you talked about art."

He paused, took a long pull on his cigar.

"Did you make Max an offer?" said Nick.

"No, no, that would have been . . ." He shook his head, not sure what it would have been—too vulgar, too mercenary. "I said I'd give him the *Heads* in exchange for *Cupid*. Like, 'Let's swap.'" Nagel laughed. Then all the humor seemed to go out of him at once. "Laverne was standing right next to him when I said it, and she saw. She saw his reaction. The contempt. The disdain. And I was his guest, right? Just this kid, and he was the great Max Taubmann. Anyway, she kind of took me aside, told me that Max didn't mean to be that way. That *Cupid* meant too much to him. And do you know what I said to her?"

Nagel turned all the way around in his seat.

"I said, 'Why?' I looked her straight in the eye, and I asked her, 'Why?' Because, looking at Max, I didn't see how he could even begin to—I couldn't figure how *that* man with *those* eyes could even *see* it. I mean, Max, he was a kind of—stuffed-shirt absurdity—and Laverne, she told me that it was because the painting was one of the first things he'd acquired, one of the cornerstones of his great collection. *Cupid*, this—this *demonic*, clairvoyant thing, was a fucking *cornerstone*? Can you think of a sadder way to express it?"

"So Max refused to swap."

Nagel batted a hand at him, frowning, thinking. He was trying to get to something, didn't want to be led.

"Then, then—and this is what I was saying to you about patterns before. The way things present themselves. Ten years. No, eleven years went by. Of course, I'd gotten to know the Taubmanns a little better in the meantime. I'd gotten to know Laverne quite well. She was kind of a queen, you know. For many of us. She had this wonderful *rectitude*."

Nick shook his head.

"But I don't understand. You wanted *Cupid*. The film gave you a way to get it. But why didn't you go to Max? Threaten to expose his wife? Wouldn't that have been more—I don't know, effective?"

Nagel said nothing, and this time his silence persisted. Nick slowed into a turn, thought he saw a light away to the left, deep in the woods. He heard a dry, chafing sound. It took him a moment to realize that Nagel was actually wringing his hands. He was straining at something, leaning forward like someone pulling on a rope.

"That was what I had in mind to begin with," he said under his breath. "But then, when I saw the film . . ." He shuddered. "You've seen it. You've seen what they did to her. Well—I was seeing her socially. Going along to Max's soirées from time to time. Laverne was different after Tangier. Quieter. People talked about her drinking problem. She'd sit there in a corner while everyone kind of whirled around her. I think probably it was around then that Max started having his affairs."

"Before Tangier," said Nick. "He was already seeing other women."

"Yes, but I don't think he really got into his stride until after Tangier. He abandoned her. This lovely, proud woman. And I think that for her that was worse than anything Frank or Reardon did. Because she loved him. It was like something she had decided on. Like a faith, a religion. And I'd see her at these parties, and I'd watch her talk, and maybe it was the way I looked at her, but sometimes she almost guessed, I think. She almost guessed that I knew what was inside her pretty mouth."

He put a hand against his eyes.

"And one time, I don't know, I think maybe I let something slip, said something about Max, something about him not deserving her or something like that, and she—I'll never forget the look in her eyes. She told me that I couldn't be expected to understand. That people like me—and she meant people who got their hands dirty for their money—immigrants as opposed to émigrés—were too crude and—

and brutish to understand them. And this was—I mean, I'd sold the business years before. I was dealing in art, for chrissakes, but for her I was . . ."

He sighed, his eyes still covered.

"Anyway, it hurt my—maybe I was from nothing, but I didn't have a tattoo inside my mouth. I hadn't gone to Tangier and gotten myself reamed by a . . ." He shook his head, took a breath. "There were other people in the room. But no one near enough to hear us. So I told her. I stuck it to her, Nick. I told her what I knew."

He took the hand away.

"I'll never forget her eyes. They got so big. She stopped breathing, I think. I thought she was going to expire right there in the throw cushions."

He pointed at a break in the trees, a low bridge spanning a dry ditch. Nick made the turn, entered a narrow track that ran sharply uphill.

"So what happened?" he said. "After you told her?"

"I didn't see her for a while after that. Then I got a note. The afternoon I went over there, it was pouring rain. Max was away boning some academic in Paris. Laverne wasn't so contemptuous this time. She had taken a lot of trouble over her appearance. She was in her fifties then and putting on weight, but still, with her *couturier* and so forth, looking very good. We had a little talk. I told her no one else knew about the film. Apart from Frank, of course, and Reardon. No one else knew I had it. I told her that with me her secret was safe."

He glanced up.

"There's a dip here. A stream. You'll need to slow down."

Nick hit the brake and rolled into a shallow gully. The car fish-tailed coming up the other side.

"She said she was ready to pay me," said Nagel. "She told me to name a price. Because I'm this German immigrant who can be bought. I pointed at the painting on the wall. This red painting that I—I *wanted*. But there was nothing she could do about that. It was a fucking cornerstone, after all. I told her to try. To talk Max around. To tell him that she could no longer live with it in the house. That she wanted rid of it. Anyway, anyway."

Foliage smacked the windshield. Branches scraped along the roof.

"We went on like this for a time. And I could see she wasn't getting anywhere, so I started . . ." Nagel faltered, looked down. "I started . . ." He took a deep breath, the cigar forgotten in his fingers. "This one time I went over there. We used to meet alone. Probably how the rumors started about our affair. She couldn't refuse me meetings. She was terrified that I'd talk. And at one of these meetings I forced her—I forced . . ." He took another breath. "She didn't understand what I wanted. This fifty-something Hungarian aristocrat. When I told her—when I explained how it was done, I thought she was going to throw up. And—I didn't understand. I mean, it made me angry. I told her. Cursed her. Called her names. 'You did it for Frank. I've got you doing it on film, you stupid bitch.' And from the look on her face—I knew that until that moment she'd had no idea. No notion of what exactly had taken place in Frank's apartment. She'd been so out of her—*skull.* She knew something bad had happened, knew that she had this fucking coil inside her lip, but . . ."

He closed his eyes.

"Anyway—anyway, for years, for *years,* this went on. I'd go around there, and Laverne—she'd get down on her knees like she was going to pray, and it couldn't have been any sadder, or more pathetic, but I was rock-hard, Nick. I was *bone* fucking hard to stick it in her mouth. Until finally—well, finally Max died."

The track turned upwards to the left, ran slanting along a line of trees. The car struggled against the slope, gripping and slipping. They passed a gate, an abandoned harrow.

"You gave her the film," said Nick. "She gave you the painting."

Nagel was sitting with his chin on his chest, eyes closed.

"But why the card?" said Nick. "The Flaubert?"

"Oh—that was—that was just—she was a big fan. Flaubert, Stendhal, Proust. She'd been raised on all that stuff. There were books everywhere in the apartment. Beautiful. First editions. Signed copies. She said reading was a passion that she and Max had always shared. Though I never saw him read anything other than the *Wall Street Journal.* It was another of those things I couldn't be expected to understand. So I went away and read Flaubert. Everything. Good and bad. I read the letters, which was more than she ever did. Of course, they were too obscene for her, too base, too vulgar. She was pretty selective about what she wanted from a genius. Anyway, I gave her the card with the film. I thought she'd get a kick out of reading that quote."

"A kick? A kick in the face, maybe."

"I had to explain it to her, of course."

Nick nodded, seeing it. Explaining would have been half the fun.

"You tortured her," he said.

Nagel stared ahead through the windshield.

"That's right."

"Why?"

"Because she disgusted me," said Nagel softly. "Her—the way she clung to this idea of Max. Of their love for each other."

Nick slowed down. They had reached the end of the track. Up ahead there were just rocks and clumped weeds. Nick put on the hand brake. For a while they just sat there. Nick thought of Laverne—the way he had bullied her the last time they'd spoken. He remembered her rage.

"When Max was dying . . ." said Nagel, his voice barely a whisper.

Nick looked across at him.

Nagel nodded, looked at the cigar, dead now, in his fingers.

". . . he wouldn't even let Laverne in to see him," he said.

Nick shook his head, not understanding. Then he got it.

"You told him," he whispered. "You told Max."

A puzzled look had came over Nagel's face. He was examining the cigar stub.

"Why did I do that?" he said softly.

"You're asking me?"

Nagel shrugged.

"You wanted what he had," said Nick. "You couldn't have it. So you destroyed him. And her."

Nagel's lips shrank back from his teeth.

"You deny it?" said Nick.

"Max was finished anyway," said Nagel. "I think it killed *her*, though. Not right away. Max's death, the business of mourning, of grieving—that carried her through the first months, and then she was in a kind of daze for a long time, paid Gallagher to keep her there. But I think that from the moment Max turned his back on her, and I mean *totally*, she died inside. Oh, she walked around with her eyes open and everything, but she was dead. You have to understand, despite everything, this was a woman who worshiped her husband. He was her first and only." Nagel looked out at the darkness, shaking his head. "At the very end he wouldn't even let her come into his room to say good-bye."

He got out of the car.

Nick felt a tingling numbness in his hands. A seasick coldness washed through him. But even then, even in his revulsion, he felt the tug of another question.

He got out of the car.

"Why did she let you have the painting?" he said. Nagel was making his way up towards the house, the handkerchief held to his mouth.

"After all," said Nick, following, "the damage was done."

"She still had the past," said Nagel, his words coming out of the darkness up ahead. "Once Max was gone, it became—I won't say easier for her, but he wasn't around to contradict her version of things. She gave me the painting in exchange for that past."

Nagel came to a halt. He struck a match. His cigar glowed in the darkness.

"You probably helped there, Nick. You offered her the chance to rebuild, to reconstruct, the past in your definitive work."

Nick had no idea where they were. The house looked abandoned, the downstairs windows boarded up. There were warnings, crudely daubed skulls and crossbones. Keys jingled in the dark. Nagel pulled open the front door and went inside. They had climbed up out of the valley and it was much colder here. Owls were calling along the Saw-kill River, their thin shrieks almost metallic in the darkness. A light came on inside—a kerosene lamp, it looked like. Then a movement caught Nick's eye. He looked up at a broken window, but there was nothing now, just a jagged shape where the glass had gone. Soft wings beat overhead. Owls.

Nagel came back into the doorway, holding a lantern.

"So?"

Nick was still looking up at the broken window.

"You think I'd bring you up here to meet Bow?" said Nagel. "You think I'd do that without talking to him first? If he knew I'd brought you up here, he'd probably . . . Well, it doesn't matter what he'd do, because he isn't here and he doesn't know."

He muttered to himself and went back inside.

Nick heard the wings again, saw a dark shape flung against the low brown sky.

He walked in through the front door. The place stank of damp and rotting boards. There were oil drums and bales of wire stacked up against one window. The moisture running down the walls made silvery tracks.

"Jesus, what a shit hole."

"Yeah, well, that's the idea," said Nagel, tugging at another door. "We didn't want any casual visitors. Give me a hand with this, will you?" He stood back. He watched Nick go past.

Nick pushed. The door jammed, then gave.

Stone steps ran down into the darkness. A smell came up on a wash of warm air. Nick put a hand to his mouth.

"Tanning fluids," said Nagel.

Nick turned, and reached for the lamp.

"You're wrong about Max," said Nagel. "I wasn't jealous. That wasn't the point at all."

He let Nick take the lantern.

"You go first," said Nick.

Nagel started down into the stink and warmth.

"The point was the picture," said Nagel. "Max had no right to it. No one does, really."

Nick had to stoop a little going down. Old brick walls pressed close, swollen with moisture, whiskery with drifting webs. Chunks had fallen away in places, revealing the dark veins of tree roots.

At the bottom of the steps Nick came to a halt and held up the lamp. There was a small petrol generator next to a boiler, lagged and wadded in the corner. In the middle of the room was a table littered with woodworking tools and tools that Nick had never seen before—curved knives of different sizes, flat-jawed grips, a bayonet in a leather sheath. There were wormy scraps that could have been bits of vellum.

There were red grains scattered over the floor.

"Poison for the rats," said Nagel, pushing past him and going across to a wooden rack in the corner farthest from the boiler. He pulled a plastic sheet away. Stood back.

Nick sucked in a breath.

In the light of the storm lantern the gold frames gleamed with a kind of Babylonian opulence. Nagel turned, nodding, pointing a finger at the smaller of the two—a hunched figure with a jutting penis head and snap-trap mouth. It was exactly the picture that Nick had seen in the Guggenheim, but different here. Nick found himself coming forward. Despite everything, despite all he knew, the picture drew him in.

"Do you feel it?" said Nagel. "Do you see how they bend the air?"

Nick glanced up at Nagel's face. There was a split second of readjustment, of seeing that something was wrong, of understanding why the old man was looking past him at the far corner of the room. There was time in the second it took him to come around on his heels, to know what had happened, and to see everything leading up to it as inevitable.

Bowyer smiled in the lantern's light, wrinkling his nose, showing squeezed brown rodent teeth.

"*Bow!*" said Nagel. "I knew someone was missing."

Bowyer clicked his teeth together. He came forward and put the muzzle of the shotgun against Nick's face. Nick clenched tight, saw Bowyer's eyes, saw food around his mouth, saw wiry red hair pushed up in a wedge where Bow had slept on it. A smell came off him: onions and cigarettes.

There was a rustling sound of plastic sheeting. Nagel, covering his pictures.

"It gets light in another few hours," he said, all business now.

Rigid, trembling, reading everything with pinpoint clarity, Nick saw the change in Bowyer's face. A blankness came into his eyes. A flatness.

"Light?" he said.

"I'm just saying," said Nagel. "Do it. Get it over, and we can bury the goddam body before the sun comes up."

Bowyer's tongue came out, searching, probing. He found a flake of something yellow and drew it into his mouth.

"Fuck the light," he said in the smallest, calmest voice. "There's no one up here to see, anyway." He stepped in closer, giving the shotgun a little turn, pressing the muzzle into the flesh under Nick's left eye. "Anyway, maybe I want to take my time."

"Bow."

"Why shouldn't I take my own sweet time? You did."

"Bow, I—"

"Two days I'm up here in the dark."

"Bow, I didn't have a chance to call."

"Strutting around with your Jew faggot friends."

"I had to think on my feet, Bow. This . . ." Nagel flipped out a hand. "He's been putting it all together, talking to the police. Telling them about Grossman."

Bowyer bit his lip and gave Nick a stiff jab with the gun, punching his head back.

"I didn't tell them anything."

Bowyer's eyes shifted lower, became still, fixing on the mark he'd made. Blood welling through an oily half-moon. He touched the barrel against it. His eyes flicked up to catch Nick's wince.

"What is it with you, Nick? This need you have to know." He narrowed his eyes, nodding, made another jab with the gun. "This need to show off all the time. Like that story you told me about the Italian guy in the woods."

Nick came up against the table.

"The *woods*," said Bowyer with a disgusted smile. "Telling *me* about the woods." He pushed the gun into the cut. "You know the hardest thing?" he said, digging, lifting flesh. "When you're skinning a head?"

Nick clamped his mouth against the pain.

"Come on, Bow," said Nagel. "Just do it."

"Not the lips," said Bowyer, ignoring him. "You can get up inside the lips, cut around the gums." He blinked, smiled, pushed. "And not the nose or the ears, because you can cut there too."

"Bow."

"*Shut up, Nagel!*" Bowyer clicked his teeth together. "Nick. Nick?"

Nick opened his eyes. Bowyer was grinning at him, his face flushed with pleasure.

"You know, for such a questioning kind of person, you don't seem very interested in what I'm telling you. But . . ." He frowned. "Maybe you already know? Do you, Nick? Do you know about skinning heads?"

He leaned in against the muzzle. Nick felt metal against bone. Blood seeped into his mouth.

"You take your knife and you unzip her up the back. Really." Bowyer was nodding. "Just like that. Like a zip. And then you kind of *peel* the skin forward until you get to the ears. Then you go very careful, get your knife in there, get the blade onto the cartilage and you make your cut."

Nick choked, retched, leaning back against the table.

"But you know what the hardest thing is?" said Bowyer.

Nick could barely move his head under the muzzle.

"That a no, Nicky?"

"Yes," Nick groaned. "I mean, no."

Bowyer sniggered, clicking his teeth.

"It's the eyes, Nick. It's those fucking eyes."

He put the gun against Nick's left eye.

Nick felt a release of heat into his groin. He tried to hold himself rigid, but that only made the shaking worse.

"The tear ducts, Nick. Getting them away from the bone without making a mess of it. *That's* a skill, if you like. That's knowledge."

He became still.

"Tell me about the copies," he said.

Staring through his fingers, waiting for the gun, it took Nagel a second to realize that Bowyer was talking to him.

"That's right, Os-scar. I really want to hear about the copies of the works that weren't ever going to be shown to anyone *ever*."

"Bow, I had no—"

"*Don't say you had no choice!*" Bow blinked, shook his head. "Don't give me that fucking line. The pictures stay in the *dark*! That was the agreement."

Nagel backed up against the wall, nodding.

"You're right, Bow. You're right. And that's where they'll go. Into the dark. No one will ever—"

"He wants to show them," said Nick. His body shook with the pounding of his heart. "He made copies so he could show the real ones later on. After—after all this screw-up with the police, he thinks nobody's going to—"

"Don't listen to him, Bow!" Nagel came forward. "He's just messing with you."

Bowyer looked along the barrel, his finger settling against the trigger.

"That right, bookworm? You want to get inside my head?"

He blinked, clicking his teeth, thinking. Stepped back.

He turned and put the gun on Nagel.

And it was like a spell breaking. Nick was suddenly able to think, and the first thought that came to him was that he was holding the light. The only reason any of them could see was because he still had the lamp in his hand.

Drop the lamp, grab the gun. The thoughts came like instructions. He drew himself upright against the table; a screwdriver rolled to the floor.

Bowyer took a step, his boots popping grit, the shotgun tucked in against his shoulder.

"Why'd you make the copies, Oscar?"

Nagel had the handkerchief against his mouth. His breath came in little puffs.

"To throw the police off the trail, Bow. To give us—"

"Thirty years I worked for you. Thirty years I spent getting you your precious works of art. And now it's done. And this is what I get?"

He was gearing up to pulling the trigger. Nick could see it.

Drop the lamp. Grab the gun. It was the single-barreled kind with a pump action. Bowyer was maybe three feet away. Nick's vision jumped with the pounding of his heart. Drop the lamp. Grab the gun. He could no longer hear the voices through the building roar in his head.

Drop the lamp.

He did it.

He saw his fingers open, saw the lamp just hang there in mid-air. Then it was gone and he was lunging forward, grabbing for the barrel. The bang and flash filled darkness that rained brick and plaster as Nick dragged sideways, backwards, deafened, yelling, pulling Bowyer with him, clutching at the gun, falling hard against the table, the man on top of him. Nick pushed backwards, striking out with his hand, knowing that there was something in his hand, something he had grabbed up from the table. He struck out, screaming—once, twice, three times—hitting Bowyer hard, hitting bone, hitting his face.

Bowyer was gone.

Nick went down on the floor, choking in smoke, ears ringing. He felt for the gun. There was no gun.

A motor started up. The lights flickered and came up strong.

Nagel was sitting upright on the floor, his left hand clutching the handkerchief. His mouth and chin and neck were starred with ragged wounds. From the bridge of his nose up, there was nothing.

Nick blinked, saw blood, saw a chunk of scalp, saw the shotgun. It had fallen to the floor in front of him. He grabbed the barrel, dropped it, grabbed it again, gripping metal that was slick with blood. There was blood everywhere. On his hands. On his legs.

He turned his head.

Bowyer was kneeling on the floor next to the generator, his back to the room, reaching for something that was sticking straight up from his shoulder, close to his ear. Nick watched bloody fingers close on what looked like a handle, then got to his feet, the bloody gun held out in front of him.

Bowyer reached and gripped, seemed to become aware of Nick then. He froze, got onto his knees, then pushed up against the wall until he was standing.

He turned.

His wedged hair was darkly spattered and two deep curved wounds opened the flesh above his temple. He looked at Nick, blinking, trying to focus, looking at the gun in Nick's hand. He wrinkled his nose, took a step, swaying slightly, reaching out to grab the barrel of the gun.

Nick backed away.

"Oh," said Bowyer, and the blood flushed out of him, hitting the floor with a smack. He looked down at himself, blinking, astonished, then seemed to remember the thing in his shoulder. His fingers closed around what Nick now saw was the handle of a chisel. A woodworking chisel, the blade jammed out of sight. Stuck somehow. Stuck deep.

"Oh!" said Bowyer, and the blood came again.

His eyes rolled back, and for a second it looked like he was going down. He lifted his chin, then turned away. Steadying himself at the bottom of the stairs, he started up, taking it one step at a time.

Nick looked around him at the bloody mess. Then he followed. Up into the kitchen. Then outside, following him out to a place where Bowyer took a seat under a boarded window. It was just a plank on two low stones. The ground was littered with cigarette butts.

Again Bowyer reached for the handle, but he was tired now, his fingers barely able to grip.

"Stuck," he said as the blood came again, rushing with a bubbling noise from deep inside his chest. He put his head back against the wall, his eyes rolling across to where Nick was standing.

"Worm," he said. "You worm."

And died.

Epilogue

Knowledge was complicity in knowing. You reached a point of understanding where sharing what you knew lost its appeal. There was no point addressing yourself to the uninitiated. Also, there were risks involved: there was a danger of being misunderstood.

Two years after Nagel's murder, Nick bought a house in Vermont—an old farmhouse in the Champlain Valley standing on 10 acres of what used to be a 250-acre dairy farm. It had seemed incredible at the time that he could just buy something like that, write a check and suddenly own it. The house was run-down, of course, needed at least twice as much spent on remodeling as he'd paid the owner. But money was no longer a problem. *Ornament and Crime* (that was the title he'd given the book), his "true" story of Frank Spira's *Incarnation,* had been on the best-seller lists for eight months, while the advance itself would have paid for the house four times over. It had been a similar story in the U.K., where Curlew had been one of the early bidders. Stanhope had argued that as publishers of the *Life,* Curlew was best placed to handle *Ornament.* It was unfortunate that they'd been unable to come up with the money.

Things had gone well for him. Even the attention brought to bear during the first weeks of the homicide investigation (Detectives Glasco and Guthry had been called in by the Kingston Police Department the morning Nick was picked up on the Sawkill Road) worked in his favor. You couldn't buy the kind of publicity the networks had given him.

And Glasco had abandoned his conspiracy case early on, seemed more or less happy with his own exoneration and reinstatement, and with a killer in the morgue. Faced with the impossibility of establishing what exactly Nick knew at precisely which moment, he was left to focus on niggling details that seemed to indicate something that stopped short of guilt but which nevertheless . . . Glasco would have found it hard to say what it was that bugged him. There was just something about Nicky Greer, something he didn't like—maybe the way he always seemed to have a plausible answer for everything. Why had Reardon invited him down to Tangier? Because he'd lied to Reardon about being able to name the Collector; he'd lied to give himself a chance of seeing what he'd assumed at that time was a painting. Why had Nagel offered the services of his lawyer the night of the arrests? Because he'd been worried Nick would talk about what he knew, and would go public with the film of Laverne Taubmann's rape that also happened to show the picture scratched on Reardon's chest. What about the film? Why hadn't he made it available to the police during the interview conducted on the thirtieth? Because he didn't see what was on it until the thirty-first, at which point he'd made his way to the Guggenheim, where he was, of course, arrested.

And then there was that night in the woods. Glasco wanted to know why Nagel had brought him up there, wanted to know on what basis that trip was undertaken. And why had Nick gone along? Hadn't he been aware of the danger? Here Nick admitted he'd lost perspective. The pictures had become something of an obsession, and Nagel was talking of a deal in which they'd fabricate a history of the *Incarnation,* establishing the importance of the copies seized at the Guggenheim. Nick said he'd led Nagel to believe that he'd go along, though that had never been his intention. Of course not.

There were certain things Glasco didn't really buy. Nick's claim, for example, that he had received the film through the mail from an anonymous well-wisher after Laverne Taubmann's death. But there was no way of finding out the truth, and so Glasco eventually eased up, even going so far as to acknowledge the importance of Nick's help and his value as a witness.

From that point on, their exchanges became a matter of clarifying how things had finally played out—Nick being taken to the house where Nagel had clearly intended to see him killed, an argument ensuing in which Bowyer had shot and killed Nagel, and Nick killing Bowyer in defense of his own life. It was a package: all loose ends neatly squared away. You could have put a bow on it.

Only one question remained, a question raised by a report published in the *Kingston Inquirer* in the middle of September.

Spira Snuff Art Still Missing

NYPD detective Eugene Glasco yesterday admitted to drawing a blank on the question of the whereabouts of the by now notorious *Incarnation* pictures tattooed by Frank Spira on the bodies of his lovers Anthony Reardon and Jacob Nathaniel Grossman. Until now the search has focused on the area around an abandoned property located two miles east of the Sawkill Road near the Zena Highwoods turnoff, where, two weeks ago, art dealer Oscar Nagel and hunter's supplier William Bowyer met violent deaths.

That the tattooed skins, taken from Reardon and Grossman, were cured and stretched in the cellar of the house seems more than likely given the workshop Bowyer had installed there and the presence of vellum scraps recovered from the floor. An NYPD forensic laboratory last week extracted DNA from the vellum that matched samples taken from the dead men's bodies.

But the pictures themselves have yet to be found. A tired Detective Glasco, speaking at an impromptu press conference on the steps of the Kingston Town Hall yesterday, said that Bowyer may have destroyed the pictures to protect himself from prosecution. "According to Nicholas Greer, Bowyer was angry with Nagel for making copies of the pictures, and this was the cause of their argument," he said. Greer, himself subject to police scrutiny in the early stages of the investigation, was unavailable for comment.

He'd gotten lost in the woods. That was what he'd told them. Covered in blood and cradling a swollen wrist, his left eye all but closed by an ugly contusion, he had staggered out onto the Sawkill Road just after sun-up on the morning of August 2, frightening a hospital worker on her way to work. She was the one who phoned in the report to the local police.

The responding officer had later described Nick as exhausted and barely coherent. With the little strength he had, he kept repeating the same phrases over and over. He had killed a man in self-defense. He had killed the murderer of Jacob Grossman. The officer called for support from the Kingston PD detective division, then, following Nick's directions, made his way back up to the house. They missed the turn twice and took over forty minutes to get to the scene.

Nick took him to Bowyer's body but would not go back down into the cellar, where the officer found Nagel's corpse sitting upright against a wall still clutching the handkerchief.

An hour later the place was swarming with police and technical backup. The local medical examiner took air and body temperatures, tested for rigor and measured lividity. His estimate for time of death was around three in the morning. Three A.M. for both bodies. The Kingston detectives asked why it had taken Nick three hours to get from the house onto the Sawkill Road. Nick repeated what he'd said before: he'd gotten lost in the woods. After Bowyer died, he'd wandered down towards the valley through the trees. He'd almost died in that cellar, he'd seen a man killed and had killed a man himself. He'd been disoriented, confused. He'd gotten lost.

It had been a relief to get back to London. By that time it was late October and Henry was negotiating a deal for the U.S. rights to *Ornament and Crime*. Nick stayed at Henry's house. It seemed that Henry couldn't do enough for him. His wife too was charming. She said she found it hard to believe that they hadn't met before. Withdrawn, preoccupied, troubled by all that had happened, Nick was nevertheless alert to the comedy of Henry talking seven-figure advances down the telephone while CNN followed Marion Martin's fall from grace. Crucible had withdrawn their advance after Barb published an article challenging the authenticity of the letters recovered from the Taubmann residence. It was Nick who had encouraged her to write the piece, Nick who had edited the final draft. And so the Tortured Walrus was finally harpooned.

He met Linda at the basement on a day of freezing October rain. It was almost comically grim, but there was nothing funny about the emotions on display—Linda watching in stern silence as he piled his books and papers into crates which were to be shipped back to New York, where he had rented an apartment.

Although she was the one who had left him, she clearly saw herself as the victim. She was angry with him for what he had done to their marriage, and it didn't help that he freely acknowledged his guilt. He said he was sorry for putting her through it all. Then added in his defense that it hadn't been clear to him at the outset how important the *Life* was going to become.

She cried when he left. He tried to tell her that she was better off without him, believing it too, that she stood a chance of happiness without him, that she'd been right all along—he didn't know when to stop, was incapable of restraint. She smiled at this, her eyes full of contempt, and said it was too easy to hide behind this version of himself. He was responsible, she said. The truth of it was that he had always done exactly what he wanted to out of selfishness and narcissism and pride.

Vermont in the fall. People talked about the crispness of the air and the vivid colors of the turning leaves, but it was the underlying melancholy of the season that stirred Nick. A sense of the land rolling into the darkness of winter—a real winter here with snow and blocked roads, not the steady damp and drizzle of his London life.

He was alone more than he would have chosen, but happy on the whole, able to work whenever he wanted to, able to spread his books and papers and clothes. But sleep was a problem, more often than not disrupted by thoughts of his night in the woods. The facts he remembered pretty clearly—remembered walking away from the house, a hand held to his bleeding face, oblivious for a time, then becoming conscious of pain—in his ears, and in his tongue where he had bitten it. He remembered standing in a gully and realizing that he'd been there long enough for the blood to stiffen in his clothes, and in that moment thinking his first clear thought—that he'd left the film up at the house, that the film was in Nagel's jacket pocket and that he had to retrieve it—never mind the police and what they'd want to examine. It was *his* evidence, hard won and, apart from the pictures themselves, the only thing that proved his story.

And so he had gone back down into that brightly lit room. He had walked in blood and scraps of flesh and he had taken the film from Nagel's pocket.

And then he had taken the pictures.

Staring into the darkness of his bedroom, it was this moment of choice that continued to evade him. Not the physical detail of it, but his state of mind. He remembered standing in the cellar and looking at the pictures inside their plastic sheet and thinking that they had to be saved, the idea coming to him like a drunken impulse. He hadn't thought it through, hadn't stood there wavering or debating. He'd just bundled them up in his arms and walked back up the stairs.

He'd buried them no more than ten feet from where they'd left the Daimler, had broken the earth with a tire tool, then scraped and delved a shallow trench.

And for the first few weeks of the investigation, he'd expected the police to find the pictures, expected daily to hear the news, and was ready to speculate with the detectives about how Bowyer, fearing imminent arrest, had decided to hide the evidence rather than destroy it. After all, the pictures were valuable if you could get them to the right collector. But the police never did find them. The investigation moved away from the woods above the Sawkill River, and he was left with time to think about the crazy thing he'd done. He still wasn't entirely clear about it but knew he preferred to think of the pictures up there in the woods rather than stuck in some police evidence room with men like Detective Glasco sneering at them.

They had no place in the evidence room. He felt strongly about that. The *Incarnation* had nothing to do with Nagel and what he had done. Just as it had nothing to do with Laverne and what had happened to her. And once you'd peeled those layers away, you were left with two of Spira's most important works. Two of the twentieth century's most important works. Two parts of a three-part masterpiece, a triptych—three figures at the base of a crucifixion.

And they were beautiful, glowing softly under the changing Vermont sky. He never did hang them on his bedroom wall. That would have been too close to claiming ownership, and he never felt he owned them. He told himself that he was keeping them safe for the day they'd be found somewhere—maybe up there in the Catskills—and be recognized for what they were, which, simply put, was art.

He never hung them, but after a few months of having them

propped against the wall, he put them on top of a plain Victorian commode so that he could see them from his bed.

It didn't seem right. What he'd done. But it didn't seem wrong. There was some madness in it. He was sure about that.

He'd waited a year before going back up to Kingston, had driven up from Manhattan in a rented Toyota. He'd moved the stones and moss and leaves with his bare hands, half-expecting someone, Glasco maybe, to leap out and cuff him. But that hadn't happened, and when he'd gotten them back to New York, unwrapping them in his tiny kitchen, he'd wept. He hadn't cried, he'd wept, had wept so hard it scared him, and insane or not, deluded or not, he *had* felt Spira's presence then, had felt the artist buzzing there under the neon ceiling light, had felt the giant's gratitude.

Acknowledgments

I'd like to thank Ellen Borakove at the Office of the Chief Medical Examiner of New York City, and Detectives Donald Cronin and Michael Walsh of the 7th Precinct Homicide Bureau. Thanks are also due to Ahmed in Tangier for paying the bribes, and to the many friends who read this book in its many guises— Sean, Beverly, Mary-Ann, Laurent, Charlie, Julian, Tina, Michael, Julia, Iris (you've been like a mother to me) and, particularly, Robert for his extensive and insightful critique. I'd also like to express my gratitude to Jim Rutman for seeing the possibilities and to Andrew Miller for his belief and support. Finally, I'd like to thank the late Daniel Farson for suggesting the idea to me in the first place, and Francis Bacon for touching my hand once in a busy London street.

About the Author

JOSEPH GEARY graduated from Oxford University in 1981 with a double first in English literature, and has taught English and worked as a journalist. He has lived in Madrid, London, Paris and the Cayman Islands and now divides his time between Los Angeles and the South of France, where he wrote *Spiral*. He lives with his wife and son and is at work on his next novel.